Heroes & Hellspawn

By

Mark R Goodrum

ACT I:

THE

HEROES

Xoran World Map

ORION

POLARIS

PYRROS

KOREGAR

TYCHON

Map of Kronos

Map of Polaris and Orion

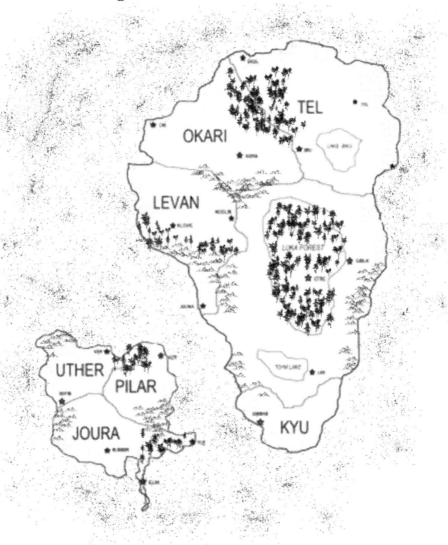

Map of Tychon

Map of Pyrros

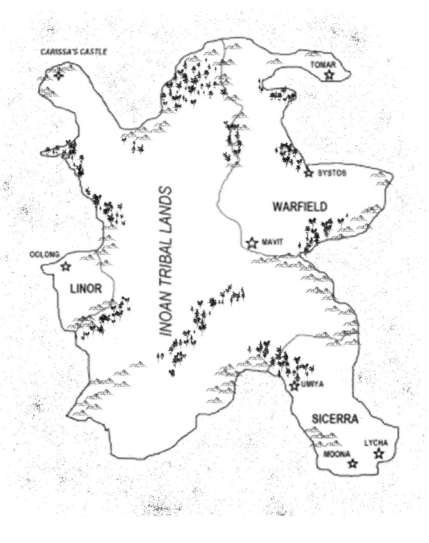

Table of contents

Chapter 1: The Goddess

Even during the day, it was dark in the Twilight Forest, but now that night had fallen, it was like the inside of a tomb. Roughly in the center of the forest, there was a God Tree that was by far the oldest and the tallest in all of Kronos. A very old woman was next to the tree, tending to a small campfire that was the one source of light and heat to be found anywhere in the cursed forest. She had lost her demon lord and his thousands of minions. Tens of thousands of humans were tricked by her demon into spreading the chaos she craved so much. The one saving grace was that she killed the only mage in Xoran. Argus was dead by her hand and now no one of any consequence stood in her way. Long before the light caught her attention, she sensed that she was not alone.

The light started out small and remarkably bright. From far off among the trees it approached at great speed, passing through trees as if they weren't there. As it neared, she could tell that it was a tall woman enveloped in a blindingly bright aura. The old woman held up her dirty, wrinkled hand to fend off the effects of the painful glare. When the woman had drawn within a few feet, the light dimmed to a bearable, though still uncomfortably bright level. The woman had long, flowing, blonde hair that was a silvery white shade. She was close to ten-foot-tall, with a medium build. She was completely nude except for a translucent veil that draped over one shoulder and wrapped around her two or three times. Her face was beautiful and perfect, and it reminded the old woman of her own face when she had been known by another name.

"You failed, Lilith," the woman said with a smile on her face.

"It has been centuries, and that is how you greet me?" Lilith grumbled.

"The Halacian killed your demon. Even though he was ancient, you should have known that he would have the strength to defeat a mere duke of hell." She floated in front of Lilith; her slender feet hung several inches above the ground. "His protégés were strong, they may also be Halacian. You were remiss in discounting them so quickly."

"I didn't expect his apprentices to take out my minions," she admitted.

"I know, I observed every mistake that you made. The human, the one that you trusted with your Gahrenna... his evil nature made him a likely choice, but he was a fool, and he wasted a golden opportunity. You expend your energy carelessly, even though you know that every curse carries a price. How can you put a plan into motion without knowing what the likely outcome will be? That's a lot to take on without a patron," she said to the crone. "My father tipped the scales ever so slightly so that he would prevail. The humans received divine intervention." She looked the old woman in the eyes, "Are you ready to accept my help?"

"You would do that Chorea? I think your father would not approve, and that would put you in direct opposition to his wishes. He takes much pride in his creation. I think you risk his wrath by dabbling in the affairs of us lesser creatures."

"It is true that Magnus is obsessed with this world. I don't understand it, but he seems to favor these humans. If it's truly your intent to open the gates to the many worlds and bring chaos to Xoran, you'll need help. Help that I can provide."

"And of course, there will be a price," Lilith stated.

The goddess floated around the clearing; her radiance continued to torment the witch. "Xoran is changing again. Magic is again blossoming in this paradise, and those humans that are born with or develop the gifts may not have yet decided where their loyalties lie. Argus approached the twin mages just as their powers were emerging. That was a triumph for the side of Law. There will be more with Halacian blood, and you need to stake your claim to as many of them as you can."

"I will recruit them, or kill them," Lilith declared. "If you help me to foul Magnus' creation, won't he punish you?" she asked the goddess.

"He loves me as all fathers love their daughters, he wouldn't touch a hair on my head. He's the strongest of us, and yet, he has a soft heart." She floated forward, not quite touching the ground. She placed a glowing hand on the old woman's face, lifting her gaze till their eyes met. "The planes are converging, and the heirs of Halacia are no longer limited by the restrictions of this reality. Magic will return, and creatures like you will gain power. And so will your enemies."

"I need to find my sisters. Can you help me to locate them?"

"I am a god," she replied simply.

"So... you know where they are?"

"I do not." She smiled evilly at the old woman. "The shockwave that freed you from your prison is a precursor to a larger merging of the universes. Your sisters, the other seasons, are not in this Xoran. In my true form, I can see and feel the coming collisions. There will be another shockwave soon, another Xoran will merge with this one. When your sisters again share the same realm with you, I will be able to direct you to where they are.

"For your blessings and information, I'm sure there will be a hefty price."

"Nothing is for free, dear Lilith." She hovered just overhead.

"I need you, so it seems that I am at your mercy. I would not have expected that our interests would be so closely aligned. I accept any blessings that you can spare this old sorceress." She bowed painfully.

"Please, spare me the theatrics. You will be my puppet, and I'll pull your strings because it pleases me, and because it perturbs my father." She floated just off the ground and drifted in a semi-circle around the fire. "Your human, Lem Lothe is coming, tail between his legs. He will beg you for... well, who cares. Use him. Twist him into a demi of the lower rings, have him raise an unholy force that will strike fear into these humans that my father cares so much about. You crave chaos. Have him as your lieutenant, spreading darkness so that when you are ready to seize control of Xoran, the road will be paved for you."

"All this, I can do on my own. How will you help me to succeed where I previously failed?" she asked the Old God.

"I must whisper into a few ears, prepare the way. You were defeated by the humans working together. I will help you to forge your own unholy alliances. I'll give you strength to find more demons that will step into this world. Evil ones that will be ready to serve you and kill your enemies."

"I'll begin again and use the last of my flagging energies. If you choose to abandon me, leave me to die in disgrace... there's nothing that I can do about it."

"No, nothing. Do as I command, and I promise that I will give you power on this plane. Power to raise armies, to pit these humans against each other." She floated down so she could meet the witch's gaze. "But you must become *my* creature. Obey my every command."

"Yes, Goddess. I will obey," she kneeled slowly and with much difficulty.

Chorea reached out her hand, and in the air just above her palm, a giant gem appeared. It was dark blue with white clouds that swirled internally beneath the shiny surface. The gem floated over and landed on the now outstretched hand of Lilith.

"Affix this to your staff, it will channel power from the lower planes. Use it sparingly, or it will try to feed from your life force as well," she said. Her halo of light grew again in intensity till it was unbearable to look at, then like the snap of fingers, the goddess was gone. Once again, the only light in the Twilight Forest was Lilith's campfire.

As she affixed the new stone to her staff and thought, *I wonder just how bad of a pact I've gotten myself into. I will do whatever it takes to bring my sisters here and join them again after so many centuries. Together, we can rid this world of mankind, and 'our' kind will flourish again. I do not trust these 'so-called' Old Gods, but if being Chorea's puppet is the price, then so be it.*

Chapter 2: The Fugitive

As predicted, he came stumbling through the forest, and when he reached the small clearing where Lilith was, he fell before her on his hands and knees. Lem Lothe had led an army of religious zealots in an attempt to convert the world to the twisted ideology of the demon. An ideology that was planted and nurtured in him by the demon that men called Quell. Instead, he demonstrated that believing in a cause with all your heart and soul was no substitute for having skill and experience. He had led his troops to defeat after defeat because he didn't value their lives, and because he overestimated his ability as a military commander.

As she looked at the failure on the ground at her feet, she could only think about her own great failure. She underestimated Argus, her former lover and longtime enemy. She had known the ancient mage for hundreds of years, ever since he was a tall awkward young man, and she was a beautiful young elemental. The demon that she had summoned with so much of her waning energy, was dead by the old mage's hand. Now Argus was dead, the last of his lifeforce stolen by her. She thought about her instructions from the goddess, and she wondered, what to do with this shell of a man. A man filled with hatred. An ambitious man who was cold and calculating, but ultimately, a disappointment.

"You failed again," she said acidly. "Quell no longer favors you."

"Yes mistress, I failed you. Now everyone in Kronos wants me dead."

"So why did you flee here to fall to the ground before me? Have you no honor? If you had fallen on your own sword, I would have infinitely more respect for you than I do right now."

"If that's what you want!" he said standing and checking himself, "I seem to have lost my sword."

"I will do one last miracle for you, but then I must rest. I've used too much of my power, and you have wasted my gifts. Down on your knees!" she commanded.

Lilith began casting her spell while holding her staff with the powerful blue gem affixed to its head. With the added power from the lower planes, she was able to pry open a pinprick to one of the many hells and summon the spirit of one of its demon lords. Lem Lothe was on his knees, the power that Lilith radiated forcing him to kneel before her. Lem screamed as red smoke streamed from the breach and entered his mouth and nostrils, filling his lungs. The demonic spirit pushed out the tainted soul of Lem Lothe, and pure evil filtered through the soulless shell and attached itself to every cell of his being. His body grew to fearsome proportions as he thinned out and his skin turned a blackish grey, the color of spent charcoal. His eyes turned red, and his entire body became covered in scales. He grew a great lizard-like tail, and horns sprouted from his forehead. He looked over at the old woman, a new level of cunning in his eyes, along with unbridled rage and hate.

"What's your name?" she demanded.

"Zaebzal," he spat. His voice was deep and subdued, reverberating with ancient dread. He looked over his new body and sniffed at the foreign air.

"Are you ready to serve me, Zaebzal? I have summoned you to spread chaos and pave the way for more of your kind to enter this world."

"Yes, Master. I'll kill as many of the humans as I can, and I'll crush the spirits of the rest. When the gate is finally cast open, this land will be an easy conquest," he said, reveling in his new body. He looked at the old crone with no attempt to hide his disdain.

"That's all well and good, but never forget who your master is. I brought you to this world and I can easily send you back!"

"Easily?" he asked with humor in his tone, "You sound like just standing erect is taxing you. Perhaps I should test you to see if you are still an all-powerful witch or just a tired old woman!" He stalked her with murder in his eyes.

When he was close enough, she reached out with the staff, touching the blue stone to his scaly hide, causing the demon to instantly writhe in intense pain. A blue fire enveloped him and despite his resistance to normal fire, the blue flames burned him, causing his thick hide to smoke and his blood to boil. She left the stone on him for long enough to make her point and then left it on him for a little longer. When she finally withdrew, he was lying on his back with his arms and legs clenched from the pain that she had caused.

"You've tested me, and now you have no doubt that I am your master?" she asked.

"Yes… master. I will do your bidding, and I acknowledge your dominion over me," he said while trying to regain his feet.

"The one who once inhabited that body before you, led an army to defeat in the swamps to the south and east of here. Thousands of freshly dead men," she sat on the log before the fire and resumed staring into its hypnotic dance, "Will this be a good start for your campaign?"

"Yes, Master. I'll gather these empty vessels and fill them with souls of the damned." The demon was finally able to stand, though still aching with pain. He dropped to one knee and bowed his head to the old woman.

"You are dismissed," she said calmly as she was now more interested in watching the campfire. The demon walked off in the direction that she had indicated. He would only travel by night, and it would take him a couple of weeks to reach the place where he would find the first of his minions. When he had built an army of the dead, he would rid the land of the living, and last on his list, would be the one he called 'master'.

Chapter 3: Zaebzal

Zaebzal had been running for a dozen nights and hiding in the shadows during the daytime. It had taken him that long to travel from the Twilight Forest to the edge of Phister Swamp. He felt more at home once he entered the gloomy swamp, with its weak lighting and oppressive heat and humidity. Here is where he would literally raise his army.

There was very little of Lem Lothe remaining in him, but enough to take note of the irony. He had led these men to their deaths, and now in death, he would use them again. He slogged his way through the swamp, and he was as hampered by the muck as the men who died here. He was given imprecise directions, so he headed inward towards the deepest, darkest part of the swamp. After almost an entire day of walking in knee-deep mud and hip-deep water, he found what he was looking for. There was more sun here, and the sky was visible because the trees in this area had been burned to cinders. He could make out the random arm and leg, sticking out of the water or caught on the brush. There was a vague memories of the mages that had killed so many of these men. The boy who froze them in place, and the girl that set the swamp ablaze.

With a deep breath, he began the spell that would allow the spirits of minor demons to enter this world. With mad gesticulations and a spell that sounded like cats being tortured, he opened a portal to his own personal hell. He was no mage or summoner, so the best that he was able to do was to open a portal smaller than the eye of a needle. That was enough though. The souls of the damned flowed like a raging river through a burst dam. Wisps of red smoke flowed out and when they found what they were looking for, they dove into the murky water. Thousands of them entered, and they spread out in all directions till they were out of the demon's sight.

The body of a fallen soldier stood up. He was nude and badly burned. His hair was gone, along with his clothes and most of his skin above the waist. Looking up, he found his master and began walking as best he could toward the demon. More followed suit. The corpses in the surrounding swamp had the flesh burned from their bones, and only a few retained weapons or metallic fragments of the weapons that they had carried into the swamp.

The swamp was now alive, with the dead. Hundreds of bodies became animated and stood up to follow their new master. Zaebzal walked North and as he picked up recruits, their burns became less severe. The pack of undead marched on through the muck and the mire for hours till they came upon more of their kind. These men had no burns but were brisling with the arrows of the Emar who had mercilessly cut them down.

When they reached the clearing where the swamp met the desert, Zaebzal had a force of some six or seven thousand undead. Perhaps not enough to win a war; but enough to bring those that had defeated his master Lilith, some well-deserved retribution. He marched his forces West where they passed through the perpetual sandstorms of the Indigo Desert. Many didn't have eyes to get blinded, nor did they have lungs to breathe in the blowing sand. It didn't matter if the storms blasted more flesh from their already rotting bodies; they could feel neither fear nor pain. These men were useless in life, terrible as fighters for the religion that they had been indoctrinated in; but now in death, they would now be a formidable force.

On a foggy moonless night, Zaebzal guided his minions through the countryside. The demons that inhabited the corpses existed only to kill. As they passed out of the desert into the neighboring lands, they would attack anything with a heartbeat, ripping at it with their rotting teeth, and tearing it with their fleshless hands. Nothing was sacred or off-limits. Rabbits and rats, deer, snakes. When they would come across a farm, they would tear apart the livestock, the dogs, and then the family. Swarming in such great numbers, a family caught in their own home would be pulled out of their beds and both parents and their children would be eaten alive. The burned and waterlogged bodies of the dead men no longer needed sustenance; the flesh and blood they consumed either fell to the ground or went to waste in their inert stomachs. The cries of terror from the adults and the tears of the children only fueled their insatiable desire for murder.

They spread across the Margera countryside like a plague, leaving death and destruction in their path. The man that was Lem Lothe would have put the resources to good use, eating the food, taking coins from the dead, and having his way with the women before putting them to the sword. The demon Zaebzal had no worldly desires, he had no interest in material possessions, no lust. Spilling blood and causing pain and misery was the only currency that he was interested in.

Chapter 4: Sisters

When Lilith finally awoke from her slumber, she had slept for almost three days and was still nowhere near her peak strength. The recent opening of gates between worlds took a lot out of her, and only something this special could rouse her from her recuperative sleep. The shockwave washed across all Xoran, touching every inch of land and water. It touched every living being from the lowest to the highest. She recognized this sensation; it was the same disruption that freed her from the prison she'd been placed in by the mage Argus. She felt it on the very periphery of her consciousness, a familiar power that could only be one of her sisters.

She snapped her fingers to light the burned-out campfire that lay next to where she slept. Her little home in the Twilight Forest went from pitch black to warm and bright in a flash. She shook the cobwebs from her head and then reached into one of the many pockets of her cloak for the needed materials. When she had what she wanted, she tossed the items into the fire and concontrated at the heart of the flames. The image of a woman took shape in the fire; she was tall and thin, and her skin was white like fine porcelain. She wore her waist-length hair straight, it was completely white with streaks of black. Her almond-shaped eyes were green and hinted at both her intelligence and her cruelty. She had a figure that would cause most men to lust after her, but she wore a tight leather jacket and long skirt with furs and silk that covered everything but her hands. She carried a long wooden staff with a white jewel set into the head, and on her shoulder, sat a great snowy owl. For the first time since escaping from her prison, the old woman's face lit up with happiness. She called out to the distant figure through the flames.

"Sister! It's me, Lilith!" She almost stepped into the fire as she got close enough to see the other woman better.

"Lilith? Is that really you? It's been such a long time. I feared for the worst."

"I trusted that mage with my black heart and he enthralled me for the last few centuries. All for the benefit of these 'humans' that the Old Gods favor so much."

"I felt the merging of worlds and suddenly, I could sense your presence in my world." She looked the old woman over from head to toe through the window in the flames. "You look terrible, dear sister. How could you let yourself wither to such a degree?" Carissa asked while staring at her with cruel delight in her eyes. "And what became of the one that trapped you?"

"I killed him, finally getting my revenge after so many, many years. I had loved him in a previous life, but that didn't stop me from taking his life force and adding it to my own. He was so near death... I didn't get more than a trickle of energy. It will take many more sacrifices before I can again look good enough to be called your sister in public."

"Be sure that you do, Lilith. I have a reputation here, and for me to introduce you in public, well... you need a lot of work," she said with little sympathy in her voice. "Have you spoken to the others? I felt you after the convergence, but Alexina and Anjaya are still missing."

"I don't feel them. They might have suffered the same fate as I."

"Or they could be dead," Carissa mused.

"They could be, but I refuse to entertain the idea. We must meet, then we can look for them together."

"Not if that's the flesh you are bringing, dear sister. Fix your house before you speak to me again," and with that, the connection was cut. Lilith stared into the fire, ashamed at how much she had let herself go. This was something that she could and would fix.

Chapter 5: Carissa

Carissa stood against the half wall on the top of the Sky Tower. From that vantage point, she could almost see the lands of Kronos, far to the North and West. What she could 'actually' see was the ocean, hundreds of feet below. Waves crashed against the rough rocks that supported her lonely castle, built into the side of the mountain that jutted up and separated the land from the sea. The whole castle, except for the outer walls, was made of stone that was milky white with swirls of dark blue, like veins beneath a maiden's skin. The Sky Tower was the tallest by far, stabbing at the bright blue sky. Next by height was the Tower of Elements, made of the same milky stone and set at the opposite end of the keep's grounds. The lowest was the Earth Tower, rising only a few stories above the main house. Three stories high, the house was quiet except for a few servants.

Carissa was not married, had no family and did very little entertaining. Most people who lived in Pyrros knew about the sorceress and feared her for good reason. Her sister Lilith had slept the last two hundred years, hidden from the world till just recently. Carissa has spent every moment of the last two hundred years haunting her own castle and planning her revenge on the nations around her. One side of her castle faced the sea, and the other overlooked Pyrros and the vibrant land it had become. Unlike Kronos where Lilith lived, the continent known as Pyrros was filled with non-human creatures and magic-using races. Especially dangerous was the Vinkul far to the South. They looked very much like humans; their most distinguishing feature was their deep blue skin. They kept to themselves and looked down on most other races. They would not be helpful, and in fact, they would destroy her if they felt they could defeat her magic.

She needed to seek out alliances. Maybe the Mavit Tomar would be receptive. If she were to travel down the mountain and cross through the unclaimed lands just south of her keep, she could reach the territory where the Mavit Tomar ran their small, but advanced empire. They were an unfriendly people, but they would be the most likely to listen to her proposal, and possibly forge an alliance. The Mavit Tomar had bodies like human men and women, but they also had sizable curling horns on their heads like a ram, and they had long spiked tails. Fur was thick on their cheeks and neck for the males, and both sexes had hairy forearms and calves with cloven hooves. They were either dark blue, grey, or white in color. Carissa was not sure if the color divided them into classes or castes; or if it was just random.

The last time that she had tried to flex her powers, she was chased away by a pack of Vinkul enforcers, and she had narrowly escaped with her life. This time she would find allies, those who would be willing to face the dangers directly, so that she would be able to exert control from a safe distance. Hearing how weak this new land was, it was an easy decision to make. Carissa packed her satchel with some items that might help out if she got into trouble, some food, and a handful of gems that she had taken while on various adventures over the conturies.

She gave instructions to her staff that she would return in a week or so. With Lilith back and her other two sisters possibly alive and waiting to be found, she felt alive again for the first time in ages. She mounted her horse and headed out for what she hoped would become a lucrative connection. The sisters had been powerful and challenged the powerful in ancient Xoran. Now that the Lords of Shadow had been banished and the Yermin were mostly dead, they would be able to crush the seven races and rule over the ashes.

Before reaching the base of the mountain, she performed a simple illusion spell to make herself look more like a member of one of the Inoan tribes that roamed the unclaimed steppe. Carissa spurred her horse on, not caring how tired the beast was becoming. Her long brown hair waved behind her like a war banner, her light armor was mostly leather with a few bits of iron to cover the more vital spots. Her arms and legs were bare except for the many ceremonial bracelets and rings that were common to the Inoan tribes. They appeared mostly human, but they had pointed ears and small rounded horns that were vestigial remains of what they had been thousands of years prior. They were thought to have been an ancient cross of human and Mavit Tomar stock, but the truth had been lost over the centuries. There were many other differences based on which tribe you were looking at. Their numbers were unknown; but there are over a hundred major tribes that live in the unclaimed lands, moving to follow herd animals or other prey.

Everyone stayed away from the white witch's castle, so it was half a day before she encountered anyone. She was riding at a brisk pace when without warning, she was surrounded by an Inoan hunting party. They looked her up and down, trying to determine which tribe she was from. Knowing that she couldn't get away, she slowed down and came to a stop. They encircled her, bumping her and her mount aggressively; their faces showed that they didn't know what to make of her.

"What is your tribe?" their leader asked. He was tall and lean, his hair was light brown with golden stripes, and he wore it pulled back in a long tail. No Inoan had facial hair, but tattoos, piercings and brands were common. The party leader had black and green tribal designs tattooed on his face and arms. Like Carissa, he wore a mixture of leather armor with mail and plate pieces sown on. "Speak up woman, before we decide to make you tribe property," he threatened.

"Okunya tribe, from the Northern plains," she said defiantly. "I carry a message to my Chieftain. You'd best not delay me!"

"This land is Zampac land, you have no right to pass through without permission from the council of elders," he said looking at the others. "Pull her off that horse, search her thoroughly!" he ordered.

"Don't you dare!" she cried out as they reached for her. Several of them grabbed at her clothing and pulled her from her horse so that she fell heavily to the ground. "Last chance!" she shouted. "Touch me, and I'll kill you all!"

As the warriors were falling on her, she touched the amulet on her chest, invoking its power. Those around her seemed to be moving in slow motion, but her speed had increased tenfold or more. She pulled a wicked-looking dagger from her hip and plunged the blade into the leg of a tall warrior that was reaching for her. She pulled it out, and watched the blood slowly shoot out and hang frozen in the air. A woman warrior had grabbed a handful of her hair, she took the knife and slashed it across her exposed midriff. She kicked a short, stocky man between his legs and smashed another square in the nose with the hilt of her dagger. When all hands were off of her, she again touched the amulet. The raiding party was shocked at how fast the woman had moved. Four of the seven of them had sustained injury, and she was no worse for wear. One of the woman warriors reached out to stop one of the men in her party from jumping into the fray.

"Zampac, hold!" she commanded.

"How can she possibly move that fast?" the leader asked aloud. The female warrior grabbed him by the arm to stop him.

"Perhaps we were too quick to attack this sister of the plains," she said to the group. "Sister, do you mean to cause our tribe any harm? Are you part of some scheme to attack us while we hunt and gather?"

Carissa wiped her blade off on the grass and put it back in its place at her side. "No. I told you that I carry a message about matters that only concern 'our' people. You will not come to any harm from our tribe, this I swear!" she stated emphatically.

"I don't believe you, maybe we should take you back to the camp for questioning," the leader said. Before he could raise his arms to lunge forward, Annika stopped him again.

"We'll take your word of honor, Sister," Annika said forcefully. The others gave her dirty looks, but she was not deterred, "Should we escort you from our territory?" she asked Carissa.

"I have a long way to go yet, I'll be fine," she said. They all watched quietly as she re-mounted her horse. The group grumbled a bit, but they said nothing as she started riding again in the direction that she had been traveling before the encounter.

Once she was out of earshot, the tall warrior turned angrily to Annika, "What were you thinking? She seriously wounded Ledo and hurt those three!" he said pointing towards the injured warriors. "Why just let her go? She's loose on our land!"

"You didn't see what I saw. When she struck, her movements weren't just fast, they were inhumanly fast. She used some kind of sorcery to make herself move as fast as lightning. If we had continued to fight her, she could have slit all our throats and left us bleeding out on the plain," Annika said.

"Should we follow her?" one of the warriors asked.

"No, I don't want anything to do with sorcery. Let's go back to camp and check on the tribe," the chief said. "I'll feel better when I know that they're okay."

Chapter 6: Mavit Tomar

When Carissa was within range of the great stone walls of Warfield, she released the illusion that had cloaked her for the last week of hard travel. She was again herself, hundreds of years old, though she was kept young by potent spells and elixirs. She wore a flowing gown that had layers of black and white panels, with a large wrap around her thin waist. Her long white hair had black streaks, that only made her pale face seem even whiter.

The gates were about one hundred feet tall, made of stones set on stones, perfectly arranged so that a minimum amount of mortar was needed to lock them in place. The trail she was on led her right up to one of the territory's large gates. The gates were designed to roll up and down and were made of steel-bound hardwood. In front of the gate were a couple of Mavit Tomar guards, dressed in pristine uniforms of dark blue wool, and no armor. They carried short swords at their waist, and ten-foot-long pikes in their hands. They wore no caps on their heads, which might cover their Ram-like horns, which were a matter of great pride among these creatures, especially the males. They challenged her when she was within hailing range.

"Halt! Who goes there!" they called out.

"I seek an audience with your Tsar," she replied as she closed the distance.

"Who are you, that we should bother our Liege Lord?" one of the guards asked.

"I have gone by many, many names in my life, but I think I'm known to your people as the 'White Witch'. I have a proposal that might interest him and bring the opportunity to obtain great spoils for the Mavit Tomar," she said, getting their respect and attention.

The first guard whistled a complex short tune, and then a few moments later, a creature landed on his outstretched forearm. It looked like a squirrel, complete with a fluffy tail, but it had long brown wings like a hawk. The guard chirped in the ear of the strange creature for more than a minute, then the small animal leaped into the air. It made wide circles as it got high enough to fly up and over the walls. The guard turned back to Carissa.

"I have sent word of your arrival, and in a while, we will get permission to let you enter, or perhaps not. Please wait here."

She knew that it could take hours for the creature to deliver its message and return with an answer, so she dismounted and conjured a tent. The guards were astonished as she went inside and promptly fell asleep.

"Thank you, Tsar Dren for seeing me without an appointment," she said sweetly. She looked at the leader of the Mavit Tomar, who cut a distinguished figure for his kind. He was tall, with light grey fur and horns that curled to full circles above his proud face.

"I think, that had I not agreed to take this meeting, we might be having it anyway, and under less pleasant circumstances," the Tsar replied. He sat in a high-backed chair that was made of hard wood with exquisite carvings and a silk cushion attached to the seat and back. In front of him was a small table with his afternoon tea and biscuits. He motioned for the witch to join him, and she graciously accepted.

"I fear you have the wrong impression of me, my Lord," she said. "True, I do have an advanced knowledge of the mystic arts, but I do not use them against my neighbors, nor against those whom I would share a venture with."

They both knew that she was lying. She'd fought with the Vinkul before, killing two of their enforcers on one occasion, and another enforcer within the last ten years. The Mavit Tomar territory was close enough to her castle that they paid her tribute to stay in her good graces. She hadn't crossed paths with the Inoans in a generation. They avoided her territory as if it was a sacred burial ground. He gave her a knowing look with his beady yellow eyes but moved on without comment.

"Yes, the guard messaged me that you have some proposal that you'd like to discuss. I have to admit, I'm very intrigued at the thought of how I can help one so accomplished and formidable."

She accepted his proffered cup of tea and took a delicate sip of the steaming liquid. She looked up at him with eyes that would melt a human man's resolve in an instant. The Tsar of the Mavit Tomar was not as impressed. To him, she looked like the Inoans, though without any vestigial horns and body modifications. He found her repulsive, though as a born diplomat, he displayed only grace.

"Your people control a large section of Pyrros, but there are the Ice Giants to the Southwest, you're not so friendly neighbors, the Vinkul, just south of you, and the roaming Inoan tribes that control the whole Western half of Pyrros. Your magic is very strong, but the Vinkul's is stronger. Your warriors are fearsome, but the Inoans are as well, and they are many."

"Did you come this far to insult me? Through strength, we've maintained peace with the other inhabitants of Pyrros for centuries," he said, a bit perturbed. "We trade with the Vinkul on a regular basis. We get along with our neighbors just fine. You are the most feared... and hated person in all of Pyrros."

"Dear sir, it's not my intention to point out any weaknesses. On the contrary, I see that you are well-balanced, unlike the others. I come with news of land that is as yet undiscovered by your people, or any of the people of Pyrros. A whole new continent. A place where your magic will be unmatched. A place where the ferocity and skill of your warriors will be overwhelming. Land that is ripe for the taking."

"Normally, I would end this conversation here, but I actually believe what you say. My personal seer has told me that there are other worlds that are merging with ours. Worlds that were separate for millennia, are now reuniting."

"It's true, my Lord. My own good sister exists there, and she'll help me, and my allies to mount an attack. The creatures there are called humans, and they are weak in every area where the Mavit Tomar are strong."

"Hmmm," he mused. "There could be much in the way of plunder."

"And slaves, my Lord. There would be enough land and resources to build a second empire on their land."

"I think we should retire to my study. Such talk should be done over a bottle of my finest brandy," he stood and led the witch to another part of his immense estate. There they spent several hours going over the details of how and under what circumstances, an invasion would occur. By the end of their negotiations, they had decided on a strategy to test the waters, and if they proved half as fruitful as she claimed, then the Mavit Tomar would commit on a larger scale.

Chapter 7: Raiding Party

Commissar Keylan Ghor watched the sorceress out of the corner of his eye. She would be considered an exotic beauty by her own kind; but to him, she was ghastly. No fur on her pale bald flesh, no horns like a proper woman should have, and no tail. He didn't trust her, not even a little; but the Tsar was insistent that he work with her and that he should follow her commands. It was him, the witch, and two dozen of his elite shock troops. The Mavit Tomar had on round helmets with cut-outs to go around their beloved ram's horns. They wore thick breastplates, armor on their limbs, and torsos. All but the sorceress sat upon giant owls, some were snow white, and others were brown or tan. Alongside them were the Zytlyx. These hunting beasts looked like praying mantis, but each was the size of a young deer. They used these insect-like creatures as their war dogs, often sending them into danger first, to soften up a target.

The sorceress was chanting and waving her arms as part of the spell. She worked quickly, and in a few minutes she opened a portal. The Commissar could see through to the other side where an old woman was also casting a spell. The combined powers of the two women allowed them to open a huge portal that was large enough for the Mavit Tomar to take wing and fly through, followed by their insect companions, and the last through was the sorceress. When they were all safe in Kronos, the women embraced, and he could hear them call each other 'sister'. They looked to be fifty years apart in age, worse yet, there was not a trace of resemblance between the two.

"Commissar Ghor, this is my sister, Lilith. We have been separated for well over two hundred years," she couldn't help smiling at the reunion.

"Such a long time, you both have aged well, all things considered," he said without humor.

"I am slowly regaining my youth. Soon, I'll appear as youthful as my younger sister."

"Speaking of which, you have gotten fifty years younger since the last time we spoke!" Carissa remarked, looking her sister up and down.

The Commissar ignored the women as he inspected this new world. The sky was bluer, the grasses were bright green, and the air smelled... different. His soldiers were also taking in the new world. A few minutes later, Carissa approached him.

"Commissar, this is the world that I promised you. As you can see, its soil is rich, the air and water are clean, and you'll see that the people are weak and ripe for enslavement. Are you satisfied yet?" she asked.

"We came here to conduct a raid, to test the mettle of these, 'humans'," he said contemptuously.

"And you shall have it, prepare your men, we are to strike a supply convoy to the South."

The Commissar smiled, then turned to his troops and gave them the signal to mount up. The giant owls flapped their wings and lifted a dozen feet or so above the ground. The witches mounted horses and started off in a Southward direction, followed from above by the Mavit Tomar, and on the ground by the huge spindly insects. They traveled for just short of an hour before coming to a quiet hilltop, overlooking a valley below, with a large highway going East to West. Far off in the distance, a caravan was heading towards them.

"About thirty men to guard a dozen wagons. Is that normal?"

"It means that their cargo is worth protecting. They may have armed guards; but if your claims are correct, they are not the same caliber as your men. Not only that, but surprise is on your side," she said with impatience. "Go forth, claim your reward!"

The owls lifted off, carrying the horned warriors high into the bright noon sky. The insects ran with their strange six-legged gaits, skittering down the hill and around trees and shrubbery. It was almost too late when the human guards saw the danger that they were in. Several of them pulled out bows and loosed razor-sharp arrows at the Zytlyx, but though some of the arrows hit, most glanced off their shiny green and black shells. Their concentration was on the low threat, they didn't see the danger from above till it was too late.

The soldiers of the Mavit Tomar swooped down at frightening speed and with their long, light swords, were able to lop off the heads of a few of the men who were trying to get off arrows. The humans had a slight numerical advantage; but when you considered the murderous insects, they were hopelessly outnumbered. They would swipe at one of the warriors attacking from above and would fall beneath the pincers of the Zytlyx. The men fought valiantly, and they were able to kill half the insect creatures and three of the Mavit Tomar; but in the end, the outcome was never in question. They all died, and the victors were able to collect the spoils. The Commissar smiled as his men picked through the wagons. There was food, spices, hard currency, raw cloth, and metal tools.

"A nice reward. After we pay tribute to the Tsar, the men will still have much to share in. These humans fought better than I had expected, but I'm still going to recommend to the Tsar that we move forward with our alliance. If we can put these men in shackles, we will have a strong workforce to produce many goods for us."

"Very good. The next time, you'll bring thousands of your troops, and I'll find a target worth taking. When it's done, you're Tsar will rule lands both in Pyrros and here in Kronos."

"I long for that day. Please create your portal, we are ready to return with our treasures."

The sisters conversed for a few moments, then together, they again created a large window to Pyrros. The Mavit Tomar soldiers took the reins and led the nervous horses through. When the whole caravan had passed through, the Mavit Tomar collected their dead, and the dead Zytlyx. Very soon, the only thing left was the dead guards and tracks that halted abruptly in the middle of an open field.

Chapter 8: Riken

The old mage's manservant greeted Landis and the twins as they returned to the site where Argus' mansion had once been. The mansion was splintered into a broken pile of wood and stone and was scattered some several hundred feet from its foundation. It looked like a tornado had picked it up and thrown it off into the rose garden, but footprints that were easily the size of a fishing boat hinted at another scenario. Riken looked down at his charges with what he probably thought was a reassuring smile. The seven-foot humanoid had sickly yellow skin, with ears that were pointy on the top and the bottom, his smile was made up of two rows of vicious-looking fangs. By far though, his most attention-catching feature was his second set of arms. The Telnor were so rare in Kronos, that Riken very well might have been the only one. His kind were known as mighty warriors, but what few people knew was that some of his people were very skilled in the magic arts.

"What have you done to the master's house?" Jorn asked the Telnor.

"It is not my doing, Young Master!" Riken said, consternation in his voice.

"I think he's joking with you Riken," Danika said, giving her twin brother a disapproving look. They were both about twenty, with dark brown hair that was almost black, and bright blue eyes. She wore a bright red riding suit, that was becoming her personal style. She was a woman on the verge of being an extraordinary beauty. Jorn, on the other hand, was very average looking, tall and lean, with his usual thoughtful scowl.

"Yes, of course I'm joking. We know that the Master died… was killed. What arrangements are you making?" Jorn asked.

"It took a couple of days, but I got a crew of workers from town to dig through the rubble till we were able to reach the entrance to his private laboratory. We found that he had an even larger chamber, several hundred feet below that. I'll show you; it's meant for the two of you now."

"Thank you, Riken. We'd be lost without you," Danika said to the giant. "Can we see his remains?"

"Yes, I think it's important that you do. He did not die a natural death, no, most certainly not natural," he said, then turned on his heel and led them towards the rubble.

Argus was laid out on a makeshift table made of stones that were probably stacked by Riken himself. The body was covered by a sheer silk shroud. The twins and Landis walked up to the still body of their mentor. They just stared, not willing to touch the cloth that covered Argus' corpse. Landis stepped up, and with respect, pulled back the cloth that covered the old man's face.

What they saw shocked them all. They had gone through a war and had seen many horrible things, but what they saw now was something altogether new. The old mage's face was unharmed for the most part, but he was shriveled like a grape left in the sun. Every ounce of vitality had been drained from him till he was nothing more than a dry wrinkled husk of a man. Without a doubt, death by magic.

"Any clue as to who could be capable of this?" Danika asked.

"He mentioned that he had a greater threat to deal with than the Quell followers. He must have battled another sorcerer or sorceress. It looks like he lost and that means there is someone out there with enough power to kill our master. We must immediately start preparations to defend ourselves, and this world," Jorn said to the others.

"That's a lot to take on your shoulders," Landis said to the twins. "I know you're powerful, but you're still only children."

"Children? Is that how you see 'me', Landis? As a child?" Danika asked. "I guess you've not noticed that I've become a woman." She gave him a look that only an adult woman is capable of. The kind of look that entices and terrifies at the same time.

"Well, perhaps we should speak of these things in private," he said with his head down, looking at his feet.

"Yes, perhaps that's for the best," she replied.

"I don't doubt you or your brother's ability. And no, I don't see you as a child; but you're only twenty and Argus died long before he could pass all of his knowledge to the two of you."

"Well, ready or not, he's dead. Jorn and I need to try and fill his shoes. I don't know how, but we must become much better, and fast."

"There's a powerful mage out there somewhere, and you two can't even sense his presence yet. I'm betting he knows about you two."

"I have an idea, I need to speak to Jorn about it first," she said before stepping up right next to him. Landis was a bit over six-foot-tall, with dark hair and handsome features. For a man who sold his skill with a sword, he was remarkably free of major scars. He had proven his almost instinctual skill in many battles and had made a name for himself. To help battle the Quell, he had been visited by Magnus himself and was given the blessed sword Soulbane. This man who was afraid of no other man alive, almost trembled at being so close to the young sorceress.

She lightly placed her open hand on him, her long delicate fingers barely contacting his firm chest. She looked up at him with a look that he'd seen a time or two, with other women. Her blue eyes were as bright as the midday sky, as deep as the ocean. He looked into them at his own peril.

"Dani… are you sure that, we…," he stuttered.

"I had a crush on you when we met, back when I was still a child. What I feel for you now is completely different. I'm a woman now, and I know what I want," she looked up at him, calm and sensuous beyond her years.

"I'm much older than you, Dani. I had a wife, and a son, and lost them both. I don't think I could ever go through that again," he said with obvious pain in his voice.

"I know you want me. I can see it in your eyes. I hear it in your voice when you speak to me. My parents are dead, you and my brother are the only people I have left, the only ones that I love."

"You, love me?" he asked.

"Since the moment we met and a hundred times more since you came back to us last year. I know you're accustomed to winning every fight, but not this time. I'll have the truth from you or burn you to ashes where you stand."

"No pressure," he said to her. Looking into her deep blue eyes. "I had a brotherly love for you when you were younger, but since coming back, I see a beautiful woman, not the child you were before." He put his calloused hand to her soft cheek, "I never wanted to fall in love again, never wanted to risk getting hurt again…"

"But…?"

"You're sexy and wild, intelligent and caring." He paused for several seconds, "I feel guilty about it, but yes… I think I may be falling in love with you too."

"I'll accept that, for now," she pressed her palms against his chest and leaned up to kiss him. "I need to work on some things with Jorn and you need to go tell King Syphon that our troubles may not yet be over."

He kissed her again, this time it was longer and with passion, "Yes, dear."

The twins sat at the dining room table in the new house that they had built. The mansion that had been there before was mostly made of stone and constructed in a very old style, it was Argus' house. This new house was still as large as the previous one, but the twins used their magic to help the laborers to build it in just a few weeks. The new house had bones of hardwood, a skin of brick, flat stones, and glass. They performed minor miracles for the local merchants and farmers in exchange for replacing some of the furniture and decorations. Now, it was their home, and the only reminder of what came before was Riken.

The giant humanoid brought in steaming plates from the kitchen and set them on the end of the forty-foot table. He turned to go back to the kitchen when Jorn caught the elbow on one of his four arms. The Telnor looked down at him in surprise.

"Yes, master?" he asked the young man.

"Riken, can you please join us tonight?" Jorn asked. "Please eat with us."

The Telnor looked confused. Even though Argus had always treated him with respect, they didn't dine together or socialize in any way. He had always been more than a manservant but less than family. With a little hesitation, he filled a plate and took his place at the main table.

"Thank you Riken," Danika said softly. "Now that our master is gone, we are trying to go on as usual. We wanted to speak to you about staying with us, in the same capacity that you did with the Argus."

"As your servant?" he asked in a low voice that chilled one to the bones.

"Yes, but also as a mentor. Your people are known to be skilled in the 'arts', and you are wise as one who is older than both of us combined," Jorn said.

"Riken, the Master relied on you so much. Jorn and I too have come to rely upon you. Please say that you will stay with us."

The Telnor sat looking down at the fair young maiden and the young man who was desperately trying to mature ahead of his time. Their knowledge of magic was still very lacking, and they could sense that the wheels of fate were already in motion. They might not survive anyway, but they would have a slightly better chance with his help.

"You have always treated me with respect and have never feared me. I like these things," he said in his icy tones.

"Of course, the Master saw you as a vital part of his household, and we always respected your age and experience. Please help us like you did the Master!" Danika implored.

"Can you sense something children?" the Telnor asked them.

Danika was going to blurt out an answer, but Jorn held up his hand, asking for her patience. Jorn closed his eyes, and Danika could see that he was concentrating. They were all quiet for more than a minute as Jorn searched for... something.

"I feel that something is, off. That the world has not changed and yet, it's mystical energy has doubled or tripled in that spaces between the material and the mystic."

"Very good. I feel it too, though I don't have a shred of your abilities. I can feel my people. They are out there, waiting for me to be amongst them again."

"You want to leave us to rejoin your kind?" Danika asked.

"I will stay as your head of household, and you both will be called 'master'; but first, I must visit my homeland. I have not been to Tel since Master Argus awoke from his slumber and I am missing that connection to my people."

"Take as much time as you need, Riken," Jorn said sadly.

"You should go with me, masters. I think that the experience may be what you are looking for."

"A trip!" Danika cheered. "I'm in!"

"An excellent idea. I'm honored that you would want us to accompany you," Jorn added. "Magnus wanted to meet your people, did he not?"

"Yes, I was going to take him, but now I will gladly take you two. I've become very fond of this world, and there is trouble on the horizon. There was another wave that passed through Xoran. The first woke up the master and also woke up the powers that lay within the two of you. The last one was another world merging with ours. I need to see that Tel, and my family are safe."

"It sounds exciting!" Danika cheered. "I can't believe it, a whole country of your people?" Riken and Jorn could both see the wheels turning in her head.

"Let's go, first thing in the morning," Jorn said. Riken flashed his best smile which was still terrifying to the twins.

Chapter 9: The Telnor

The trip was taking a lot longer than they had anticipated. Danika watched her brother for signs of trauma. The last time that they had traveled by boat, their parents were murdered by pirates, and only by releasing their magic were they able to survive. For days he had been quiet and just stood on the deck, staring out towards the horizon. They chartered a ship at no little expense. The crew was terrified because they were sure that if they kept sailing North that the ship would soon sail off the edge of the world. Some wanted to turn around and forget the pay, but when they saw the girl with a fire fairy dancing in her palm, they held their tongues and continued sailing.

All of the fear and resentment changed several days later when they spotted land. A huge landmass that appeared on no map in all of Kronos, was now off their port side. They got closer and closer till they were able to see that it was not an island, but a continent. Per instructions from the Telnor aboard, they did not stop and instead, they followed the coastline for several more days. Now they were getting close to their destination. Ahead was what appeared to be a port city. In many ways, it was just like the great port cities of Kronos, and yet somehow this port was much larger and had an alien feel about it. Giant cranes, shaped and carved to look like the arm of a Telnor, reached into the holds of giant ships and pulled out incredible amounts of cargo. Entire ships were lifted onto cradles for cleaning, painting, and repair. Most astounding to both the twins and the crew was that everyone in sight was a Telnor.

They looked at Riken who as usual, assumed his wide-fanged grin that was meant to be a warm smile, but instead put fear into all who didn't know him. Riken had grown more excited with each league they traveled, though he tried to hide it. They were soon met by a ship that sailed out from the port to intercept them. The ship was of strange design, the wood was dark red, and the fitting were made of gleaming brass. The top edge of the ship was a mass of intricate carvings, designs of foreign flowers, beasts not known on Kronos, and of course, brave Telnor warriors. The Telnor sailors lined their deck, staring at the soft pink creatures in the ship across from them. When they were close enough, they tossed over a line that the human crew used to secure the two boats.

Half a dozen uniformed Telnor boarded the human vessel, and seeing Riken, turned to him for answers. They all wore fancy long jackets with high open collars, cinched at the waist with leather straps and signs of rank on the back. They wore scaly leathery breeches and knee-high polished black boots that went well with their charcoal-colored ensemble. They all carried knives tucked into their belts, and two short swords at their hips. The leader was bald and older; the others had thick shiny hair that fell to the tops of their pointed ears.

The leader began speaking and was asking questions in their strange language. Riken answered, his low tones that seemed to be the norm for their race. The talking went on for several minutes before Riken broke from the conversation and walked over to consult with the twins.

"Masters, the port police are willing to let me and the two of you come ashore. The crew and the boat must return," he informed them.

"Will we be able to get back?" Danika asked, seemingly alarmed.

"Do not worry Masters. I will arrange for our return, once we have seen all there is to see!" he replied with growing excitement, "Let's cross over to their ship now and they'll take us to the customs office." He turned and went back to the boarding party.

They informed the crew that they would not be landing, and for almost all of the men, that seemed just fine. The leader gave Riken a short salute with two of his four arms and then turned to lead them aboard the glorious Telnor vessel. The humans made all possible haste to adjust the sails to turn back on their course. Some looked fearful, but others stared in wonder at the sparkling city that was now so close they could almost smell food cooking in the streetside stalls.

When they had arrived, and finally stepped off the ship, Riken went to his knees, put all four hands on the ground, and touched his forehead to the dusty pier. He mumbled what might have been a prayer, then returned to his full seven-foot stature. His smile was still horrible, but the twins were glad for their friend to see his homeland again.

"Welcome to Tel," he said in his sonorous tones.

"You're our guide," Jorn commented. "Where to first?"

Jorn and Danika walked after their manservant and friend Riken almost at a run, due to his long legs and longer stride. He was average size for a Telnor at about seven feet tall. Some were taller, a few were shorter. The women were only about six foot and half foot tall, otherwise they looked a lot like the males except for mostly modest breasts and wider hips than the males. They too came in both the bald and spiky-haired variety, a few wore their black shiny hair in braids that fell to the collarbone. Both males and females wore a lot of jewelry, including wide gold bracelets, bangles, chains, and piercings of varieties that humans had never dreamt of.

They were enjoying the city of Tel, or was the whole country Tel? The twins were never sure, but they marveled at the metropolis. Where human cities in Kronos were generally one or two stories tall, the Telnor built their cities to the sky. At the heart of the town, which seemed to be where Riken was leading them, there were more than a hundred buildings that reached thirty or forty levels. They could be seen for miles and miles, and they were made to shine like ingots of silver in the midday sun. The humans were used to cities and towns with dirt streets, and on rare occasions, cobblestone. They were not prepared to find that there were wide avenues all over Tel, and each had been produced from countless hours of laying hand-sawed stone. The lamps in the windows of the stores were shaded with colored glass, which created multicolored designs on the snow-white plastered walls.

Compared to the citizens of Tel, Riken was dressed very strangely; but with two humans in tow, he got no looks at all. Men, women, and children alike stared at them, wondering what exactly they were. If the twins had not spent the last six years with Riken, their expressions and incredible height might have frightened them to death. Riken led them to a public conveyance. They climbed into a coach pulled by a team of creatures that resembled Lynx but with longer legs and a more protruding snout. Six of the beasts, carried the car along with passengers and driver, at a remarkable pace. The cacophony of city sounds, and the dazzling multicolored lights had the twins mesmerized by the delights of the city.

They passed through the central districts and headed West towards greater Tel. The country, not the city. The modern construction gave way to equally enchanting countryside. For some time, they passed through what Riken loosely translated as a crystal forest. There were a few yellowish vines and sparse Orange grasses, but the most prominent feature was the crystals; most of which were over fifty feet high, and a dozen feet in diameter. They were predominately clear; but some were milky white, milky white with blue streaks, and a few that were black and opaque. Once past the forest, the carriage soon came to a residence set in what they guessed was a farm.

Riken led them to the door, and without announcing his presence, walked in. There was much shouting in their low voices as the twins followed Riken inside. When they were in the house, they saw their normally subdued servant pressing his head and palms to a series of male and female Telnor. When the excitement had died, they all turned their attention to the aliens in their midst. A small child hid behind the skirts of a female Telnor, the rest just looked in wonderment, while shooting questions at Riken.

"Master Jorn, Master Danika, this is my family," he said with his scary smile, wider than ever and waving his hand in the direction of the other Telnor present.

"Really?" Jorn asked. "I never would have guessed."

"It is true!" he exclaimed, then he did a round of introductions. "Tonight, we have a Telnor feast. Tomorrow, I will take you somewhere very special!" The twins were not afraid of the Telnor, but they secretly were afraid of what they might be expected to eat.

In the morning, the twins joined Riken outside the home, where he had already saddled four of the cat-like beasts. Jorn and Danika both had to be helped up into the high saddles, Riken easily put his foot in the stirrup and jumped up, into place.

"There is someone very special that I want you two to meet," Riken said. "It is half a day's ride from here, but very much worth the time. Don't worry about steering the Zeerah. Your Zeerah will follow mine and my brother Mora's."

"We can't thank you enough for letting us meet your family. Thank them again for the food last night, it was... interesting," Danika said happily.

The small group started slowly but soon picked up the pace. The first couple of hours they traveled through fields with long blue grasses, huge bushes with white bark, and deep purple fruit. They finally reached a point where the scenery made a drastic change. The twins looked up to see what looked almost like a wall where the fields ended, and the 'forest' began. There were thousands of trees; but they had no leaves, so there was plenty of light. They followed a trail and saw that there was no underbrush, no leaves on the ground, nothing but bare earth.

"There's something strange about these trees," Danika said aloud.

"Can you tell how they differ from the trees you remember from home?" Riken asked.

"They look dead," she replied.

"Try and burn one," the Telnor instructed.

Danika easily conjured a small fireball and tossed the flaming sphere right at a tree that was a dozen feet from them. The fireball struck the trunk of the tree and broke into pieces that fell harmlessly to the ground. She looked at Riken with a questioning expression.

"They are stone!" he replied. "They once lived, but for a thousand years, this forest has been a forest of trees turned to stone. No one knows what turned the trees to stone, and probably no one ever will."

They followed the trail till they came upon a house, just off to the side of the road. It looked like it had been constructed from fallen stone trees. Riken and Mora dismounted, then helped the twins down from their saddles. They all approached the front door, where Riken took up a horn that was hanging on a peg and gave it a mighty blow. The sound echoed creepily through the dead woods. They heard a shuffling, then the door opened to reveal an ancient Telnor within.

"Madam Elna, I don't know if you remember me. My father is the one who comes by and sells you meat and vegetables," Riken stated.

"Riken, son of Rika. Yes, I remember everyone that I've ever met," she said proudly. "How can I assist you, and these…, what do you call them?"

"Humans. Don't you remember my telling of my master Argus, the great mage of the new lands?" he asked. "They come from the new lands, and they were training with my master, till he was killed recently."

"Is that so?" the old woman asked. She was so bent over by age that she was almost as short as Jorn was tall. Her clothing was not new and brightly colored like most of the Telnor that they had met so far. She definitely marched to the beat of her own drummer. "I may be wrong, but I'm starting to get a feeling of what you might be here for."

"Madam is known for both her intelligence and her perception. The training for these two was cut short, and now with the intrusion of the other planes on this one, their people will be helpless," he pleaded. "Please impart some of your knowledge on them, and when you are done, I'll take them back to their country."

"Why should I do such a favor? Do you think I have nothing to do all day but teach strange creatures my long-held secrets?"

"They are my Masters, and I vouch for their character. I think that you 'do' have time to teach them and that you might need their company more than they need your teachings."

"Do you, now? You think that I'm an old woman, desperate for company?"

"In the end, aren't we all, Madam? They will be respectful, they will follow your commands, and if you let them, they will become like family."

"I will try and teach them. If I find that they have no power, no skills to work with, I'll send them back to you in an instant."

"That's fair Madam. Can you cast a spell so that they will understand our language?" he asked hopefully.

The witch recited an incantation in the strange low-toned Telnor language. The twins just stood there and allowed the magical energy to surround them, to penetrate them; fully trusting their servant Riken.

"Can you understand our language now?" Riken asked in his native tongue.

"I can!" Jorn exclaimed in Telnor. "You must be a powerful mage!"

"I'm glad that you approve Masters. I will leave you with Madam Elna, she is now your teacher! Please follow her every command without question or hesitation." The twins looked at each other in surprise. Riken introduced them, stayed for a few more minutes, then returned home.

Chapter 10: Learning

She moved her hands precisely as she had been taught and chanted the words that would engage the spell; the air before her began to warp and fold. A huge circle formed that touched the ground and was ten feet in diameter. Within seconds, the circle became a window to another world. On her side of the portal there was the petrified forest, and on the other side was Riken's home. She finished her spell and marveled at what she had done. Jorn was less impressed and stepped through to be followed by his sister. Instantaneously they were transported a full half day's ride from their previous location. The older male Telnor was surprised to see them appear as if out of nowhere, his son Riken was not surprised and greeted them with his toothy grin.

"Very good! Which one of you did this?" Riken asked, referring to the portal.

"I did!" Danika said excitedly. I was having trouble remembering the whole spell, and this is the first time that I was able to create a stable holo," she said happily, then looked at her brother. "Jorn picked it up a couple of days ago. He is able to go anywhere in Tel."

"Well, I think that's just wonderful. I'll prepare Father's weekly shipment, and you two can take it back with you," Riken said before walking towards the barn.

"That would be a relief. I've made that trip a thousand times over the years, getting to take a week off would be a blessing!" Riken's father said. His mood changed to a more somber one, "So, another week or two and you are going back to your country? Riken has already said that he is going to return with you."

"Yes Sir," Jorn replied. "He can stay here if that's his wish, but he is like family to us, and we have come to rely on him."

"He makes me very proud," the tall Telnor said. "Not many of our kind would be able to live among humans, for an extended length of time without being around other Telnor."

"Well, if this convergence of the planes is permanent, then he will be able to visit you as often as he likes," Danika said cheerily.

"I know that he really cares for you two, but he is missing so much by being the only one of his kind there in your world," the old man dropped his gaze, becoming thoughtful. "If he had a wife to keep him company, that would be good for him."

"Is there someone special in his life right now?" Danika asked.

"What? No, it doesn't work that way," he said with a chuckle. "If you could stay for a month, I can begin immediate negotiations for a wife. It won't be easy, but I think I can find him a good match if I have a few more weeks to work with." The twins just stood there for a minute, not sure how to react.

"If you do find a wife for him, she too will be welcome in our home. We will treat her like family, just as we do Riken," Jorn offered. The old man smiled and jogged off to the barn to tell his son.

"Let me get this straight," Jorn said to the old Sorceress. "You can summon reptiles, birds, monsters, and even giants, but you don't know how to conjure food and drink?"

"Really?" Danika asked. "That was the first thing that our master taught us. Literally, the first thing," she said laughing.

"No sorceress knows every spell, and besides, if I did start conjuring food and drink, then Riken's father would lose me as a customer. He's been so good to me over the years," the old woman stated.

"Well, he cares about you too. That's why he's never told you that he loses money by coming this far out to deliver to you," Jorn added.

"Ok, I've shown you many things this last month and a half, crammed it in your small hairy heads. I guess it would be only fitting to learn something from you in return."

"How generous of you," the twins laughed and soon Madam Elna was laughing too.

"Children, I know that you leave me in the morning, and truthfully, I'll be sad to see you go. I know you came here to learn things to help you fight the evil that is creeping into Xoran. I ask that, even though you will be facing great dangers, please be careful. I couldn't bear to outlive either of you," she said with tears welling in her cat-like eyes.

"I have no intention of getting killed," Danika offered. "I have too much to live for."

"Both of you do. I have a gift for each of you," she said digging into one of the inner pockets of her voluminous purple robe.

"That's not necessary, Madam!" Jorn said emphatically. "You have been more than generous, more than we had any right to ask of you."

"True, but I still want to pass these tokens on to you. I have no children, and I'm old. Very old." She pulled an amulet from her pocket, a large ruby set in pewter with ancient carvings around the stone. "This is for the female," she said looking from one to the other.

"Still me," Danika said, taking the gift.

"Of course." She then pulled a dagger from another pocket and handed it to Jorn. "The amulet… oh yes, you read the inscription and become bonded with the amulet. It will know the last spell that you cast, and when you grab the stone firmly, it will recast that spell." She turned to Jorn, "The dagger is a family heirloom. If you throw it at your enemy, it will always find its mark, and as long as it touches him, it will drink his life essence."

Jorn looked again at the ten-inch knife with its wrapped leather handle, plain iron cross guards, and its engraved two-sided blade. Words in Telnor were carved along its length, and no doubt were the source of the enchantment. He smiled and nodded his thanks to the old woman as he slipped the knife into his belt. They said their goodbyes, had dinner, and went to bed for the night. The next morning, they ported to Riken's family's farm.

Chapter 11: Roku

Roku sat alone in the meditation area of the master's courtyard. It was very early, and even though there was some light, technically the sun had not yet risen. Master Kakta entered, and when he saw one of his most gifted disciples already hard at work, he walked on cat's feet so as not to not disturb his disciple's meditation. He spread out his rug and sat upon it, allowing his conscious mind to fly forth and seek other planes. He felt a very strange feeling, a feeling of weightlessness that he usually only felt when he was deep in a trance and was traveling outside of his earthly body.

Opening his eyes, he found that his senses had not deceived him and that he was floating two feet above his prayer rug. A few feet away, Roku was watching him with quiet interest. The master willed himself to return to the rug which covered the hard, stone floor of the patio. Roku waited till he was safely landed before speaking.

"That was amazing, master. You have achieved a new level of awareness?" he asked.

"So, it would appear," he said with more surprise in his voice than Roku was expecting. He looked at his disciple with interest. "You haven't beat me to meditations for ten years, not since you were a neophyte, trying to impress me and the other senior clerics,"

"You're wondering why I'm here so early?"

"Yes, what brings you here at this ridiculous hour?"

"It started while we were still on our return trip from fighting the followers of Quell, back East. I felt…, it was like a vibration in the universe. Even now, I feel that something is… different," the usually quiet monk explained to his senior. "You know that I've never been able to travel the planes like you and the senior masters. Even my sister can leave her body and explore the infinite with relative ease. Since I felt the reality quake, or whatever it was, I can now see into at least one of the other planes of existence."

"That's wonderful brother! I am so happy to see you achieve this new level of Ammun. You have been working very hard for so long."

"I wish that it was a cause for celebration, but I fear that there is a huge storm coming. Can't you feel the disturbance, master? My instinct is that it's connected to our growing strength to travel among different worlds. It should be a cause for celebration, but I fear that a great evil will use this power against us."

"I have to admit, I have yet to feel anything," he said as he closed his eyes. They both sat in silence for several minutes. Again, the old master began to levitate above the ground.

"Roku, now I am sensing what you were so in tune with. Thank you for bringing it to my attention. It is so subtle that I allowed myself to write it off as my being tired or being too tied to this world. There's energy seeping in from one of the other dimensions into this one," he drifted down till he landed on his rug again. "Please brother, summon the masters here immediately. Perhaps together we can decipher this riddle."

From all over the temple, the masters were woken and urged to join Master Kakta in the main hall. The Ammun temple sat atop a small mountain that took up half of their island sanctuary in the middle of Silver Bay. The day had begun, and a pleasantly cool breeze washed through the temple. Far below, the ocean surrounded them on all sides, filling the air with that salty smell that many found to be refreshing. They listened while the Master explained what he wished for them to try.

The monks, young and old, man and woman, all sat in their standard relaxing positions. They were instructed to calm their thoughts, to turn off the active, alert parts of their brains; and to allow the deeper, more primal areas to rise to the front. Master Kakta slowly rose from the cold stone floor, and soon, several of the other masters too were hovering a foot or two in the air. The Master reached out with his spiritual self, looking for his fellow devotees. Looking down, he saw his own body, relaxed and safely floating in the brisk morning air. Instinctively, he knew that he was not on another plane; and yet, he was no longer part of the material world.

In the air around him, they started to appear. He saw first, the young woman who was one of his most promising monks. The ghost of Melina was still an attractive young woman, her ability to focus herself was astonishing for one so young. Unlike her brother Roku, who was perhaps a perfect physical specimen, she was formidable in both flesh and the spirit. She saw her mentor and smiled as she willed herself to fly over to where he was. Before she could speak, several more of the senior masters condensed into the air above the open air patio. They looked at their corporeal bodies, astonished at what they had achieved, then they too went to join their master.

Last to the party was Roku. Though it was his heightened senses that had caused this assemblage, he found it difficult to achieve the proper state of nothingness in order to leave his body. When he saw himself as a translucent copy of the person a few feet below, he almost cried from joy. He too joined his sister and the others who surrounded the old Master. Despite his old age, in the spirit world, the master glowed with youth and vitality. His long white beard glowed white in his spirit form; his small frame seemed to radiate the power that he normally hid from others.

"I was right master, something is transpiring!" Roku said to his mentor. "There is a change in the world that not only affects the material, but also the ethereal."

"Brothers and Sisters, Roku told me that he sensed a shift in the bonds between worlds. He couldn't put his finger on it, and neither could I. But this!" he shook his thin hands at the swarm of floating bodies that surrounded him, "This is proof that our vision of the universe is at least partially correct." He relaxed and even in his astral state, they could see him close his eyes. "Can any of you detect something... irregular?"

They all looked at each other in confusion, then one by one, they closed their ghostly eyes. No one spoke for several long moments till Roku broke in.

"Master, I feel that another plane of existence is trying to merge with this one. In their universe, our powers are commonplace, and the reality that we have always taken for granted is out of the ordinary."

"You have captured it brother," Melina said to her older brother. "I have always tormented you for your lack of ability in this most important of our pursuits; and yet, you are the first to grasp the gravity of what is happening." She beamed at her sibling, "I am so proud of you, brother!"

"What you say rings true," the master said. He reached out to touch Roku's arm. Their formless bodies started to combine like drops of water on a smooth surface. "Fear not brother!" the master said as he pulled Roku in till they were one person, larger than either of the two original entities. Melina drifted over and flowed into the glowing ghostly entity. The amalgam had features of all three of the spirits that had combined. The others knew that it was safe and didn't fear for their individuality. They flowed into the growing entity that was now the mix of more than three dozen different beings.

The new lifeform was large, though the size was immaterial in this form. It had eyes on all sides of its head, it was neither male nor female, and it stared emotionlessly at the vast multi-verse. With the combined intellect of so many, it could see the planes, how they lay in layers like playing cards, and how others cut across the stack, touching them all, and yet not interacting with them. It flew up through the solid stone ceiling of the temple and was now far above the mountain that they called home.

It soared above the world they knew as Xoran, and time and space lost all meaning. They were higher than any bird dared to fly, and soon they were looking down on the world and could detect the intruder. Far to the West was another whole universe, like a million stars painted onto a giant dinner plate that was almost parallel to their own. Another was approaching from the East, another from the opposite direction. They could see that this other reality was in motion and that in a minute, or maybe a million years, they would be level with their own, and the many universes would merge into one.

At the speed of thought, they soared towards one of the newcomers, the countries of Kronos below them, flashing by with no visible borders, no differences between the people of Chuo, the citizens of Rubina, or Tebron. When they reached the sea that no one had ever been able to cross, they kept going. Below was a vast inky colored body of salty water that seemed to have no bottom and no end. They flew, and because there were no landmarks, they had no idea if they were cruising leisurely or traveling at the speed of light. Below, they saw the occasional sea monster, fish the size of warships with huge fang-filled maws.

Squid the size of whales swam below, ignorant that they were being observed.

Ahead was the intruding plane, the oceans were melting into one great body of water, and not far beyond was a new landmass. A continent that rivaled Kronos in its enormity. They could see the great forests that covered much of the land. They saw huge deserts and mighty rivers. Mountains split one of the islands almost in half, its peak, much higher than anything found on the well-manicured land of Kronos. They tried to pass over into the new universe, but it was still at a very shallow angle to their own world, and even though they were no more substantial than a wisp of smoke, they could not yet cross over.

They thought as one and were able to reach a consensus with little difficulty. They must return and let their allies know of the changing reality of the universe. There would be more opportunities and undoubtedly, more dangers. Instead of retracing their voyage, they just willed themselves to return, and they were back in their temple. The unified being fell apart, the individual monks were tired and almost fell into their waiting bodies. Roku was the first to regain his senses. He saw that the lower monks were guarding their bodies, as was their duty, and he felt great relief. When the last of them had recovered, they were addressed by the master.

"Such an incredible thing we have done! Please, all of you, take food and rest, we will meet here again when the sun is high in the sky and talk about what our next steps should be," he said in his best fatherly tone. No one objected, and they all stumbled to their respective cells and quickly fell asleep. Roku approached Master Kakta as he was slowly exiting the patio.

"Master, do you fear that this… whatever it is, is dangerous?"

"I do, brother. There are scrolls that only the senior masters even know about, and I am one of the very few that has read them. What I tell you must go no further," he sat cross-legged on the floor, and Roku followed his lead. "Many millennia ago, Kronos was the center of a much larger world. We had lands to the North, East, and West. Kronos and Tychon were for man, and the other lands were for the other races." The master scratched his head, trying to recall the details. "If I remember correctly, there was a dispute among the gods, and to settle their differences, the world was split, and the pieces were cast far apart. They can still be reached by means of powerful magic, but they are beyond the reach of our spiritual selves. That is where we lost track of the other continents."

"That still doesn't explain why you feel that there is a danger. If there are more people out there, there's no guaranty that they would be against us."

"That part only worries me a little," he said to his student. "There are creatures that look like men; but with wings, and fangs, tails, and who knows what else. There are tales of giants, and golems, dragons and demons."

"I don't know what any of those things are, master," Roku said.

"I'm not sure about all of them, but it sounds like we might find ourselves no longer the masters of this world." His expression became thoughtful and grim.

"I don't think that we are ready to take on such changes."

"We need to warn the King's Table."

Chapter 12: Wever Bran

Wever Bran sat on his 'throne' and allowed the senior fathers to come and go, each with a demand for money or bodies to help their local churches. He had the ability to deal with his day-to-day bureaucratic responsibilities without consuming all his attention. He would pass judgment, give here, take there, and the whole time he would be dwelling on the big picture. The church suffered the most in the war with the Quell. Unless he was able to find a miracle, that loss and failure would wind up being his legacy.

These kings wage their wars. The people and the church are left to pick up the bill.

Wever was the High Father of the Panist Church, a religion that followed and revered the Old Gods. Wever was tall and very thin, his light brown hair cut short enough so that his scalp was visible. Unlike the priests in his charge, he wore robes made from the finest silk that money could buy. As the head of the church, it was important to display the power and wealth that is possible through the grace of the gods. His specific patron was Magnus, the father of the Old Gods. Despite what he allowed to be common knowledge; he had never actually spoken to Magnus. To be more accurate, Magnus had never spoken to him.

"Lehna," Wever called for his assistant. The young woman came from behind his chair with a stack of papers.

"Yes, High Father?"

"I'm losing my patience. Any word yet from Syphon about getting my soldiers back?"

"No, High Father. There is an older father from Cozar waiting, should I put him off?"

"Not to worry. Show him in," he instructed.

These kings think that they can use the church as a personal treasure chest and that we can provide them with wealth and workers that rightfully belong to the church. Damn Syphon, he should not try to put the monarchy above the church. He thought to himself.

An old priest shambled in the main door of the great hall and made his way down the long red carpet. He looked to be a hundred years old, with no hair and skin that was covered in age spots and deep wrinkles. The old priest had a robe on that looked like he had owned it for longer than Wever Bran had been alive, and he walked the long hallway with great effort. When he finally got close enough to have a conversation with the High Father, he lifted his face, and he had a devilish twinkle in his eyes.

"Good morning, High Father," the old man said as a matter of custom.

"Good morning, Father. I'm sorry, they didn't give me your name."

The old priest raised his right hand, and there was a halting of time. Wever felt it immediately, he looked around the room; he and the old priest were the only ones that didn't seem to be frozen in amber. The ancient face with the youthful eyes looked at him appraisingly. He nodded before going on.

"The name doesn't matter Father," the old man said. "I have just borrowed this shell, and after we have spoken, I will abandon it." The older man moved closer so that he need not yell, "You have been waiting your whole life to speak to me, I think. Do not take it as an insult that I have waited till now to address you personally."

Wever was in a state of shock and stood to face the priest. He sat face to face with the one entity in the universe that he held in higher regard than himself. He almost fell in his haste to drop to his knees before his god.

"Lord Magnus! Is it truly you?" he asked, his voice quivering.

"Am I not the one you've been waiting to meet?" the old man asked. He climbed up and took a seat on the High Father's throne-like chair. "So good to rest these old bones."

"Praise Magnus!" Wever almost yelled. "What can this humble servant do for you, Lord Magnus?" he asked, his forehead pressed to the carpet.

"My son," he said with a sigh. "Do you believe that the kings of Kronos were chosen by me personally? That I looked at of the hundreds of thousands of people in this world and decided that 'this' family should rule, while 'that' family should sweat and till the earth?"

"I don't know, Lord Magnus. That is what your ancient scrolls teach us."

"Scrolls that were written by the hands of men. Kings are men who were bold enough to claim power, by whatever means possible, and then to have the impudence to look at their countrymen and say that they were chosen by the gods to rule over them."

"So... the men and women that call themselves queens and kings are 'not' your choice? They don't rule by 'divine right'?"

"Let's just say, if you built a world, gave life to man, and had him populate the world. Whom would you want to be in charge?"

Wever thought for a long moment, not wanting to answer too quickly and to offer the wrong answer. "If it were my creation, I would want to oversee it myself."

"That makes sense, doesn't it?" the old priest asked the High Father, with a peculiar glimmer in his eyes. "Man has been allowed to control his own destiny for a hundred generations, and what does he do? Wars, false religions, slavery... man can no longer be trusted to govern himself. He needs the guiding hand of the gods."

"What exactly are you saying, my Lord?" Wever asked.

"I am commanding you as the head of the Church, to go forth and do my will. When you're done, all of Kronos will bow to the authority of the Church, and by extension, to me," the old man chuckled at his own statement. "This last war that you men started has left many Monarchs dead, along with their noble houses. Claim those lands in the name of the church and combine them till this land is united. Form a single country, with you at its head. I will be there to guide you, behind the scenes."

"I should become the King of Kings, then?" Wever asked.

"No, no more kings. Men may call you a prophet, or you may take the title of 'Supreme Leader' after you have assumed power."

"Yes, my lord," Wever said, his head bowed in thought. "I will desperately need your assistance. These kings will not want to share power with an outsider, especially a holy man."

"I will help you. From time to time I will visit you, but never in the same form. When you know that it is indeed me, you must obey without delay or question."

"Yes, Lord Magnus!" Wever said dropping to his knees and placing his hands and his forehead on the ground.

The old man stood up and walked around till he was again between the throne and the door. He casually waved his wrinkled old hand, and everyone started moving again. Wever looked up in awe. He watched as his savior shuffled down the long hall and out the door. The feeling of euphoria was almost too much for him to contain. He called for his assistant.

Where is that woman when I need her? There is so much work to be done.

"Lehna," he said to the young woman who served him faithfully. "I have had a vision. Get rid of these rabble, prepare a supply train. We are going North to claim the first of many countries in the name of the church!"

The old priest walked around the corner and changed to his true form. She was nearly ten feet tall and glowed brightly like a miniature sun. She said nothing and just smiled as she floated up and through the ceiling and on into the heavens.

Chapter 13: The Power of the Church

The supply train moved slowly through the ravaged countryside. Many countries were spared the direct effects of the war, but Preston had been directly in the path of the Quell. They were one of the first countries to fall before the Quell hordes, and many of their citizens had either been conscripted to fight or were slaughtered for praying to the wrong deity. Most buildings were burned to the ground, and the crops were either abandoned or burned.

Wever bran looked at the land, and what he saw was an opportunity. King Syphon had finally released the Church's troops that he had commandeered for the war. They were meant to be a small force in each country, tasked with defending the local temples and just as importantly, collecting taxes to fund the Church's initiatives. He had ordered that all of his soldiers should meet at the abandoned castle of the former King Kenshin. Not only was he dead; but the entire Kenshin line had been publicly tortured and murdered by the Quell. This was now a land without a lord, without leadership.

It would take a lot of work, but Wever felt that this was the perfect place to begin his holy work. Preston would have to be renamed, and the Church would govern this land. His destiny as he saw it and outlined by who he had thought was Magnus himself, was to spread church control to all of the lands in Kronos. They rode all the way to the castle itself and right through the smashed gates. Once inside, they saw the extent of the damage. Everything that could be burned or sold was gone. There was no need to consult an engineer, the place would have to be razed and the new building would have to be built from the ground up.

"Lehna, send a few riders out and collect as many workers as they can find. We'll rebuild this castle into a mighty church. I need men of all trades, as many as we can find."

"Yes, High Father!" she said while running off to begin her task.

A bulk of the men relieved of service by King Syphon had now arrived at the once thriving town of Norman, which lay in the shadow of what would become the Temple of Magnus. Though they were not tradesmen, there was still an abundance of plain old labor that needed to be done. The senior priests were organizing and overseeing the efforts when one of the former nobles arrived to visit the new tenants.

"Lord Anders, to see the High Father," the man said to the outer guard.

He was shown into what had been the throne room, which now served much the same purpose, though it would never be referred to as a 'throne room'. He walked up till he stood directly before the table where Wever Bran was laying out his various projects. He stood for what seemed like a very long time before the High Father deigned to look up and acknowledge his presence.

"Yes?" Wever asked callously.

"High Father, on behalf of the few nobles left in Preston, we'd like to welcome you."

"Thank you, but Preston is now a theocracy, I'm not sure if there's even a place for 'nobles'."

"Preston was never a rich country, the noble houses were tasked with governing their districts and supplying the capital with men, food, and taxes. If you don't have at least one level between yourself and the farmers and bakers, the administration alone will drive you insane," the man said earnestly.

"You might have a point there," Father Bran said, considering the idea.

"Count Rhone Anders at your service Father. That's not the only reason that I've come to you today, milord."

"What else troubles you, Governor Anders?" Wever said, stressing the new title.

"The Twilight Forest. It's huge, and it lies half in Preston and half in Jaga-Koba. No one goes there because it is said that some great evil lives there."

"I've heard stories," Wever replied.

"They're not stories, Father. For a year, devil dogs would creep from those woods at night and seek out the blood of man, woman, and child. Nothing that enters those woods ever returns."

"What would you have me do?"

"You'll need a lot of wood to rebuild your temple and to help your citizens rebuild their homes and businesses. I would cut down every single tree in that damned forest."

"Let me pray on this brother. I will see if the gods think that it's the right course of action."

"Pray all you want, Father; but you have a cursed forest in your lands, and by the gods, it will only bring you suffering," with that, he bowed and left.

Chapter 14: Syphon

Kel was glad to be home. He had tried to summon Magnus, to no avail. King Kell Syphon was widely praised for defeating the followers of Quell with a minimum loss of life. It was the wish of Lord Magnus that he retain his leadership over all of the lands in Kronos. Even though he was respected for his victory, none of the other kings, aside from King Herron, seemed to be willing to bow to him as King of Kings. The last thing that he wanted was to try and take the title by force. The Quell had wiped out six of the nineteen royal families and their houses, leaving those lands ungoverned. They had also drained the land of young men. Disaffected and unhappy men, to be sure; but no country could afford to lose so many healthy hands.

Ravi Syphon walked into his brother's study, papers in hand. He was Kel's younger brother and shared his tall, good looks. They were both dark, their skin the color of rich growing earth, and both wore their hair cropped short. Ravi had a beard without a mustache, and though he was four years younger, looked like the older of the two. As usual, he greeted his brother and king with a grim look on his face.

"Brother, some dispatches have just arrived. I have not read them, but judging by who sent them, I can only imagine what they portend," he said, handing over the rolled scrolls.

"Best not to imagine, especially when the truth is literally 'in hand'," he smiled at his brother.

He opened the first and scanned it, then handed it over. "Sarutendo is trying to put off the special King's Table meeting that I requested. Typical of him." He opened the next, read it, and handed it to his brother. "High Father Wever Bran is demanding the release of their soldiers from service. They shouldn't even be allowed to build their own private army." He skimmed the last dozen notes, then gave them to Ravi. Kell sat at his desk and picked up his pen while pulling out a fresh scroll. He stared off into the distance for more than a minute before Ravi broke the silence.

"Kell, how are you going to unite the kingdoms if Sarutendo is going to block any meetings of the King's Table?"

"If he's going to be that way, I can bring the kings here, or meet with them one on one."

"I don't think that they'll believe that Magnus told you personally to become the King of Kings," Ravi said to his brother.

"I can show them my hand. They all know that I lost it fighting monsters a year ago, and now Magnus has returned it to me. Surely a miracle will convince some of them."

"You would think so; but they, like you, are men who were born to be kings. Though you are not asking them to give up their birth rights, they still can't imagine bending the knee to any 'man'. They cooperate in times of crisis, but the war is over and now they won't feel like they need you anymore."

"I'm going to start with what I hope is an easy one. Let's invite Prince Heron for a state dinner." Ravi nodded and watched as his brother made out the dispatch, rolled it up and sealed it with wax and an imprint of his signet ring. Taking the papers, he left the king alone in his study to contemplate his next course of action.

Olehya looked at her husband as he paced back and forth in their dining room. She enjoyed the title of 'princess' but knew that the chances of being upgraded to 'queen' were very slim. Her brother-in-law, was very popular with the people. He had more than his share of women, and it was only a matter of time before he chose one, or one was chosen for him. Once he becomes a father, all other branches of the family tree are effectively cut off. She was tall and curvy; her skin was as black as midnight and shone like polished ebony. Her black hair was long and straightened into a waist-length ponytail. Pressing a hand to her lower abdomen, she imagined the child that had just taken hold there. In her mind, the child was a boy and he would of course be tall and strong like his father, and smart like his mother. For this child to not become king was an injustice that she could not allow to pass.

"What do you think about this, 'King of Kings' idea? I've heard Kell's thoughts, I'm more interested in what you think, my love," she cooed to her husband while massaging his tense shoulders.

"He is a great warrior. I saw the beast that he brought back from his hunting trip. It would kill most men without leaving a trace. He claims that Magnus himself spoke to him and that Magnus gifted him with a hand to replace the one that he lost," Ravi said to his wife.

"So, the kings of Kronos should bend the knee to your brother? Is he truly so wise, that he can make decisions for everyone in the world?"

"I think it would be more of a 'wartime' title. I don't think that he would try to meddle in the day-to-day decisions of their individual countries," Ravi said earnestly.

"Really? What about the issue of slavery? It's legal in the North; but here in the South, most countries outlawed it generations ago. Would he be bold enough to declare slavery illegal, and then back it up with force?" she asked her husband.

He looked confused for a moment. "I don't know, we haven't thought this idea out to all of its possible ramifications.

Would he be just a wartime leader? Or would he be a true king of all the peoples of Kronos." Ravi looked uncomfortable with the direction that the conversation had taken. "I don't know for sure; but from knowing him, I think he is inclined to let the kings rule their own lands and he would exert his authority only when there is a crisis that affects all countries."

"I know him too, and you're probably right; but is that what Magnus wanted him to do? To take less than total control might be exactly the opposite of what He has commanded. The king that I want to follow is one that is decisive and carries out god's will with single-minded devotion. He must, without question, enact the will of Magnus," she stroked his scalp with her strong hands while speaking. Enjoying the massage, he closed his eyes. She continued, "You follow the will of the gods without question, do you not, my husband?"

"Of course, my dear; but they have never sat around a fire and spoke to me one-to-one as they did with Kell."

"If you are happy to live forever in your brother's shadow, that's fine. I thought that the man that I married was more ambitious. If you think that he is so deserving of everything, that he can do no wrong, then at what point would you draw the line?"

"What are you talking about woman!" he said rising to his feet. She was tall for a woman, but he was taller still and quite imposing. He looked down at her like a man who had been pushed to his limit, "What evil are you trying to foster?"

"Evil? Me? Dear, I just want what is best for you, and for your son, that is even now growing in my womb. I just need to know that the father of my child is committed to me and to Chuo. Our country needs a king that is willing to do what is needed to expand our borders, and still protect the common man. A god-fearing king, who obeys our Lord on High without question."

"What you are saying is treason, wife! I can forget this conversation, but I need to know that you do not really harbor these evil and traitorous thoughts!" Ravi said, shaking his wife like a rag doll.

"Don't call me traitor!" she screamed at her husband. "I tell you that you are to be a father, and all you do is protect your brother!" she said as tears ran down her flawless cheek.

"A baby," the words hit like a sledgehammer. "What a blessing," he said looking at his feet. "This is great news, my love."

"Yes, a blessing from the gods themselves. We have tried for so long. I'm so happy that we'll soon be graced by a son. I just want a country where he'll grow up to be safe, and yet proud of his father. Kell is a politician. You my dear, have the soul of a warlord!"

"A warlord?" he asked.

"Yes, I can see you at the head of one hundred thousand men, with all of their banners, subordinate to the Chuo banner. I see you, sword raised high, leading them into battle against the tide of evil that Magnus has said is coming." Ravi stood there thinking of his wife's words for a long time. They did not speak of it again that day, or for many days to come.

Chapter 15: The King's Tables

King Syphon had his great hall cleared out and left nothing but the giant dining table and accompanying chairs. He had a second table made and used it to increase the occupancy for the special meeting that he had called. All the remaining monarchs of Kronos were invited, along with other important, and or notorious characters. For days they rolled into the port town of Kilburn, the largest city in Chuo. The capital was a thriving city and a staple for travelers of the Iron Road. When all the primaries had arrived, he called the conference to order.

King Kel Syphon was in his best suit, a garment that was both rich in its materials, and regal in its cut. He stood tall and proud, looking over those who were his peers. He was a man that was known for his bright smile and his warm nature. Today, he stood as stoic as he did when leading the combined troops of Kronos off to battle. "Brothers, Sisters... many of you are weary as I am. Tired of fighting, tired of war. I thought that defeating the Quell would allow us all to go back to our previously peaceful lives, but there is growing evidence that our troubles have just begun," he said to a room full of groans.

"Before you get started Kel," said King Sarutendo. Everyone took note of his familiarity, and how it was, at best, a rude breach of protocol. "This is not the King's Table. In fact, it's two rather plain tables just pushed together. I've heard your requests for convening 'The Table', but frankly, they just weren't convincing," Sarutendo said, spite thick in his voice.

"I may be wrong, but I'm guessing that you speak only for yourself. You have no position of authority, and as such, have no right to decide when the King's Table convenes." King Syphon checked each face to see if there were any dissenters and found none. "I was visited by Magnus and was told by him personally, that there were new lands in the world, across the seas from Kronos. Whole countries that were wild and filled with strange and dangerous creatures."

"That's blasphemy!" Wever Bran cried out, as he leaped to his feet, "How dare you say that you've had an audience with the King of the Gods when you are not even a regular attendee of the church! The gods speak to me, and through me only!" he screamed.

"I hate to be contrary to the High Father, but that's just not true. If you remember, at the last King's Table, I showed you all my wounds. I showed you all where a creature had bitten off my hand? Well, look at this." He pulled off his gloves to show the room his two good hands, long dark fingers stretching to show that they were real, "As a blessing, he returned my hand, and told me that the fight had just begun. He also said that we must be united, and to truly be united, we must have one leader. A King of Kings."

"And I suppose you're talking about yourself for the position?" Sarutendo said from the far end of the table.

"His hand was definitely gone," interjected Renata Rin, the Warlord of Inram.

"I saw the wound before the war started," Landis Stone added. "Only some very powerful magic, or a miracle could grow back a lost limb. Such magic is far beyond what the Anant twins can do, and their mentor Argus was killed while King Syphon was leading the army."

"Who could kill the most powerful mage in all of Kronos?" asked the Master Trader, Genia King. "Only a god or a demon could kill such a man."

"Jorn tells me that there is an evil sorceress in the Twilight Forest and that she is the source of the evil that plagues us. She's still alive and is again gathering power. She's actively seeking aid from demons and summoning creatures from different worlds. We have to bolster our defenses and gather allies to our cause. When she feels she's strong enough, she'll unleash her minions on all of us, regardless of our imaginary borders."

The bald-headed monk near the center of the table stood. He was in a black jacket, with loose white pants. He was calm, but his presence radiated power. "Brothers, Sisters, I am Roku. I am here to represent the Ammun. Some of you know me already."

"Who cares! How did you get invited to this meeting!" Sarutendo yelled from his end of the table. Everyone looked at him in disbelief. He sat again, fuming.

"Our order is very in tune with the spiritual world, and we often leave our bodies and let our souls travel between dimensions, visiting the different planes of existence. Recently, our powers have increased dramatically, and we believe that it's because other planes have merged with our own. Where there were many worlds, soon there will be only one." Everyone else at the table was confused by the warning, but they all respected the Ammun's reputation for truth.

"The twins have gone on a voyage to visit the land of the Telnor. Their Telnor servant said that his homeland is now accessible by ship, so he has taken them with him. I believe that there may be one or more continents, every bit as big as Kronos, just across the sea," Landis informed the group.

"If there are more countries out there, filled with people, we should try to contact them. It might be a good way to increase trade, and find allies as well," Genia added.

"This is heresy!" Wever screamed, still frothing at the mouth. "I don't know what trickery was involved to help you recover your lost hand, but it was 'not' from Magnus. He speaks to me and tells 'me' his wishes." Everyone was looking at the priest in disbelief. "We have claimed Preston in the name of the Church. The former king and most of the great houses are all gone, murdered by the Quell. Now the people cry out for proper guidance. Preston will become a country ruled by the Holy Church and will prove to be a guiding light for all heathens!"

"You can't just claim land and declare yourself King!" King Syphon roared.

"Why not? Didn't each of your families come from nothing? Instead of being 'blessed' with royalty, instead of being 'chosen by the Gods', your ancestor just took what they wanted."

"There is something to what he says," the Warlord chipped in. "I overthrew the ruling house of Inram, and now I rule with the permission of my subjects."

King Jalen Hardine stood, "Much of the North is now leaderless. I think that having the Church in control of Preston is a good thing. We can't allow so many to remain leaderless. House Hardine claims the lands in Jaga-Koba east of the Langloo river."

"Impossible!" said King Vivek Fionn of Margera, standing and pounding on the table. "That would almost double the size of your holdings!"

"That land was taken from us almost three hundred years ago. We are just reclaiming what is rightfully ours," Hardine shot back.

"That's enough!" King Syphon barked. "If we start debating who took what from who, we'll be here forever. For now at least, let's vote on the Church claiming Preston, and on Kees expanding their borders."

"I would like to add one more agenda item to this conversation," a finely dressed man said from the back of the room. "My name is Lectr Vaughn, I am the owner of the Far East Trading Company, as most of you who live East of here are familiar," he said walking up to the table. Many of the attendees were not familiar with his face but they were all familiar with his name and his company. The man was a bit over six foot tall, with short dark hair, no facial hair, and a large scar that ran from just under his right eye to the crease between his cheek and chin. The quality of his suit was matched only by Genia King's, and he carried a gnarled walking stick with priceless gems set into a band just under the hand grip.

"This is a special meeting of kings, and today that would include the kings of industry. Please say your piece," King Syphon said.

"Thank you, milord. I have heard rumors about creatures and magic, and I very much believe what you say. War is coming again, and we need to prepare. I have vast resources at my disposal, and I am willing to pledge a considerable sum to the cause."

"In return for...," Prince Herron interjected.

"As a child, my family used to summer in Ursina, and if any of you have been there, it's one of the most beautiful lands in all of Kronos. For three years now, they have not had a leader or any real law and order. I would like this table's blessing to become the King of Ursina, of course with hereditary rights. I can provide all of the required records of lineage, titles, and such."

Several of the kings, especially the remaining Eastern kings balked at the ascension of a regular citizen to a royal position. On behalf of the Church, Wever Bran strenuously objected, though he didn't get a vote. Genia King, the only other business person there, was also strenuously against the proposal. She too had no formal say in the matter. They finally came to a majority consensus after promises were made to help fund a new compound for the Church in Preston, and other payments were promised. Lastly, and most importantly, the presentation of a lineage that showed the Vaughn family having descended from an ancient royal line. They took a couple of quick votes, and both of the other claims narrowly passed. The tempers around the table were rising and they were getting to the point where no one was listening to anyone else.

Genia King, the Master Trader stood to address the group. She was of average height for a woman, her dirty blonde hair cut short and her suit worth more than anything worn by the room full of monarchs. "Business is just war by different rules. We must act immediately and decisively," she said firmly, looking at each of the powerful men and women in turn. "I will provide a ship and fund the venture to make contact with these new continents. We need to make allies, and fast."

"And you will be able to open trade routes and increase your wealth! Filthy opportunist!" King Sarutendo screamed from just across the table, his look was venomous.

"Calm down Imanol," she said using his first name in a show of great disrespect. "Yes, I will profit, but King Vosbarra will gladly accept the taxes that I pay. When my business was in your kingdom, you deserted me when I needed you the most," she said turning the knife. "You all talk about kings and gods, etcetera. It's business that makes life possible. Business puts people to work and creates the wealth that everyone in this room has benefitted from. Business pays for the food that your armies eat, for the armor they wear, and even the swords that they carry." She looked at the host, "King Syphon, do you accept my donation to our common cause?"

"Gratefully, Madam," he replied. "I would suggest taking Roku and Landis there," he said pointing at the former sellsword. "Both men are supremely competent," Kel offered.

"I'm familiar with Sir Stone's abilities, with and without a sword," she said to the shock of many, and to Landis' great embarrassment. "Landis, will you lead a team across the great sea?"

"Yes Miss. I'll bring Father Sebastian and of course, if Roku is willing, his skills would be greatly appreciated," he said looking to Roku. The monk nodded.

"Excellent! My ship, the Alexandria, will drop me in Goldport. After that, she is yours for the length of your mission. I suggest we leave at daybreak in the morrow." There were no objections, and so it was decided.

Chapter 16: The Mission

"Landis Stone, to see your Highness," the clerk announced.

Kel looked up from his writing and smiled his usual bright smile. The sword for hire had proven to be a reliable and highly skilled weapon in his arsenal. He waved to the clerk to let the man come forward.

"My king, I'm sorry to arrive without an invitation or an appointment," Landis said, bowing his head.

"Nonsense! You are welcome in my home anytime that you wish. How are the twins doing?" he said rising to clap the warrior on the shoulder.

"They are fine milord; but without their mentor, they are sorely in need of education. I think that is partially why they agreed to journey to the Telnor homeland."

"Really? I didn't know that they had mages. I figured that with Argus dead, the twins were the newest Arch mages of Xoran."

"Unfortunately, that's not the case. The old mage died at the hands of an evil sorceress. One who was as ancient as he was, and equally skilled in the arts. She was behind the rise of the Quell and those wolf creatures that attacked the knights of O'Bell."

Kell fell silent at this troubling news and motioned for Landis to sit at the table. "What, if anything, do we know about this sorceress?" he asked.

"Nothing really. Argus never spoke of her, but Jorn seems to think they shared history. Jorn tells me that she opens portals to other planes, allowing all manner of evil to enter our world. He and his sister are very worried that our troubles are not over, that in fact, they might have just begun."

"You heard Roku told tales of how another universe was trying to merge with our own. If that's true, then men and beasts will be able to travel back and forth at will. We can barely withstand war against our own, much less fight off creatures that fly or breathe fire!"

"I fear the same, milord. The twins are going North to a land that only their manservant Riken knew existed. I'm told, it is also where the Emar are originally from. Hopefully, they will pick up more experience. The boy has visions, and he has seen a terrible war in our future. It will be much larger and more devastating than our battle against the Quell."

"Let's hope they can learn something useful, and possibly find potential allies. It sounds like you're familiar with this Genia King?"

"I worked for her several years ago. She's a ruthless businessperson, but she pays well."

"It sounds like you received more from her than coin," he said with a wry smile. "She is providing the ship. I'm guessing she'll be looking for exclusive trade contracts if you are able to find some far-off country full of regular people."

"It may as well be her. She is the dominant trader in the West. That Lectyr Vaughan seems to control almost all trade east of here."

"I'll trust her for now, but she was disrespectful towards Sarutendo. He's a turd of man, but he's still a king."

"He demands respect, you command respect milord," Landis said plainly.

Chapter 17: The Team

Landis stared out at the ocean, watching as the sun rose and turned the black water into a beautiful blue-green sea. Only minutes ago, they had departed from Goldport and were now making their way out of the bay. Father Sebastian was still below, catching up on his sleep. A few feet away, the usually quiet monk was meditating. The warrior was getting lost in his own thoughts until he felt a hand on his shoulder.

Landis turned to find a man about his age, also dressed as a sellsword. The man was just under six-foot, a few inches shorter than Landis. He wore a hood that covered his dark curly locks and had a thick beard and mustache that had hints of grey. He wore leather armor in the style of the Lochmar Riders and carried a huge bow on his back.

"You're Landis Stone, are you not?" the man asked.

"I am. Should I assume that we have a mutual acquaintance?"

"I go by the name Tennyson Coe. I was asked by Genia King to accompany you, and the two religious types on this journey. Never hurts to have another sword, eh?"

"Father Sebastian is no fighter, that's true; but that one over there." Landis nodded in Roku's direction, "He's deadlier with his bare hands than most men are with a longsword."

"Still, strength in numbers, right?" he said with a grin.

"True, it's good to have another wandering soul to travel with. They," He indicated everyone else, "can't understand what it's like to take a fee, and then be ready to die for a new employer." Landis looked the man up and down again. "The way you wear your leathers..."

"I was one of the 'Riders' for many years; but when they were almost wiped out at the battle of Yost, I found myself without a home. I've been a mercenary ever since."

"And the bow you carry, it's one of the Lochmar Giant slayers?" Landis asked.

"Well, I've never met a giant, but it'll take down anything on two feet." He tapped on Landis' steel breastplate, "It'll go through plate like a quill through wet paper."

"I guess it's a blessing that you'll never be aiming that blasted thing at me."

"Not to worry friend. I accepted the contract, I'm your man till death claims one of us, and if it be you, then I'm to continue the mission," he stated.

"Genia is practical, I'll give her that."

After rounding the devil's tongue on Agron's northern coastline, they headed out to the open sea. The men of Kronos didn't have complete maps because they feared the vast open ocean. The ship that the King Trading Company had lent them went due West, and with every league, they traveled further than anyone in their homeland had ever gone. Days went by, and there was no land in sight, not ahead, and no longer in their wake. A week passed, and then two, and the crew grew restless as they were sure that they would come to the world's end. Only Landis' dominating will and his faith in the people that he turned to for guidance kept the crew from mutiny or madness.

"Sir Stone!" the captain nearly shouted, though they were standing close to each other. "Give us the order! We need to turn around before we reach the edge! I feel it in my bones, we are a day's sail, maybe two, from reaching the end of the world!" he implored his passenger. "The money to take ya out here was great, but it wasn't worth me life!"

Landis gave the man an icy stare. No words were necessary, the captain knew that Landis could cut him down in a one-on-one battle. If the stories were correct, he could cut him down in a ten-to-one battle. Seeing no break in the man's resolve, he slunk away, beaten. The wind kept the ship moving forward at a brisk clip, the sun was bright and the weather exceptional. The passengers were enjoying a delightful trip, but the crew, fed by the captain's uncertainty were scared and miserable, till...

"Ahoy, land ho!" Came the call from the crow's nest. A young lad, who spent most of his time aloft, called out the sighting of land. "She's not an island, she stretches as far as the eye can see!" he called out from his perch.

Landis looked at the captain from his vantage point near the prow of the boat. The man tried unsuccessfully to hide the tears of joy and relief that came to his eyes. The crew abandoned their various tasks to rush to the front of the boat to hang on the rails. They strained to see, and soon it was evident that the lookout was correct. A massive landmass lay directly in their path. Landis, who was only twenty percent skeptical, felt vindicated about his treatment of the captain and crew.

"You don't have a definite destination, do ya Sir?" the captain asked as he approached Landis, relief in his expression.

"No. We're all of us explorers. We're going where no man of Kronos has ever gone, and for that, we should all be proud," Landis said to all who were close enough to hear.

"True, true; but I'll be skirting the coast till we find something that even vaguely resembles a port. I figure, if we put you in a city, things will be easier on all of us."

"Sound like a good plan." the warrior said, clapping the captain on his shoulder.

It took almost two days of sailing parallel to the coast before the crew saw signs of life. The nearby shore was full of fishing vessels, and hours later, they came across what must have been a commercial port. There were warships, traders, fishing boats, and luxury craft. Setting anchor, they put a skiff into the water, and Landis, the priest, Roku, and Tennyson all piled on, along with a small contingent of sailors to row them ashore. They were not met by anyone and made it all the way to the piers before anyone noticed that they were not locals.

As the ship pulled up to the pier, the dock workers stared at the ship and crew, and the crew stared back at them. Everyone on the docks, and on the other ships in the port had black skin. King Syphon was black, as were his family, and about half of his citizens; but in this new land, every single person was dark-skinned. They looked at the crew which was predominantly white as if they were some aberrations of nature. Landis made it a point to be first down the gangplank. He was approached by a few workers, and a tall man who by his dress, looked like a supervisor.

"Greetings," Landis said to the man. "We are new to this country, we come in peace."

"I know that your new here. I just wonder if you are spies of the Doreh," he said grimly.

"I don't know who the Doreh are, we come from Kronos, across the great sea," Landis said while pointing in the direction from which they had come.

"I don't know about such things. You'll need to come with us to the city magistrate."

91

Landis turned to the ship, "Tenn, Father, Roku, come with me. You other men, tell the captain, please keep the crew onboard till we return."

"Yessir," one of the sailors replied happily. Landis stepped onto the pier and was followed by his small group. They followed the supervisor down the long pier till they were able to set foot on land.

"What is the name of your country, Sir?" Father Sebastian asked.

"You really don't know?" the man asked incredulously. "This is Koregar, one of two countries that make up Tychon. The Doreh occupies the other half of the continent, their country is called Hadon. We Uzor, occupy all Koregar." They walked down the main street; every eye was on them as they walked toward the city center. "You have no Uzor in your country?" he asked Landis.

"You mean people with dark skin like yours? We do, in fact my lord, King Syphon is a man whose skin is your shade, and there are some others, but they are a minority in our country."

"Well here, 'you' are the minority," he said with no little satisfaction.

Landis and Tennyson both accepted the glasses of wine that were offered; Roku and Father Sebastienne declined in favor of cool water. The Magistrate, Aren Lamont, waved for them to take seats in his private study. The man was very dark, his hair was cropped to less than an inch from his scalp, and his beard and mustache were much longer, the beard being tied with a gold ring a few inches below his chin. His clothes were made of fine yellow silk with white trim. He looked every bit of what he was, half businessman, half politician.

"Please tell me again where you say that you're from?" he asked the group.

"We call our continent Kronos. It was created by Magnus, the King of the Gods. Each country in our land has its own royal house. We were sent here by King Syphon on behalf of all the leaders of Kronos. We seek allies for a coming conflict."

"Really, I have never heard of this 'Kronos', and the Uzor are well known for their seamanship. You say your land is two weeks due East?"

"Yes, Magnus told our king that other lands would appear, and so it seems that they have. I think a month ago we would have found only open ocean here and now we are in your homeland."

"Of course. You are from a different tribe than these others?" the Magistrate asked Roku. The monk looked startled at being addressed.

"Yes, my people are from an Island in the North. I am a monk of the Ammun religion."

"This is all very fantastic. Is there any proof of what you say?" he asked them.

"Are we ourselves, not proof?" Landis asked. "You say that there are light-skinned men in the North. Are we like them?"

"No, no you are not. They are a savage and war-like people. They only have fishing boats, they don't have any seaworthy vessels like the one that you arrived in," he said rubbing his scalp. "What is it that you seek? Why have you come here?"

"Our patron wants to find markets for trade, and our king looks for allies in a conflict that we fear is coming to us sooner than we can prepare for it."

"This all sounds like it is far above my station," he said looking over the strangers. "I'll have to contact the capital, to inform King Lollando," the Magistrate turned to his secretary, "Westa, bring the Speaking Pool."

In a minute or two, the young man came in, pushing a large basin of water on a sturdy wooden cart. The basin was about two feet in diameter, almost a foot deep, and made of copper with intricate designs carved in it. The Magistrate stood and walked over to the basin and looked down at the still water. He chanted a series of words that activated the device.

The water blurred, and shortly, a face appeared. The woman looked at him, questioningly. "Yes?"

"This is Aren Lamont, Magistrate of Omar. I must speak with the king."

"I'm Linea Bkar, the royal mage, and councilor. You can speak with me. What is so important Magistrate Lamont?" she asked.

"Madam, strangers have arrived at our port, and they claim to be from a large landmass far to the East. They are white, but they do not seem like they are Doreh."

"And you believe what they say?" she asked, "They sound like Doreh spies."

"I will leave it to the crown. Do you want me to send them to the capital?"

"That won't be necessary. I will come myself to collect these spies."

"When can I expect you?" the Magistrate asked.

"I told you that I am the royal mage. I will be there within the hour," her severe expression left no room for doubt. "Do not let them get away, or it will be 'you' that I drag before the king."

Tennyson, Roku, Landis, and Father Sebastienne sat at a café near the Magistrates office. They were kept on a short leash, awaiting the arrival of the king's advisor. They sat marveling at the city, that according to the Magistrate, was a shadow of the capital. The roads were paved, and a few of the buildings were built so that they were a dozen stories. Brightly colored signs adorned every door, and banners were stretched across the road at intervals. The bright colors, the trees and flowers that were planted in esthetically pleasing locations, and the sculptures gave the city a positive, life-affirming feel. A thought came to Landis, that Kronos may 'not' be the most advanced society in this new world.

They were enjoying a strange new drink called coffee when two very attractive black women approached them. The one who looked to be in charge was petite, perhaps five feet and a couple of inches. Her straight black hair was pulled back in a ponytail that reached the middle of her back. Her facial features were small and delicate like a child's. Over her white blouse, she wore a knee-length black coat, high black boots, and blue silk pants. She wore an amulet that seemed more than just an accessory, and she carried a wooden staff that was several inches longer than she was tall.

Behind her was another woman, much taller and with skin that was a few shades lighter. She had short curly hair that just touched her collar. She wore brown leather pants, thigh-high black leather boots, and a puffy light blue blouse. She wore many pieces of jewelry, several earrings in each ear, gold and silver rings on her fingers, gold bracers on each wrist, and a leather collar with emeralds set into it. Landis looked at her wide brown eyes and instantly had difficulty breathing. She could tell when a man was attracted to her, and she was one to use it to her advantage. Unlike her friend, she wore a curved saber at her shapely hip, and a dagger tucked into her wide leather belt.

"Obviously, you are the strangers that the magistrate notified us about. I am the king's councilor, Linea Bkar, and this is my younger sister, Anisha Bkar," she said indicating the tall woman behind her.

Both Tennyson and Landis stood to welcome the women with slight bows. Linea stood evaluating the foreigners, her skepticism clearly showing in her expression. They looked at the very tall young man in a plain brown hooded robe. They saw the soldier who was dressed for war but claimed to be on a mission of diplomacy. The hooded man with his ever-present bow and smile, and the monk who didn't mix with his own people, much less the native Uzor.

"Please sit with us, the coffee here is very good. I want to bring this drink back to my people," Landis said. The women didn't smile and continued to stand rigidly.

"I'm told that you claim to be from a large country to the East, but we know that there is nothing there. You are liars, of that I have no doubt; but I'm trying to find out why you would approach us with such a wild tale."

"I don't much like being called a liar, Miss!" Landis hissed at Linea. "If you'll not listen to reason, perhaps we must speak directly with your king."

"You'll meet him, to be sure. We are going to take you before King Jarondo Lollando, and if he too sees the liars that I see, you'll die in the tourney."

"Only your sister carries a sword, and you're going to take us to some kind of trial? What if we resist?" Tennyson asked the very serious young woman.

Linea said a few words in the strange language of magic while making signs with her long, bejeweled fingers. Almost as one, the men fell asleep, their heads literally bouncing off the table. Everyone around took notice; but when they saw the panther crest on her breast, they turned their heads. Linea then worked her magic, and a rift opened in the air beside her. She turned to two large men at a nearby table.

"You two! Help carry these prisoners through the portal!" she commanded. The men grabbed Landis and the father and carried them through, to dump them in cells on the other side. They then came back for Roku and Tennyson, again carrying them through the hole in space. When they were done, the Bkar sisters stepped through the portal, and then the portal folded in on itself and was gone.

Chapter 18: Recruiting

Lilith dropped the various components that she had collected into the cauldron. The boiling liquid fizzed as the last of the powders was added to it. The smell of the smoke was horrible, but it was what told her that she had mixed the potion correctly. She stirred it absent-mindedly, her thoughts strayed to the task ahead of her. When she felt that it had cooked for the proper length of time, she poured some of the liquid into her humble clay cup. The rest she poured into crystal vials and stoppered them for later use. Tilting the cup back, she downed the whole contents of her cup in a single gulp.

The change took place almost immediately. Falling to the ground, she writhed as her body changed into a twenty-foot serpent. Her arms became long leathery bat wings, and her legs lengthened and melted together till she was a snake with the same rough body mass that she had prior to downing the potion. Now her skin was smooth and scaly, with brilliant green, yellow, and orange stripes. Flapping her wings, she lifted from the ground and flew up and out of the dense forest.

Making her way south, she flew high enough so men couldn't shoot her down with bow or bolt. Her wings beat at the black night sky and her tail undulated as if she were swimming through the air. She didn't make great time, but it was still much faster than traveling by horse or carriage, and she was still able to reach her first stop by the time the sun was breaking the horizon.

Seeking out a specific farmhouse, she flew into the barn through a hole in the roof and settled into the hay piled up on the upper level. The cocks were crowing, but she was tired and quickly fell asleep. When she awoke hours later, she was again, an old haggard crone.

"Ma'am," the boy called up to her. What ya doin' up there in our barn?" He was early twenties and was a fairly handsome young man. She inspected him from her perch. He had long black hair that touched his shoulders and he seemed fit and healthy.

"Help an old woman down, young man?" she called to him.

"Of course; but that still doesn't answer my question of who you are, and why you're sleeping in my family's barn," he grabbed a coil of rope and climbed up to her. He could tell that she was frail and that her climbing down the ladder was a recipe for disaster; so, he looped the rope around her a couple of times, then lowered her down, inch by inch, till she was safely on the ground. "Don't know, for the life of me, how you got up there in the first place."

"Why, by magic of course," she said plainly.

"Magic, ya say?" he said laughing down at the old woman. "That's a rich one, by the gods! Why would a powerful mage such as yourself sleep in my father's hay pile?"

"I flew all night to get here and felt that I should rest before evaluating you," she said taking a seat on a hay bale next to the wall. "You scoff at the mention of magic, and yet... some strange things have been happening to you recently, no?" she asked.

"Like what?" he asked, a hint of fear seeping from within his confident outer shell.

"Like things happening around you that can't be explained. When you get angry, afraid, or anxious, does something happen that can't be explained?"

He stood there thinking, looking down at the ground. Lifting his head, he looked at the woman, and his whole demeanor had changed. "There were a couple a times..." he said hesitantly. "A couple a days ago, I was collectin the herd out yonder, at the far end of our property, and these men come. They knocked down our fence and were taking our cattle," he said, anger flashing across his face, just thinking about the theft.

"What'd you do, boy?" she asked him.

"I didn't really do nothin. At least, I don't think I did. Every animal that we own is a hundred hours of my father sweatin and workin away to make our ranch successful. To see them strangers take our property, taking my father's labor... There were a half dozen of them, and there weren't nothing that I could do to stop em," he said fighting back tears.

"What did you do boy?" she nearly screamed at him.

"I felt helpless, and at the same time, I felt a burning hate for 'em! I wanted 'em to suffer and die!" He looked her in the face, "They saw me and was gonna ignore me; but then they started coughing, and scratching. It looked like blood was coming from they eyes and noses, mouth and ears. A minute or two later, they was all lying dead on the ground. They looked like they had caught the plague."

"You did that, boy. You have the power, and your hate, fed by your magic, killed those men," she said, her face alight with anticipation.

"No! That ain't possible!" he screamed while taking a few steps backward.

"Of course, it's possible. I'm telling you what, in your heart of hearts, you already know. You're different from the rest, from the masses, the regular people. You have natural abilities that set you apart from the common folk, abilities that make you 'better' than them."

"I, I don't believe you," he stuttered.

"The more you deny it, the more you know deep down that what I'm saying is true. You want to know how I 'really' got up in the top of the hay barn?" she asked. "I transformed into a winged serpent and flew many miles to find you. I want you to leave this life of drudgery and sweat, and to join me. What you did by instinct is the tip of the iceberg, compared to what I have to teach you."

"My family needs me. What'll they do without me to help out?"

"You're not the oldest son. When your father dies, your brother will take over, and you'll be... redundant. They only see you as free manual labor. You are meant for so much more."

"How do I know that any of what you're saying is real?" he asked.

Lilith gave him a quiet chuckle, then looked at the rope that was lying on the ground near where he had let her down from above. With a casual wave of her hand, the rope came alive. Coils of the thick rope flew at the young man, wrapping around him a dozen times till his arms were pinned at his sides and his legs were held together. He watched in panic as the rope started to constrict. He was being crushed and he was having a hard time breathing.

"You have two choices, boy. Free yourself, or die," she said casually as she again sat on the hay bale.

"I can't move my arms! Hard to breathe!" he gasped. He looked to the old woman for help or support, but she looked at him with cold dispassion.

He knew at that moment that he was on his own and that no one would come to his rescue. Through blurry eyes, he saw the rope that was slowly strangling the very life from him. He concentrated on the rope, and how he wished that it would crumble and break so that he could be free. The rope responded to his wishes, by starting to smolder. The fibers grew dry and brittle and began snapping as they aged and withered before his will. In what felt to him like an hour, but in reality, was only a minute or two, the rope was sufficiently withered to allow him to flex and break his bonds. He looked at the old woman incredulously, not able to vocalize what he was feeling.

"Very good. You have the natural ability, very strong. With my guidance, you'll be able to be a master of the natural world, a diviner of the mystic world, a person of... substance."

"Let me say my good-bye's," he said as if asking permission.

"Be quick. We have another stop."

Lennox shuddered, trying to shake off the sensation of having been transformed into a reptile. The wings were gone, and his strong arms were back where they belonged. What had been a tail was again a set of long legs, and scaly skin was replaced by the soft flesh of a human. A dozen feet away, the old woman was having what appeared to be a heated discussion with a young woman who was about his age. The girl was blond, average looking, but with a very serious and responsible demeanor as they spoke. He couldn't hear a thing and felt it would be impolite to move any closer.

The discussion went on for a long, long time. Just as he started to get bored and started dreaming of having a nice white mouse for a snack, the fireworks started. The younger woman was enveloped in a yellow glow, energy that he could feel even from as far away as he was. She looked like she was ready to unleash this power when the old crone grabbed both of her wrists. The girl growled in anger, but soon, her cries became panicked and mournful. He saw the back of the old woman and was facing the girl as she became old and withered. Her eyes closed and she dropped to her knees, only being held up by the old woman. Her skin cracked, like the pages of a book in a fire, flaking off and turning to ash.

Lilith let go of the girl and stood a little more erect before turning around. When she did, her appearance shocked Lennox. The crone was now just an older woman, perhaps his grandmother's age. Where before, she had looked every day of her hundreds of years, she now looked to be healthy and in her sixties.

"By the gods!" he exclaimed. "What just happened?"

"She didn't have your common sense, to join us in setting up the new power structure in Kronos," she said to the young man. "And I must insist on no more of that 'Gods' talk. We don't follow those gods" She smiled at him, "We have our own."

Chapter 19: King Herron

"I'm sorry to hear about your father, Gabriel," King Syphon said solemnly.

"It was a long time coming. Considering how he suffered at the end, it was more of a blessing," Gabriel replied. He seemed taller, almost six feet tall now, his light brown hair combed to the side and his spindly limbs were starting to grow and take on some definition.

"So now we're equals, as you once predicted," Kell said, giving Gabriel a sly look.

"We are equal in title, but you know that I don't consider us on the same level. I'm still in favor of you becoming the King of Kings," Gabriel said.

King Syphon regarded his friend and ally critically. A week ago, he was a prince, and now he was the king of Khatuna. A year ago he acted like an under-achieving, over-indulged brat. His good looks, quick wit, along with his large purse let him skip through life without a care. Then the Quell came, and because of his father's poor health, he was forced to be the leader of his country's army. Since then he had grown up a lot. He still had his looks and his good humor, but he was cognizant of his responsibility to his country and to all of Kronos.

"Have you found a wife yet?" Kel asked his junior.

"Found a wife?" he asked laughing. "You're a fine one to talk. The most desired bachelor in the world, and you're wondering if I am off the market. You're safe milord, I'd be happy to pick from your rejects."

"The time for wine and women will come, but I have a mission for you," he said returning to his usual grim self. A year ago, he too was wild and immature, but now he had the weight of the world on his broad shoulders.

"Anything, my king," the younger king replied without hesitation.

"War will come again, and we need to be prepared. I'll need every man and woman that is competent with a blade to join us. Fools like Sarutendo think they can play politics while our enemies gather their strength. People like him and the High Father must be worked around. Whoever does not join us voluntarily, will join us by conscription. I may not have the title of High King; but in everyone's best interest, I'm going to start acting as if I do."

"I'm with you, Sire. The men of Khatuna are never more than a few hours from being ready to ride," Gabriel said proudly.

"Very good. I need you to sweep East and collect armies and stores from the kingdoms North and East of you. Put them into your army, create a great fortress, and be prepared to march in any direction at a moment's notice."

"I'm with you, but if this evil comes later, as opposed to sooner, we'll both be driven out of our keeps and strung up for treason," the younger man remarked.

"True, but I believe the predictions of Magnus and am willing to risk my life, and I guess your life too, that we are doing what is right," he smiled at Gabriel.

"I'll return to my home in the morning; but for now, let's have a drink or two, and celebrate life."

"Gabriel, are you sure about this? Your father is barely in the ground, and now you're taking such decisive actions!" the queen mother asked.

"I think that it's very wise mother. A military fortress within our borders will cost a fortune, but it'll also bring jobs and outside money to Khatuna. I'm going to put it right on the Iron Road, and a town will spring up around it." His valet walked into the room. "Send a message to Jorn and Danika Anant, asking them to please come to House Herron as soon as they can."

"What's that about?" his mother asked.

"They are the mages that I told you about Mother. They are very powerful, and I think with the right enchantment built into my fortress, it might help us to repel the invaders."

"I don't believe in such things. Monsters, and demons. Really!" She shuddered at the very thought.

Chapter 20: Legacy

Octavia Sarutendo looked in the mirror, fighting back tears. She was twenty-five and had yet to find a husband. She was not a classic beauty, but her face was more than pleasant. Her body was young and firm, and her long honey-colored hair fell to her waist in long gentle curls. When she was younger, she would stand beside her mother as she dressed, and watch as the queen would finish off her ensemble with a diamond-studded tiara, a necklace with an emerald the size of a walnut, gold earrings, bracelets, and broaches. Now, her mother no longer had such luxuries, their father had lost so much of the family's wealth since becoming king that they had to sell almost all of their trinkets. As the princess, she had nothing to wear, and she had only a single servant. Without a sufficient dowry, she would never find a husband.

Walking down the long hall of the family castle, she entered her brother's room without knocking. The young man was just over twenty and looked very much like his father. She didn't like her brother much; but to be honest, she didn't like anyone very much. She knew that if things were allowed to proceed as they were, she would be doomed to be an old maid. She knew, like almost everyone in Tebron, that her father's ill-treatment of the trader Genia King was the beginning of the end of House Sarutendo. Octavia hated the woman who almost single-handedly destroyed her family and their good name. She had very little love for her fool of a father, whose greed was the beginning of his downfall. She hated King Syphon of Chuo for making her father look like a fool by illegally convening a King's Table. There were many enemies, and few allies on the road to redemption for House Sarutendo.

"Brother, we need to talk," she said while standing over the younger man. He was chatting up one of the chamber maids, who upon seeing the wild-eyed princess, ran from the room. Octavia sat on the bed next to him, putting her arm around his thin shoulders. "Brother, our legacy is in danger. If things continue as they have for the last six years, we will no longer be 'royalty' when it's time for you to ascend to the throne. Providing we live that long," she added for emphasis.

"I know things are tight, but we should have faith in Father," he insisted.

"Why? He had a good thing going, then he stabbed that businesswoman in the back. That bitch has been very cunning and has been the cause of all of our troubles. Obviously, Father needs to go. He's nothing but a liability at this point."

"What you're saying is treason, sister," he said shocked at her forwardness.

"Yes, but it's in the best interest of House Sarutendo, and of the people of Tebron. How can they hold their heads high, when their monarch is leading a pauper's life?" she asked.

"I do get a lot less respect when I'm in town. I feel that they are speaking ill of us behind our backs," he grumbled.

"Exactly! If Father is content to piss away our legacy and leave you without a crown, and me without a dowry, we must take matters into our own hands!" she looked him in the eyes.

"What manner of treason do you propose sister?" he asked.

"First off, we must have new leadership. I will find someone to do the deed. I want you as our king before winter," she said without remorse.

"Then?" he asked.

"We have many enemies, they must all be dealt with. Harshly, and in the correct order."

Octavia sat in her father's drawing room behind his great desk. She had called for one of her father's lower functionaries to report to his office. The man was shocked that instead of appearing before the king, he was to have an audience with the princess. Damon Cern was only twenty-seven, but he had high ambitions and was known for being a closet intellectual. He was shorter than the average man and was thin and frail. Octavia had noted his cunning side and had decided that, even though he was sworn to her father, he would become 'her' man.

"Damon, have a seat," she instructed.

"Yes, of course, milady," he said nervously.

"How do you think that my father has been performing as king and ruler of Tebron for the last ten years since he took over from his father, my grandfather?" she asked.

"He's a great king, my princess! I'd follow him to the bitter end if that was my fate!"

"That's unfortunate. I'm his daughter, and I've lost all faith in him. Tebron is the joke of Kronos, where we were once an economic powerhouse, we're now paupers and everyone knows it."

"Everything that you've said is true, my princess; but what would you have 'me' do about it?" he asked carefully.

"I think that we need to go outside Tebron to find resources to help with 'regime change'."

"That's a very dangerous road to go down, my princess," he said, warming to the conversation.

"I know the dangers," she stated. "I've studied everyone in my father's employ and you're a smart, ambitious man, who under the current administration will never, ever, reach the top."

"Really?" He seemed shocked by this blunt bit of information.

"Father's man, Lord Luton, hates your guts. You made a small joke at his expense three years ago. He never forgets, and he never forgives."

"So, I've wasted my time here," he said bitterly.

"No, on the contrary. You caught my attention. When my brother becomes king, you'll be an important person in the new administration. On the rise." She leaned forward, pushing a small sack of coins towards Damon, "Leave in the morning. Don't come back till you have experts who can clear the path for my brother to assume the throne. Your star will rise with his," she smiled at the cunning little man.

Damon Cern waved the barmaid over to order another round of drinks. Across from him was a fat, fiftyish go-between. The slimy type who could, for a price, procure anything. Damon had traveled two weeks to find this tavern. The Black Bull was renowned in central Kronos for being a place where you could get into trouble or find services that couldn't be acquired in a respectable society. He had devoured a full meal of the tavern's best steak, potatoes, and followed by rich deserts, two servings. Finally, they had capped the evening with several rounds of expensive Cozar whiskey.

"It has been a pleasure dining with you, but it's time to get down to business. I've already told you what the job is, can you handle it?" Damon asked.

"Son, what you're asking for is very dangerous... and very expensive."

"That's why we are looking for out-of-town specialists."

"Are you prepared to pay half in advance? No refunds, regardless of what happens, and if any of this comes back to me. You'll die a very slow and painful death."

"Agreed," Damon said, pushing a pouch of coins across the table. "There can be 'no' collateral damage. Take out the target, no one else may be harmed."

"No problem, the man I have in mind is a master at precision. When the job is complete, a week later, a man will appear at your office to collect the balance. I don't need to tell you what would happen if you were to be even a copper short."

Black Adder had a tiny crossbow attached to the back of his left hand. Instead of crossbow bolts, it shot long darts. Two silent shots took down the gate guards. He usually used one of his lethal, fast-acting poisons, but today he used a blend that caused temporary paralysis. He was under strict orders to kill the target only, with no other casualties. Security was light because the target was no longer a man of wealth, in fact, he was relatively poor for one with his title. After a few more darts and a lot of walking slowly and softly through the huge castle, he was at the entrance to the king's private chambers.

He peered into the inky blackness inside the bedchamber. The queen had her own bedroom down the hall. King Imanol Sarutendo was fast asleep, dreaming of regaining his wealth and position. The assassin walked over till he stood over the man, watching him sleep. Pulling a special dart from his waist pouch, he pushed the point into the sleeping man's neck. The king bolted upright in bed, with a small cry from the mild pain.

"What's going on here? Where are my guards?" he demanded.

"They are laying about, where I left them," he hissed.

"You need to leave right now! If I had my sword, I'd run you through!"

"It's too late for that. You're already dead. The poison I used on your guards was non-lethal. The poison that I just injected you with is very lethal. You have two or three minutes at best."

Imanol looked crushed. He was defeated, and he knew it. "Why, why would you do this?"

"For the money, of course. Nothing personal."

"But... why?" he pleaded.

"My guess is because you're a bad king," Black Adder said as the king started to droop.

"I... yes, you're right. I am a bad king," he said before dying.

Chapter 21: Lollando

King Lollando rested his large, calloused hand on the neck of his pet and friend, Eko. Hardly a cat, Eko was a pure white Panther that was huge, even for a breed that was the largest of the felines. She was calmed by his touch and didn't react to the strangers that were in her midst. He sat on what was a throne for two, the small couch-like seat was draped in exotic furs from the various predators in Koregar. He wore a turban of white silk, bound with a silver netting which held a two-inch diameter gem of the deepest and most captivating purple. He wore a vest of the same white silk, open to reveal his bare chest, strong from years of fighting in defense of the Uzor. He wore simple pants, baggy at the bottom where they met his shin-high boots, his pants were high-waisted and had several blades tucked into the sash of his belt. Beside him was his queen, Amara Lollando. The queen was very dark-skinned, like her husband, but her skin had a luster to it as if she was carved from flawless ebony. Despite her beauty, she was dressed in a long tan cloak with a hood, beneath she wore a simple brown shirt and tan pants. She had gold at her ears and on her wrists, but she was otherwise without excessive adornment.

The strangers were brought before the king and queen and were marched down the long, carpeted path that stretched from the chamber entrance to the throne. He studied the strangers as they approached, taking note of their manner, their expressions and demeanor. By the time they reached the petitioners circle, the king had formed a few conclusions. In front of the small procession, was his advisor and sorceress, Linea Bkar. As usual, she carried herself with more than a little pride, and as usual, she had a displeased expression on her face. Behind the group was her sister Anisha, pushing the strangers along as if they were already prisoners.

When they came within a few feet of the throne, the warrior and the archer bowed, the monk bowed even lower, and the very tall priest just stood quietly. They had all been stripped of their weapons before being allowed an audience.

"I am Jarongo Lollano, and this is our queen and my wife, Amara," he said acknowledging his mate. "Despite my councilor's misgivings, I am not yet convinced that you are Doreh spies."

"That's good, your Highness because we have never heard of the Doreh, and to be honest, we've never heard of the Uzor either," Landis stated.

"See how he lies, my king!" the sorceress proclaimed. "The Uzor are known throughout the world as the highest and most advanced civilization. Even the lowest Doreh knows of our greatness!"

"You answer your own question, witch," Tennyson chimed in. "We are not Doreh."

The king stood and raised his hand, and everyone abandoned their defensive stances.

"You put me in a difficult position. My heart tells me that there is truth in what you say, but I have relied for many years on the advice from my councilor and sorceress," he said to the newcomers. "I have decided to leave it in the hands of the gods. Trial by combat will decide if you lie or speak the truth. Choose your champion, we can settle this, here and now."

"If it is to be armed combat, I'm your man. If unarmed, brother Roku is our choice," Landis offered.

"My usual champion is away on assignment. In his stead, I would have Anisha Bkar represent the crown," the king stated, then turned to the young woman who stood in the back. "Anisha, do you prefer armed combat or unarmed."

The young woman blushed at having the attention put on her. She looked at her sister, whose expression was angry, but otherwise indeterminate.

"My king, I thank you for your confidence. I am highly skilled in the saber, and prefer armed combat," she stated.

"So be it. You, what's your name?" he said to the leader of the foreigners.

"Landis Stone, your Highness. I must object; I do not fight women."

"You feel that women are beneath you, Sir?" King Lollando asked.

"On the contrary, your highness. I revere the fairer sex. I could no more strike a woman than strike my own sainted mother," he said with all sincerity.

"I have no such qualms, Sire," said Roku, stepping forward.

"Very well then, clear the circle," the king commanded, indicating a circle that was prescribed on the floor with smooth, red stones set into the tiled floor. The royal couple watched from their position directly in front of the circle, and everyone else but Roku backed out. Anisha Bkar stepped into the circle while pulling out her three-foot-long saber. The curved blade gleamed in the subdued light of the hall. She stepped forward, her face both nervous and anxious. Landis noticed her fighter's body, toned from countless hours of sparring, and felt a quiver in his loins.

"You have no weapon, outlander!" she called to Roku. "Arm thyself, or this will be the shortest trial in many a year," she warned the monk.

"I am content to fight without weapons. They are, after all, just extensions of ourselves," he said. Without waiting for an answer, he stood straight, stiffening his body, then he spread his legs wide and put his arms forward, forming a circle in front of his body. All those watching, which was everyone in the hall, could see him relax his whole body in an instant. He went from firm and unyielding to calm, relaxed, and pliant. With his eyes closed, he took several controlled breaths, calming his body and focusing his chi. When his eyes finally opened, Anisha took it as the signal to begin.

She opened the contest with a very deliberate slash at Roku's neck. Not a serious strike, but more to see if he had any skills at all. Dodging easily, he slipped to the side, watching her moves and storing the information for later. She lunged at him with a feint and then followed with what she was intending to be an actual attempt to connect with the unarmed monk. He could read the feint in her eyes and ignored it. The true lunge, he side-stepped and allowed it to come within an inch of connecting. She started getting perturbed by his refusing to be struck by her and redoubled her efforts. She began a series of slashes, strikes, lunges, and each time, the monk blocked her. He met her wrist, stopping her chop, and when she would lunge, he would sweep his hand, turning her blade to the left or right. The whole time, he never struck her or even attempted to harm her. The fight went on for several minutes, Landis and the king both admiring the show of skill. Linea watched her sister being outclassed and stood there galled by the display. Anisha started to get weary of the fight, but Roku not only showed no sign of slowing down and he refused to even break a serious sweat.

The king stood again, and with a commanding voice, ended the contest, "Halt!" he bellowed. "It is clear that our guests are skilled, and yet have the courtesy to not harm their hosts. I declare Roku the winner of this challenge, and through his efforts, you all are found innocent of any charges of espionage," he said, then took his seat.

"Tonight, we shall feast and get to know these strangers. Please be prepared to indulge us with stories of your country and its people," the queen announced. "Ikala!" she called out to her handmaiden. "Please find quarters for our guests, and attend to even their smallest request," she ordered.

Again, the men from Kronos bowed and took their leave, following the servant to their quarters on the far side of the compound. When they were settled, Tennyson turned to Roku.

"Very diplomatically done, friend," he said to the monk.

"Not at all. I too, do not believe in striking females. I would have let her cut me to pieces before harming her seriously. I'm glad that my skill was such that my death was not necessary."

"What do you make of these pale-faced strangers?" the queen asked her husband.

"I don't believe that they are Doreh. Perhaps what they say is true, and there is a landmass to the East. I should send ships to verify that part of their story at least."

"The bald one made a fool of the Bkar girl."

"Both Bkar sisters lost face today. I am glad that no one got hurt; I would hate to lose Linea's sister. Despite what we saw today, she is quite skilled at combat. Gods only imagine if the other one had fought her. He probably would have been forced to kill her or stand fast and be executed."

"If only Wanaka were here, I think he would have taught the lot of them a lesson," the queen said, referencing the king's preferred champion. "Have you heard how his sabbatical is going?"

"I've not heard from my fiercest warrior and closest cousin in a month. I hope that he's safe."

"I'm sure he's fine dear, the man is un-killable. With any luck, he's trying out potential wives. I'll be glad to see him settle down. He's the only person I know who prefers spilling blood to sex."

"That's unkind of you my queen. Completely true, but still, unkind," he said smiling.

Roku sat cross-legged on the ground in the queen's garden. Linea Bkar was there, also sitting with her legs crossed, though she was not as comfortable with the pose. Roku had been there for ten or fifteen minutes with his eyes closed; he continuously chanted the mantra of the spirit self. She watched him, very skeptical that anything that he had said to this point was real. When she was just about to officially give up, her patience gone and her attention wandering, it happened. She was looking about the garden, smelling the fragrant blooms and looking at the myriad of bright colors when in her peripheral vision she saw the remarkable. The bald monk with dusky skin and exotic features began to levitate where he had sat. He appeared to not be conscious of it, his body floating several feet above the ground and his calm expression remained unchanged. She was accustomed to many schools of magic, but this seemed very different. She tried to sense if he was gifted with arcane skills; but after trying exhaustively, she determined that what he was accomplishing was not magical in nature.

The monk soon returned to his physical form, and his body slowly floated down to gently rest where he had been sitting. Opening his eyes, he was the picture of calm. He looked at the sorceress and saw that she was suitably impressed by his demonstration.

"You saw the levitation? That was for the most part, unintentional. The true miracle was what you could not see, with your physical eyes," he said calmly. "When in that heightened state of relaxation, where the body is shut down, the spirit is given the freedom to roam. With proper training and dedication, one can leave the material world behind and travel the astral plane. When your consciousness is free to explore the dimensions that lay on top of ours, you are truly free."

"I don't understand, Roku," Linea admitted reluctantly. "Are you saying that you can become… a ghost?"

"No, and yes," he answered cryptically. "Your spirit can travel at the speed of thought if you train it to. When I was in that state a few minutes ago, I was able to visit my homeland and see my sister at her chores. Then with a thought, I was back at our ship back at the port where we landed. From there, I flew through the air till I came to this magnificent city of yours. You brought us here unconscious, and I assume we traveled by some spell. I know that we are two weeks ride from the port and that this city is by far the largest in your country. The biggest I have ever seen."

"Everything you say is true. With such abilities, are you not the perfect spy?" she asked.

"I guess that is so," he answered thoughtfully. "Now that we know that you exist, I can let my astral form fly here any time I wish. The material world is not even aware of the existence of the immaterial, and only a few highly perceptive individuals are able to 'feel' that they are in the presence of a person in his spiritual state." He looked up from his kata, regarding the sorceress, "Please tell me, if you will, how you came about your powers. In Kronos, we only had two magic users that I know of. Their master having died recently."

"Only two? There are many magic users here on Tychon, though the Doreh don't trust magic, and kill anyone they suspect of having the gift," she mused. "I still have my mentor, though I haven't seen her in ages. It makes me want to visit her."

"Where is your teacher?" Roku asked.

"She is very old, though she was old when I met her as a child. Her name is Monoka, and she lives in a small village several days from here."

"In a world where magic is possible, and where a person can travel the universe at the speed of thought, don't you think that your king will entertain the possibility that what we say is the truth?"

"I know that he now believes you, after the trial by combat," she said painfully. "He heard my advice, yet even before the contest, I think that he believed your people."

"I have a different culture and a different religion than the others, but I have no doubt that their character is beyond reproach. If they can negotiate trade, and perhaps even an alliance, I hope that would bring our peoples together."

"Well Monk, against my will, I'm coming around to your side."

"If you have goods that my people desire, a trade pact is an easy first step. As far as being allies, I'm not sure what the benefit is for the Uzor," King Lollondo stated plainly.

"Maybe nothing," Landis said. "Our lands have always been without magic, without demons and beasts; at least as far as I know. There are legends and stories that only children believe, but the times are changing. There are holes between the planes, and hordes of creatures are spilling into our world. Their goal is to exterminate us. If you start to have the same problem, wouldn't it be good to have our people fighting beside you?"

"Mr. Stone, I won't say 'no' yet; but you are very far from a 'yes' right now," the king said waving the servant over. They sat near each other at a very long dining table, but they only used the head of the table and the seat next to it.

"If you could send a representative or two back with us to see that the dangers we speak about are real, maybe then you would reconsider," Landis proposed.

"Perhaps. Maybe you should speak with the Doreh. They are no friends to the Uzor, but they are white like you, and maybe their love of fighting will make them more likely to join you. I warn you though, they are a savage people. You will find no city in the world as grand as this one. By comparison, the Doreh are still living in homes of wood and thatch, and many of them live by raiding amongst themselves. Sometimes, they dare to cross into Koregar. We push them out, kill some; but I have no desire to have open war with them, their numbers are too great."

"Could you help to broker a meeting with their leader?" Landis asked.

"There are many tribes, they have no 'one' leader. If you could convince one of the larger tribes to join your cause, then you would have a powerful ally," Jarondo sipped his wine and thought. "I will ask if my counselor would like to at least escort you to the border. I hear that her stance against you and your friends has softened a shade or two."

"That is generous of you, Sire," Landis said, lifting his cup in salute.

Chapter 22: Peace Mission

The last of the group stepped through the portal before Linea closed it. They took in their surroundings, with different responses. Linea and Anisha Bkar were nervous, they were a short walk from the border between Hadon and Koregar. The two peoples, Uzor and Doreh had fought so many wars to no effect, and now they maintained a tenuous peace.

For the Kronos group, this was an adventure. The air was cold and crisp, and when they spoke, steam issued from their mouths. The trees were of a variety that they had never seen before, instead of broad green leaves, they were covered in dark green needles, with brown cones on the branches. The border was a frozen river that stretched as far as the eye could see from west to east. They walked out onto the ice, and finding it solid, crossed into the country of Hadon where the Doreh's power was absolute. They were not invited, but there were no diplomatic relations, so there was no one to ask permission.

Far in the distance, they saw huge creatures roaming around in packs. Each one was covered in thick fur, the adults were the size of houses with huge ears, ridiculously long noses, and giant white tusks coming from their mouths. The herd grazed a few hundred feet away, seeming to not care about the humans in their midst. The young hid behind their mothers; but the bulls looked at the group menacingly, as a warning. The group worked its way around the herd, leaving enough room to let the creatures know that they did not pose any threat.

"Wow, those animals are huge!" Tennyson exclaimed.

"They're called Mammoths," Anisha said.

"A little on the nose, don't you think?" Tennyson said chuckling.

"They sometimes roam in Northern Koregar, but mostly they are found in Hadon," Linea explained.

The sky was cloudy and windy, snow started falling softly, soon to be replaced by a driving storm. They had prepared and brought thick hides for each of them, their bodies were remarkably warm, but their faces were painfully chilled by the cold. They walked on for hours, not seeing anything but deer and moose. Far above, a hawk circled, and each time it came around, it flew lower till it was only a few dozen feet over their heads. Landis looked at the bird of prey and could swear that it was staring at them.

"That hawk had a ring on its foot, looks like it is scouting us for the Doreh," Anisha stated.

"The bird is a spy?" the Father asked.

"They are trained to scout up and down the border, to look for interlopers like us. Before we get much further, they will know that we're here," she said with almost regret in her voice.

"Well, we are here to meet with them, see if there is room for an alliance," Landis said.

"I think we are risking our lives on a very slim hope," Linea said. "King Lollando might come around if his scouts return with news that what you say is true. The Doreh are savage and difficult at best. Only our skill at war keeps them north of the frozen river back there."

"Fear is not in Landis' vocabulary, and I go where he goes," Father Sebastienne proclaimed.

"The Doreh don't care if you fear them or not," Anisha said as they marched on.

An hour after the hawk had flown away, they could see activity on the horizon. Many miles to the left was a wall of the strange trees, and to the right and ahead was nothing but snow-covered plains. They could see for a long distance, and there was nowhere to hide. There were a couple of dozen black dots, heading in their direction. The dots grew into men, mounted on the backs of war horses. When they got closer, they saw that the men were also trailed by wolves, larger than any breed found on Kronos.

Both men and women were riding shoulder to shoulder at the fastest speed their mounts could run. Without exception, they all had long blonde hair, the men with long thick mustaches and beards. They wore thick coats of animal skin, the blue, grey, white, and black fur keeping their bodies warm. On their heads, they wore nothing and seemed not to feel the cold on their faces. When they got close enough, they started chucking spears at the trespassers. Linea cast a spell that caused all of the missiles to lose their forward momentum and fall harmlessly to the ground between them.

"Hold!" Landis yelled, walking forward and holding his hands up, in a non-threatening gesture. "We come seeking peace," he said to their attackers.

"We ask that you grant us safe passage to speak with your chief," Linea said.

While they were talking, the Doreh had closed the distance and now formed a circle around the men of Kronos and their Uzor guides. Their leader dismounted and walked closer till his chest was almost touching Landis'. His skin was even paler than Father Sebastienne, his golden hair was wild and looked like a Lion's mane. His black eyes had a cunning cast to them, their ill intent was reflected in his menacing smile. He was several inches taller than Landis and was built thick all over like a tree stump.

On his back, he wore a wooden shield, painted bright red and blue to represent the colors of his clan. He stared down at the soldier in gleaming armor, his hand resting on a long sword that most men couldn't lift, much less wield.

"You're not Doreh," he stated. "Where ya be from, stranger?"

"I come from across the Great Sea. We traveled a long way, more than a score of days to reach the shores of your neighbors, the Uzor."

"They didn't kill you, so you join them to invade our land?"

"We are not invaders. As I said, we wish to parlay with your chief or king, whomever you follow."

"Parlay? Sure. Come with us, we'll take you to our king," the man said with a smile that did not instill confidence. "King Svengard is a fair man, and I'm sure he's open to hearin your story."

"I like this, not!" Anisha whispered to the group, "I don't trust these people!"

"A little late for that," Tennyson commented. The savage warriors collected their weapons. They were surrounded and were then escorted further North, away from the border and deeper into Doreh territory. The men of Kronos checked out their hosts as they were traveling. The women dressed and acted much like the men. They all carried small axes, daggers, and wooden shields, and they wore furs and dark-tanned skins. The men and the women had designs permanently etched on their skins, thick and thin lines of black, red, blue, and green that formed intricate designs. Their horses were also marked with paint that coordinated with their riders, and they had thick fur near their ankles to keep them warm while traveling in snowy lands.

After riding for a few hours, they reached the outskirts of a city. Ahead were dozens of buildings, all built from raw logs, stacked and cemented in place. Thatch roofs and smoking chimneys were on every building that was for housing or meetings. There were hundreds of men and women roaming here and there, carrying food or supplies on their backs. They bore knives but were obviously not of the warrior class. They gave the strangers a quick look, then lowered their heads and returned to their labors. The raiding party that served as their escorts, or possibly their captors, walked them through the maze till they reached the main thoroughfare.

When people saw the Uzor women, they took notice and were openly hostile towards them. They saw the two white men, who were obviously not Doreh, and another man who was different from both races, and they were confused. They had only gone a few blocks before the locals started tossing vegetables, rocks, mud, and even a few eggs. They ducked what they could, but after a few blocks, they were covered in trash, and Linea was bleeding from a cut on her cheek. It took all of her self-control to not unleash hell upon the townspeople. They slowly rode for endless blocks through the primitive-looking city, with every eye on them, hating them. Father Sebastienne caught up with Linea, and before she could object, he placed his large, yet soft palm on the still-bleeding wound. A soft light escaped from between his hand and her cheek, and she was startled by the heat of his touch. They went along for a minute or two, till he felt the task was complete. She looked at him in stunned silence while touching her cheek, only to find the wound completely healed. He replied only with a humble smile.

"Sir," the Father asked. "Where are we going? It seems more like we are prisoners being paraded for your own glory than as emissaries seeking audience with your king."

The savage, giant of a man, hauled off and struck the priest hard enough to knock him from the saddle. The Father tried to rise only to be kicked again by the savage. The whole party laughed at the hilarious scene.

"Coward!" Landis yelled, "He's a peaceful man of the gods! Face me instead!"

"Shut up, cur!" the larger of the party yelled. "You foolishly surrendered without a fight and now, I'll sell you to the games. Even if the price is low, and I fear it will be, I lost nothing in the capture of you lot," he couldn't help chuckling as he prodded the Father along with the head of his war axe.

"What's your name, you bastard?" Landis asked.

"Why do you ask, slave?" the man demanded.

"When I'm committed to killing a man, I feel it's only proper that I know his name."

"You think that you can kill me?" the man asked incredulously. "Okay then, I be Gallard Engal, cousin to King Svengard. The closest that you'll come to meeting the king is for him to see you die in the arena."

"All of you, mark this!" Landis said aloud, making eye contact with each man in the party. "When I leave your country, it'll be when I choose to leave, and your blood will be ice cold before I leave these lands." Landis smiled with the assurance of one who had faced far more dangerous threats.

The usually verbose Gallard Engal was stunned into silence. The man in his custody was a sturdy type, but much smaller than he or many of his closest clansmen. The Engal clan consisted of large men and sturdy women. They feared no one and wore their physical superiority as a badge of office. This outlander seemed supremely confident in his ability, and his lack of doubt made Gallard second guess his decision to profit from this encounter instead of bringing these strangers to his king. Sucking up his resolve, Gallard turned to the crowd that had gathered, while still speaking to the stranger. "You talk a good game stranger, but 'the arena' is the true test of a man." They all cheered at his words. "When you face the best that Tychon has to offer, you won't be singing the same tune." He paused for effect, "You'll be dead."

The crowd cheered at their local hero's words. They again pelted the prisoners with whatever object they could lay hands on. The others, including the Father and Tennyson ducked their heads in shame to try and dodge the thrown objects. Landis rode on with his head held high, not letting the impact of garbage on his person affect his posture. He looked at his persecutors with pity and contempt. Anisha lifted her head from time to time and was heartened to see that one of their party was still a proud man of honor.

The ride of shame ended after traveling dozens of blocks toward the center of the village. They came to an impressive construction, compared to the rest of the city. Dug into the ground was a pit where they would be expected to fight for their lives. Above ground it was maybe three stories high; but the pit was deep so that once inside, there was seating for thousands of spectators. Landis and his team, along with their Uzor guides, were finally pulled from horseback and dragged through tunnels under the stands to an area where hundreds of other prisoners were already being held.

Without ceremony, they were pushed into dark and dirty cells. The men were put in one area, while the women were taken to another part of the catacombs. The floors were roughhewn rock, and poorly crafted iron bars were set into the stone both below and above. There was a bucket in the corner for the latrine, and each cell was packed with disgruntled, unwashed Doreh men. They all had the typical wild, dirty blonde hair, with untamed beards and mustaches. Most were bare-chested and bore the scars of numerous battles. They looked the newcomers up and down and didn't know what to make of them. At first, the Uzor were sure that Landis, Tennyson, and the Father were Doreh. The Doreh were never confused for even a second that they were outsiders.

"Do you think we're in danger in here?" the Father asked.

"I can take most of these men, but I'm helpless when sleeping," Landis answered. "Just in case though, I'm going to sleep for a couple of hours, you stay on watch. Wake Roku for the next shift." Landis leaned against the wall and was quickly asleep.

Chapter 23: The Arena

The prisoners flowed as a single entity from deep in the cavern, up a ramp and into the bright early morning sun. With the wind blocked by the high walls of the arena, it was comfortable, though the smell of unwashed bodies kept it from being pleasant. The prisoners from Kronos, along with twenty or more of the Doreh prisoners were herded into the very center of the contest floor. After adjusting their eyes to the bright sunlight, they could see the large oval floor and the stands. From the floor of the arena, the stands looked to be ten stories high. There were thousands of people, men, women, and children, all settling in for an afternoon of entertainment. They drank heartily from horns or wineskins and ate huge hunks of meat from heavy wooden platters. It was the first match of the day, and the crowd was not yet near full capacity.

At the center and a couple of levels high, was the king's private box. The space could have seated thirty of the masses comfortably, but this area was for the clan chieftain and guests. They sat on large chairs, carved from the bones of Mastodons, draped with furs and silk-covered cushions. King Igurt Svengart looked on with only mild interest; he seemed to be more consumed by a conversation that he was having with his wife, Queen Anahilda. The king was shirtless and wore loose brown pants, brass armbands, and a short sword. Anahilda on the other hand, looked like she was prepared to go to war; with her long blonde hair tied back, her full body chainmail armor, wolf skin cape, and both long sword and short sword. He had won her hand from a clan far to the North which had the reputation of constantly warring with anyone and everyone.

The king's right-hand man, Wulf Olric, whispered in the king's ear as the first match was nearly ready to begin. Wulf was taller than most Doreh and was long and lean whereas most of them were wide and thickly built. His hair was dark, and his skin was dusky in color. His people had been wiped out a dozen years ago, and after becoming a champion in the arena, he was given his freedom. His intelligence, patience, and quiet aggression had served to propel him up the ranks, till he became a trusted advisor to the king. They spoke privately for several minutes, and when they were done, Wulf retreated to his own, much smaller box. The king leaned forward, taking interest in this warm-up match.

At ground level, there was a device set into the ground, inside the first ring of the stands with a massive horn attached to it. A large man with his long blonde hair pulled back and braided into a rope, stepped up and grasped the horn, and brought the small end to his mouth. He started speaking and the sound echoed and filled the whole arena. He announced the commencement of the first match of the day. As he did, the dozen or so guards that formed a loose circle around the prisoners started cracking their whips, urging the men to fight each other.

The Doreh prisoners were very familiar with this scene, though until today they had probably been amongst the spectators. For whatever crime it was that they had committed, they were now the entertainers and not the entertained. The melee started and reached peak intensity almost instantly. All of them were nearly naked, only having coverings for their groins and feet. Men were punching and grappling with each other, doing their best to knock out an opponent with a single thunderous punch.

"Father, stay behind me!" Landis shouted. He blocked all comers, keeping himself between the holy man and the numerous attackers. Father Sebastienne had never thrown a punch in his life, and even if he were inclined to do so now, his great height would only serve to entice the large savage Doreh to seek him out. Instead, they had to go through a smaller man that most of them towered over. Landis was a master with a sword, but his abilities were born of a man who was a consummate athlete at heart. Instead of headhunting, he drove his powerful fists into the tender gut of his opponent, hitting the kidneys, punching the liver, and when they wore out and were tired of having their bodies smashed to bits, then he would strike at their unguarded chins. He easily beat four or five before the fight was over.

By contrast, there was Roku, who was not only accustomed to unarmed combat, he preferred it. These huge men of the West never even considered using their legs as weapons. At first they scoffed at the little man, bald and almost hairless. His skin was a different color, and his facial features set him apart from everyone in attendance. His face was calm and expressionless as he easily ducked under haymakers, sidestepped lunges, and diverted any and every punch thrown in his direction. It took him only seconds to gauge his opponent's abilities and to find counters to their moves. His attacks took advantage of their weaknesses, which by his standards, were many. When on offense, he was a flurry of motion, landing kicks to unprotected groins, uncovered abdomens, and roundhouse kicks to the face. His punches and chops were designed to be efficient and subduing. A chop to the throat, a focused punch to the solar plexus, anywhere he could hit a nerve cluster and bring a man down, he struck. No one died at his hands; but very soon, he was surrounded by a pile of whimpering Doreh who had not lost the desire to fight, just the ability to do so.

Tennyson held his own, dropping three opponents till he met a giant of a man who didn't feel his punches. The giant picked him up and slammed him to the ground. Roku distracted the man before he could kill the unconscious archer, and quite easily humbled the towering Doreh. When the scrum was over, only the four men of Kronos stood tall. They looked up at the king who by now was intently watching the action. He heard the roar of the crowd; they longed for the blood of the trespassers, but as king, he did what 'he' wanted. Despite their objection, he stood and gave the 'thumbs up' signal, that they should live and be allowed to move on.

Landis climbed the ramp and again found himself in the bright sun that had trouble warming the country of Hadon. A week ago he was fodder for the machine, and now he was a gladiator. The crowds roared at the sight of the white man who was not Doreh. Now he had a sword, a breastplate, and a heavy steel helm. He walked the distance from the gate to the center of the arena, to be met by his opponents. There were four Doreh, all dressed similarly. They all turned to honor the king, who now watched the games with renewed interest. He wondered aloud who these strangers were; but because of public pressure, never called them to speak with him directly. Instead, he fed the people's insatiable hunger for blood and let his questions go unanswered.

When the match was signaled to start, the four men rushed the outsider. In the back of their minds, they were concerned about his lack of fear, his utter and complete confidence. Landis spun the long sword in his palm, measuring the weight of it, the balance. He ducked the first strike, the second, and the third with ease. His opponents were physically larger than him, and the war axes that they attacked him with would split a man in two, armor or not. In his mind, this bit of swordplay was like any other; what they had in common was that each battle had its own rhythm. He saw the strike, strike, strike, pause; and after that, it was all but over. The fourth man who didn't have time to bring his weapon around was stabbed through the heart. The sword that he was given was by no means the match of Soulbane; but in his hands, it was more than enough to deal with this lot. He pushed the slightly dull point of the sword through the man's breastplate, past his sternum, and into his heart. Knowing that his thrust was true, Landis pulled it out and rejoined the contest. Thrust, thrust, thrust, pause. In the heartbeat of time where steel was not flying at him, he jumped in and hacked at the man on the right. His blade caught the large blonde man under the arm and above the top of his armored torso. The attack was not, in and of itself, fatal; but it bit deep into the pour soul's flesh, and at least momentarily, took him out of the fight.

The crowd, usually boisterous and opinionated, was nearly silent as the deadly ballet continued. The crowd could almost sense the foreign fighter smiling as he dodged and weaved, not taking any damage, and yet inflicting painful and debilitating wounds on his opponents. The third suffered a chop to the neck that half separated his head from his shoulders. The last fighter, though a very large man, a man who was probably accustomed to dominating any room that he was in, was now quaking in anticipation of his demise. Landis didn't make him wait long. The two traded slashes and thrusts, the tall Doreh man was obviously trying to score a lucky blow and part the other's head from his shoulders. Landis spun around, blocking if he had to, ducking when he could till an opening presented itself. He jumped inside of the larger man's reach and thrust his sword upwards through the larger man's throat and into his brain, then out the top of his skull. He died instantly and dropped to the ground like a sack of rocks. Landis went to the injured man and smashed him on the head, knocking him unconscious.

Being the only man standing and the undisputed winner of the conflict, he walked till he was in the position to present himself to the king and queen. The crowd roared with approval at the violence and the level of skill that had been displayed.

Landis bowed and saluted with his blood-soaked blade. The king gave him an enthusiastic thumbs up. After basking in the love from the crowd, he was ushered back to the pits.

"How do you see this playing out?" Tennyson asked Landis. "They are going to continue to stack the deck till we find a match that is finally beyond our skills."

"You worry too much friend," Landis said to his comrade. "We are providing them not only with entertainment; but if they start to wonder how only three of us can defeat so many of them, we'll gain their respect, or their fear. I'll take either one."

"I see your point, Landis," Roku interjected. "But I too fear that we will reach a point where we can no longer win. If we die here, our mission will be a failure," the monk said grimly. "I'm not afraid to die, but the mission is far too important for us to fail."

"Father?" Landis asked, turning to the priest.

"Brothers, Landis has faith, as do I. Magnus watches over us and wants us to succeed. On the first day, we were nothing but sticks of wood to be tossed on the fire; but with each victory, we become real people, men with names. Soon we will have the audience we came for, and when we do, we'll find out if these people are worthy to fight by our side."

"Landis!" the captain of the guard called to the rising star of the games. "Today you'll be fighting against an Uzor that we captured near our borders. Like you, he has faced and defeated many challengers, and has come out without a scratch."

"I'll kill Doreh all day, but I have no problem with the Uzor. They're good people."

"We've been at war with them for generations. You may think that they are not hostile because they put on a show for you. We caught one of their spies checking out our defenses. That's when we captured him and his patrol."

"What if I say that I won't fight this Uzor of yours?"

"If you want to keep the holy man outta the ring, you'll have to do as you're told," the guard said so that all could hear. "Otherwise, he fights in your place. The Uzor will chop him to pieces without a second thought."

"As a slave, I have no right to ask; but could I again wield the sword that I carried when we were taken prisoner?" Landis asked of the guard.

"I can grant such a simple request if you can guarantee a memorable match." He smiled wickedly at Landis, "The next match will be a very tough one. This Uzor is better than any you have so far encountered. You'll face him to see who's the champion of the arena."

Landis stood in the center of the ring once again, Soulbane was in his right hand, and he had a large wooden buckler on his left arm. Instead of his preferred plate armor, he wore thick leather armor on his arms, legs, and torso. In the weeks that he had been imprisoned, he had gone from a hated interloper to a fan favorite in the arena. He killed when he had to, but he often just incapacitated his opponents. The crowd hated it when they were denied the blood that they came to see, but they marveled at the stranger's skill. He could clearly kill any man that he had faced in the ring. His moves were economical, he expended no energy carelessly.

For the first time since the first day, he stood in the ring as the challenger. Pacing back and forth, he waited for his opponent to emerge from his tunnel. The crowd noise started low but started building, accompanied by the banging of plates and utensils on the stands. They were shouting 'U-zor, U-zor, U-zor' so loudly that it was starting to hurt his ears. The time for the match to commence had arrived. His opponent trotted up the ramp and emerged from the opposite tunnel. He was black as midnight, and he wore the same armor as Landis. They were similar in height. Both were about six feet two inches tall, but where Landis was solid, the Uzor was thin and wiry.

If he's reached this level, he could be the toughest challenge I've ever faced man-to-man. I have nothing against this man, but I can't desert the Father after he saved my life. Landis thought to himself while watching the Uzor fighter stretch.

The combatants approached each other, and Landis saw that the man carried a very unique sword. The weapon was definitely not of Doreh design; it looked sharp as a straight razor and was a longer version of a machete, wider and thicker at the point than at the handle. When they were a dozen feet apart, they both turned to the king's box. The king stood and raised his right hand to signal the crowd to silence. The announcer stepped up to the horn and prepared to make the official announcement.

"Brothers! Sisters! Today is the day we've been waiting for. For weeks, we have seen these two outsiders rise through the ranks of fighters. They have easily defeated the weaker Doreh from the Mori clan, just as our brave warriors did when they took them prisoner. Today they face each other in a battle to the death! We'll find out if our night-skinned neighbors to the South are as strong as they claim to be, or if the pale stranger from parts unknown is the better fighter!"

With a downward chop of his hand, the king signaled the beginning of the contest. The crowd immediately went wild, most of them chanting for the Uzor. Both fighters turned to each other, gave a respectful bow, and then prepared to wage war. Each of them circled, gauging the physical strength of the other and watching the way they held their weapon, the way they wore their meager armor and the way they carried their weight while walking. Landis felt energy flowing in his sword, he looked down to see that Soulbane was glowing faintly. *What on Xoran is happening? Soulbane has never 'glowed'!* He looked over at his opponent, *his sword also had a faint glow to it. Maybe he too carries a blessed sword!*

The Uzor was the favorite, and he eventually felt the pressure to attack. He feinted and then swung his sword in an arc that would have opened the stomach of a less experienced fighter. He followed with a series of thrusts, each narrowly missing Landis' flesh. Landis was going to duck another slash, that at the last minute, became a smash to the side of his head with the pommel of his opponent's sword. Landis shook his head to reduce the ringing in his ears, while his opponent pressed the attack. With both hands, the Uzor warrior chopped down at the upturned sword of Landis, trying to break his will and wear him down. The blows were heavy, and they drove him down to one knee.

With his head now clear, he saw an opening. As the Uzor warrior reared back to strike again, Landis punched as hard as he could with his left hand into his opponent's side. He heard the wind leave the other fighter and then he pushed him back to create space. Landis got to his feet just as the other fighter had recovered and was charging in again. Landis thrust Soulbane at the charging man, and even though he impossibly halted his forward motion and tried to retreat, the blade itself sought him out and pricked his ebon skin. The man looked stunned for half a second and then redoubled his attack. His limbs seemed to move with inhuman speed, his heavy sword crashing again and again against Landis' buckler or his sword. Landis had to shelf his plans for offense and put all of his skill into not missing any of the rapid-fire attacks. After two dozen attempted strikes, the Uzor man was able to slip behind Landis' buckler and stab his bare arm. The sword opened a six-inch-long gash, not too deep but painful and bloodletting.

Landis thought to himself that this may not be the most technically proficient swordsman he had ever faced; but his total package made him the deadliest. The other man's celebration lasted for less than half a second. He almost smiled, but that was enough time for Landis to open a slight gash in the man's side. A wound that looked infinitely worse than it actually was, but it led to a second cut on the man's off arm. Then a third cut to his thigh, a fourth across his chest, and finally a scratch along the man's left cheek. The Uzor fighter was stunned, not by pain or loss of blood; but more by the fact that he was no longer untouchable. He had won so many fights, and taken such little damage, he had grown overconfident.

His anger growing and his pride hurt, the Uzor fighter lashed out with his small shield and hit Landis' sword hand, causing him to drop his weapon. Thinking that the pale-faced demon was now helpless, he raised his sword with two hands to prepare for a death blow. Before he could gain any momentum, Landis grabbed both of his wrists, the sword high above them, and lunged forward, driving his knee into the man's solar plexus. The breath gushed out of him, and he was helpless while the white demon let go with his right hand and punched him full in the face with his gloved hand. Blood from his nose now joined the half dozen or so wounds to his person. Landis tackled the man and proceeded to rain down several more blows to the Uzor's head and shoulders. The people's favorite was helpless, and Landis could have finished him with his bare hands. A most undignified ending for a swordsman. Instead, Landis stood up, walked over to where he had left Soulbane, and picked up his enchanted weapon. Turning, he saw that the favorite had regained his weapon, but was barely able to stand.

His face full of both anger and desperation, he grasped the weapon tightly and spoke his first words. "Panther claw! Aid your master now!" Energy sizzled in the air all around them. Everyone in the arena except the Uzor fighter had no idea what was happening. The sword disappeared, and in the space between them, a towering creature blinked into existence. A large black panther, as tall as an elephant was suddenly in the ring. It crouched in a protective stance, guarding the one who had summoned it. Landis felt his grip on Soulbane weaken as his sword had a will of its own and was bound to exercise it. Soulbane faded from this world and in its place a winged reptile sprang from nothingness, as big as the Panther just a dozen feet away. The serpent had a Cobra's head with a flaring hood, the wings of a bat, and a snake's tail. It looked at the giant panther and hissed in anticipation of a fight. The two semi-transparent Titans attacked each other. Soulbane wrapped its long snake-like body around the panther's body and snapped at its face with its gigantic fangs. The panther swiped its mighty paws at the bobbing snake head.

Shouts of terror erupted throughout the stands as spectators ran for the exits. The king was standing and shouting orders at his attendants, the queen had already fled with her retinue. Guards were supposed to rush the field and take the combatants into custody, but they defied their orders and stood in the doorways, fearing for their lives. Landis looked over at his opponent who looked as shocked as Landis felt. He ran over to the man and shook him by the shoulders as the battle raged on in the air over their heads.

"What's your name, man of Uzor? I am Landis of Kronos" he yelled above the shouts in the background.

"I am Wanaka of Koregar," he shouted.

"Wanaka? You're King Lollondo's champion?" Landis asked.

"How do you know that?" the man asked incredulously.

"You're king sent me along with my three friends and guided by the Bkar sisters." He looked around at the chaos around them, "We should get out of here!"

"If Anisha and Linea are here, we must break them out first!" Without waiting for confirmation he turned to the giant apparitions battling to the death above them. "Panther Claw! Return to me now!" The giant panther faded and became the sword that fell to the ground at his feet.

"Soulbane!" Landis yelled, "Return to me!" The same action happened, and once again, both men were in possession of their blessed blades. "Let's go this way, I know where to find my crew!" Both men trotted off as quickly as they could, despite their various injuries.

They approached the entrance to the pits and were met by a dozen men of the city guard. Landis charged the guards and killed the first one before they could adjust to the new threat. He swung the long rune-etched sword as if it weighed nothing, opening throats and lopping off hands with what looked like little or no effort. Out of the corner of his eye, he could see that Wanaka was less into precision and more about overwhelming his opponents. He hacked at them with Panther Claw and cut through their rusty swords like they were made of glass. They cut down the guards in a minute or two and moved on down the ramp into the pits.

They ran through the dark, dirty halls, looking for their comrades. There were a couple of guards trying to block the hallway, but the champions cut them down without breaking stride. Prisoners yelled at them for their freedom, but they ignored their cries. They searched hall after hall till they found a relatively empty cell. Inside were the three men of Kronos. Wanaka pulled keys from a dead guard and quickly had their door open.

"About time!" Tennyson complained. "As you know, I'm an archer. I barely survived with my, still advanced, sword skills," he helped the Father up, and Roku followed.

"You're all odd looking Doreh," Wanaka stated.

"Oh! For Magnus' sake, were not damned Doreh!" Tennyson groaned. "Do we really all look alike to you?"

"Enough, let's get the women," Landis said, as he led them down deeper into the pits. They ran on for what felt like miles, trying to navigate the narrow maze of the slave pits till they came to the women's section. They looked around till they found the Bkar sisters in a cell. Most of the cell was crowded with over a dozen women, the other half of the cell was open and occupied only by the sisters.

"Ready to go?" Landis asked them.

"About time!" Anisha stormed. "Find the key for these handcuffs!" she said showing that her hands were secured behind her back. Linea was in her own cell, cuffed and gagged. When they saw their champion, they were filled with joy.

"Wanaka!" Anisha cried out.

They opened the cell and freed the sisters. Their reunion was spoiled by the sound of what must have been dozens of guards heading their way. Landis and Wanaka each faced a different direction, holding their swords, prepared to fend off the Doreh city guard. When the guards arrived, there was a familiar face among them.

"Gallard Engal, is it not?" Landis asked aloud. Everyone inside and outside the cells stopped to hear the response.

"It is foreigner! You can't escape these dungeons. You should fall on your sword!"

"I promised to kill you," Landis said to the tall Doreh. "I'm a man of my word." With his threat still hanging in the still air, he launched at the Doreh giant. With Soulbane in his hand, he was faster and more accurate than any swordsman alive. The tall blond man was already holding his war-axe and barely brought it around in time to avoid a devastating strike. Landis attacked with speed that the Doreh could only dream of; he soon had inflicted several painful, though not debilitating wounds on the large man. Gallard could barely use his large weapon in the confined space of the dungeon, with the dark walls and ceiling seeming to close in on them.

"Landis, time to go!" Tennyson called out.

Landis nodded at his companion and pushed forward. Gallard almost stumbled as he was backed into his own men. Landis used the man's half a second of faltering to thrust his sword into the large chest of Gallard Engal. He ignored the big man's expression of surprise and horror, and pulled out his sword, letting the corpse fall face-first on the ground. He took advantage of their shock and killed both of the guards that were with him.

"Everyone, inside the cell!" Linea yelled. They turned to her in disbelief, "Trust me! Now, get in here!" They followed her instruction and piled into the cell. She slammed the door shut and locked them inside. The guards roared down the hallway from each end and met in front of the closed cell. They looked confused because they expected to have to capture the outsiders, but here they were already in a cell.

"Now that my hands are free and I can speak," Linea started chanting and making signs with her hands. The guards seeing what was going on started to try and unlock the cell. Landis stabbed two of the guards before they took the hint. Seconds later, a portal was opened to King Lollondo's audience room. Landis kept watch while ushering their party through the hole in space. They all stepped through, and Linea being last, passed through and closed the portal behind her.

Chapter 24: Home Coming

Riken had to duck to fit through the portal that Danika had created, her arms stretched to their limit and her portal was still not as round as he was tall. The twins stepped through the portal first, followed by Riken and his new bride. Among other skills that they had picked up from the old Telnor woman, they had become skilled at creating holes in the fabric of space. On the outgoing trip to Riken's homeland, they had taken several weeks to travel by ship. Now they were now able to return home in the time it took to cast a spell. The twins were glad to be home again, and even though he left his people and his homeland, Riken also felt a kind of relief to be back at the mansion.

The mansion itself was completely different from before. The old house had been suited to its former master's taste, but Magnus was dead, and the twins now owned the mansion. They designed their home in a more modern fashion. Some of the mysteries that they had become accustomed to no longer worked without the life force of the old mage to power them. They summoned their combined skills and changed the house till it had three distinctive sections, that if seen from above, formed a triangle. Jorn and Danika each wanted a wing to themselves, and now with their manservant happily married, it seemed only fitting that he have a wing to himself. After a little small talk, they all drifted away in their own directions.

Jorn tore into the food that the cook had prepared. Telnor food wasn't necessarily bad, but he had been craving the familiar. The roast was swimming in a rich, dark brown gravy with lots of mushrooms, potatoes, carrots, and familiar spices. Danika picked at the meal; her thoughts were a million miles away.

Landis had taken a couple of his adventuring buddies on a secret mission and was overdue to return.

A messenger arrived the next day with a request from King Herron. She noted the change in title and felt compassion for Gabriel. He was their age, and now with his father gone, he was the newly crowned king of Khatuna. She had lost her parents to pirates years ago, but the pain occasionally flared up like a forest fire that everyone thought had been put out. Herron had been one of King Syphon's most trusted generals, even though the boy had no experience in battle when the war against the Quell had started. That was not so long ago, and he had grown up considerably. As king, he was responsible for the safety of hundreds of thousands of his citizens.

"Jorn, are you going to Khatuna?" Danika asked.

"Yes, of course. Why do you ask?"

"Landis is overdue, he should have been back weeks ago. I'm concerned and was wondering if I should stay here and wait for him."

"That's a terrible idea. You're the most impatient person I know. After I leave, you'll pace a permanent path into the flooring. Usually, I would go out with Gabriel to have some drinks and a few laughs; but I'll tell him that you are coming along. You need to spend time with people your own age."

"I guess you're right. I'm sure Landis is going to be fine." She tried to smile, but something made her feel like there was a shadow that had just passed over her, and that her life would never be the same.

Chapter 25: Betrayal

Olehya Syphon read the private dispatch, then read it again. Dispatches sent by pigeon or raven went directly to the king's coops. Even if the messages were marked for her 'eyes only', the chances of one of those dolts in the dispatch department reading it were high. Too high to risk. This dispatch came by human messenger. It was a costlier and much slower method of communication, but far more secure. For this special project, security was of ultimate importance.

Damon Cern had replied to her request to hire an assassin. The message was heavily coded in case it was intercepted, but she deciphered it and was pleased with the results. He would send his best man, due to the prominence of the target. The cost would be... astronomical; but if it succeeded, she would become queen, and her resources would increase a thousand-fold. The game that she was playing was a dangerous one, but she believed in her husband, and even more, she believed in a man who listened to every honeyed word that she poured into his ear. She loved her husband dearly, but she was not so enthralled that she didn't see his limitations. In a world dominated by men, through her husband she could still wield ultimate power. Power not only over Chuo but over all of Kronos. He would be the strong face that they followed, and she would be the mind and the spirit that controlled the throne.

Quickly she put together a confirmation of the order and pledged an amount of coin that was in reality, much more than her husband could afford. It all relied on the assassin's ability to kill King Syphon. Her husband Ravi would ascend to the throne, and the riches of Chuo would be hers to manage as she saw fit. She was the financial head of her family and the ultimate decision-maker. She loved Ravi and with her pulling the strings, he would become a legend.

Black Adder scaled the wall to the apartments of his target. He had already passed over the outer wall and was able to avoid detection by the outer ring of guards. He waited almost an hour to cross the hundred or so feet from the outer wall to a shadowy area that lay at the base of the king's keep. From behind a stack of oil kegs, he waited another hour or so till the moon was blocked by passing clouds to start his climb. The wall was two hundred feet straight up. Hand over hand he climbed, looking for a purchase to place the toes of his soft leather boots. If it were daytime and he had permission, he could have climbed the wall in twenty minutes. At night, with no illumination and no permission to be there, he took almost two hours to reach the level where the keep's master would be sleeping. According to his intelligence, Syphon slept before ten every night and rose at dawn. He should, by all rights, still have several hours to complete his assignment before anyone would notice the assassination.

After many hours of creeping and lying in cold ditches, climbing cold stone walls, and scaling sheer stone towers, he was tired. This was by far the most lucrative kill of his career, and that was the only thing that made it worth such an ordeal. He was clad in his traditional black gear, black hood, and cape over black leather armor. His boots were soft leather, as were his gloves, both dyed black to match his pants and chest gear. He wore a mask that only revealed his eyes and covered the rest of his face. In shadow he was all but invisible, and he used this to his advantage. If someone were to look up towards the king's apartments, it wouldn't be unreasonable for them to totally miss the black spot attached to the tower's wall.

He found himself climbing the Southern face of the main tower, and when he finally reached the royal floors, he found a small window to wiggle through. On the other side of the window, he found himself in a laundry room, several rooms away from where his target would be sleeping. At this ridiculous hour there should only be a few guards around to get past. He took a long time opening the door to the hallway to avoid making any squeaks. He turned the corner, and before a large door were two men at arms. They were awake but were not as alert as they should have been. The assassin fired off two poisoned darts before the guards knew that he was there. Both guards fell where they had stood, dead from the powerful toxin.

Feeling emboldened by dispatching the guards so easily, he pushed his way into King Syphon's private bed chamber. By the dim candlelight, he could see that the king was not asleep. He was quite naked, making love to one woman from behind while sharing a passionate kiss with a second woman. Both of the women shrieked at the intruder and the king yelled for his guards. Black Adder put the dart gun to his lips to fire a poisoned dart at his high value target. What he didn't expect was that the dark-skinned woman who had been in the king's embrace put herself between her lord and the would-be assassin. The other woman, a much lighter-skinned woman, picked up and threw one of the heavy candlesticks at the assassin, causing him to drop his blowgun.

Kel leaped out of bed, over his murdered mistress, and closed the gap between himself and the assassin in half of a second. He kicked the man, sending him flying out into the hallway. He gave chase, just in time to see the hooded man pull a stiletto from his sleeve. The king knocked the hand with the knife away as his other hand now held a short sword. Naked and covered in sweat, the Kel was hard to hold onto. The men were maneuvering around, as Kell held each of the assassin's wrists in his strong warrior's hands. His anger gave him extra strength and he kicked the assassin in the side of his knee, wrecking the joint. He applied pressure with his mighty hands, veins exploding from his strong dark arms. Black Adder's sword fell noisily to the ground. King Syphon yanked with his dominant hand, pulling the man's arm out of its socket. Now that he had a free hand, he gripped the intruder's neck with crushing force.

"Who sent you, assassin?" he demanded.

A good assassin will take the name of his employer to the grave, and Black Adder was the best. Kel looked into the man's eyes, and did not see anger, nor did he see fear or regret. What he saw was a glimpse into the spirit of a man who has already resigned himself to his fate. Angry that he would get no answers, Kell squeezed the man's neck ever tighter and was surprised to hear a loud 'snap'. The eyes went from a dead expression to just dead. The body became limp and Black Adder slumped lifelessly to the floor.

Guards poured in from the lower floors, but Kel ignored them. He looked down at his hand, still very much under his control; but somehow it had the strength of ten men. At that moment, he knew that this gift from Magnus was more than it seemed.

It had been three days since the assassination attempt, and life in House Syphon was almost back to normal. The king would spend most of his time behind his desk in his business office, but today he sat on the throne brooding. He didn't resent being the target of hatred, when one is successful, one naturally collects enemies. What bothered him most was the needless loss of life. He had said many prayers, thanking the gods for the sacrifice of his lady friend and his guards. It also bothered him that this person that wanted him dead didn't have the intestinal fortitude to face him directly. Hiring an assassin was, in his opinion, the most cowardly of acts.

Before he could fall too deep down the well of self-pity, a racket arose outside of the throne room. He looked up to see his brother dragging his wife by her arm in a most unkind manner. The woman's face was a mask of fear. His brother had struck her from time to time, just to try and amend her behavior, but he had never treated her in such a publicly hostile way. He pulled her along faster than she was able to walk, so she stumbled and almost had to run to keep from being dragged the length of the throne room.

"I must have a word with you, my king!" Ravi said loudly. Ravi was fond of his special permission to refer to the king as 'brother', so to ask his king for an audience instead of having a word with his brother meant that he didn't feel comfortable addressing him informally.

"Of course, Prince Syphon. How can your king be of service?" Kel asked.

"I have found the traitor in our midst! My wife Olehya is the one who hired the assassin that breached our security and attempted to take Your Highness' life." The king turned to stare directly at Olehya.

"Why would you want me dead, sister?" he asked with true hurt in his voice.

"Because your brother should be on the throne, and I should be Chuo's queen!" she spat. "This baby that I carry in my womb is meant to be a king!"

"How do you feel about that, brother?" he said turning to Ravi. "Do you agree with your woman's ambitions for you?"

"Allow me to show you sire! I love this woman; but let 'me' be her executioner, right here and now!" Ravi pulled his sword and raised it high above his head. He had her by the collar with his left hand and was poised to strike with his right.

"Wait!" Kell yelled to his brother. "How did you know of her crimes?"

"She had voiced her ambitions in the past, but I would never have guessed that she was a serious threat to you, brother," tears were streaming from his eyes, his shame had broken his manly resolve. "A messenger arrived just an hour ago, demanding monies to keep her secret. I was able to extract from the man that he was sent by the broker, Damon Cern. He's one of House Sarutendo's men."

The king sat on his throne, taking in the scene before him. His beautiful sister-in-law was a disheveled mess on the floor, her golden robes torn and muddied from being dragged across the courtyard. His loyal brother, a proud and strong man, was now so ashamed that if he were asked by his brother to take his own life, it would be granted instantly.

"Your child grows inside her, even now?" he asked his brother.

"Yes, sire."

"Take her to her quarters where she will stay under constant guard until she delivers. The child is not guilty and should not suffer for her crimes. After she gives birth, you will take the child, and she shall be escorted to our borders," he leaned over and spoke to Olehya directly. "I curse you woman for the harm that you have caused my brother. I show mercy so that my brother can raise his child. Who knows, maybe it will be a boy, and maybe, just maybe, he will be king someday. But you will never know. Once banished, you must never enter Chuo again under penalty of death," with that he waved his hand to dismiss her and the whole matter. The guards took her from Ravi's grasp and escorted her from the hall.

Ravi looked like he had just run a marathon, he was sweating, crying, and looked like death warmed over. He walked up and knelt before his older brother. "My king, I am not worthy. I offer you my worthless life," he started crying uncontrollably. Kell came down and put his arms around his brother and held him tight.

"Not to worry brother. I see into your heart and know that it's true. Put her from your mind, and when you are holding that baby, make sure that it is raised to be a worthy member of our family."

Chapter 26: Prelude

The training grounds were like a miniature version of the arena that was at the heart of the Koregar Capital of Nanoan. There was an oval of about fifty feet by thirty-five feet and surrounded by a dozen or so rows of seats. In the center, Landis and Wanaka were shirtless in the cool air. They set aside their enchanted swords in favor of wooden ones. The two looked as different as possible, and yet they both shared a love for a good-natured challenge. After a short warm-up, they were ready to commence.

In the stands were Father Sebastienne, Tennyson, Anisha Bkar and a handful of the king's private guards. Everyone stopped their own routines to witness what promised to be the sparring match of a lifetime. One of the guards approached the Father and Anisha who were sitting together.

"Last chance to place a wager! The smart money is on Wanaka. How about you stranger?" he asked the tall priest.

"I'm not sure if wagering is a sin..." He looked at Anisha who only shrugged her shoulders. "If it is, I'll do penance later. All that I have on Landis," he said as he pulled a handful of coins from some hidden inner pocket of his plain brown robe. The guard accepted the coins and couldn't help smiling like he had taken candy from a baby.

"You're pretty sure about your man?" Anisha asked. "Wanaka trained me and is the king's champion for a reason. I'm afraid your man will be beaten badly," she said trying to goad the monk.

"I didn't see you risk any of your money. Perhaps you fear that your master has finally met his match," he smiled at the young woman.

"For a holy man, your words have evil intent," she smiled her brilliant white smile to let him know that she was joking. "All of your money is gone, priest. What would you bet with me?"

"Well… on our ship, I have a keg of Wolvig brandy. I find it an essential elixir for loosening the tongue and making new friends." He smiled at her, "What would you wager?"

"If your man wins, I'll squire for him till you are ready to return to your home."

"Excellent! Landis will appreciate having his armor and horse tended to. To celebrate, since I will still have my brandy, I'll share it with all!"

"You are overconfident my friend," she responded.

"I saw Wanaka in the arena in the Doreh city, and he is extremely talented," he looked her in the eyes, "But I have been protected by Landis' strong arm and sword more than once, and he fights as easily as a fish swims. Just watch."

Wanaka was used to fighting without much armor and felt buoyed by the supportive cheers from the stands. As the fighters began to circle each other, the king and queen quietly filed in and found a seat in the upper stands. Neither of the combatants seemed to notice them. The champions were now engaged in a match that seemed to carry much more weight than a simple practice session. Wanaka swung the wooden practice sword around, getting used to its weight. It was heavier than Panther Claw and seemed more like a bulky club than a sword. With a grin, he charged at the tall pale stranger.

Landis too was off put by the crude weapon. He had only recently acquired Soulbane but had grown to rely on the weapon's speed and special abilities. Without his bulky plate, he felt freer than when he was encased armor. He stretched his long frame, flexing his strong chest and shoulders, and felt the wind blowing the light-colored hair that covered most of his chest and upper torso. His gut was tightened in anticipation of an attack, the abdominal muscles formed a half dozen squares just above his belt. His strange but muscular frame caught the attention of Anisha and the queen, though they would never admit it.

Wanaka's attack was a clumsy downward chop that Landis easily dodged. With the flat of his wooden weapon, he smacked the champion on the shoulder, the slap of wood on flesh echoing in the small bowl of an arena. All were shocked by how quickly the first point was scored. As Wanaka shrugged off the slap, he seemed to notice the king's presence for the first time. He was now fighting for his king's approval more than anything else. Slower than he would have been with his enchanted sword, Wanaka was still frighteningly fast. He struck again and again, and though Landis was able to block the attacks, he looked to be half a beat slower. What was harder to see, and only the warriors in the crowd took notice, was that Landis conserved his energy and used the minimum effort to block or deflect Wanaka's advances. After a flurry of motion, the Uzor halted for literally half a second to take a breath, and that's when Landis pressed his attack. With only soft breeches on, his range of motion was greatly increased, and he was able to land a kick to Wanaka's ribs. The heavy leg hitting the solid muscle made a loud slapping sound, and almost everyone could feel the blow.

Landis spun his wooden blade in his grasp, giving everyone including his opponent the perception that he was calmly toying with him. He slashed at the champion and was blocked; he thrust and was pushed aside. He walked the shorter man down, his attacks not as fast; but each had strength and his pursuit was relentless. Wanaka was surprised when he took yet another backward step and found himself with his back to the short inner wall of the training ground. In an unexpected move, he dove to the side and rolled head first on the ground. When he again gained his feet, he was several feet away from the strange white warrior and had regained his breathing room. Wanaka began leaping wildly, spinning and whirling around like a top. The unconventional style caught Landis by surprise, and when Wanaka stopped abruptly, he was able to land a solid strike on Landis' ribs. *In real combat, that slash would have carved me up,* Landis thought. *I need to take into account that these people are not classically trained.*

The two went on for several minutes, one attacking, then the other. They seemed fairly evenly matched, and both men were now sweating freely. Landis was struck a few more times till he was able to adapt to Wanaka's wild fighting style. The king cupped his hands to amplify his voice.

"Sir Stone. If you win, I'll send men with you back to your country. When they return to me, I'll decide if it's in our interest to form a bond with your people."

"That, plus, I've bet all of my money on you. A vow of poverty is good in theory but terrible in practice," Father Sebastienne called to his friend.

Landis smiled warmly, and this seemed to cause Wanaka a bit of unease. A change came over Landis, his movements went from rigid exactness to a more fluid style. His face lost its tension and he seemed to enjoy the encounter even more than he had before. Unlike the fighting style of formal dueling that most knights were brought up on, his movements were organic and natural. Many years of war and a god's given natural talent had built memory into his muscles. He didn't need to consciously act or react; the correct movements just came to him. It was like an orchestra had started playing just for him, and he let his instinct take over. He landed point after point on Wanaka, and after a dozen or so unanswered points, the champion conceded.

Both men turned to the royal couple and bowed. Wanaka felt shame and the beginnings of anger were showing on his face, but Landis put his arms around the man and pounded on his back in the way of teammates. Anger fled from Wanaka, and he thought to himself that perhaps this loss would give him a goal to strive for. The king was amused and amazed; the queen had already left the arena. Those in the stands were exchanging coins, and the priest waved Landis over.

"Landis, Anisha doubted your skill, and now is obliged to squire for you till we leave."

"Is this true, milady?" He was amused at her discomfiture.

"At first I thought it a harmless wager and was sure that I'd be drinking the monk's brandy; but after what I just saw, perhaps serving you would be a boon to me." She looked up at him, her eyes glimmered like torch light on a still black pool. Her breath came in deep gulps as she stepped into his personal space. "I can learn your strange ways if you're willing to teach me."

"I've never had a student, but I must say that I do like the idea," he said, trying his best to look her only in the eyes, and not let his gaze travel up and down her tall, muscular, yet curvaceous form.

Seeing the king approach, she collected Landis' weapons and armor and made for the weapons storage chambers under the stands. King Lollando approached and despite having his champion bested, was still in fine spirits. He offered his arm, and the two men grasped each other in a forearm handshake. The king motioned for Landis to sit, then he joined him on a stone bench that was warming in the sun.

"You bested my champion, and am I right in thinking that you could have done so sooner?"

"He's a fantastic warrior, my Lord. When we fought for the amusement of the Doreh, it was actually much closer," Landis said humbly.

"You didn't answer my question. Were you trying to spare his reputation by keeping it close?"

"Perhaps I didn't fight with the same intensity that one uses in a real battle, but your offer was too valuable for me not to give my best. My mission here is to grow our world and to make allies. I will introduce your emissaries to my king, and they will report back to you that your world also is larger than you had thought."

"If there are many more like you in your homeland, I would be foolish to not try and befriend them. I will speak with your king, and we will talk of many things."

"Whom will you be sending?" Landis asked.

"I need Wanaka here with me. I feel naked without his sword between myself and danger. I will send the Bkar sisters and my trade minister. If I understand these things, once she has seen your country, Linea will be able to use her magic to travel back and forth."

"That would speed up the process. She can even help you visit our king, just like she transported my friends and me after she knocked us unconscious."

"I think you're as averse to magic as I am. I like you more than I should after knowing you for such a short amount of time. I hope that I can count you as a friend, Landis Stone."

"You can Sire, and I would call you friend as well. Despite the difficulty when we first met, and being taken captive by the Doreh, I am glad that we made this journey. Indeed, your lands are remarkably beautiful, and I hope that I will live long enough to explore them."

"It seems that my king is quite taken with you," Anisha said while polishing Landis' plate armor. She sat on a wooden fence made of rough-cut lumber, inside the barn where the horses were kept. She wore a brilliant white blouse that brought out the rich brown color of her skin. Her leather armor was set aside, along with her scimitar and knives. She still wore her leather pants and high boots.

"He reminds me of my own king, King Syphon," Landis said to the woman warrior. "I mean, they are both dark-skinned and have a... regal-ness about them," he said, trying to choose his words carefully. "It seems that your king is so well suited to his station that he cares not for appearances. My king was supposed to have been the wild and playful type; but since the war, he has become so serious."

"Does it bother you to follow a man who is not of your race? You are so light-skinned, and we Uzor are a much more pleasing shade," she smiled at the former sellsword.

"You'll call me a liar; but I never gave it much thought. King Syphon is a man of such integrity that I would follow him to the gates of hell and back."

"It never registers that you are... different?"

Landis looked up from sharpening his short sword, "Different can be good. It can make one appreciate both what they have, and what they have to gain," he said looking at her a second longer than he had intended. "You don't really have to be my squire. I won't hold you to whatever bet you made with Darus."

"A bet is a bet. As a soldier in the royal guard, I'm held to higher standards than most." She smiled at her knight, "Besides, I don't really mind. It's been a long time since I met someone that I thought that I could learn from." She looked at Landis with a look that was difficult for him to fathom, "I think that I could learn a thing or two from you, master."

Anisha pressed her attack. Not only was she graceful in her moves, but she was much stronger than she looked. Her beautiful face twisted into an odd grimace as she concentrated on the match. You could almost see the battle play out behind her eyes. Her concentration was all consuming. There was a lot of Wanaka in her fighting style. The speed, the ferocity, the flexibility, all were obviously traits that he had beaten into her over years of training. Each time she blocked, she tried to turn it into a counter. She was perhaps even faster than her master.

Landis caught her overreaching and kicked her lead foot out from under her. She lost her balance, and he scored a point that in a real battle would have left a fatal chop to the shoulder. Recovering, she turned red with anger.

"That's not part of sword fighting!" she yelled.

"Is that what we're doing?" he asked. "I thought we were just 'fighting'. There is a difference you know."

"Oh?" She lunged forward, trying to pierce his lower extremities.

"When a judge evaluates you, and says that you have won? That is sword fighting. When you live and the other fellow's dead, that's fighting," he said while knocking her weapon from her hand. She bent to retrieve the weapon, only to find the tip of his sword against her throat, lifting her back to a standing position. "Do you want to be right, and dead? Or are you willing to learn to do what it takes to win when it counts?"

"You are a very different master," she replied.

"I've never been a master. In my land, I used to fight for money, whoever would pay me the most." She looked surprised at this. "I do what it takes to win; because no one values the life of a 'sellsword', a 'mercenary'. No ransom would ever be paid for me. No rescue if I were to be captured. When I can, I spare the life of the one that I'm fighting; but in a pitched battle, you have to put your enemy down and make sure they stay down. Your whole body is a weapon. I always knew that, but Roku taught me ways of fighting that complemented what I was already doing and made me even deadlier."

"You are willing to teach me more?" she asked.

"You and your sister are both coming back to my country. We'll have a lot of time on the ship to train. I can learn from you, you can learn from me and from Roku, and maybe even from Tennyson," he laughed.

She stepped very close to him and lazily reached out her hand to touch his side. Her fingers traced a scratch, and she lifted them up to show him the drops of blood. She looked up into his blue eyes and smiled like the mouse that caught the cat.

"Perhaps you're not untouchable, Master."

"Are you done packing master?" Anisha called from the doorway. She stood there studying the strange man who she had just met a month ago. He was tall, strong, and his fair skin showed a dozen wounds from battles hard fought and won. He had a devil's blue eyes and a wicked smile. Staring at him, naked from the waist up, she allowed her imagination to roam. She imagined being swept up in his strong arms, arms that made a sword sing, arms that crushed those that stood in his way. He was so different from her people, and yet his beauty was magical. Just as her thoughts were getting ever more intimate, he looked up.

"Yes, and enough of this 'master' business. Are you ready to ship off tomorrow?" he asked.

"I am, though I admit, I do not like travel on the sea."

"I'm the same. If we were meant to travel the seas, we'd have fins and a tail, no?" When she giggled at his stupid joke, he began to worry.

Chapter 27: Wanaka

Wanaka turned the blade over and over in his strong hands. The silvery color of the blade contrasted with his coal-black skin. He was a handsome man, an inch or two over six feet tall, with wide shoulders that tapered to a very thin waist. His legs seemed long and were as strong and wiry as the rest of him. Around his cousin's castle, he never bothered to wear his armor or any sign of his rank. He was the official King's Champion and a prince, though he was not in line for the throne. He studied the alien runes that were carved all along the long straight blade, they made no sense to him. Swinging the sword around, Wanaka marveled at how light it was. The sword did not reject him outright, but he was not the master of this weapon, and part of him thought that the sword knew it too. He handled the enchanted sword belonging to the tall 'not Doreh' man who stood across from him.

"Truly a marvel of craftsmanship, friend Landis," he said, handing the sword back.

"As is yours. I think we both suspect the same thing, that our swords are brothers."

"How did you come about yours?" Landis asked.

"Ahhhhh, a very good story!" Wanaka's face lit up. Over a couple of glasses of beer, he told the story of his youth as a squire to his cousin, King Lollando. They were near the Northern border, hunting Doreh raiding parties. There was no love between the Uzor and the Doreh, and years of border wars had shown the Doreh that the Uzor would not take their incursions lying down. The king had just recently ascended to the position due to his father's retirement, and despite having the right name, he still felt that he had to prove himself. Not only to his father and his subjects but most importantly to himself.

They were tracking the Doreh raiding party along a riverbank, looking for tracks of the men or their mounts or any traces that they had passed that way. Not finding anything and because it was growing late, they decided to make camp in a clearing near a small dam in the river. After a few hours of cooking up some small pig-like creatures and swapping a few stories, Wanaka decided to go off by himself and get fresh air. It was not his usual nature to leave a gathering till every drink was drunk and every story told, but he had a strange feeling and knew deep in his being that he needed to be alone.

A manly voice woke him from his own thoughts. It was strong, but quiet and seemed to echo through the nearby forest. He wasn't sure if he was hearing the voice with his ears, or with his mind; but it was so compelling that he stumbled through the near darkness, to answer the call. He followed the voice till he came to the river, the voice was coming from beneath the still water behind the dam. Not knowing exactly why, he walked into the water's edge, took a deep breath, and dove in. Under the water's calm surface, he opened his eyes and was surprised that he could still see. The light from the moon filtered through, but it seemed much brighter here under the cool water. Then he saw him. There was a man there, calmly drifting in the water. The man was smiling at him in a fatherly way. His skin was black as night, and he was old enough to be Wanaka's grandfather. Despite his years, he was still strong and imposing. He wore nothing, and bore the scars of many battles, and the ritual scarring typical of the ancient people that pre-dated the Uzor. He waved the young warrior over and when he spoke, Wanaka heard him as if they were on dry land.

"Come to me Wanaka, proud son of the Uzor, warrior of the Lollando clan," his voice was rich and deep. His smile was enchanting.

"I am Wanaka. How do you know my name?" he asked the stranger.

"It's not boasting when I say that I know everything. I have watched you since you were conceived and have waited till now to reveal your destiny."

"My destiny?" Wanaka asked, not understanding. "You're a stranger, how can you possibly know about my destiny?"

"We've never met, but I am no stranger. You call out to me whenever you are troubled and in need of solace."

"I am confused by your words, and how are we able to breathe and talk under water?"

"What I have to say if for your ears only, so I found this place for us to have privacy. Only a few men are born each generation whose lives are touched by the Fates. It is their destiny to fight and defend, to protect others, and if necessary to die in the defense of my design for this world," he smiled at the young warrior.

"As you've recognized, I'm a warrior for the Lollondo clan, its already my destiny to fight beside my cousin. Of course I would die for him, or anyone in our clan!"

"Of that, I have no doubt; but as you get older, you must think larger, think beyond your clan and be prepared to do what is in the best interest of all the people in this beautiful world that I've built for you."

"You built this world?" He could barely believe what he was hearing, "Are you then, the one known as Yob, King of the Gods?"

"I go by many names, my son," the older man said, he smiled like a father to a son. "Yes, I am He. I have seen a great future for you. You will grow to become a hero, a champion of your people; and as such, you will need any blessings that I can give." He held out his hands, palms up, and an enchanted sword appeared, laying across his open palms. He reached out, in a gesture that was meant to invite the young warrior to take the sword from him.

When Wanaka touched Panther Claw for the first time, he knew that he had found a part of himself that had always been missing, and only now did he know that he had been incomplete. As he wielded the sword, it occurred to him that the weapon felt like an extension of his arm, as if it were part of his body. It sang to him, a comforting and soothing melody that played only in his head. He tied the sword to his waist, and again looked at his benefactor.

"I can't thank you enough, master!" he said, bowing his head.

"No need, my son. Thank me by protecting your king. Even now, he and your party are about to be attacked. Lead the others and put yourself between your king and all harm."

"Yes Master!" the boy said quickly, then turned to make for the shore, never looking back. He knew that the Yob was already gone.

The king was in danger and that was all that mattered. Dripping wet, his clothing clinging to his thin frame, he ran back to the camp. He was just in time to see the man on guard being taken down by a brutal chop of a war axe. The large, crude blade bit into his shoulder and sliced through his body till it was buried deep in the poor man's torso.

With a traditional Uzor war cry, Wanaka ran around the campfire and threw himself at the Doreh attacker. Panther Claw seemed to almost fly into his grip, and with a powerful swing, he easily took off the attacker's hand. The calloused white hand and the weapon it held fell to the cool jungle earth. The man howled in pain, as from behind him, a dozen Doreh raiders melted out of the jungle. Panther Claw felt light as a feather in his hands, and he swung the blade so fast that instead just a single blade, it looked as if he was surrounded by a ring of steel. Two more warriors fell before they even realized that their prey was awake and ready to defend themselves.

The king was beset by two of the huge savages. He was the picture of composure as he defended against both of the raiders, and patiently waited for his moment. His sword was long and thin and didn't have a hand guard. Because of its light weight, and its multiple folded steel manufacture, it was strong and moved faster than any Doreh blade could hope to match. He slashed at one of his attackers, opening a deep gash on the man's axe hand, causing him to drop his weapon. He deflected the other's attack, and then returned to the now, unarmed opponent, and used the thin blade to pierce his throat. The attacker fell to the ground, clutching at his severed windpipe with his beefy hands, and died just before his fellow raider fell to the king's relentless strikes.

Most of the party of Uzor were fighting one on one with the Doreh raiders; but Wanaka was not satisfied with those odds, instead taking on three of the raiders simultaneously. His enchanted sword almost wielded itself, dragging his arm along as it moved to intercept blow after blow, slash after slash. Knowing that it was his destiny to become the king's champion and protector only caused him to attack with even greater ferocity. His speed was impressive before, but now he seemed to move faster than the eye could follow.

As the others were finishing their individual battles, Wanaka was facing three enemies. King Lollondo watched as his young cousin fought not for his life; but for the joy of doing his duty. His second in command was going to jump in to aid the youth when the king held out his arm to stop him. The man didn't ask for a reason, and Jarondo made no effort to give one. The remaining half dozen warriors stood watching young Wanaka. The Doreh raiders were covered in bleeding cuts on their arms and legs. A puncture to the gut for one, a slashed face for another. Wanaka knew that to kill one of them too soon would leave him vulnerable to the other two. He wore them down, drained their blood and their spirit. He was, as yet, unharmed. Blood and sweat covered his dark skin, causing him to shine brightly in the moonlight. His eyes were wider than usual, he could see things sharper, and faster than he could before. The dueling went on, and Wanaka blocked or evaded every slash, thrust, every swing of the huge war-hammer.

The raider that was wielding the war hammer seemed to be getting tired. The head of the hammer was essentially a small anvil with tribal etchings and runes, mounted on a hardwood handle wrapped in treated leather. Each swing got slower, and with every miss, he got angrier and more tired. He attempted to cave in the Uzor boy's skull with a crushing swing that came from behind his head, over the top, and was intended to land square on the Wanaka's skull. Wanaka easily evaded this, stepping to the side, and using the man's own body to block his fellows, brought Panther Claw down across his arm. The hammer fell to the ground, soaked in his lifeblood. He screamed in pain, till his cries were cut short by a slash that opened the front of his throat and windpipe.

The other two raiders screamed in anger, hurling their insults. Wanaka kept up his airtight defense, not reacting to their taunts. With more room to move, the other two raiders increased the pace of their attacks but were standing still compared to the reborn Wanaka. Using the speed granted to him by Panther Claw, the young warrior opened an additional, half-dozen cuts on each of the men he was facing. Soon they were covered head to toe in their own blood, they became weaker as their life flowed out in sheets of crimson. The Doreh raiders slowed and looked dizzy. Knowing that the time was right, Wanaka lunged forward, his sword penetrating the large man's chest, cleaving his slowly beating heart in two. The other lurched forward, to have Wanaka slip to the side and bring his sword down on the man's neck. The head dropped from its place atop the large man's body and hit the ground with a meaty thud, then rolled off into the brush.

Turning around, Wanaka faced his cousin and the others in his party. The young man had a satisfied look that was mixed with just a touch of the mania that it takes to kill three larger, stronger men. Doreh blood covered his face and arms and chest. He grinned widely like some raving maniac, then calmed himself and bowed to the king.

"What is that weapon that you carry, Wanaka?" the king asked, his hand outstretched to receive the sword.

"I was blessed by Yob and was given this sword. He named it 'Panther Claw', and so I shall call it," he said plainly.

Jarondo hefted the sword, and felt its perfect balance, admiring the inscriptions carved along its length. He swung the blade around his head, performed a few movements with it, then handed it back to its owner.

"It's not right for a king to envy one of his men, and yet, now I do. Yob has never appeared to me, despite my being head of the Church of Oyan."

"You're right Wanaka, a very good story. Let me now tell you about how Magnus gave Soulbane to me," he said, filling his new friend's cup.

Chapter 28: The Seasons

Carissa poured wine from a long-necked crystal decanter. She filled her sister's goblet, then her own. She was not accustomed to serving anyone, even herself; but being around her older sister gave her new life. The servants were given the evening off, and they fled to their wing of the mansion to wait until tomorrow when they would again be on duty. Lilith sipped at the heady beverage and purred like a contented kitten. The two sat on an open balcony in the Tower of Elements, the middle-height tower attached to Carissa's home. From there, they could see far out along the peninsula where the White Witch lived and held sway.

"Perhaps you are right sister. Why not enjoy some of what life has to offer."

"Exactly! True, you still look hideous, but that's no reason to sleep under the stars in that rat-infested forest. It's time to upgrade your lifestyle, my dear."

"I had a thought, sister. Since I have brought you in on my plans, you should meet my matron. She gave me this crystal on my staff. It has doubled, maybe even tripled my strength," Lilith gushed. Her old eyes had the spark of a much younger sorceress.

"As long as she doesn't kill us, I'm game," Carissa said. "Begin the summoning, I'll join you."

Lilith stood up and waved her staff in circles as she began chanting the summoning spell. Carissa stood and added the power of her staff to the mix. They tried casting their spell for several minutes before Carissa grew tired. Undaunted, Lilith continued to expend her reserved energy to perform the summoning spell. A rustling sound came from behind them and

172

several feet above where they were standing. Looking up, they saw the goddess Chorea. Lilith shielded her eyes because of the blinding glare, but Carissa stared at her like a troll seeing the sun for the first time. Chorea floated in the air a few feet above them, a full ten feet tall, nearly nude, and glowing like an exploding star. She looked down at the women with an amused expression.

"You know, you can summon demons, but you can't summon a god," she said smiling at the women. They both turned their head from her radiance.

"I wanted you to meet my sister. We are working together to plunge Kronos into chaos."

"I want you to plunge all of Xoran into chaos, but you can start with Kronos." She looked at the younger of the two women, "You're Carissa, the Autumn Witch?" Chorea asked.

"You ask, but you already know the answer. Yes, and Lilith is the Winter Witch."

"How long has it been since you saw your other two sisters?" the goddess asked.

"The Spring Witch, Anjaya... I saw her two hundred years ago," Carissa said. "Alexina, the Summer... almost three hundred years ago."

"I was trapped in the forest where I slept for several hundred years," Lilith added. "Perhaps the others are also imprisoned."

"Or dead," Carissa added.

"They are both alive," Chorea informed them. "Anjaya is in a far-off land called Tychon, in the country of Koregar. She's under a strong spell and doesn't know her true identity. For these many hundreds of years, the locals have thought of her as one of their own, as a Shaman. She predicts their futures, heals their wounds, gives them spells for growing crops and defeating enemies in battle."

"How terrible!" Lilith exclaimed, "We must rescue her immediately!"

"Magical energy is increasing in your Xoran due to the convergence of planes. So far, it looks like a few universes have collided and are merging into one," Chorea explained. "At the behest of my father, Argus split you four and imprisoned three of you to weaken your combined power. He favors these 'humans' and has given them advantages. He can't stop magic from entering his creation, but he is doing his best to tilt the scales in the human's favor."

"The timing seems a little too coincidental, if you ask me," Lilith stated.

"Perhaps because you are awake, and there's a renewed magical presence in Kronos, the planes are becoming attracted to each other. With the two of you working together, and the energy you're expending; you're probably at least part of the reason that the planes have veered back into each other."

"So, these lands where Anjaya is, and where Lilith lives, are accessible by ship?" Carissa asked.

"They are now. If you sail North West from here, you will find Kronos. If you sail East of here, a long way, you will eventually find Tychon, where Alexina is in the North, and where Anjaya is in the South. The lands of Orion and Polaris are North of Kronos, but no humans live there."

"Alexina! She's alive too?" Lilith cried out, "Where can we find her?"

"I can tell you where to find her, but you must hurry," Chorea urged. "Men from Kronos have traveled to Tychon, and they are, as we speak, seeking alliances to stop you. Magnus will be watching over them; but he will not personally intercede, just as I only offer advice. Free your sisters and combine your strength. The four of you can get the humans to war against each other, then you can easily defeat whoever survives."

"You said that Anjaya is bewitched and doesn't know her true identity. What of Alexina? Where can we find her?" Carissa demanded.

"She has been entombed in the Cave of the Five Tigers in Hadon." Chorea turned down her light and looked at each of the sisters. "I've said enough, probably too much. Get to work, and don't stop till every house is burning, every castle is razed to the ground, every life… extinguished." She faded and was gone.

Chapter 29: Recovering the Lost

The two women didn't even try to hide their identities as they walked through the small village. Both women were seeking something special. They found a young man working steel at the local smithy. Like all the Doreh, he was tall, wide of shoulder, and had a head full of long, uncombed dirty blonde hair. His muscles said that he was a man, but his failed attempt at growing a beard showed his immaturity. He was working briskly, pulling red hot iron from the furnace, placing it on the anvil, and pounding it into shape with a large hammer. He saw the women enter but didn't want to stop what he was doing because that's how fires start.

"Boy!" the old woman yelled. He looked up and gave the signal that he would be with her in a second. "Boy, put down that hammer. I need something from you!" Looking perturbed by their interruption during a vital step in the process of working the hot iron, he put down the hammer, placed the iron back into the furnace, and turned to the women.

"What d'ya want? Canna ya see I'm workin?" he asked the old woman. He looked over at the other, she wasn't necessarily his type, and yet to some degree, she was every man's type. He unashamedly ogled her in her long, skintight dress. She wasn't really dressed for the weather, but perhaps that's what caught his attention. "Ya say, ya need somthin from me?"

"I do!" wailed the old one, "I need your youth!" her voice cackled as she grasped each of his wrists with her claw-like hands. He was caught by surprise by how quick she was. By the time he felt that something was terribly wrong, it was too late. The boy's face took on a look of horror as he felt his lifeforce flow out and into the old woman. In seconds, his skin started to deflate and wrinkle like a rotting fruit. He fell to his knees, no longer strong enough to stand, and still she pressed on. She had a supremely evil look in her eyes, a ravenous smile on her face as she stole every year, every last bit of vitality from him. The life of a youth was delicious, but the life of a youth with innate magical ability was ten times the treat. When she finally released his dead hands, all of his youth had been transferred to her. Lilith looked at her sister Carissa for her opinion. Carissa smiled and nodded in approval.

"Now, I'm finally proud to call you sister. You're every bit, your old self," she handed Lilith a mirror. Gazing at the image before her, Lilith beamed with joy. Her skin was taut and pale as snow and her green eyes shined with a youthful brilliance. She was again, the woman that she had been three hundred years ago, young, beautiful, and glowing with unearthly power.

"Excellent! We do need to do something about those clothes though," she said as she began a simple spell. The fabric of Lilith's robes dissolved, and then in a tornado of cloth, a new dress formed on her perfect body. She wore a long white flowing gown with cobalt blue sparkles and trim. Her long white hair was held in what looked like a crown of thorns. Carissa looked at her older sister and smiled. "That's more like it. Let's get our Spring sister. She's been trapped by these savages for far too long."

The cave was not as hard to find as they thought it would be. They only had to capture and torture about a dozen people to get the location. The Forbidden Mountain lay In far Northern Hadon, in land controlled by one of the smaller Doreh clans. All through recorded time, it had been intentionally left off of maps. It was forbidden to travel up the mountain, though going around it was allowed. Forgotten Mountain was the largest mountain, in total area, and the tallest mountain in the entire continent of

Tychon. Per instructions, they were told to go nearly to the top and to look for the cave entrance on the Western face.

Witches didn't normally climb mountains, and you can't port to a place that you can't visualize. You also can't fly as high as the cave that they were seeking, it was thousands of feet up where the air was cold and thin. To make the dangerous journey, they had to enlist the help of the Hill Giants. They inhabited the range of mountains that lined the Northern shore of Tychon and were the absolute rulers of their snowy domain. In return for a few ponies to snack on, and a vast amount of iron, they agreed to carry the witches up the mountain.

Unlike their giant brethren, Hill Giants were a very simple race. They separated themselves from the rest of humanity and often were thought to have the intellect of children. They liked Iron for making tools, especially axes and hammers. Though they are on average twenty feet tall, they are the shortest of the giant races. Their thick hides and hairy limbs and bodies allow them to mostly ignore the cold in the upper reaches of the mountains where they live. They all had what humans would consider thick, rounded facial features, great muscular legs and arms, and huge bellies filled with goat or human flesh.

Lilith cast a very simple charm, and the Hill Giants were happy to pack the women up the side of the cliff. They created backpack-type baskets for the witches to sit in and enjoy the view as their bearers slowly climbed the thousands of feet, nearly straight up. After nearly a whole day of scaling a nearly vertical cliff face, they were at the level of the cave. The giants set them down on a flat area that gave them access by foot to the cave mouth.

"There may be danger within. Can you go into the cave with us?" Carissa asked her carrier. She smiled her most innocent, yet seductive smile up at the brute.

"No!" He shocked them all with his loud reply, "Me no enter! Forbidden! Danger!" the giant yelled. He flashed his gnarled rotting teeth at them, then started running down the path that worked its way down the mountain. His friend was quick on his heels.

"Guess we should be thankful for them getting us this far," Lilith mused. "What could be so dangerous, that it would send a couple of giants running down the mountain?"

"They call this, 'The Cave of the Five Tigers. I guess there are some ferocious felines inside?" Carissa wondered aloud.

"Only one way to find out," Lilith said as she cautiously walked towards the mouth of the cave, Carissa following close behind. They did their best not to make a sound, but their steps crunched icy snow with every step. The air was cold, and the wind was almost strong enough to pluck the women from the mountain's face and fling them into the open air. From their vantage point, they could see the range of mountains, stretching both left and right from their peak. Ahead lay the ocean, and behind was the continent of Tychon, and more specifically, the country of Hadon.

When they reached the cave, it was barely large enough for two people to enter walking abreast. They peered in and found no movement. Feeling emboldened, they walked in softly. The cave inside wound to the left and when they had gone quite a distance, they realized that without direct light, the inside of the cave was black as pitch. Lilith took a torch from her pack, then conjured a small ball of flame to light it. The cave went on for a hundred feet and got narrower as they went deeper.

"I'm starting to feel confined in here," Carissa complained.

"Try being trapped inside of a tree for a few hundred years, then come to me and complain."

They crept on, coming to a slight turn to the right. The passage opened up to a large chamber that looked like it was carved from the living stone of the mountain. The floor of the chamber went down, and the ceiling was a dozen feet above. It appeared to be an almost spherical hole in the heart of the Forbidden Mountain, and on the far side, a hundred feet away, was a dais. On the stone table was a woman's form, laying in a supine position with a delicate shroud covering her from head to toe.

Filling most of the chamber were five statues of Doreh men, though they were bigger than any Doreh man known to exist. The statues looked like warriors that had been frozen while in supplication to some higher power. Their every muscle was taught, and their faces showed both pain and need. They wore the traditional Doreh half armor and the weapons at their sides were fearsome, despite having the rust of hundreds of years on them. Lilith looked at the men, their finely toned muscles, flat stomachs, firm thick legs, and luxurious blonde hair. She reached out to touch the stone-cold flesh of the statue nearest her. It had been so long since she had touched a man or was touched by one. Her long delicate fingers stroked the muscled thigh of the petrified guardian, and she almost shuddered with desire.

Her sister Carissa, who had not been completely depriving herself, was far more cautious. She saw her sister reach out her hand, and she instinctively knew it to be a mistake. She called out for her to stop, just as Lilith allowed her hand to glide up the stony flesh. The statue came to life, and he moved slowly for only a second before coming fully to life. The Doreh warrior was close to eight feet tall, and he was a perfect specimen of manhood. Seeing the invaders, he reached for the massive war axe at his waist. His stone eyes still had the look of a man in agony, and his silent scream would have been heartbreaking, if the sisters had hearts. He swung the massive iron blade and only missed taking off Lilith's head by inches. Carissa's reflex took control and she cast a spell that didn't require any components or complex casting rituals. She sent a battering ram of water to impact the warrior's torso, knocking him off his feet and tossing him back several dozen feet.

Both sisters noted that waking one warrior also woke his four fellow tigers. They now faced five of the oversized fighters, who were trapped there for centuries to guard the seemingly dead woman behind them. Lilith's go-to spells always involved fire, and she started firing balls of white-hot fire at the guardians. She was feeling young and powerful like she had in her youth. She launched fireballs, cones of fire, and waves of pure flame. Carissa stepped behind her for her own safety. When she had expended a tremendous amount of energy, she stood back to see the fallout. When the smoke cleared, the Doreh Tigers were unfazed.

They were cursed to guard this tomb forever, their skin turned to living stone. To the witches, they reeked of enchantment; not even their hair or clothes had been affected by Lilith's fire. They lumbered forward, each of them reaching for their axes or hammers as they drew near. Their main problem was that they were so large, and the witches were so small by comparison. They could barely fight one on one, much less two or three-on-one. The golem that Lilith had touched was still in front, and he again swung his axe, trying to chop her in twain. Lilith ducked to the side; the wind displaced by the swing tossing her hair.

Carissa was concocting a spell, and when her sister was out of the line of fire, she launched it at the closest guardian. The stone around his feet turned to liquid, and he immediately sank to his knees. She then let the stone harden so that it became solid again. The guardian, who was now more creature than man, roared in frustration at being trapped. Taking his massive weapon in both hands, he started hacking at the stone around his legs, trying to free himself.

One of his fellows pushed past and confronted the sisters at the edge of the cave, near the entrance to the tunnel. He was almost his predecessor's twin, the only difference being that he carried a massive war hammer. He swung the hammer like it weighed nothing, and it nearly took Lilith's head off. Carissa touched the amulet at her breast, and time seemed to stand still. She carried her sister into the cave and placed her safely by the dais where their other sister lay. Then she returned to the horrid scene of a seven-foot barbarian with his weapon cocked, poised to strike. His every muscle was stretched, and he was prepared to contract his mighty chest and arms, bringing the hammer down in an attack that would kill, even if it only struck a glancing blow. She cast a quick spell that weakened the stone on the floor of the cave where the frozen golem was standing. She knew that the spell was effective, even though with time nearly frozen, she could not yet see the effects.

Carissa again touched the amulet, and from her vantage point at the back of the cave, she could see the rock beneath his feet crumble and fail. The whole front of the cave sheared off and slid down the mountain. The stone warrior had a look of horror as his momentum carried him over the edge. He still held his weapon, out of instinct, as his body fell thousands of feet straight down to a certain death below. His face looked almost relieved as he knew his long centuries of servitude for a master he hated, were now at an end.

The inside of the cave was large, but there was not enough room for the remaining guardians to swing their huge weapons. Unperturbed by their brother's death, they charged forward, huge dirty hands reaching for the soft flesh of their prey.

Lilith was being stalked by a man nearly eight feet tall, with long thin limbs and wide shoulders. She ducked under his first clumsy attempt to grab her, but he moved much quicker than she expected, and he was able to scoop her up in his long sinuous arms and he started squeezing the life from her. The first constriction forced all the air from her lungs, and she tried in vain to stay conscious long enough to think of a spell.

Carissa was being chased by two of the giant men; and for the first time in centuries, she felt fear. They were resistant to fire, to water, and who knows what else. One of the men caught her with a wild swing, it didn't have more than a fraction of his full strength, and yet, it sent her flying across the chamber. Her limbs were intact, but she felt like there was real damage internally. It was far too soon to be able to use her amulet again, so she desperately thought of another way to either protect herself or strike down the statue men. She used the brief separation to start casting her spell. Lilith saw that her sister was in danger and cast a light spell that temporarily blinded the guardians. With a brief respite, Carissa completed the spell, and a portal formed between her and the men. Both men that were attacking her were confused by the rift and leaped at it, disappearing to the world on the other side. She quickly closed the portal to keep them from returning. She then turned to see how her sister was faring.

Lilith looked like she was near to passing out when her spell took effect. Her body began to flow like hot candle wax. She grew and grew and grew, her skin becoming mottled grey with lots of hair and deeply cratered skin. Within seconds, she achieved her nearly twenty-foot height. She now towered over the barbarian that seconds before had seemed so large and unbeatable, she had transformed into a female Hill Giant, with all of their size and strength. She roared with anger, remembering being struck and almost choked to death. The barbarian pulled out his axe and opened a two feet long gash on the Hill Giant's calf, she growled in pain and anger. She moved with the slow deliberate movements of a giant, the Doreh Guardian seemed to move at least twice as fast. He inflicted another long gash on her forearm and across her stomach before she could anticipate his movements. Her body was huge and hard to manage, but her mind was as sharp as ever. Seeing his movements, she was able to predict his movements. After slicing her thigh, he was exactly where she thought he would be, and when she reached out her giant hand, he almost fell into her palm. Her hand easily grasped his whole lower body. She grabbed him from the waist up with her other hand and twisted. The pale rock-hard guardian was ripped in half and died instantly.

Carissa was there to catch her sister as she returned to her own form. Lilith was bleeding from several wounds and seemed to be drained of energy. She tore bandages from her own skirts and wrapped Lilith's wounds to try and slow the bleeding. When her sister was stabilized, she looked at the destruction around her. The cave was littered with the remains of the guardian that the Hill Giant killed, there was a guardian trapped to his knees in solid stone just inside of the cave mouth, and then there was her other sister, laying on a table of stone at the back of the room.

Walking carefully across the uneven floor of the cave, she slowly approached her still sister. The figure under the thin shroud appeared young and beautiful, as did all the Seasons. Unlike the others, Alexina the Summer was blonde, with thick wavy golden hair that fell to her waist. Lilith the Winter dressed conservatively, covering herself from neck to foot, Carissa the Autumn also dressed in a very conservative manner. Alexina, by contrast, wore next to nothing. She had on a sheer wrap that barely covered her more than ample breasts. Her perfectly formed midriff was bare, as were her arms and legs, and she wore another wrap that served to protect her modesty, at least somewhat. Normally her skin was bronzed and almost glowed with life and vitality. In her current state, she was like a fire that was nearly extinguished.

Carissa felt exhausted but knew that she couldn't stop now. She dug all of the required spell components out of her bag and began drawing the runes on the stone around the table. A curse powerful enough to trap one of the Seasons would be performed by a very high-level mage. To break such a curse, it would normally take all of her energy along with all of her sister's as well. She looked over at Lilith who was not near death yet but was far from being well. She would be of no help. When the preparations had been made, she began her chant. Words in an ancient language that may have even pre-dated the arrival of man, fell from her mouth. She placed a special herb under her tongue, hoping that the extra stimulation would help her through the process. She recited all the words of the spell, and when she came out of her lucid dream, she saw that nothing had changed. Alexina was still as lifeless as she had been before she started.

Carissa the Autumn slumped to the ground, her back against the dais where her younger sister lay in a death-like trance. She didn't despair, there was nothing to be gained from that; but she couldn't help the feeling of helplessness that pervaded her mood. She could take Lilith home and come back at some later time; but if anyone monitored this prison, they might move her younger sister, or just kill her. She felt hungry, and her mind was starting to wander when she was surprised by a strange voice.

It sounded like the voice of a child, a young girl to be exact. She peered around the stone pedestal, and there in the mouth of the cave was a young girl around ten years old. The girl skipped across the rough stone floor and ignored the flailing of the trapped guardian and the various body parts that littered the chamber. Her golden hair bounced joyfully as she worked her way back to where Carissa was resting. She wore a simple white and gold dress with soft leather sandals.

"Looks like you're having a bit of a problem, yes?" she asked with a knowing smile on her pretty face. She skipped over to Lilith and placed her tiny little hand on one of the more serious wounds. The skin seemed to weave itself back together. She did the same with the next few wounds until the Winter Witch was completely healed. Returning to Carissa, she laid hands on the Autmn witch, her touch healing the internal damage that she had incurred. After healing the sisters, she pulled a small iron cook pot out of seemingly nowhere and placed it on the corner of the large stone table. She then produced two small bowls of very common crockery and two wooden spoons. Carissa sat silently, watching her as she ladled out a helping of the stew from the pot at gave it to her. "Eat this, it will refresh you!" she said happily. Then she offered a bowl to Lilith. She had to hand feed her the first couple of spoonsful, but soon the woman had the strength to feed herself.

Both women started feeling better, their energy and strength returning as quickly as they downed the heavy broth. Carissa saw that her sister was regaining her color, though she was naturally very pale. Blood returned to her face and gave her cheeks the slightest rosy hue. Her own hands were no longer shaking, and her mind was no longer clouded.

"Thank you for the refreshment," she said to the child. "I've never tasted such an invigorating dish." She gave the girl a respectful bow.

"I don't imagine that you would have tasted this, it's a recipe of my own design. I call it, 'Food of the Gods.'" She laughed lightly at her own joke, her childish voice sounding like music to the ear, "You'll be fine now, and I'm off!" She bounced to her feet and skipped through the cave and out the front. Carissa and Lilith both watched as it appeared that she danced right off the edge and into space.

"Do you feel strong enough to help me break this curse, sister?" Carissa asked.

"To be honest, I haven't felt this good in centuries. Let's do it!" Lilith got to her feet and stretched her long lean form. She didn't have the pure sexual attraction that Alexina had; instead, she had strong, sharp features and a physique that exuded strength of muscle, and perfect proportion. She looked at the work that her younger sister had started. "I'm sorry that I was not able to help, but it looks like you have nearly completed the spell. Your skill is still unmatched, dear sister."

"Thank you, but enough of that. Let's finish this and be on our way." She again began chanting the language of some people who long vanished from the worlds they now shared. Lilith joined in, their voices in harmony as they sang-spoke the words of the spell. Lilith held her sister's hand, and with her other hand, invoked the power of her clear blue crystal. The gem on the head of her staff glowed with energy far more powerful than what she was previously capable of. Her new patron had done more than her share, and Lilith wondered in the back of her mind what exactly would be the price she would eventually have to pay.

The enchanted sorceress that lay on the cold stone table looked every bit a corpse. A beautiful corpse; but still, completely devoid of any sign of life. As the ancient phrases were uttered, the smoke of burning incense made from sacred herbs filled the air. The runes that were written all over the chamber, with ink made from the blood of a virgin, began to glow. The sisters poured their power into their spell casting, and they were delighted that they could see the color return to their baby sister's skin. She again had the golden glow of Summer itself, and when her eyes opened, they knew that their efforts and sacrifices had not been in vain.

"Lilith! Carissa! Where am I?" Alexina asked, sitting up slowly and surveying the room.

"You've been trapped here in an enchanted slumber for the last three hundred years," Lilith said to her younger sister. "I too was trapped; but the planes are again converging, allowing all of us to be in the same world again."

"Where's Anjaya?" she asked, trying to stand after so long laying on her back.

"She's bewitched. Our next stop is to free her, and then, we take our revenge on this world!" Lilith said, the other two nodded in agreement.

Chapter 30: Anjaya

The women arrived in Nanoan by one of Alexina's portals. Alexina had seen the Koregar capital a few hundred years ago, but it was all new to her sisters. Aside from the display of magic, the three white women, two with long white hair and the third, with blond hair, seemed very out of place in an Uzor city. All eyes were on them, but they ignored the people around them as one would ignore ants beneath their feet. They marveled at the city; it was the largest that any of them had ever seen. The streets were paved with interlocking stones of deep reddish brown, and the buildings were stacked stone, held together with mortar. Most of the buildings in their immediate vicinity were one or two stories. Further off, towards the Western part of the city were the larger buildings that housed the royal family, the government buildings, and trading companies. The buildings were visible from afar because they reached twenty stories high.

Every building had glass windows and solid wooden doors. Flowers and vine plants were everywhere, and it was apparent that they were planted and well maintained. Above the streets, lines were strung across the road to support flowering vines. Many people stopped in these naturally shaded areas to stop and talk, or in this instance, to stop and stare at the foreigners. Men, women, and children alike stared at the women, and despite having a thousand questions, they instinctively knew to give them their space. Even the constables who were quickly on the scene, chose to join the growing crowd of onlookers. Finally, Alexia walked over to an older woman.

"You have a sorceress in this city?" she asked the woman. The old black woman stared at her golden hair, her ample bosom, and her tanned white skin with interest bordering on disbelief. "Answer me!" she demanded.

"There are many sorcerers and sorceresses here in Nanoan," the woman replied.

"Is there one who is superior to the rest? A woman, who has been alive for hundreds of years, and yet does not die of old age?"

"I've heard of such a woman, she is old enough to be your grandmother, except she is black like me," the woman said. "She lives very far from here, in a city in the North called Konto."

"Very far, you say?" she said turning to her sisters. They shrugged in a show of indifference. "All right then, have her summoned! We'll wait in this café," she said, pointing towards a nearby outdoor eatery. "Bring her to us before the sun goes down, or we will conjure a swarm of demons to drink your blood and claim your souls!" she shouted her demands to the crowd. Almost every onlooker turned and ran.

"Too much?" she asked, laughing at the townspeople's discomfort.

The women walked calmly to the café and sat. They were instantly served tea and biscuits and carried on their own conversation, catching up after their long time apart. The regular people ran for their homes, and the constables ran back to their station to send their demands up the chain of command.

Anisha Bkar stepped through the portal, followed by Wanaka, and finally by Linea Bkar. The three approached the seated sisters and stood waiting for them to give them their attention. All three sisters looked over at the newcomers. Lilith looked specifically at Linea, ignoring the others.

"We didn't ask for you girl. We are looking for a sorceress who has lived here for many generations. A much older woman than you, much more powerful."

"I'm powerful enough," she stated testily. "I'm the crown's personal sorceress, and I'm here to take you before the king. If you're Doreh spies, you'll be sent to the pits to await execution."

"I can feel your power, sister," Carissa said. "You are strong, true enough, but each of us is more than a match for you. Three of us? You should run off and find the one that we're looking for."

"Do you think they are looking for Monoka, your old teacher?" Anisha whispered to her sister.

"That sounds promising," Lilith interjected. "Bring her to us now, and we will spare you and this city. At least for today," she laughed out loud, and her sisters joined in.

Linea could feel their power, just as they could sense her ability. She knew instinctively that she was outclassed by each of them, and together they would be nigh invincible. Without a word, she opened the portal and pulled Wanaka and her sister through. When they were again in the castle, Anisha looked at her sister, who was standing there infuriated, her anger more evident than it had ever been since they were children. Anisha knew better, and let her sister walk away.

The portal opened, and Linea walked through with a very old black woman on her arm. She was followed by her sister and Wanaka. They walked the dozen or so feet over to where the witches were seated. Eyes were peering out from all the windows around the square; but only the waitress remained and was tasked with keeping the sorceress' calm and satisfied. Alexina stood and walked the rest of the way to the old woman, who was standing there, hunched over her staff. Bending down, she held out her bronzed hand and caressed the old skin of the woman's cheek.

"Anjaya, what have they done to you?" she asked with tears welling up in her eyes. She stood up, and her gaze panned around the square. "What have you creatures done to her? By the demon, you'll all pay for this!"

"What are you talking about, you crazy Doreh whore?" Monoka yelled at the blonde.

"She doesn't know you, why are you harassing an old woman who has not harmed you!" Linea asked, putting her arm around her former mentor.

"Harassing? We're not harassing her. She's our sister, and we're here to right an injustice. You 'people' have captured our sister and now hold her prisoner in this decaying body, this fictional life!"

"You're all crazy!" Linea shouted. "Monoka, tell them that they're wrong!"

"How can we be sisters? We are literally as different as night and day!" The old sorceress croaked.

"We are the seasons, dear sister. I'm the Summer, and you little sister are the Spring. You are the embodiment of life itself, it's an ironic crime that they've imprisoned you in this decaying shell," Alexina said with tears in her eyes.

Carissa and Lilith joined Alexina, and the three of them surrounded the old woman. They all laid their hands on her and began to chant. Linea took a step back, her face showing her concern. Even those with no magical ability could feel the raw energy in the air, and they all feared the worst. Linea was attuned to such things, and what she felt overwhelmed her senses. Her old mentor had been very strong when she was still under her tutelage; but even at her peak, she was nothing compared to these women. Part of her wanted to run or dive through a port to anywhere else, but she needed to know. It was important for her to witness and report back to her lord.

The chanting increased in volume, and the already high level of energy continued to increase as the sisters tried to break the spell that held their lost sister. A strong wind swept in from every direction, the sky directly above grew dark with the sudden appearance of rainclouds. Lightning began cracking off in the distance, and the air grew bitterly cold. They tried for many long minutes, and the face of the old woman looked both confused and scared at the same time. The very air around them became electric and the glow coming from the ancient sorceress' was becoming blinding. The lightning and the wind swirling around built and built and built... then stopped.

The women all looked spent by the procedure, but they were happy with the result. The old woman now had a vastly different light behind her eyes. She was no longer a kindly teacher of young magic users, no longer a loyal Uzor. She was much more. She strained, stretching out her back so that she could stand straight. The sisters again laid hands on her, and they each lent some of their energy to her. Before everyone's eyes, the years fell off the one who was called Monoka, and she became Anjaya the Spring. She was now as tall as Carissa, seductive as Alexina, and as serious as Lilith. Her skin was dark brown and shone as if lit by an internal flame. She had short hair, held by golden combs. Her now youthful face was beautiful, her features sharp and noble. She had a long thin neck that topped strong shoulders and a body that rivaled Alexina in its perfection. She cast a quick spell that destroyed the rags that she had been wearing and replaced them with a form-fitting dress that was bright green, blue, gold, and brown. Around her ankles, she wore anklets of silver and strings of shells. Her midriff was bare, showing her flat stomach. She smiled brightly at her sisters, but her eyes had menace in them. She was finally free, but she resented the loss of her freedom for gods knows how many years.

"Who did this to you, sister?" Lilith asked.

"I don't know his name," Anjaya said ruefully. "He was a tall, good-looking, rather thin mage. He Had a short beard, and light brown hair down to his shoulders. I poured us each a glass of wine, we drank, we… kissed, and then I woke up here, now."

"Did he have the sign of the demon inked on his skin? Across his back?" Lilith asked.

"He did!" Anjaya said, shocked at her sister's knowledge.

"I know the mage that cursed you sister. He's dead by my hand; but ah… in his youth," Lilith seemed to almost be lost in her own dreamy world. "He was so powerful."

"I was trapped in the body of a human, forced to live their lives of drudgery for hundreds of years, and now that I'm myself, I'm denied my rightful vengeance?" Anjaya shouted, "All of you are complicit!" she said accusing the faces behind the windows. "Anjaya is herself again, and all of you will pay for being party to my imprisonment!"

Wanaka pulled the girls away from where the Seasons were reuniting and whispered in her ear. "Go tell the king, right now! Bring as many men as possible and any mages that we have. This will get bloody, and very soon!" he ordered the Bkar sisters. Linea created a portal, and they were gone in an instant.

Chapter 31: Spring's Revenge

Mere minutes had passed, but already the chaos was well underway. Landis was the first through the rift, his plate armor gleaming brightly in the late day sun, Soulbane already in his grasp. He was followed by King Lollondo, and then Tennyson, Roku, Father Sebastienne, and the Bkar sisters. After them came a flood of the king's elite guard and a half-dozen mages that were Linea's disciples.

A dozen Hill Giants were storming around the dining district where Anjaya had been awakened. At their feet were the corpses of men who had died in Phister Swamp back in Kronos and were now animated by minor demons. Anjaya was making the dull-witted giants carry out her revenge like mindless puppets. She laughed at the massive destruction they were causing, and her sisters joined in on her celebrations.

Zaebzal screamed orders to the dead, urging them on with a twenty-foot whip. Light from burning buildings around him danced in the reflection on his shiny red and grey scales, Lem Lothe was not even a memory, this new being was truly evil to the core. The demon was a lower-rank type, and completely in Lilith's service. A woman tried running for safety behind him, his long, spiked tail whipped with incredible speed, striking her, and sending her broken body flying in the direction that she had come from. At his master's direction, he personally supervised the dead as they hunted down and ate Uzor civilians.

Wanaka was hacking away at the undead fighters, everyone that he chopped down was replaced by two or three others. He was starting to become a little concerned until, in his peripheral vision, he saw a knight in shining armor. Landis chopped his way toward the champion, leaving severed limbs like fallen leaves in his wake. Wanaka acknowledged him with a nod of his head.

"You started without me, friend?" Landis asked as he deftly removed the head from a decomposing soldier.

"I didn't have the time to wait for you to get dressed in your shiny suit," he joked with his former rival. "I'm actually not as worried about this lot as I am about the giants."

"Giants... I've heard bedtime stories of giants, but I never thought that I would ever see one in person," he said, taking a second to look up at the twenty-foot-tall brutes.

"Seeing one would be quite a thing to tell your children. Seeing a dozen rampaging through the streets is more than just an old war story. They're stupid, like children that are twenty-foot-tall and bent on killing and eating people."

"Well, I brought one of the Lochmar Riders with me, let's test his skills," Landis offered.

"I really have no idea what you're talking about, but make it happen!"

"Tennyson! Get over here!" he called to his friend. "Time for your bow, let's see if it can live up to its name!"

Tennyson ran up to the champions and sheathed his long sword. From his back, he pulled out the giant bow that he always had on his person. From the quiver on his back, he pulled out a long iron arrow. The shaft was more than four feet long and the broad head was razor sharp. He only had a dozen 'special' arrows, each blessed by a priest to carry out the will of the gods. Landis gave him direction by hand signal, then turned to Wanaka.

"I'm going to get the giant's attention." He pointed at the closest of the Hill Giants, "Keep these others away from me, and more importantly, away from him," he said, hooking his thumb toward Tennyson. Wanaka, not one for excessive conversation nodded in agreement.

Landis charged at the giant, knocking down a couple of the undead on his way. When he was close enough, he slashed at the huge ankle, severing the giant's Achilles tendon. The huge child-like beast screamed in pain, his dull expression turned to one of anger and agony. He wore a simple robe, tied at the waist with a large rope, the kind that kept ships in place while in port. He wore nothing else, and Landis did his best to not look directly upward. Tennyson Coe came in on his right side, bow nocked and ready to fire. The giant turned his massive body and reached for the human that had caused him pain.

Despite not being a large man, Tennyson had remarkable strength through his chest and arms that he didn't make a point of advertising. His hood back, legs planted firmly on the rubble strewn street, he pulled back the bow that was nearly as long as he was tall. The sinews of the silk bowstring were near to bursting as he pulled the bow back, folding it nearly in half. With a silent prayer on his lips, he released the built-up tension, sending the arrow at terrific speed and with unmatched force in all of archery. The giant was just about to grasp Landis with his huge thick fingers when the arrow plunged through his eye and buried itself deep in what passed for his brain. There was no cry of pain, just the sound of a couple tons of dead meat falling flat on the city street.

"Giant Killer indeed!" Landis called out to his friend.

Wanaka was cutting down the dead warriors, flinging their shriveled limbs to and fro, and separating fleshless heads from rotting bodies. He was joined by Landis, and the two heroes fought back-to-back, stacking up corpses till they were standing on a hill made of bones and decaying flesh. Flanked by his elite guards, King Lollando joined the fray. With a long, heavy scimitar, he hacked at the animated bodies, wiping out one or two of the undead soldiers with every slash of his mighty sword. Linea was directing her disciples, having them fight against the dead, and working to protect people and property.

Tennyson was able to strike down another two of the giants before he ran out of his special arrows. He returned his bow to his back and pulled out his long sword. Along with Anisha, he was able to push his way through the enemy to reach Landis and Wanaka. Most battles were bloody affairs, but the dead warriors had been bled dry long ago. He found his friend Landis covered in scraps of decaying skin and flesh, and other substances that were hard to identify.

"How are you doing friends?" Tennyson asked.

"They are easy to kill, but there seems to be no end to them," Wanaka replied.

"The giants are destroying the city!" Anisha shouted to the group. "My sister may be able to kill a few, but her magic isn't without its limits!"

"Wanaka!" Landis called out, "Can you summon the spirit of your sword?"

"Yes, we both must summon our sword's inner spirit! When we do, we'll be weaponless and easy targets!"

"I'll protect you!" Anisha said, looking directly at Landis. Even in the heat of battle, he remarked to himself, how desirable she was. *My God, she's fantastic. I should focus on the task at hand, but I can't get her out of my thoughts.* Her curly hair was wet with sweat, her flawless skin was coated with perspiration that steamed from her long sinuous limbs. Her eyes had a fiery glint. She looked like Nan, the Goddess of War.

"Wanaka!" Landis called to the Uzor fighter.

Wanaka held his sword out in front of him and concentrated on his summoning. Anisha, Tennyson, the king, and his guards all formed a circle around the two champions. Wanaka called out loudly, enticing the highest power of his enchanted sword. The blade faded from his grasp, and in its place, a huge ethereal panther appeared. The titanic black feline was proportionally as large, compared to the Hill Giants, as a real panther would be to a regular-sized man. The great cat leaped forward, and with its massive paws, it knocked down the closest giant. The surprised giant was taken easily to the ground, where the panther ripped at his throat with its nightmare-inducing fangs. Kegs of blood splashed everywhere, and the giant's dying cries caught the attention of everyone on the field of battle.

"What kind of magic is this!" Alexina screamed.

As Alexina was reacting, Landis was invoking the spirit of 'his' sword. Soulbane faded, and in its place, a giant winged serpent filled the air above him. The body coiled around one of the giants, while the snake's head snapped at another, filling his veins with deadly poison. The witches watched as their giants were being murdered by colossal mystical defenders. Lilith grabbed her younger sister by the arm and pulled her away from the action.

"Let's go, sisters. We have much bigger plans in the works," she created a port back to her forest in Kronos. The witches known as the seasons stepped through and were transported thousands of miles away. In their wake, they left half a dozen rampaging giants, thousands of undead warriors, and one furious demon. The witch Lilith had just an hour ago ported them from raiding peaceful farming villages in Kronos to a battlefield where people were fighting back.

Zaebzal was shouting orders to his troops, and out of the corner of his eye, he almost missed seeing the sisters slip away. When the portal snapped shut after them, he knew that he was now on his own. It was difficult for a creature that is fueled by rage to get angrier, but he somehow managed it. From a strap around his back, he pulled out a Morningstar, three feet long and forged from black iron with four-inch spikes. He swung the weapon in huge circles, taking out soldiers, two and three at a time. His scaly, four-foot-long red tail slammed into anyone trying to attack him from behind.

Linea saw that the tide was turning and was able to devote more of herself to the fight. She had always had an affinity for water and conjured a huge bubble of water to envelope the demon. Zaebzal was furious at being trapped in water. No matter how much he flailed, he couldn't break free. Being a creature born of fire, he drew on the hellish heat that raged inside of him, and the water that was trapping him started boiling. Soon, he had evaporated enough of the water to break the surface tension of the bubble and he was free. Seeing the sorceress, he charged after her, flames dancing on his scaly hide. She put up her hands to cast another spell and waited for the demon. Running at full speed, he smashed into the invisible shield that she had formed between them. Wiping the blood from his mouth, he howled in rage and began hammering at the shield with his oversized iron weapon. Being Iron and wielded by a creature with demonic strength, it only took a dozen strikes before her shield shattered and she was helpless. He closed the few feet that separated them and struck her with all his power. The sheer force of the blow crushed the bones in her arm, shoulder, collarbone, and a few ribs. The spikes bit deeply into her soft skin. Linea was knocked a dozen feet through the air and fell to the ground unconscious and bleeding.

Zaebzal ran to where she had landed and raised up his weapon to deliver the death blow. He didn't even see the other Bkar sister who came at him from behind. With both hands, she chopped down with her scimitar, the blade almost missed him, but was still able to tear a long gash down the demon's back. He cried out in pain and turned to face his new attacker. She stepped in and attacked with the fury of a mother bear, but unfortunately, not the strength of one. The demon easily deflected several of her strikes, and when she was caught off balance for just a second, he whipped his tail around and knocked the sword from her grasp. He jumped forward and kicked her straight in the chest. The force of his kick sent her sprawling backward, knocking the wind from her lungs. She clutched at her injury with her right hand and glared with murderous hatred at the demon. A trickle of blood flowed from her open, gasping mouth, and she knew that she had been hurt badly.

The demon stood between the sisters, deciding which to kill first when the knight stepped in. The giants had all been dealt with, and now Soulbane was again in its master's hand. The demon almost didn't notice the tall man in blood-soaked armor, but at the last minute, he smelled the enchantment on his weapon.

"Demon! Are you the same hellspawn that has been terrorizing cities in Eastern Kronos?"

"I am... human!" he replied, a smile on his face.

"And now, you're fighting women? You're such a fearsome demon, should I fetch you some children to fight next?" Landis taunted.

Zaebzal sniffed the air and stretched his mighty frame. Unlike his former human host, he was now several inches taller than the knight, his muscles were intimidatingly large, and he was covered in the blood of the Bkar sisters and the Uzor guards. He launched himself at the human who had dared to mock him. He swung his morning star with enough force to cave in the knight's armor, if it had connected. Landis dodged his attack with surprising speed and dexterity. He chopped downward, opening a gash on the Demon's left wrist. Howling in pain, he whipped his tail around, trying to catch Landis unawares. Again, with surprising speed and strength, he leaped the whip-like tail. Zaebzal tried again, but this time Landis caught the tail with his offhand and hacked at it with his sword. The demon screamed in agony, and by reflex, flexed his wounded tail flinging his attacker several feet away.

Landis landed in a heap and painfully got back to his feet. With renewed determination, he charged in, buckler held high. With one good arm, the demon attacked; but the force behind his swings was cut by more than half. Landis blocked a downward strike with his buckler, the small shield shattering beneath the blow. Though he was driven to one knee, he still had the strength to plunge his sword into the stomach of the demon. Pulling to the side as he withdrew the blade, a wide gash opened in the demon's abdomen allowing his intestines to burst out in a shower of blood and gore. The demon again howled in pain and used his injured hand to hold his insides, inside. With his other hand, he again attacked the knight. It was now child's play for Landis to dodge or duck his swings. Landis cut him several more times, injuring both legs, the demon's side, before giving him a particularly gruesome cut to the side of his neck.

Zaebzal knew that he'd been defeated. The part of his nature that was a coward won the day and he turned to flee the human who was slowly cutting him to pieces. He ran fast for one losing so much blood and having so many injuries, but Landis gave chase and easily caught him. Landis slashed at the tendons on the backs of his legs, bringing the demon to his knees. He took Soulbane and ran the creature through so that a foot of his blade came out of the demon's front. Zaebzal howled in pain while showering the knight and all humans present with insults and bile. Landis pulled the whip from Zaebzal's side and wrapped a couple of coils around his wounded neck. Putting his armored foot between the demon's shoulder blades, Landis pulled back with both arms, using all of his strength to strangle the demon.

Ignoring the sword that completely pierced his chest, and the opening that his guts were spilling from, Zaebzal clutched at the whip that was cutting off his air supply. He still thrashed with the strength of several men, but Landis held on and torqued down on the pressure. Several minutes passed by till the demon's arms fell lifelessly to his side, his head slumping forward in death. Landis released the whip and kicked the demon forward onto his face in the same motion. To be sure, he pulled Soulbane from the demon's back and hacked at the scaly neck till the horned head rolled awkwardly on the ground. Winded and exhausted, he looked up to survey the battlefield.

The battle was over, and they had won. King Lollando, Roku, Tennyson, and Wanaka all stood together staring at Landis, exultant in victory. They all had the same expression of awe. Some of the credit would go to his enchanted sword, but they had watched a man, an ordinary soldier, almost single-handedly defeat a demon.

Looking for the Bkar sisters, Landis found both being attended by Father Sebastienne. Landis rushed over to see how he could help, and for the first time since losing his wife and child, he felt completely helpless. There were no cuts to tend to, no bones to set. Both women were suffering from internal injuries, the kind most people died from. *Lord* Magnus, *please lend Father Sebastienne your strength to save these noble women.* Landis prayed.

"Priest!" Anisha called out. "I will live, save my sister if you can," she pleaded. The father nodded and took his hand off her. Picking up the smaller woman, he held her against his chest. He called out to Magnus and the other gods, and energy flowed from him into the broken body in his arms. Landis got down on his knees so that he could pull off his glove and touch it to the woman's neck. The pulse felt weak, fading.

"Father, you must push harder! She is nearer to the gates than she is to life." Landis pleaded.

"You must concentrate on your inner spirit," Roku offered, also on his knees. "We will offer you our energy as well. Accept the flood and heal her with all your might!"

Roku grabbed Landis' hand and placed the other on the priest's back. Landis took Tennyson's hand, who took Wanaka's. The five of them were enveloped in a warm yellow glow, a pleasant light that was in stark contrast to the horror around them. An inner radiance returned to Linea's ebony skin, showing that she was indeed improving. Many minutes later, Father Sebastienne ceased his prayers and removed his hand from the young woman. He looked tired and turned to the others.

"I've done all that I can do for now. She needs rest and fluids. I can help more in the morning after we've both slept." The father said, looking around at the allies. He found Landis sitting on the bloody ground, holding Anisha in his arms. Wearily, he made his way over to them.

The good father placed his hands on Anisha and again began his supplication to the gods of Kronos. For an hour, the Father tended to the woman warrior, while Landis held her close to himself. When he was done, the Priest almost passed out, just as Anisha was regaining consciousness.

"It's remarkable what that man can do," the king said to his champion.

"They are all remarkable, my king," Wanaka replied.

"When the sisters can travel, I will be looking forward to learning more about their land. If there are more like them, then I think that we must count them as allies."

ACT II:

THE HELLSPAWN

Chapter 32: The Castle

Work had started weeks ago, but nothing substantial had yet been accomplished. The first part of the construction was the accumulation and staging of materials. No castle could be built without a mountain of stone and a forest of timber. For weeks the caravans had traveled far and wide to bring the supplies that would be needed to make a fortress that would be the vanguard of the allied Kronos forces. King Gabriel Herron had left his own castle in southern Khatuna to build this behemoth on the Iron Road. He had worked with engineers from all over the continent to develop the blueprint for a castle that was not only aesthetically pleasing but as impregnable as could be.

Jorn had joined him just a few days ago to offer both advice and assistance. They had spent hours going over the plans with the engineers, and when the final plans had been decided on, Gabriel gave permission for the construction to commence. They had the dimensions of the castle all staked out and were prepared to start construction when Jorn stopped his friend.

"Your Highness, I have a present for you and these men," he said loud enough for all to hear. The workers looked on with great interest. "I know that every great castle needs a proper dungeon, winter food storage, escape tunnels, and sewer tunnels; so I studied very hard, and came up with a solution." They all watched skeptically while Jorn set a small cage on the ground in the middle of the cleared area where the castle would go, then began his spell. Though fire was more Danika's specialty, he started a small fire to aid in casting his spell. He spoke words in an ancient language of magic that only a few people in the world understood. As he recited the spell, he added small bits of this and that to the fire. The smell and the smoke that came from it were unpleasant, at best. The tempo of his words and hand gestures increased, and everyone could start to feel the energy that was growing in the air around the fire.

The cage burst open and a dozen creatures started growing in the open area where the castle was to be built. They were moles, but they grew to the size of a draft horses. Jorn spoke again in the magical language, and the moles not only seemed to understand but were happy to carry out their orders. They all began digging furiously. The humans stood back because of the flying earth; but watched with great interest as in only a couple of hours, the moles had dug a huge underground area for the dungeon, etc. At Jorn's command, they also dug escape tunnels for miles and miles in each direction. Some tunnels went to a nearby forest, and others exited in neighboring lands, far from where an invading army might be camped. They even created a sewer to carry away waste and a well system to provide fresh water.

"Amazing, Jorn!" Gabriel said. "Won't they tear up the whole countryside though?"

Jorn looked at where the sun was on the horizon. "No, they should be returning to their normal size about now." He smiled at his friend, "I think we all deserve a drink on you, your Highness!" Thinking of the thousands of man-hours that he had just saved; he was more than happy to buy a few rounds.

"I'm hopeful that with these shortcuts, we'll be ready in time for the dark days to come."

"There is still a lot of loose dirt to move, and they have to set the foundation; but while they're doing that, I'll help the stone cutters."

"How's that?" Gabriel asked.

"They create cracks in the stone, fill them with water, and I freeze the water. It's what nature does; but a thousand times faster. Much better than carving each individual block."

"I'm really glad that I brought you in on this project. Plus, since becoming king, I don't have any peers to spend time with."

"That's nice of you to say, Gabe. Danika will be here in a week or so, and we have a few ideas for the defenses that we'd like to try out. My visions tell me that what we'll be facing makes the followers of Quell look like a schoolyard threat."

"You've had more visions?" he asked.

"I feel that I have to check often now; things are changing from day to day," Jorn said thoughtfully. "The sorceress that killed my master is stronger now and she has been joined by her sisters. One of these witches was too much for my master, now there are four of them."

"Not to worry, Jorn," Gabriel put his hand on the thin mage's shoulder. "Magnus is on our side, and somehow, someway, we'll defeat these witches and protect the people of Kronos."

"Let's hope your right friend," Jorn said.

Chapter 33: Interlude

Landis stood at the bow of the ship, staring out at the endless sea. He was deep in thought when Father Sebastienne put his hand on his shoulder. The Father said nothing and waited for Landis to speak first. Landis just looked at the tall thin priest with a pained expression.

"Are you all right friend? Despite some setbacks, we are returning with both war and trade allies," the Father said.

"I have another problem that troubles me, Father. A subject that is not my specialty, and certainly not yours."

"Women?" the priest asked.

Landis stared at him in shock, "Yes, Father. I'm sorry that I dismissed your help so quickly."

"Well, in the realm of the female, I'm probably the last one you would turn to for advice, but some truths are universal. If nothing else, you'll feel better getting it off your chest."

"Ok, Father. It all started..."

There was a knock on the door to Landis' cabin. As the leader of the group and the sole reason for the trip, Genia King had made sure that he got first-class accommodations.

"Come in!" he called from his seat behind a small desk. The door opened, to reveal a tall dark-skinned woman with oiled black curls in her hair, wide bright brown eyes, high cheekbones, and a strong chin. She opened the door, but would only peek in. "Anisha, come in," he said almost hesitantly.   She walked into the small room, and sat on the edge of his bed, only a few feet from where he sat.

"How is your sister?"

"Much better, thank the gods for your friend, and of course, for you too." Landis looked at her and could tell that something was troubling her.

"You have something on your mind?" he asked. *She smells so good, like some exotic spice, and her skin seems to glow in the candlelight.*

"How long did you say that this trip was?"

"We left three days ago, it'll be another two weeks, give or take."

"I hate traveling by water," she grumbled.

"Me too. I've no taste for the up and down, and the side-to-side makes my stomach queasy."

She leaned forward and placed her hand on his knee. He could feel her breath when she spoke to him, and her closeness made his blood race through his veins.

"I know that the priest healed my sister, and he healed me too, but I wanted you to know how much you meant to us. That demon would have killed both of us, and I doubt that the priest could bring us back from that." She leaned in to kiss him on the cheek. "I'm a warrior, I've been fighting since I was a young girl. The king and queen often trust me with their lives, but compared to you..." She placed her hand on his cheek. The warmth of her hand filled him with a feeling that was more than mere animal attraction. "You're the most dangerous man with a sword that I have ever seen. You might be the best in both of our countries."

"I...," he said looking deeply into her eyes.

She cut him off, "I saw you speaking with the priest. You spoke for a long time, and you seemed... troubled."

"I recently began something, with someone back in my country. A woman."

"Are you promised to her?" she asked. Her forwardness appealed to him.

"Well... no, not formally. There is an age difference. I knew her when she was a child, and now that she's of marrying age... there's this attraction."

She held his face in her strong hands so that their eyes met, "Tell me she owns your heart, and I'll leave now. I'll leave, and this conversation will have never taken place."

"I've been with women before. Many women," he said while reaching for her hands. "I was married once and thought that I could make a happy peaceful life with her. An enemy came and killed her and our son. Then I reunited with this girl after many years of being absent. She had become a woman, and I thought that I had found my ideal mate; but..."

"But what?" she said, drawing even closer.

"Since the first time that I saw you, I've had feelings that are new to me. I want you, your body, your lips, your hands... I want to stand next to you in battle, to fight together, to defend the things that we both hold dear, together."

"Can you decide now? Right now?" Her eyes were wide, and he body grew tense. "You have two women who crave your embrace, but I don't share with anyone. If you choose her, gods bless you. You'll always be my master and my friend." She leaned so close that her ruby-colored lips were almost touching his ear. "If you choose me, be prepared to never make love to another till one of us dies."

He pulled her close, "I feel ashamed... that making this decision is not harder than it is." He leaned in and kissed her long and passionately.

Anisha stood at the far end of the candle-lit room and slowly untied the lengths of cloth that held her bright white blouse together. She looked her man directly in the eye as she revealed her pert breasts, small and firm. She undid another knotted cord, and her skirt fell to the ground. Stepping out of her sandals, she sauntered closer so that her lover could devour her with his eyes. Her stomach was flat and firmly toned, though it bore the scars of a few deadly encounters. At his behest, she spun around, showing her wide, firm buttocks and solid thighs. She had an athlete's body; her curves were the byproduct of muscles that had been forged by thousands of hours of training.

Landis stood before her and let her help him off with his clothes. She pulled off the shirt and smelled his manly scent. She touched his chest and ran her fingers through the hair. His chest muscles that were wide and taut, his perfect physique made her envision the Uzor God of War, though he was white, and all the gods were of course black. She undid the cord at his waist and pulled down his black cotton pants, leaving them both completely exposed. Reaching out, he touched her face, her hair, her neck, and slowly worked his way down her blemished, yet perfect body. His fingers traced the scar on her shoulder, and he smiled at the thought of her in battle. He squeezed her breast and found it as firm as it looked. Trading motherhood for battles had helped her to stay in peak fitness. She his junior, but the age difference was only a few years.

Pulling her close, he held her body against his. She could feel his heart beating quickly against her chest, and she could feel his tumescence down below. He placed her gently on the bed and kissed her tenderly on the neck and throat. She moaned in pleasure, but suddenly rolled him over so that she was on top. She leaned down and kissed him savagely, her tongue finding his, her lips smashing his, her breath in his mouth. She rose back to an almost sitting position. His eyes took her in, and as she rocked back and forth. His hands explored, touching her softly, then firmly. Every inch of her was tight like a drum, and responsive to his touch. She put her hands on his shoulders and then began to aggressively make love to him. He tried not to become overwhelmed by the sensations; he was accustomed to setting the pace and being in control. He felt helplessly dominated by her blissful assault. Her body was everything he thought it would be, the coupling was everything that he had hoped for and more.

He tried to divert his own attention, in an attempt to delay the inevitable. He thought of war, so many battles, so much destruction. It was working for a moment; but then thoughts of Anisha, nude and swinging her scimitar filled his mind. She was hacking at undead fighters, blood was flying everywhere, her skin was covered in the sweat and the blood, her face was a mask of manic joy, her war cry ringing out. The vision of her as some kind of crazed Berserker only added to his excitement and caused him to reach a thunderous climax that lifted them both off of the bed. Reacting to his conclusion, she almost immediately erupted in a series of earth-shaking tremors. She continued to ride him as if he were her mount and she was fleeing from a pack of wolves. Soon, she slowed, then halted, and they both laughed out loud.

"You're a fighter on every battlefield," he remarked, catching his breath.

"I'm no fair maiden, no damsel in distress. You offer, but I take in the manner that pleases me."

"It pleases me as well," he looked her up and down, the sweat beading on her coffee-colored skin. "Stay here tonight, and every night going forward."

"As you wish, milord. Love only me, and I will serve you, above all others."

"When your country or my king needs us, we will both serve," he said pulling her down so that she was lying next to him. "Otherwise, we will travel this new world and see everything that there is to see."

"Agreed. You have saved me, and now, in every way, I am yours." She smiled as they drifted off to sleep.

Chapter 34: Long Live the King

Regina King stood at a huge table studying the new map. The center of the map was dominated by a fairly accurate map of Kronos. In these newly revised maps, there was land to the North, as verified by the crew that delivered the two young mages and their Telnor companion. The map showed a large continent to the North and a bit East of Kronos. All they could provide was a long stretch of coast that presumably was the East coast of this new continent. With less than half the coastline defined, it was impossible to determine exactly how large this new land was. According to the Telnor, the continent was roughly two-thirds the size of Kronos and had double the people. The inhabitants were mostly Telnor, but even Telnor had to buy things. The thought of virgin markets opening up filled her with excitement. She would immediately send a swift ship to circumnavigate the whole continent, marking the entire coastline, and whatever ports, rivers, and mountains that could be seen from offshore.

She then turned her attention to the West. Where there had once been a vast endless ocean, there was now a large continent full of people. The map that she had purchased from the Uzor was very detailed and cost her a small fortune, but it was worth every coin. They had people and a market that she could easily understand. She needed to speak to King Syphon to see about setting up an embassy and then a trading post. The barriers to starting a trading business were high, including the cost of ships, and the ability to obtain credit. This kind of expansion was almost impossible for a small firm to accomplish, and she liked it that way. She controlled most of the trade in Western Kronos and with newly forged alliances that gave her not only access but control. The Telnor sounded like they would be open to trade and could become friendly allies to the men of

Kronos but reaching westward seemed like a more rational first foray into this brave new world. Going East and North, she would have to move caravans through countries where her competitors held many advantages. Going West, she could ship from ports that were friendly to the King Trading Company. The Uzor were eager to sell their wares, and they wanted to sample what Kronos had to offer.

Turning to her faithful assistant Karl Goodwin, she asked about the most recent numbers and received his report. She would need to contract for a dozen ships, just for starters. They would have to pay for a trading post and some warehouse facilities in the Uzor land of Koregar. The list of staff and supplies that she would need to purchase would be extensive. She decided to take a working dinner, as she often did. She walked with Karl to her carriage, followed by her bodyguard Naoka.

They rode from her trade house in Goldport to a restaurant that she was told had the best seafood in all of Kronos. When they arrived at the restaurant and parked the carriage, there was the soft whistle of missiles parting the cool night air as a volley of arrows struck them. Karl fell instantly, two arrows hit him in the back and a third entered his neck from the back and exited through his trachea. The silent giant Naoka was struck seven or eight times, all the arrows sticking out of his back. He had heard the arrows and managed to maneuver his bulk between Genia and her attackers.

"Go, my Lady!" he said, speaking more than he normally would in a year.

She couldn't yet see who was shooting the arrows, but she could tell from which direction they had come. The assassins were somewhere in, or on the roof of a warehouse that lined the seashore. The restaurant was down towards the end of one of Goldports two main piers. Each had scores of eateries and entertainment venues and stretched out hundreds of yards into the bay. It was late in the evening and the traffic on the pier was much quieter than during the daytime hustle and bustle. She had on white linen pants, with a dark brown leather long coat, and high black leather boots. Unlike more traditionally dressed ladies, she was able to break into a full run. She made a dash for the far end of the pier, hoping to find a constable or at the least, a crowd to hide in. She had made it two dozen feet before an arrow pierced the back of her right thigh. She had no time for the pain, so she kept running. She had almost reached the end of the pier and was right in front of a restaurant when another arrow hit her in the side, just above her waist. The pain she could worry about later; but the blood she was losing was a more pressing matter. Looking down the long pier, she could now see six men, dressed in dark hooded coats, with masks over the lower half of their faces. They looked like mercenaries of the Legion. They were stalking her, bows in their hands and reaching into quivers to load the next volley.

Genia ran into the building and through the dining area where only a handful of patrons were still eating their dinners. She caught everyone's attention as she stormed through, knocking servers and other patrons aside. She was bleeding from two wounds and had to drag her right leg now that the pain had set in. Taking a napkin from the collar of one of the diners, she rolled it up, pulled the arrow from her side, then applied the cloth. The room had only normal family types, no soldiers or constables, and certainly no knights. When the Legion men burst through the front door after her, she knew that she couldn't count on anyone there for assistance. She was already towards the back of the dining room, and she ducked into the kitchen as two men shot arrows and a third threw a knife.

The kitchen was still steamy from the many cookpots, and the floors were wet with water and fish entrails. She almost slipped as she darted around the cooks and made her way toward the rear. When she got there, she opened a door that let out into space. Twenty feet below was the ocean, and the killers were hot on her heels. There was only one choice, she gave them a parting glare, then jumped into the cold ocean water. The assassins ran after her till they reached the doorway and looked down. The first one turned and shrugged at the others. They were not going to dive after her.

Genia swam underwater for as long as she could. She had grown up on a lake in Tebron and was actually a very strong swimmer. When she had swam to the limit of her lung capacity, she rose to the surface for a breath of air. The pier was not yet out of bow range, but they had no idea which direction she had gone. Seconds later she was again swimming underwater and getting farther and farther away. When she had taken her first breath, she headed towards the 'Manticore' parked at the next pier over. It was one of the five ships that she had in port right now. When she reached the side, she called to the night watch who sent down a ladder and called for the captain. She was now on home territory, surrounded by dozens of strong sailors who worked for her and would protect her.

"Who do ya think sent the cowardly dogs?" the captain asked, as the surgeon tended to her wounds. She was in his cabin, stripped down to her under britches. Genia was not the shy type, and her clothes were bloody and wet. The fire and a cup of warm rum soothed her while the old surgeon sewed her skin shut.

"I have no idea. My two worst enemies are both dead," She winced as he tugged at the cat gut, "I'll find out though, and whoever is responsible will suffer as much as I can arrange before they die." She got a little melancholy, "They killed my bodyguard!

I've had Naoka at my back for as long as I can remember. He was a true and loyal servant."

"Only a few of the men know that you're aboard Miss, and I've sworn em to secrecy."

"Good. I'll need an armed escort back to my home in the morning. Tomorrow night, an extra ration of rum for the whole crew, courtesy of King Trading Company."

Chapter 35: Distant Relatives

King Kell Syphon stood when the women entered; he was attended by his brother Ravi, his team of advisors, and one of his most trusted knights, Landis Stone. He looked at the beautiful Bkar sisters who were every bit as dark as he was. They walked with a regal air about them, the shorter one seemed very confident in her own skin. They both approached and at a dozen feet, stopped and bowed their heads. Landis came alongside and dropped to one knee, trying to convey how to show proper respect by example. Anisha smiled at him and dropped to a knee also. Linea stood as proud as ever. Standing at his brother's side, Ravi spoke first.

"Welcome to House Syphon, masters of the country of Chuo. King Kell Syphon wishes to personally thank you for making such a long and arduous journey."

"I can speak for myself, brother," Kel said lightheartedly, stepping down from his elevated throne. He wore a violet jacket over a brilliant white silk shirt and dark brown leather breeches He walked over and clapped Landis on the shoulder, "It's been a few days, but I wanted to formally welcome you back Landis. As always, you've exceeded my expectations," His smile was infectious, and started working its magic on Linea. Addressing the sisters, "You've crossed an ocean of water, then an ocean of land to be here. Please join me for refreshments!" he said as he waved them to follow him to his private dining room.

"On behalf of King Lollondo of Koregar, we would like to extend a hand in friendship, and would invite your highness to visit our country at your convenience," Linea said woodenly. Then she looked the king and his brother over, "I think you would find yourself at home among the Uzor, your Highness. In Koregar, everyone looks like you and me, unlike this place where the people are kind, but still, make me feel like an outsider. Who knows, your clan may even be distant relatives of the Uzor. With our worlds separating, then reuniting, there may have been a time long ago when your ancestors boarded great ships and explored this land; only to find that their homeland had disappeared."

"I'm sorry that you feel that way. My being of a different clan than most has never hurt my ability to rule this diverse land. I see where you are going with the theory that we have common ancestry, and I wish there were a way to know for certain. Whether we share ancestors or not, I accept your invitation. Please join me for some wine and refreshments."

Landis turned to whisper to Anisha, "Do you see the difference between how your people greeted us, and how we welcome you?"

Anisha gave him a look, "That's my sister's doing! I think that the king liked you from the first." She squeezed his hand and kissed his neck, "As did I."

After a cordial snack and a couple of bottles of good Khatuna wine, the group was relaxed and in good spirits. Landis chuckled to himself, noting how his ever-present companion, Father Sebastienne was free of most vices, but enjoyed a drink as much as the next man. Anisha had a few glasses, and that usually led to a vigorous session in the bedroom. The new king of Tebron, Varin Sarutendo looked as disinterested and stupid as ever. He drank too much and contributed nothing. Finally, there was Linea. She drank little, and as usual, didn't seem to be having any fun. Landis remembered his ultimate mission and stood to address the mixed crowd.

"Linea, do you have the strength to create a portal to your homeland?"

"I do, Landis," she replied.

"Can you take King Syphon to meet your master? After the attack of the Hill Giants and the undead fighters, all of them taking orders from those witches; I think King Lollondo may be ready to discuss the forging of an alliance. The sooner we get these two great men together the better."

"When should we go?" she asked.

"Right now," Kel said, he was relaxed but sober. When he stood tall, he was an inspiring figure. "As a show of good will, I will go alone with you, little sister, and I'll leave my sword and shield here. Landis vouches for you, your sister, your people and your king. That's good enough for me."

Chapter 36: Fallout

Construction on the castle's tower had been completed only days ago. Landis stood at the parapet, looking down at the vast countryside below and the Iron Road, far off to the North. Behind him, Danika paced tensely, as if she wanted to wear a path in the newly placed stonework. It had taken weeks to cross the sea and reach Western Kronos. Instead of chartering a ship to Khatuna's shallow ports, they chose to travel by land. By horse, it took several weeks to cross from the Western coast to the newly constructed Castle Herron. Danika had been told of the changes in her relationship with Landis by raven, but today was the first time that they could speak face to face.

"I've waited months for you!" she yelled, tears clogging her voice. "And years before that. Years!" Even though it was not intentional, energy danced off of her pale perfect skin and her hair blew backward, even in the absence of wind.

He stood his ground, not wanting to upset her, and not able to cower. "I won't lie to you and say that I'm sorry that I fell in love with another because the feelings I have are new to me. I've found someone who understands me on a level that few can. Not the woman I was married to, and not even you. I do regret hurting you though. I swear that it was never my intention to cause you any pain."

"You regret hurting me? Well, I guess that makes it all better now, doesn't it!" she shouted, miniature bolts of lightning cracked around their heads. "You said that you loved me. Why would you lie to me!"

"I didn't lie to you. I do love you, but I see now that it's more of an infatuation. For you, I was a replacement father figure, a man who was willing to risk death to protect you." He waited for a reaction, she closed her eyes and sobbed, "For my part, I saw someone who I very much cared for, a girl who had blossomed into a desirable woman, and who wanted me. It was wrong of me to allow such a thing to start..."

"Afraid that everyone will see you as an old lech?" she asked.

"I was taking advantage of you, and your... inexperience."

"What do I do now?" she demanded. "Go live the life of an old maid? Maybe I should make my home in this lonely tower." Her tears flowed.

"Old maid? You're still... a child." Her look shook him more than battling the demon had. "I mean, a beautiful, smart, funny woman, and no disrespect to your brother; but you're the strongest sorceress, possibly in the whole world. Your options are... limitless. When you're ready, kings and princes will be lined up to kiss your hand."

She walked over and hugged him for a last time, "If I'm so great, why don't you want me?"

"Jorn, tonight we feast, and we drink!" said King Herron as he approached his friend. Gabriel was still in his mid-twenties, his dark brown hair a bit too long, but cut stylishly. He was tasked by King Syphon to build the fortress and to be the protector of the East. He was also a major contributor to covering the astronomical costs involved in its construction. Never in the history of man had such a formidable structure been erected so quickly. "We still have time for a drink, yes?" he asked.

"I've checked my visions, and the time the enemy will attack is growing nearer; but yes, tonight we can drink to this monument to... yourself?" Jorn said, raising an imaginary cup.

"Hey! Why not! I did pay for most of it," he said, putting his arm around the skinny mage.

"You're rich, not completely unattractive, have a decent sense of humor, and you're the king. So why can't you find a girl?" Jorn joked.

"I find plenty of girls. Perhaps, too many." Gabriel looked around conspiratorially, then whispered to his friend, "I hear that your sister is... unattached."

"That's true, but she's a bit of a wreck right now. I'd give it, some time."

Chapter 37: Legion

Lectr Vaughn reviewed his newest troops, just arrived from the training grounds of the Legion. The legion created assassins, and they were very expensive, but their main products were mercenaries. A few years ago, they had given homeless men minimal training and sent them into battle with false hope and a rusty sword. Their poor reputation had almost ended them. By increasing their standards for both new recruits, and those that they considered 'fully trained' mercenaries, they had again become dominant in the field. Now, one thousand men, bought at great expense were his to command.

Lectr Vaughn found out that he could buy the land, and even buy the 'hereditary' title, but he couldn't buy the loyalty or respect of his subjects. They would no sooner shed blood for him than join the Quell. He taxed them, as was his right; but some paid, and others did not. People 'may' pay out of civic duty; but they 'will' pay, when asked at the point of a sword. He didn't have enough swords or men to use them, and the entire infrastructure died along with the previous Noble House. Now with the beginnings of a military force, he would be able to run the country properly.

Wever Bran was the head of the Panist Church, a religion devoted to all of the Old Gods. Wever specifically prayed to Magnus, King of the Gods; but the church encompassed Magnus and all his progeny. After taking over the country of Preston, which was in the northern part of Kronos, he started a subtle campaign of reestablishing churches in every country, starting with those that were geographically close. Only Wolvig separated Preston from King Vaughn's precious Ursina. On a routine basis, Panist missionaries were crossing his border and setting up churches and temples without even thinking to ask the crown's permission. Lectr saw it for what it was, a soft invasion. Five years from now, his own people would be demanding his head and would be trying to install the Church as the head of Ursina. That is something that he would not allow to happen.

Father Luther was just finishing up the Restday service, praising Chorea, Goddess of secrets and deceit. An odd choice to attract followers; but the Panist church revered all of the Old Gods. A man with short black hair and a trimmed beard and mustache walked boldly through the door, causing the Father to pause his sermon and look at the intruder. The man wore mail armor, and over it, the Black Stallion crest of House Vaughn. He had both a long sword and a short sword, yet his manner was the most menacing thing about him. He stomped slowly down the aisle, till he was standing directly in front of the priest.

"Father Luther, I am Edmond Arnaud, captain of the king's guard. I am sure that you know, but just to keep things legal, I will inform you that the territory of Ursina is now under the rule of House Vaughn."

"I know that. I am merely spreading the word of the gods," the priest replied.

"You don't have the crown's permission to proselytize. You crossed into Ursina and started trying to influence our citizens, of which you are not one."

"The Church has never needed to ask permission to spread the word of the Panist Gods! How dare you enter this holy house!" the balding priest whined. He shook his thin finger at the captain.

"This house is owned by King Vaugh," the captain informed the whole congregation. "You Sir are trespassing. By divine right, this land belongs to House Vaughn."

"King Vaughn! A rich trader who paid his way into royalty, based on forged lineage papers! He is not one to tell the Church where and when to hold services!"

The captain smiled to himself, then turned to the congregation. "Traitor!" he yelled. "You would question the veracity of the legal liege of this sacred land?" The captain turned to his fellows, "Guards, take this man outside. Crucify him!" The crowd gasped in shock, several women fainted or broke into tears.

The guards pulled the priest from his pedestal and bodily dragged him from the church. Once outside, the lieutenant slapped the man across the face and knocked him to the ground. The others ripped his clothes off and then dragged him over to a flag pole that was planted in the middle of the small town. They lifted him up and drove a spike through both wrists and into the wood of the flagpole. They did the same with his ankles. He howled in pain for hours, then whimpered for another day. By the morning of day three, he had already passed. The guards set fire to the church, packed their camp, and headed for the next town where there would be more lessons to teach.

Chapter 38: Forging Alliances

The two women rode side by side, chatting often to pass the time. Queen Renata Rin, formerly known as 'the Warlord', was a small woman but had combat skills that eclipsed most others, male or female. She normally wore her breastplate when not in her castle; but for the road, she wore linen pants and her doeskin boots. Her hair had lightened from spending a lot of time in her personal garden, and it was now past her shoulders, though in public, she always pinned it up. Her companion was Queen Lydia O'Bell. The O'Bell clan was a female-dominated society and was known to be a bit stand-offish when it came to the politics of greater Kronos. Lydia was tall, even in a land of women who were unnaturally tall. She wore only her leather armor, knowing that her personal guard was behind them, fully armored and ready for any contingency. The countries of O'Bell, and Inram were in the far Northeast of Kronos, and for them to travel to this new castle in Khatuna was quite a trip.

"So, what really happened to your husband?" Renata asked.

"I allowed him to claim 'health issues'; but the truth is, either he was going to kill himself or I was going to kill him. He's pretty enough, but the only thing he succeeded in was giving me attractive children. He's only a half-step above the eunuchs that bathe me."

"When you say that, it makes me wonder if I'm missing anything by not having children."

"Well, first of all, you'd have to sleep with a man," she said, chuckling under her breath.

"That might be a deal breaker," the Warlord replied. "What about you then? Who shares your bed these days? Man, woman, both?"

"I'm taking a break right now. The girls are in need of a strong role model, and I want to be able to devote more of myself to them right now," Lydia said to her friend.

"What does your mother think about that? I doubt she's pleased. She's been grooming you to lead O'Bell since birth. No doubt, she's already looking for another strategic match."

"She's not in charge anymore. If she needs something to do, she can find herself a man."

Riding ahead of them were the O'Bell soldiers, each and every one of them, a strong statuesque woman in full battle attire. They wore highly polished armor that gleamed in the midday sun, and on their chests, they wore the crest of the Virgin Queen. Behind rode the Inram troops, mostly men, but they were a mixed force. The Inram troops also wore full battle gear and, on their chests, and banners were the new crest for House Rin, the 'Angel Heart'.

The women rode in silence for quite a while, till Lydia broke the silence. "Before we get there, perhaps you and I should understand each other's positions," Lydia said.

"I'm listening," Renata replied to her younger cousin.

"It feels like we just finished the last war a few days ago, and already these 'men' are talking of preparing for the next one. Do they even know the meaning of diplomacy?"

"Normally, I'd agree with you; but it was less than a year ago that the Quell invaded your country. Those men would have loved to rape and kill every one of you, and I think you were lucky to have driven them off," Renata said to her young cousin. "I have pledged my sword and my lands to King Syphon, and if half of what they say is true, they'll need every soul to stand and fight."

"What you say is true enough, but I wish that we had time to replenish our people and our supplies," she said bitterly. "I'll probably side with you and that tall, dark, handsome king; but I'm going to need a very persuasive argument."

The old King's Table still existed in a dusty old hall, deep within the castle of House Sarutendo. The new King's Table was now at Castle Herron in Khatuna. Kings, queens, and other dignitaries had been invited from all over Kronos. They were flooding in from all corners of the new map. For three days they arrived, some came alone, and others came in pairs or more. Almost everyone had a cadre of armed men with them for their personal security. Fortunately, the newly erected castle was built partially for these types of gatherings. There was plenty of room within the high stone walls for hundreds of horses, thousands of men, and supplies to outlast a year-long siege.

The Ammun had chosen to send their master this time. Master Kakta came by foot, accompanied by his trusted disciple, Roku. They were one of the few that traveled without an entourage. The Master seemed to be of the same clan as Roku, his long white beard showing him to be an elder member of the sect. They were both weaponless and were confident in their abilities to defend themselves using their unarmed fighting techniques. They always wore humble robes in their island temple, but today they wore silk robes of bright red for the Master, with gold trim and intricate embroidery, and dark green for the disciple, with black and silver designs.

The queens of O'Bell and Inram arrived together, as they often did. The women were cousins and Renata Rin had been an O'Bell warrior before being sold to House Laima in Inram. In a world dominated by the strong arms of men, the women warriors were the exception to the rule. Everyone had to respect Queen O'Bell for her station, and everyone respected the Warlord for her skill on the field of battle.

Wever Bran, the church's High Father, arrived with his usual pomp and circumstance. He had two dozen men, all mounted and riding before and aft of his carriage. They all wore the sign of the church, a fist gripping crossed lightning bolts that were the symbol for Magnus. Their colors were dark blue, black, and silver, which were also associated with the King of the Gods. Along with his security, the Father also traveled with his assistant, his private butler, another manservant, his own chef, and two buglers that immediately started playing as he exited the carriage.

Though they were traveling separately, King Klaas of Agron and the new King of Tebron, Varin Sarutendo, arrived at almost the same time. Klaas had a score of trained knights to guard him, Varin brought only two men at arms. King Benjamin Vosbarra arrived alone from Rubina. Bargo Odila of Cozar, Jalen Ilordine of Kees, Plel Tomislava of Wingard, and Vivek Fionn of Margera, all arrived in ones and twos over the three days leading up to the conclave.

Genia King arrived on horseback, surrounded by six of the toughest, meanest warriors that she could find. The memory of being targeted for assassination and losing her bodyguard Naoka was fresh in her mind. She had a lot of business to attend to at this conference, but her main motivation was to find out who was after her head, and to take theirs.

The guest list was almost complete except for the host. A portal formed, and King Syphon stepped through, followed by King Lollondo, Wanaka, and finally Linea. When they arrived in the throne room, the visitors took a moment to look around at the alien surroundings. The Uzor throne room had more wood and much more ambient light. This brand-new meeting space was typical of Kronos architecture in that the room was long, with a high ceiling. There were stained glass windows high up on the walls, and the diffused, colored light that they provided gave the room a light and airy look. Jorn and King Herron were there to greet them.

"Welcome to my new home!" Gabriel said cheerfully.

"Several of us chipped in to pay for it," Kel added.

"True, but I built it, my vision... and I do live here."

"Thank you for having us, King Herron," the Uzor king said politely.

"Jorn Anant," the young mage introduced himself with a respectful bow. "Let's mingle with the others. There's a reception outside of the King's Table, and there is plenty to eat and drink." He turned and led the way. They made their way through huge rooms, still waiting to be decorated. The fact that the lord of the manor was a bachelor did nothing to speed up the process. A few hallways later, they found themselves in a courtyard on the roof of the third-floor guest quarters. Grass had been planted on the patio, and wooden chairs were set around a dozen small round tables. There was a table that held every possible dish, including a whole roasted boar. Bartenders were bringing around cups of local wine and pints of rum, mead, whiskey, etc.

Landis was there with Anisha on his arm; they were chatting with Roku and Father Sebastienne. Wever was trying to ingratiate himself with some of the lesser-known kings of Kronos, ever on the campaign trail. Tennyson was sharing a brandy with Lectr Vaughn as they talked of war and trade. The roof was alive with conversation and good times. King Syphon personally walked around, introducing King Lollondo to the various guests.

Everyone was calm, till a strange sound, accompanied by a warping of the air near the door caught everyone's attention. A large portal opened, and through it walked two Telnor, a dozen Emar, and Danika.

The Telnor spell caster Lohar was the first one through the portal. He had the typical pale-yellow skin of a Telnor and was just under seven feet tall. He wore long gloves on all four hands and was bald with a short triangular beard, he wore a long maroon leather vest that almost reached the ground, matching pants, and he wore no boots. With him was Andor, several inches taller and covered in leather straps and partial mail armor. He had short spiked red hair, and his beard was twisted into two long tails. At his side, he carried a sword that was longer than Danika was tall. He was the royal war advisor and envoy.

The Telnor did not send their leader, but the Emarian emperor came to represent his people. Like all Emar, the emperor was tall and very thin with oversized eyes, entirely too much hair, and a weak chin. The few people that even knew that they existed sometimes called them shades, for their ability to literally vanish in shadow and re-appear in a shadow elsewhere. He was dressed in a long purple robe with no jewelry or other show of wealth. He was known as Emperor Haku, and the rest of his party were his personal guard.

Danika's appearance was every bit as shocking as the company that she kept. As usual, she dressed in red, but now she had deep cleavage, revealing that she should no longer be referred to as a child. Her dress was slit, so that at times, her shapely leg could be seen almost in its entirety. Her lush black hair fell in curls around her shoulders and her lips were bright red. She wore several jewels and rings that accentuated her stunning beauty. The crowd was dazzled to have such a group transported into their midst. The guards were directed to go downstairs as the dignitaries were introduced around.

Jorn pulled Danika aside, "Dani! It's too dangerous to make a port this close to people. What if someone had been standing there?"

"What about it?" she asked testily. "No one really knows if it's dangerous."

"Accidentally killing a king or some other important person is not the way to find out. And what's with this?" he asked, tugging at the sleeve of her sheer red gown. "You look like a tart!"

"You're my brother, not my father!" she said, pulling out of his grasp as she walked away.

"My friends," King Syphon began. "Some of you have recently had invasions into your lands by small armies of raiders. Inhuman raiders that were more goat than man, riding on giant owls." Three or four of the leaders nodded in agreement. "One of our most powerful mages has predicted this and much more. As proof that much of the world as we know it is changing, I have invited King Lollondo to speak. His country Koregar is as big as all of Western Kronos, and his people too have been the victims of aggression by magical forces that seek to usurp mankind."

King Lollondo stood, and with the input of his champion Wanaka, and the Bkar sisters, told the story of the Seasons. Many at the table had heard whispers about the Winter sister, Lilith. Now there were four of them, and they had demons at their beck and call. The need to prepare for war was becoming clearer to the assembled kings and queens. The Uzor king described the battle with thousands of undead soldiers, led by a minor demon. He recounted the attack by a dozen Hill Giants, each so strong that they could lift a horse and toss it like a child's toy.

Kell Syphon stood again to address the crowd. "I am but one voice here, no more, no less important than any of you. I asked King Herron to construct this fortress, which he has done in an amazingly short time," he nodded toward the younger monarch. "If you believe what you've heard today, I ask that you contribute not only coin to help defray the cost that a few of us have already paid out; but to support us with enough men to create a standing army. The days grow few, and we need to be prepared."

"Why do you think that they will attack us here?" the Warlord asked.

"The idea is wherever they choose to strike, we flee here to make our stand. If we can choose the field of battle, we'll have the high ground, and we'll have an advantage," Gabriel said.

"Now that all four of the seasons have been reunited, it only seems logical that they will accelerate their plans to wipe out humans. I don't know for certain that the attacks of these goat-men are related to the sudden arrival of these witches, but I'm not a big believer in coincidences. The witches started by attacking King Lollondo's people, and there are raids here in Koregar. They have great power and unknown resources, but with a dozen Hill Giants and a few thousand undead fighters, they wreaked havoc in the Uzor capital."

Landis stood to address the table. Many now knew his face and all of them had heard of his deeds. "Yes, we need money, supplies, and men. What we need even more is competent leadership. I have no official capacity here, but I propose that you select King Syphon to be our King of Kings. With that, he be granted unlimited powers, only to be exercised in time of war. In times of peace, he can act as arbiter for disputes between warring crowns."

There was a lot of grumbling, followed by a vote, and another vote, and on the third vote, after much haggling, King Syphon was made High King and Supreme Commander of the Army of Kronos.

Chapter 39: Romance

Lydia stood at a table near the edge of the patio, sipping a very good glass of wine and listening to her friend Meisha. The two had been friends and sparring partners for as long as either of them could remember. Meisha was happy to play second fiddle to her friend, and now her queen. She was tall for a woman, though not as tall as Lydia. Her long black hair fell in waves that hung past her naturally tanned shoulders. She had lost the love of her life recently, the Quell had killed him as he was saving her life. Despite an intense feeling of sadness at his brutal murder, she was an O'Bell knight, and she would go on.

Much to her own surprise, as to anyone else's, her friend Lydia O'Bell preferred the company of men in her bed. She had to be shamed and coerced into consummating her arranged marriage, but now she had the sexual appetite that most twenty-year-old men could relate to. It had been six months since she sent her husband back to his homeland. On the outside, he was perfect; but in her estimation, he was too sensitive. She couldn't understand why he couldn't gratefully accept her criticism. There were a lot of powerful men at this party, indeed, every man of high enough station was in attendance.

She was a desirable woman, and she knew that. She didn't have the prettiest face, nor did she have the perfect breasts, the most flawless skin, the silkiest hair; but she was a queen, queen of the mightiest warriors in Kronos. Her house had as much land as they wanted, as much coin as they needed, and more. What she lacked in social graces, she more than made up for in strength. She was a mighty and feared warrior in battle, she recognized no equal, except for the Warlord, or possibly that Landis Stone fellow.

A few cups of wine and thoughts of sleeping in an empty bed were enough to put Lydia O'Bell on the prowl. The host, King Gabriel Herron was without a wife and was a very handsome man; but he was still a child, and she doubted that he had the fortitude to put out the fire in her loins. Landis Stone would have been a fine choice, but he was quite obviously enamored with the black female warrior. One thing an O'Bell would never do would be to take a man from another strong woman. Finally, her gaze fell on what should have been the obvious choice. King Kell Syphon. He was tall, strong, and masculine. After the voting, he was now the most powerful man in all of Kronos. Especially for the party, she had put on something other than armor for a change. Her sleek silken gown accentuated her figure and showed more skin than she was accustomed to showing. Her hair was cut short these days and she had it colored to look like fine strands of copper. She caught a last glimpse of herself in a mirror and smiled in approval.

She walked over to where Kings, Syphon and Lollondo were chatting, and flowed into their circle. Both men looked up, King Lollondo let the words that were hanging on his lips drift off unspoken. Lydia placed her hand on the strong round shoulder of Kell Syphon. Just touching his shoulder through the white cotton shirt made her blood flow faster.

"Can I join you?" she asked, looking at both, but allowing her gaze to linger on Kell.

"Of course, Queen O'Bell," King Syphon said genially.

"Please, call me Lydia."

"O'Bell?" King Lollondo asked. "Are you not the leader of the tribe where the women are the warriors, and the men serve them?"

"Most of the men in O'Bell are slaves," she said to the raised eyebrows of King Lollondo. "They are not like the men you find here in this room. No, they are weak of body and spirit; hardly men at all." Both men gave her looks that conveyed their disapproval. "They are very well treated, and appreciate the food, shelter, and mostly, the security that we provide," she said in all sincerity.

"We abolished slavery over a hundred years ago, back when my ancestors conquered the other Uzor tribes and united all of Koregar," the Uzor king said. "The Doreh still take slaves, but they work theirs into the ground. No slave of the Doreh ever dies of old age."

"We too stopped slavery, many years ago," Kell said to the pair. "Someday, we'll have to discuss why you in the North still maintain the practice."

"We can discuss it now if you like. Privately."

"Kell, I should mingle some more. Still hard to believe that there are so few of our kind in your country," Jarongo said, slipping away from the tension-filled conversation.

When he was out of earshot, "So, you are ready to discuss the slavery issue?"

"I am, but not now. These are dangerous times, and not all of us will survive them. I think that we should look at this occasion as a last chance to relax before the 'real' problems begin."

"Perhaps you're right, Lydia," he replied as he unashamedly looked her up and down.

She waved her hand towards one of her servants in a summoning fashion, and almost instantly, a middle-aged man, who looked happy to be at his queen's beck and call came to her.

"Bring two bottles of my special reserve to my quarters, at once!" she ordered. The man, in the livery of a servant of House O'Bell, jogged briskly away.

"Let's retire to my quarters. I know that this castle is as new to you as it is to me, I hope we can find my rooms. That Herron boy did a spectacular job on this fortress. And so quickly, too!"

The king took her hand as they walked away from the party and towards the guest chambers below. By the time they got to her room, the servant was already opening a bottle of the finest O'Bell reserve, with a second bottle at the ready. He poured two glasses, just as a second servant was arriving with a plate of fruit, jerky, and an assortment of cheeses. Kell thought to himself how well trained her people were, and for tonight at least, tried to forget that they had no freedom. She snapped her fingers, and her servants disappeared.

"We're not here to talk about your policies, are we?" he asked.

"You have no woman, correct?" she asked him, her face just inches from his.

"None of any import," he said, looking her over appraisingly.

"I need a man, a real man," she started pulling at the sash that held her dress together and you're the only one worthy of my time." She pulled at a silken cord and the pink and silver cloth fell to the floor around her feet. With her elevated sandals, she was as tall as he was. Stepping into his open arms, she leaned in for a kiss. He held her so that she fell just short of her target.

"In O'Bell, you are the queen, but I'm the King of Kings. Know that I rule everywhere, including the bedchamber." His

242

long dark arms completely circled her pale, yet muscular body. He squeezed her like she had never experienced before in her life and pulled her in to place a passionate kiss on her waiting lips. Scooping her up, he carried her the few feet to the bed. With ease, he tossed her into the middle of the bed that was heaped with furs and pillows. She lay there breathless as he ripped the clothes from his own body, never breaking eye contact.

Lydia lay there, her blood was hot and surging through her veins. She watched quietly as he removed his clothing; her eyes drinking him in from head to toe. Before he was even finished, she was convinced that she had made a very good decision. As he climbed on the bed, he was on all fours and looked every bit the predatory animal that he was. It was at that moment, she realized that she was just the most recent in a line of perhaps hundreds of women to lie in this exact spot. He was experienced, but not jaded, and it just fed the fire inside her.

"You have no children?" she almost whispered to him.

"I'm careful," he said plainly.

"Don't be."

The party was starting to wind down. Gabriel was pleased to host such a successful gathering, and he was glad for the commitments that the various factions had promised. Standing by the bar, he ordered a dark beer and surveyed his new castle. A woman approached him, and though she was a few years older, she outshone all the women who had attended the party. She was as tall as he was, and she looked like trouble. Her black dress did little to hide a body sculpted by years of training and activity. Her long black hair was pulled back in a clip, her caramel-colored skin and bright brown eyes drew him in like a moth to a flame.

"King Herron?" she asked.

"Gabriel. My father was 'King Herron'. It's been difficult getting used to having people address me that way. I'm sorry, I don't think that we were introduced," he unashamedly looked her over.

"Not surprising. I'm Meisha, a personal friend of Queen O'Bell. I generally keep her out of trouble, but tonight I guess I failed," she confessed.

"I saw her leave with King Syphon. I never would have foreseen that one."

"Me either. You were in the running, but she thought that you were too young."

He looked at her with a shocked expression. "What? How could I come in second to him? He's... old. I also happen to have one of the richer countries as my holdings."

"Are you trying to impress me, Sire?" she flashed a devilish smile.

"Maybe. Is it working?"

"You were too young for her, but I am more open-minded," she feigned coyness.

"For the old folks, the night is pretty much over; but for us? The night has just begun."

"That's what I was hoping that you'd say. Be warned, I can be a handful."

"I have two hands."

Chapter 40: Accusation

Lectyr Vaugh was very pleased with himself. Being a king was everything that he had dreamed about since childhood, though it didn't pay the bills. He had started from nothing, and by his fortieth birthday, he had created a trading business that brought him unheard-of wealth. As a member of the King's Table, he had naturally contributed his share to the war effort. More than his share. Since the fighting was again likely to take place in lands where his influence was dominant, he was able to secure contracts with the table for transportation, supplies, and even hard currency loans. His generous contributions would likely be paid back in triplicate.

He stood in a corner sipping a particularly expensive and warming brandy when she walked over to him. Genia King was the only trader in all of Kronos whose wealth came close to approaching his. To him, she looked and dressed like a man-hating dyke. With her short, boyish haircut and her pants and jackets, she looked more like a pre-pubescent boy than a grown woman. He could feel her hatred of him from a dozen feet away.

"Genia? So nice to see you," he said with his best attempt at civility.

"I wish that I could say the same, Lectyr. You did well at this conference."

"The alliance needs things. I sell things. Why would you begrudge me some business? You don't have a significant presence east of here. This is where the fighting is going to take place if what they say is true."

"That's fine. I don't have the infrastructure or the connections to service this war; but that's not why I'm here," she crossed her arms, looking at him with venom in her stare.

"What is it then. What have I supposedly done to you."

"I was attacked by a bunch of Legion assassins a few weeks ago, and I hear that you've recently acquired thousands of them on a permanent basis."

"So? That's not a crime. I don't have the loyalty of my subjects yet, and conscripting farmers only breeds contempt. Now my country has the beginnings of its own military force. War is coming in case you haven't heard."

"You claim to have nothing to do with the attempt on my life?" she demanded.

"By Magnus, I swear. I am already richer than you. By a sizable margin. With these new territories, there will be more additional business than either of us can handle," He looked her directly in the eyes, "I have no 'reason' to want you dead. You're going to have to look harder."

"All of my enemies are dead. I made sure of that," she said plainly.

"Are they? When you bury a man, check to see who attends his funeral. You'll find that you may have more enemies than you thought. People that you've never spoken to may be out for your head."

"The Sarutendo's?" she asked aloud.

"Wasn't your main enemy, Imanol Sarutendo assassinated recently?" he asked her. "Your intent was to bring Imanol down, but you brought down their whole house."

"I apologize for accusing you unjustly. I'll have to look into this. Thank you for your suggestions," she loosened up, and was ready to turn and leave. "Let me know if you hear anything from your Legion men. As the gods are my witness, someone will die for what happened."

Lectr Vaughn was preparing to head back to his country, when he was stopped by the High Father. The tall thin man brushed his thinning hair from his eyes, and walked gingerly, trying not to get his robes soiled. When he was within conversational distance, he laid his hand on Lectyr's forearm.

"Mr. Vaughn, I need a word," the father said.

"King Vaughn is my proper title, High Father," he said with open contempt.

"I'm sorry, I didn't know that typical courtesies applied to purchased titles," he said without an attempt to make it look like it was an innocent mistake. Vaughn turned to mount his horse when the High Father again grabbed him by the arm.

"I know that you're a priest; but if you don't unhand me, I'll have your hands removed forcibly!"

"You'll listen to what I have to say, you greedy upstart! All the churches that I authorized in Ursina have been raided by your men. The churches burned and the priests, jailed or killed! I won't have it!" he screamed at the trader, turned king.

"There's nothing you can do about it, Wever. I know that you're setting up churches in my cities is a precursor to trying to establish a theocracy. The others here don't see it, but I do. You will build no churches and do no missionary work on my land. If you do, I'll send your priests back in small boxes. If 'you' personally enter my land, I'll do the same to you, and no one will ever know where to look for your body."

"Why! How dare you!" the High Father blustered. He turned so red that he resembled a tomato more than he did a person. "Men, seize him!" he commanded his dozen guards. As one, they dropped their spears to a horizontal position and marched towards King Vaughn.

Seemingly from nowhere, a dozen heavily armed Legion soldiers, wearing the crest of House Vaughn appeared. They were led by the notorious Captain Arnaud. The man had the look of a trained killer, and everyone present could see that he was akin to a wild dog, pulling at the leash. They knew that if King Vaughn were to unleash the man, he might just kill the High Father and all his guards by himself. Every man behind him also had the look of hardened, trained killers. The head of the High Father's guard looked up at the High Father to see if he was going to be ordered into a fight that he was sure he would lose.

"Ok, stop this!" Wever yelled. "We are on neutral territory, and if we start a ruckus, we'll incur the ire of all of the other kings." He waved for his men to lower their spears, then turned to King Vaughn who was now on his horse. "You refuse the church at your own peril, trader," he said angrily. "From this day forth, I consider it open season on any man from Ursina."

"Talk all you will, priest. I'm a man of action, and you'll never see your end coming," Lectr dug in a vest pocket, "You crave money and power? Here's my tithe," threw a gold coin on the ground at Wever's feet, then turned and casually rode away. His trained killers mounted and followed, still eyeing the Father and his guards.

Chapter 41: Settling Scores

Damon Cern sat at a roadside inn having a sumptuous meal of roast leg of lamb, with potatoes with carrots. He was in especially good spirits these days, his work on behalf of the princess had landed him a cushy position, with a salary to match. Now, instead of the types of meals that were eaten by students and young men on the rise, he was able to regularly treat himself to the foods that were reserved for senior tradesmen and traders.

Damon had just returned from a trip on behalf of the new king of Tebron, under the orders of Princess Octavia. He was not well known in either social circles or professional circles, so he had no need for security. The blessing and the curse of being a low-level functionary was that you were not important enough to want dead. Normally. He looked around as he enjoyed his feast, conscious that not everyone in the establishment could afford what he was enjoying on his own. He saw a particularly rough-looking character across the room that looked him over more than once and with more than just passing curiosity. He was deciding on his next course of action when the man came over and sat at his table.

"Good evening," the man said plainly as he sat across from Damon.

"Good evening. Is it your custom to sit, uninvited, with strangers?" Damon asked.

"You're Damon Cern, correct?" the man asked, though it was plain that the question was rhetorical.

"I am." Damon was becoming very uncomfortable.

"For a man of such minuscule influence, you carry out deeds of great import."

"I'm sorry, but I don't have the slightest idea what you're talking about. No offense."

"Allow me to elucidate," the older man said. He was around thirty and his hair was black, greasy, and cut short. He had a wicked scar on his chin and a tattoo of a black snake on his neck. He wore simple clothes that gave no clue as to his profession or station. "Deals have been struck, contracts… issued, and accepted," he looked deeply into Damon's eyes. His gaze seemed to brush away any pretense of making an excuse. "Your own king lays dead, by an assassin's hand. Another king was attacked, and almost killed."

"Are you talking about the murder of King Sarutendo? I had nothing to do with that!" he flatly denied. "Who is this other king that you speak about?" The man just stared at him. "Are you talking about the trader, Regina King?"

"I'm glad that we are able to cut to the heart of the matter," the man said, his words punctuated by a dagger that seemed to appear from nowhere. "You have information that I require, and you should know that when I ask people for information… they always provide me with answers."

"Yes sir, I'll tell you anything you need to know," Damon stammered, not able to take his eyes off the man's knife, "Just please don't hurt me."

"We'll see. Now, there was recently an attempt on the life of Regina King. Who paid for the Legion assassins that went after her?" he asked.

"The… the princess!" he got out. "It was the daughter, Octavia."

"The princess? Not the boy?" he asked, truly surprised by the answer.

"The boy had nothing to do with the father getting killed, and he bore no grudges against... well, anyone. He's a very mild person, not quick to anger and he doesn't bear ill will towards anyone. The girl wanted to repair the family name, and to increase her dowry, when and if they could find a suitor."

The man held his knife tight to his chest, allowing his jacket to conceal it from the rest of the patrons. He stared into Damon Cern's face, his attempt to determine if the man was being truthful. He leaned in to whisper.

"You would not be dissembling, would you Damon?" His voice was full of menace.

"What?" Damon asked in a confused tone.

"Dissembling, prevaricating, misleading... lying?"

"No, sir. No raise is worth dying for," he stated, looking the other in the eyes.

The man read his honesty, thought to himself for a few moments, then the hand holding the knife reached out, slashed Damon's throat, and returned to his sleeve so fast that no one around them knew that anything had occurred. He got to his feet as Damon Cern reached up to feel his mortal wound. Without a sideways look, he casually walked out into the night.

It had been many weeks since she lost her operative, Damon Cern. He was a weasel of a man. Luckily, his kind was the kind that was easy to replace. She wasn't sure how he'd done it, but her brother had finally negotiated a marriage for her. She was to wed the eldest son of the king of Agron. The Klaas family had ruled Agron for centuries and were generally well thought of. Their oldest son, Raymar Klaas was an average-looking young man, who, when he would eventually become king, would have his father's deep pockets. Octavia had long ago given up on the fantasy of marrying for love.

Octavia was certain that if she gave this husband a son, he would gift her with one of the small coastal islands off the shore of Agron. There, she could lie in the sun on some of the finest beaches, drink and eat till she weighed a thousand pounds. She would surround herself with luxury and with the most handsome stable boys and valets. She happily climbed into a carriage. It was not nearly as nice as the one that her family had owned ten years ago when they were flushed with cash; but nice enough. The wedding was to take place in her father-in-law's castle in Agron, and in three days she would be a wife!

The trip was pleasant enough and Octavia was falling asleep when the carriage jerked to a stop. She perked up a little and pulled back the curtain to peer out the window. There was nothing but an open sky and a little fog on a cool evening. She got closer so that she could stick her head out the window. The carriage was stopped on a bridge over a deep and rocky chasm. She couldn't hear the driver or her four-man guard, so she knocked on the wall that separated the cabin from the driver's seat on the outside. No answer. She waited a minute, then opened the door and gingerly stepped out onto boards that were the floor of a bridge. Walking around to the front of the carriage, she saw that her driver had an arrow in his chest. He probably died instantly. The four horses that her guards were riding were walking around aimlessly, and she was just in time to see a dozen or so large men toss one of her guards over the edge of the bridge. They all stood and listened as the man screamed all the way to the rocks far below.

"What's this!" she demanded, "How dare you attack a royal coach in transit!"

A woman with short, dirty blonde hair walked up from behind her and came around till they were face to face. She wore pants and a jacket like a man, an expensive suit that was made of the finest buckskin. On her hands were a few rings that each would be more than Octavia's dowry. She wore the crest of the King Trading Company on her left breast and there was no doubt as to her identity.

"Regina King! By the gods, why won't you just die!" she screamed.

"You killed your own father? Octavia dear, you've been a bad girl."

"You killed my father when you sank that ship full of our goods and gold! That's the day his spirit died. I just helped his body along."

"You think that I started this? I was loyal to Tebron and to House Sarutendo, but when I needed the crown's protection the most, your father screwed me and left me for dead financially. When someone messes with me, that's one thing; but when it affects my business, that's another thing altogether. I get mad, and then I get even. Regenia King always pays her debts."

"I don't care what you say. You were on the list of those that contributed to the fall of House Sarutendo. I ordered your assassination, and I'm not sorry!" The hate in her eyes was like nothing that Regenia had ever seen.

"Your brother seems stupid but harmless. I'll let him live, but today is your last day, bitch!" Regenia said, pulling a long dagger from her hip.

"I curse you, and all yours till the end of time," Octavia spat on the ground. "With my last breath, I'll steal from you the vengeance that you think you are owed!" she said before running to the side of the bridge. Perhaps the first time in her life she was described as being graceful. She leaped over the edge in a dive, arms outspread, her dress flowing after her like sails on a ship as she flew out over the edge into space. Time froze for an instant as she levitated there, then fell to the earth like a wounded dove. Genia rushed to the edge, and watched as she got smaller and smaller, then bounced awkwardly off the jagged stone below. Even from that great height, they could see the blood form a halo around the fallen angel.

"She had more honor than her father," Genia said, turning back to her horse. "Escort me home and receive your payment."

Chapter 42: Sisterhood

The pool was deep in a mountain cave with luminescent plants and algae giving it a warm, soothing glow. Four women sat in the steaming water, naked and unembarrassed because they were in the company of their sisters. There was some catching up, some levity, but soon their talk turned to their plans for wreaking havoc in Kronos.

"Sisters, we're finally together after centuries of being hunted and imprisoned. What should we do now?" Lilith asked the others.

"Quite obvious Lil, we must get our revenge," Anjaya said without hesitation.

"We must kill all of them, all of the humans must die!" Alexina added.

"And the rest. The seven races must fall," Anjaya said.

"It's hard for me to know how you've suffered, sisters. I'm the only one who's been free these last two hundred years. Only this convergence of the universes again has allowed us to travel back and forth," Carissa said.

"Do you think that this 'convergence' is permanent?" Anjaya asked the rest.

"Well, the 'Gods' say that they created the heavens, the land, and the seas; but I doubt even they know if magic and the supernatural creatures have returned for good," Lilith stated. "Perhaps we should summon Chorea and find out if she knows."

"Do you really trust her, sister?" Alexina asked. "From what you've told us, I wouldn't be surprised if she's playing some cruel game; having us create chaos for her amusement."

"I admit, she is both lifesaving and confounding at the same time," Lilith grumbled. "She offers her assistance; but only when and where she pleases. Her assistance is not something that we can rely upon."

"I agree. Let's form a strategy that doesn't include anyone's help, aside from what the four of us can do on our own. If she aids us, then it'll be an additional blessing," Carissa declared. They all nodded in agreement. "I've made a pact with the Mavit Tomar, a humanoid race from my land. They are more than happy to help me conquer and enslave the humans here in Kronos."

"I think, that with a little trickery, a little persuasion, I can get the Doreh to fight for us. They can't beat the Uzor because they refuse to unite, but I bet they will sweep across this land like locusts!" Alexina offered. "They may be mindless barbarians, but their numbers are great, and they fight like Berserkers."

"I can enlist more Giants. There are more Hill Giants in Tychon, and I know of a secret island far to the North where dozens of the mindless brutes live."

"That sounds promising, and if we can coordinate our attacks, we have a chance," Lilith mused. "It's still not enough though. You all saw what happened when we freed Anjaya. Though weak in magic, they are not completely without weapons and allies." The four women lay in the steaming water, thinking about what else would be needed to assure their victory.

"I have an idea, sisters," Lilith said. "When each of you has brought your pawns to the board, you can join me in my forest where we can open portals to bring in the help we need. It's more than I can do on my own; but together, we can hold the gates of hell open long enough for an army of demons to come through."

They all nodded in agreement. Lilith smiled at the thought of getting her revenge, even though the one who trapped her was dead now. She would crush everything that he held dear. It never made sense to her. Why did he care for these humans so much? Then there were his apprentices to deal with. Of course, would have to die.

Chapter 43: Barbarians

Aliana Ragnar walked confidently into the city of Geltz. She rode a tall grey horse and wore a fur coat that almost matched her horse's coloring. Her golden blonde hair was tied in a loose braid that fell below her slim waist. She had red stripes tattooed around her eyes like a raccoon's mask and she wore high boots that disappeared under her long coat. At her side, she sported a two-headed battle axe that was wider than her shoulders, and nearly as long as she was tall, which was nearly six feet tall.

Geltz was a town of several hundred thousand and was the home base of the Friodor clan. Even though it was not a small town by any means, they had a knack for knowing when someone is an outsider. They saw the self-assured posture, the sly way she looked around appraising everyone, and her style of dress. All of these things shouted 'stranger'! She had worked her way through miles of suburban streets, where the common folk sold and bought food and clothing, weapons, slaves, and trinkets. The markets gave way to the city center, where the buildings were taller than most; but still, pitiful shacks compared to the magnificence of the structures found in the Uzor cities a thousand miles south.

As she slowly rode down the main road of the town, a couple of young boys near manhood, took off in different directions. They were, no doubt, going to report that a stranger was in town, the kind of stranger that demanded attention from the ruling clan. Indeed, that's what she got. Before she could got much further, her path was blocked by a couple of men who looked like they had seen hundreds of battles in their careers.

"Who be you?" the leader asked. His long blond hair was pulled back in a tight ponytail, with leather ties, his beard cut short, and his hand resting on the hilt of his longsword.

"Ragnar," she said. "Alianna Ragnar. I've come to see your king," she said smiling, though her eyes sent the opposite message.

"I doubt that he wants to see you, girl," said the second ruffian. He was tall and fat, but his scars and leather armor spoke of a man not to be toyed with.

Alianna got off of her horse and handed to reigns to a young man nearby. She opened her coat and threw it across the horse's back. Underneath, she wore a leather bra that held her sizable chest tight to her body. Her stomach was bare and flat, and she had a skirt that covered her modesty but fell several inches short of reaching the tops of her long leather boots. She had a wicked knife at her waist along with a small drinking skin. Taking out the skin, she pulled at the tie and knocked back a healthy swallow of the drink.

"I've done this too many times already, boys. You're under orders not to let me anywhere near the king's longhouse, right?" she asked the leader.

"He'll never know you were here," he stated flatly.

"Even if I did make it to the king's hall, he would need some kind of... demonstration," she pulled her war axe from its holding straps at the horses' side. "So this is how it'll go. I'm going to kill the two of you, then one of these other nice people will lead me to Osmund Friodor."

Both men dismounted, the leader taking out two medium-sized axes, meant for speed in battle. The second pulled his longsword. They lined up, side by side, effecting a roadblock, even though she had already made it clear that she intended to go 'through' them.

"Last chance, girl. Surrender now, and maybe I'll not kill ya after I have my way with ya."

Instead of answering, she leaped forward with viper-like speed, her axe opening a gash in his chest that was large enough to see daylight through. The second fellow gripped his sword, still having a hard time processing how quickly his partner died. The crowd gasped in surprise at the huge man, that was now a lifeless mound of bleeding flesh. Alianna stood there, her smile more predatory than ever as she spun the axe around easily in her hand.

The second fighter held his sword out, swinging it around so that he had a buffer zone between them. He slowly walked towards her, a very intent look on his face. What a scene it was. A hardened warrior, huge and imposing, and he was swinging his blade in front of him to keep his distance from a sultry, half-dressed warrior woman. They clashed steel several times, he tried to get past her whirling, double-edged axe, but her speed was too much for him. Time and time again, he would lunge, only to be pushed away. He would chop, only to find her no longer where he was swinging. He took both hands and with all of his might, sliced at her with a horizontal chop about breast high. She met his blade with the edge of her axe, and his sword snapped in half like an icicle at the beginning of spring. As he stared dumbfounded at his broken sword, she spun around and took off his head with a single swing of her axe. The cut was so precise that the head remained in its position on his neck for just a moment, and then fell neatly at his feet.

The crowd stood around in stunned silence as the woman collected the head, then took the other man's head, and placed them in a canvas bag that she hung from her saddle.

Putting on her coat again, she turned to a young woman in the crowd.

"Which way to your king?"

The woman nervously pointed in a direction, then ran off the other way. Alianna rode casually till she found the longhouse, a building so much better than the rest, that she knew she had arrived. No one dared to follow her from the scene of the crime. She dismounted and dragged two heavy bags behind her. The guards at the door turned and allowed her to enter unmolested. Both bags were stained with blood and obviously contained grim souvenirs. Osmund Friodor and his inner circle were ready for the outsider; news of her coming had caused him to send the first two men. News of their easy defeat men made this audience possible.

A large man with white hair, cut flat on top and short all around, stood between Alianna and Osmund. He stroked his bushy beard and mustache as he watched her drag her bloody sacks. When she was a dozen feet away, he put up his hand, indicating that she should approach no further. He wore a warrior's garb, a one-shouldered robe without sleeves, and a kilt of sorts. He had on thick leather bracers, short brown leather boots, and both a long sword and hand axe.

"Halt!" he commanded. "Your name?"

"I go by the name Alianna Ragnar. I hail from no great clan, though I would someday be the head of one," she answered.

"You claim to be a person of no standing, yet already the tales are that you dress and look like a succubus, and fight like a demon of the lower realms!" he said for all to hear.

"I'm not without talents, or blessings," she said in response. "I've come to enlist a clan in a raid like no other. A raid that will open new lands, tens of thousands of slaves, nearly endless resources, and of course, gold and silver."

"If you talk of taking on the Uzor, we are too far from the border. The Engal clan is much closer to their lands," Osmund said, standing up in front of his wooden throne.

"First off, good sir, I return to you the heads of the men that you sent to discourage me from meeting with you." She took the smaller sack and pulled a cord so that it opened up and the heads of the men that she had just killed rolled out onto the floor of the cabin. They were still fresh, the wounds still wet. "And here is why I won't be doing business with the Engal clan." She opened the other bag that she had been carrying, and the heads of King Svengart, his brother, and Queen Anahilda all rolled out onto the floor of the longhouse.

"So, you would kill me and my bride if we choose not to aid you?" Osmund asked.

"I guess it's all in 'how' you turn me down. I can have a bit of a temper." She smiled at the men standing. "I'm not talking about the Uzor, there are lands owned by white men, far to the East. These men are soft and not at all war-like. They'll fight back, but they don't possess the warrior spirit of the Doreh."

"How do you know of these people? Have you been to their country?" the queen asked.

"I've just returned, and there is much wealth to be had. Like the Uzor, they have animals just waiting to be eaten and turned into leather. They grow grain, and grapes for wine. They make weapons and tools of a higher grade than those found her in Hadon." She walked to the nearest table and grabbed a wineskin. Tilting it back, she took a long slow draught before returning her attention to the royal couple. "Unlike the Doreh, very few of them are warriors. The rest are just slaves without masters."

"My people rely on me to constantly find new lands to conquer, new towns to raid. If we choose to go with you on this raid, what is your price?"

"There will be land and slaves, too many treasures to be counted. I want a country of my own, land where I can put down my own longhouse and have wealth, start a clan of my own. I assure you; it will be a small fraction of the spoils. Each man and woman in your clan will share in riches beyond their wildest dreams."

The king looked to his queen and his councilors, and they all smiled.

Chapter 44: Black and Blue

The Myoran pools were not well known, but those lucky few that did know about them found them to be one of the most beautiful spots in all of Koregar. High up on Mount Lanth, there was an exclusive getaway and a series of cabins for skiing, and relaxing. It was a place for the well-funded and well-connected to mix and mingle. Along the trail that wound up the hillside to the resort was an unmarked turnoff that led to the pools. You had to follow the trail through several passes, and through quite a bit of forest before coming to the clearing. The pools were naturally heated springs that lay hidden in an alcove that still managed to get sun for a third of the day.

Wanaka lay naked in the pool, letting the healing waters soak into his tired muscles. The morning had begun with extensive stretching and meditation, followed by a healthy meal of Uzor delicacies, a shower, and finally a soak in the pools. His lord had decided to trust the white devils with their black king and had formed an alliance. Over the next weeks, he would be gathering troops and materials for war. The crown appreciated his recent efforts and knew that if they got him away from the logistics of preparing for war, that he would be more effective when the time for fighting arrived. Wanaka was not a diplomat, or a bureaucrat, or even the kind of general that sweated over maps and secret messages. He was the tip of the spear. He was a weapon that was best when used often, and only for its intended purposes.

At any given time, there would be only a handful of guests at the resort, so he was surprised when he heard another person walking from the cabins toward his pool. She walked very quietly, but Wanaka had a battle sense that regular people couldn't even imagine. He only opened his eyes, not stirring his body from the steaming goodness. His mind was in a state of shock, but he was too disciplined to show it. She was like nothing he'd ever seen or heard of in his life.

The sun was bright, though filtered through the surrounding trees. Even in the diffused light, he could see that she had bright blue skin. She was the color of the sky as the sun was halfway over the horizon. She had long black hair that was woven into braids that fell to her waist, with streaks of blue tint that could only be seen when the light was just right. She was clearly a warrior; her broadsword was as long as Panther Claw and twice as wide. Her blade had a faint glow, and when he looked at Panther Claw, he saw that it too was radiating energy. Her high leather boots had dull-colored metal plates riveted to them, a twist on scale armor. She wore leather pants and a shirt, with a wide fur collar. Her mail vest hung to her knees, and like all warriors, she had a buckler and dagger at her side.

They made eye contact, and she eased his tension by resting her sword on a stone bench above the pools. With deliberation, she undressed till she was as naked as he was. She had pointy ears, and sharp features, but he still found her to be both mysterious and alluring. She had tattoos in darker blue ink all over her back, in the shape of a large mythical creature, complete with wings, teeth, claws. Her arms and one leg had what looked like writing and decorative designs. The whole of her art appeared to be along a theme that he couldn't quite make out without knowing her language and culture.

She stepped confidently into the pool till the water completely covered her to the neck. She leaned her head back and looked directly at him. She neither smiled, nor gave hint that she meant him any harm, so he remained calm, knowing that his sword was close and could be reached if she made any aggressive moves.

"So many questions. Where do I start?" he asked.

"My name is Cresta, I'm a scout for the Vinkul parliament," she replied.

"I don't know what any of those things mean," he replied.

"We are an ancient race from the land of Pyrros. Thousands of years ago, our world was connected to your world, a time when the pre-human races controlled all of the lands. The Emar, the Telnor, the Goran... we lived in our own areas because there was so much land, that they didn't need to fight each other or even associate with each other. Then your kind came into being. Your people claim that gods created you and gave you the land and all it possessed. This conflicted with the people who already lived in those lands. Legend has it that the gods warred amongst themselves, and there was upheaval in every land as the world was ripped apart. Xoran was once a land populated by the seven races, along with a host of wild creatures, but after the gods separated the world, the pieces were sent drifting apart. One world became many, and those who were not with their kin were cut off. Most died, but some were able to live in their own enclaves."

"Are you saying that the black men in Kronos are originally Uzor?"

"Yes, and the white men in Doreh were once a sailing tribe of the white men of Kronos. The pre-humans had a better understanding of the magic world, and they could sometimes move between the planes. That is why you can find some Emar and Telnor on Kronos; but in my land, for instance, there are millions of souls, and none of them are human."

"So, your people are called...?"

"Vinkul. Unlike you humans, all Vinkul practice magic of some kind."

"And… you're all… blue?"

"We are, just as the Telnor are all a shade of yellow, the Emar are dusky, and the Goran are green. When these gods came along and made your race, they made you every color from darkest black, like you Uzor, to pale white, like the men in Northern Kronos."

He thought for a few moments, "Why are you telling me all of this?"

"Because, Wanaka, I'm tasked with contacting your kind to see if there should be peace between our tribes. We share a land with a race called the Inoans, who are very similar to the race of men, as are we Vinkul, we also share our land with the Mavit Tomar, who walk on two legs; but are very different from men."

"How do you know my name? I didn't even know that your people existed till a few minutes ago."

"I'm a scout, it's my task to know things and to approach your people in a way that would not cause any kind of mistrust or panic. By 'measures', I meant that we could choose to hide, and it could be years or even decades before you would find our country."

"Well, stripping off all of your clothes has certainly put my mind at ease. The sword you carry had me concerned at first."

"It's a family heirloom. It was given to my great grandfather by Tanus himself. It's a special weapon, like your own." She scooted back and sat straighter so that the top half of her chest was out of the water. She had a design on the space between her breasts that he assumed was a family or tribal marking. "Do you think that your people will be open to all of the knowledge that I've given you just now?"

"My king always prefers diplomacy to conflict. Perhaps he could meet with your king?"

"We don't have royalty. Our people vote on all important matters, and the parliament is tasked with carrying out the wishes of the people. We do have different casts, but they're all equal in the eyes of the law."

"I can take you to meet our king then. Just seeing your skin and your ears will make him take your words seriously. We can be there in a couple of days at an easy riding pace."

"I can get us there much faster; but let's go after a soak. This is a remarkable custom of yours." She smiled, allowing the water to soothe her.

Chapter 45: Curses

Wever Bran sat brooding on his throne-like chair. The last of the churches that he had authorized in Wolvig had mysteriously burned. Of course, it was the mercenaries hired by Lectyr Vaughn, but even if he had proof, whom was he going to tell? Did he really think that King Syphon would interfere for or against him? They had much bigger fish to fry, and only full-scale war would get the attention of the King's Table.

Normally, every waking second of the High Father's day was consumed with matters of state. Not only was he the head of the main religion in all of Kronos; but he had gotten permission to run the State of Preston after their royal house had been wiped out by the Quell. He had much loftier ambitions though. Magnus himself had essentially laid out that this world should again come under the control of the gods, through the actions of the Church. It was his destiny to spread the theocracy of the Panist gods to every country. His attempt to infiltrate his neighbors to the West had failed, his churches had been burned, and his priests had been crucified. King Lectr Vaughn of Ursina was to blame.

All morning, the handlers, priests, and functionaries had wisely chosen to not bother the High Father with their constant need for approvals and decisions. Much of the burden was taken on by his assistant, Lehna Miraslav. Though she was not a priest and had no 'official' function within the church, she had served as the High Father's right-hand man for many years and was respected as if she were second only to the High Father himself. She didn't notice the small boy walk the long hall till he stood before the High Father. No one but Wever Bran could actually see the boy.

"Father?" he asked in his high-pitched, squeaky little voice. Wever looked up to a boy of about seven, with dark brown, uncombed hair. He was pale and had freckles across his cheekbones and the bridge of his nose. He wore the clothes of a homeless child and was covered in dirt.

"Child, where's your mother?" he asked, with genuine compassion.

"I have no mother. I have no father," he said sadly.

"Poor child. I'll have my assistant bring you food and water."

"That's very kind of you. It's good to see that you're a moral man, even when you don't think that you're being watched," the boy said. His eyes took on a hardened mature look that no child could duplicate. The High Father started to realize what was happening, and his face broke out into a wide, loving smile.

"Yes, Wever. I sensed your pain and have come to see how I can help you."

"Lord Magnus, I have been trying to spread the influence of the church, but at least one king has vowed to stop the church from operating in his lands. He sees it as a slow invasion, meant to win the hearts and minds of the people. He has killed 'your' priests, my Lord. He has burned 'your' churches," Wever held his forehead in his hands and massaged his temples. "I can't go to war with him, he has superior forces, and almost unlimited resources."

"What would you have me do with him, son? Should I kill him for you? I could kill him this instant, and then what would your excuses be?"

Wever thought for the briefest of moments, then replied. "This is a test, but I will pass it. Of course, wishing death on one who does me evil is no less evil. What can I do to stop this man, without becoming just as much of a sinner as he is?" he asked.

"Do you have anything of his person, an article of clothing, a hair, his blood, a token of some kind?" the boy asked.

"The only thing I possess of his is a coin that he threw at my feet. I kept it to remind me of whom I'm dealing with." Wever dug into an inner pocket of his vast robe and produced a small gold coin. He tried to hand it to the boy, but the child refused to take it.

"Hold the coin in your palm, think of this 'Lectr Vaughn', and repeat my words," the boy commanded.

Wever Bran held the coin tightly in his bony hand, his thin form shaking from the intensity of his concentration. Strange alien words flowed from the boy's mouth and the High Father did his best to keep up and to repeat the words precisely as he heard them. The coin began to get hot in his hand, but he ignored the sensation and continued to chant the words that he was given. Before too long, it was over, and the High Father looked up, sweat beading on his forehead. The small boy stood there smiling at him.

"There you go, priest. You've cursed your enemy, and soon, affairs of state will be the least of his problems."

"Cursed?" the priest asked. "Isn't the use of curses forbidden by you, my lord?"

"No. I don't forbid any tool that helps us to achieve our final goal. Once this man is out of your way, collect your forces, and storm through your neighboring country, and into his lands.

He's not a true believer in the gods and must be taught a lesson that the rest of Kronos can learn from."

It was mid-day, and Lectr Vaughn was attending to his business. Aside from his regular contracts that were extensive, he now had the sole right to provision the new fortress that King Herron had built. The foodstuffs alone were more than some countries consumed in a year, and he had to subcontract with almost all of his competitors. In the end, everyone but the taxpayers across Kronos would profit. He was standing at his desk, looking at the big picture with his junior partner, Koren Ash and a stream of lower executives when the pain struck him.

Lectr was mid-sentence when he felt the pain in his chest like a cold steel dagger had been thrust into him. He doubled over, only barely catching himself so as not to fall to the floor. The beehive of activity came to a halt, and everyone closed in to see if he would be all right. He doubled over, and they eased him into a plush leather chair. He became very pale and sweaty, his breath coming in gasps. The royal doctor was close, and when he saw Lectyr's rapidly failing health, he instructed the others to carry him to his personal chambers, where he could recline and try to catch his breath.

For two days, the doctor tried every medicine, herb, tonic, and treatment that he could think of. On the third day, he came out of the King's chamber, his face drawn and defeated. He finally summoned the strength to declare the king dead. Koren was distraught and knew that the mission of informing Mrs. Vaughn and their children would fall on his shoulders. The men pleaded with the doctor, bribed him, they even called out to the gods, asking for a reprieve for their master. When all hope was lost, and they had all hit rock bottom, there was a noise.

Turning, they all watched as the knob to the bedroom door slowly turned and Lectyr Vaugh came out to address them all. They stood in shock, and rightfully assumed that the doctor was either crazy and was playing some cruel joke on all of them; or that perhaps he had seen many of the signs of death and had jumped to a premature conclusion. Lectyr was even more pale than usual, though he seemed to be out of pain and merely suffered from hunger, thirst, and exhaustion. Everyone present gave thanks to the gods, either privately or out loud, without reservation.

For the next several days, Lectr tried to eat and drink; but nothing would stay down, and he was quickly losing both weight and strength. Koren was doing his best during the day to keep the business running the way Mr. Vaughn would have wanted, he often had to work long hours and late into the night. The newly crowned Queen Catherine Vaughn was doing her best to keep up with the royal responsibilities. Like her husband, she was in her early forties, and unlike him, she had blonde hair with just the right amount of white to give her a very mature and regal look. She managed their five children, while at the same time handing down royal decisions when they were called for.

Lectr was lying in bed one night, having difficulty reaching deep sleep, when a smell awoke him. The iron smell was not completely foreign to him, but it was still difficult to place. The smell grew stronger, and he opened his eyes to see one of the young chambermaids in his room. Though she had tried to hide it, as women often do, she was in her 'time of the month'. The smell of blood triggered an insatiable hunger in him, one so strong that he couldn't resist his body's demands for sustenance. His animal instincts took over, and he lunged to a sitting position and reached out to grab the girl. She tried to scream; but he grasped her windpipe with one of his strong, bony hands, and with his long sharp nails, he ripped the soft flesh from her body.

Blood began fountaining out of the dying woman, and his instinct took over. Lifting her limp form to his mouth, he began to guzzle the hot blood as quickly as her failing heart could pump it. When he was finished, she was dead, and he was covered mouth to waist in her blood. The bed and sheets were a total loss. But he felt better. In fact, he felt better than he had since he was a child. For the first time in ages, he was without aches and pains, his vision was crystal clear, and his hearing so sharp that he could hear his wife's heartbeat several doors down the hall. His sense of smell was sharper than the many hunting hounds that he owned. His sense of touch was finely tuned, he could feel each hair on his arms move, as the light breeze wafted in from the open window across the room.

Feeling both horrified and invigorated, he walked into the private bathroom and cleaned himself up. Then he made his way to where his wife was still sleeping. Soundlessly, he entered her room and stood over her, watching her sleep. Her heartbeat was like a melody to him. He hungered to drink her blood as well, to feel the warm brackish liquid slide down his gullet and fill his aching stomach. Instead, he grabbed her shoulder and gently shook her awake.

Cath, as he called her woke slowly, not sure where she was or what time it was. When she was able to pry a single eye open, she saw her husband standing over her and she let her relief wash over herself. He had not been on his feet for so many days, and now he stood there, the strong man that had wooed her and given her children. He looked healthy; but there was panic, sadness, and guilt in his expression.

"You feel better?" she asked him groggily.

"I do. I feel... like a new man. Come with me," he said, taking her hand and helping her to her feet. She put on her slippers and robe and followed him down the hall. She watched him walk in front of her and noticed that indeed, he seemed fully recovered; perhaps, even stronger than before.

They walked into the murder scene. On his bed lay the dead maid, her lifeless eyes staring off into nothingness, her mouth twisted in a silent scream of agony. Her lifeblood was everywhere, half the bed was soaked, and his clothing lay in a pile in the corner. Only by putting his hand over her mouth, did he stop her from letting out a tremendous scream. Her eyes were wide, as she turned them to look to her husband for an answer.

"I don't know exactly what happened. I was half asleep, she was in the room doing… something, and I smelled her blood." He let go of his wife and looked downward in disgrace. "The smell of fresh blood drove me mad. I tore into her and drank and drank till my stomach was full, and I wanted more."

"What are we to do, my love?" she said trembling with fear. "Not even a king can do this, without…"

"Repercussions? Consequences?" he said sharply. "We have to get rid of her, then explain where she's gone. Most importantly, I need to know why I did this?"

Catherine put her arms around her husband and just held him. She cried into his shoulder, and he tried his best not to join her. After several moments they calmed themselves and looked at the problem more rationally. She stepped back and opened his shirt. Above his left breast was a black symbol that looked like it had been burned into his skin. It was nothing that either of them had ever encountered, and yet when she touched it, she knew.

"I think you've been cursed, my husband. This smells of evil sorcery," she said grimly.

"Perhaps, but I don't know who is even capable of such a thing, much less, who would wish it on me," he said perplexed.

"I'll get one of the hounds from the yard. We can put some of the blood on his muzzle and blame it on him. After that, we must find out how often you need to take blood, and if only human blood will suffice."

"I hope so. I've never taken a life before, and by the gods, I hope never to do it again."

Chapter 46: Invasion

There were well over a thousand workers, and they had been toiling from dawn till dusk, trying to finish the required number of boats. A sizable forest that had lined Hadon's East coast had been completely cut down. Hundreds of women set aside their normal chores to completely devote themselves to the fabrication of sails and rope for the rigging. They sang and gossiped while joining great sheets of dyed canvas. Even the children were put to work, collecting stores and carrying them to the docks to be loaded on the ships. Some men were steaming and bending lumber into the desired curved hulls. Others were taking the raw lumber, stripping the bark and branches, and doing their best to make them square. The sounds of the nearby sea were drowned out by the sounds of sawing and hammering, and the songs that men sang when they were focused on long, hard work. A couple of months later, the finished ships were stacking up in the harbor. With the completion of each ship, they were getting closer to the day they would be able to launch their invasion

Even though the Friodor clan was one of the largest, they saw the benefit in bringing in other allied clans to cover the cost and take on some of the risk. After four months, they had created a thousand ships, and fifty-thousand battle-hungry barbarians were ready to set sail. They consulted an old wise woman who was often relied on to predict the future, and when she said that certain stars were aligned, the ships full of war-hungry raiders were launched.

In the lead ship, Alianna Ragnar stood with King Osmund Friodor. Both wore long fur coats to fight off a chill from the cold sea air. Neither spoke much; but for different reasons, they looked forward to the end of what was to be a several weeks journey. The king looked forward to the plunder of course, but even more, he yearned for blood. Life in Hadon had become stagnant, with a few large clans controlling most of the country, none of them could make any move that wouldn't incite the others, and spell certain doom for all. If he could increase his land, and increase his population both of warriors and slaves, then eventually, he would be far too large for the other clans to compete with. Alianna, who was really Alexina in a thinly veiled disguise, was looking forward to the beginning of a genocide that would be the beginning of the end of man and would weaken the Old Gods.

Behind them were legends of Hadon, three warriors known for their superior skill at war. Agnar Yoren of the Friodor clan was King Friodor's right hand man. He bucked convention, and wore his white hair short on top, shaved on the sides and back. He had scars from many battles, and now wore armor that was a mix of plate and mail. His weapons of choice were the hand axes that many of the barbarians favored; but each of his axes were larger than most men could wield single-handedly. Beside him was Gunner Sigifrid, formerly of the Engal clan and now a sword for hire. He wore his long blonde hair, including a mustache and beard in the typical barbarian fashion, wild and unkempt. He had on a kilt, with thick leather boots, and a sash that went over one shoulder and met where he hung his giant broadsword. The last of the three was Reinhold Lothar. He was a brooding man, well over six feet tall with long dark hair, and darker skin that was typical of the Northern clans. Each man had made his reputation over the course of their lifetimes, and now, they wanted to make some money, so they could afford a few passing luxuries.

After three weeks on the open sea, they finally spotted land. A few hours later, they saw the coastal traffic, trade ships and fishing craft. By the time they were close enough to wade ashore, the whole coast was a beehive of activity. The women and children were nowhere to be seen, and several hundred men had lined up, including the city police. When they saw the tens of thousands of men and women coming ashore, they sent a man out to offer their surrender.

A city policeman walked out to the beach, his sword still in its scabbard. He tried to offer his surrender. "Welcome to Tebron…" His words were cut off, along with his head. The weather at the beach was warm as it was almost midday, and Alianna was in her typical nearly nude state. The king watched her with both lust and admiration at how she could be so sexy while taking a man's life. She waded ashore, the Doreh veterans just behind her, with the rest of the raiders following behind. They all wore paint on their faces, to scare the enemy, and to show their devotion to war and to the Doreh gods.

The men of Tebron knew that there would be no quarter, so they lifted their swords, crouched behind their long shields, and prepared to take as many of the invaders with them as they could before they died. Alianna smiled with pure joy as she swung her oversized axe, taking off arms like dry twigs in a hurricane. With more force than should be possible from such a thin, hauntingly beautiful woman, she mowed down all that she faced. Indeed, she was the living embodiment of the 'angel of death'.

Gunner was the first man to hit the beach, and without a shield or armor to speak of, he charged the front line. He brought his mighty broadsword down in a chop that found its way between two shields and split open the head of one of the defenders. He was followed closely by Agnar who also was likewise, without a shield, and used his strong legs to slam into the weak shield wall. Once the gap was created, he took the men apart with his war axes. The green and blue streaks that he had applied to his forehead and cheeks were now bright red, splashed by the blood of their enemies.

Behind the two more dynamic warriors was Reinhold the Grimm. Unlike the others, he bore a regular sized round shield, and a longsword that was the right size for single-arm combat. The others expended great amounts of energy and bowled over the enemy by sheer force and power of will. Reinhold considered himself more of an artist. He blocked attacks, dodged when it was called for, and struck out when the enemy was open or off balanced. Looking down on his fellow Doreh, he thought to himself that though they had reputations as large as their massive bodies, he could easily pick them apart in a fair fight. Those that had seen him fight, thought of him as quite possibly the most skilled swordsman in all of Tychon.

Behind them followed the rest of the barbarian hordes. They were short on defense, but long on enthusiasm. Many of them fell to archers, spears, even thrown bricks; but their numbers would not be denied. In less than an hour, the beach was King Friodor's. He stepped ashore, ignoring the buckets of blood that the waves were washing in at his ankles. At his side was his queen, Frida. They carried weapons that were spotlessly clean.

"It is as you say, they are soft and ripe for conquest," he said to the fiery blonde with the bloody axe in her strong hands. She was covered head to toe in blood and gore, her eyes shone brightly from behind the gruesome mask she now wore.

"Aye, and this is just the coast that is closest to our country. We can fight our way East for months, even years to come. This land is larger than all of Tychon, and if you plan the campaign correctly, all but a small plot of land can be yours."

"You speak of your own country, where you can be queen of all you behold?" he asked with a condescending tone.

"That was our deal," she growled.

"What I see is a coalition of fifty thousand of my men and women, a thousand boats, supplies, weapons... all these things are supplied by me. Perhaps I can gift you a village or two; but of course, you will always bow to me, and call me 'King'." He smiled deviously at her.

She returned his smile, her blue eyes smoldering behind the mask of blood and mud that covered her flawless face. She turned away from him, hefting her huge axe in both hands up level with her chest. Even with his wife standing there, he unashamedly stared at her shapely, muscular buttocks. When she turned away, he cried out. "How dare you turn your back..." His words were cut off. She spun with incredible speed, the razor-sharp edge of her axe blade slicing through his windpipe, and half of his neck. He clutched at the opening in his throat, his expression no longer one of a victor, but of a fool.

"Typical human," she said, as he fell to his knees. "I have to thank you for being so very predictable." She threw the axe to the ground, and then turned and ran towards town. She moved so fast that even the seasoned warriors were dumbstruck as they watched the whole scene play out. Eventually, at the queen's request, bands of men were sent after the blonde demon; but she was long gone.

Chapter 47: The Iron Road

The line of refugees stretched in both directions for dozens of miles. They came dragging children and cattle, and little else. The road was also filled with armed men on horses, and wagons to carry the weak and infirm. The evacuation had begun weeks before, and now, only the very stubborn were left to face the wrath of invaders. The rest of Western Kronos was moving towards Castle Herron as quickly as they could. King Syphon stood over the map of Kronos with his host and lieutenant, King Herron, trying to plan their next step.

"Do you think that they'll take the bait?" Gabriel asked.

"To them, conquering is the taking of land. You can't just move in and call it home. You have to kill the former owner. Then and only then, can you call the land yours."

"So, they'll keep marching on till they find an enemy to fight?"

"Basically. They will see the trail leading toward this castle and will not bother to go north or south. I think if we infuriate them, it will only cause them to throw caution to the wind and run headlong into any traps that we can put in their path."

"There are so many of them! By the gods, I knew there would be thousands; but I fear that they can afford to lose half their strength and still overpower us by three to one."

"Let's hope that the friendships that we've formed will be strong enough to get them to come to our aid. Otherwise, I'll go down in history as the leader that presided over the fall of humankind."

Chapter 48: War Plans

"Good work, Alexina," Lilith said to her younger sister. "Fifty-thousand barbarians on the march. Too bad that you had to give up your place with them," she said, looking into a sphere of water suspended above a stone basin. In the water's ripples, she could see each of her sisters as if they were all together.

"It was past time. I had to spend months among them. The same creatures that allowed me to be trapped a death sleep in their mountains for several hundred years," she replied. "I killed their king, and now along with fighting the locals, they are fighting amongst themselves to see who will run the clan when all is said and done."

"There is very little resistance from these humans. They run when the Doreh hordes get close. The barbarians are rolling through, looting, and burning everything in their path. Most of them have already fled east."

"No matter. We can trap them between your barbarians, and Carissa's Inhumans."

"Carissa, how is your part of the plan going?" she asked the Autumn Witch.

"Well enough. The Mavit Tomar are ready to go at my command, along with their Owl mounts and their hunting beasts. There are too many of them to transport through a portal, so they have been constructing boats, and will launch in a week, maybe two."

"I've convinced the Hill Giants to aid us, I can have up to two hundred of them at a moment's notice," Anjaya added.

"Then it looks like we're ready," Lilith declared. "You two march from the West, kill everything that you come across.

Carissa, you bring in your allies and attack from the East. When we meet in the middle, we can mass together and finish the continent by going North."

"And what will you be doing, sister?" Alexina asked.

"I have some surprises, and I'm going to save them for just the right time!" she cackled.

Chapter 49: Jorn

Jorn returned to the mansion to gather a few things that he didn't want stolen or destroyed by the coming hordes. For two days, Riken dutifully followed him around with the purple cloth bag that Argus used to always carry around. For a reason that neither of them fully understood, the bag had an infinite volume inside, where the outside was roughly two cubic yards. They stuck in paintings, vases, and it took half a day; but they loaded Argus' entire library in the bag. Two men, six arms, working furiously to save the priceless texts. When they had saved the absolute essentials, Jorn let Riken take a break to eat with his wife. The yellow-skinned giant knew how important their work was, but he was still pleased to have the time off.

Jorn worked his way down to the lowest chamber, to the place where his master had been murdered by the old crone, Lilith. The old mage had become a second father to him, and the old man's loss hurt deeply. In an open area near the entrance to the chamber was a pyre where the eternal flame roared, and a dozen feet away, the endless fountain poured into a shallow pool. Two of the most powerful elements of nature, which often opposed each other, were content to occupy their own space in the secret chamber. Jorn ignored the ball of fire, it was the tool of his sister, who was a master of fire. Contrary to her being known as the Winter Witch, Lilith was also a devotee of fire. Jorn preferred the power of ice and water. The visions that he sought while in water were the most vivid, the deep truths. He didn't really have control of the process; he immersed himself in the living water and it took him where the visions led him. Though it often felt like hours, his dream state lasted only a few minutes at most. He had the time and thought it wise to see what else might be revealed to him.

Stripping down to his bare skin, he climbed into the pool and sat on the rock floor of the fountain's bowl. The water was numbingly cold. He sat with his eyes closed and allowed the discomfort of the cold to seep into his every cell. Since he could remember, he was largely immune to the effects of cold. Cutting off the physical world from his mind, he drifted into a state of lucid dreaming. The water around him stopped flowing and was drawn to the young mage, where it formed a sphere of water with Jorn at its center. He didn't breathe and yet, he was in no real danger of drowning. This time, something different happened.

"Jorn," came a familiar voice, that sounded only in his mind.

"Master?"

"It is I," came the reply.

"You died. I burned your body," Jorn thought.

"I am dead, my son. You found the remains of my physical body, but my spirit can never be completely extinguished. I have a weak connection to this world, and soon, I may lose it completely, but for a short time, I can communicate with you."

"Thank you, Master. Many enemies are converging on us now, I could use your guidance."

"I was killed by the Winter Witch. I had just destroyed her demon, a demon lord from the lower pits, and she caught me at my weakest. I guess it's only fair. Even though we had been lovers hundreds of years ago, I didn't think twice about trapping her in the tallest tree in the darkest forest in all of Kronos. Now she's back and her sisters are back as well. I scoured the many universes for them, and I found two more of them. The Spring

Witch is an ebon-skinned beauty, powerful and cruel. I used one of my most powerful enchantments and made her forget who she was. For the last two hundred years, she's been a servant of her community. She was not cursed like the others. Alexina the Summer Witch… how I wanted to bed her. She must be part Succubus, her every curve, every word, every move made a man's blood rage through his veins. I saw that despite her perfection of form, she was every bit as evil as the others on the inside. I put her into a long-lasting sleep, and hid her body in the mountains, overlooking the lands where the bear-men live, and where the tribes of barbarians have formed a nation."

"They are all free now, and I fear that even with you at our side, we might not be able to stop them," Jorn worried.

"A reasonable concern. Let me tell you the story, as much as I know of it, of what the witches are and how they came to be. I will also tell you about my origins, and about you and your sister. I know that we seem human, but we Halacians are an ancient bloodline, and we have been the protectors of humankind for many millennia. I can tell you about yourself and your sister, things that you thought that you knew, but were never told the truth."

"What kind of things?" he asked.

"You and your sister are not the offspring of simple farmers. "You are more like me than them, and you were conceived with a purpose," the disembodied spirit said. His training involved being in control of his mind and emotions. Jorn was able to take his feelings of shock and fear and put them aside for later consideration. He controlled his heart rate, his air consumption, and he willed himself to relax.

"I'm ready Master. Tell me everything that you think I need to know."

Chapter 50: Horns

The ships reached the shores of Lourens and flooded the beach with Mavit Tomar troops, their owl mounts, and their Zytlyx, the mantis-like hunting beasts that accompanied them into battle. Commissar Ghor watched as his men and supplies arrived on the unguarded shore and was sure that his crack troops would tear through the local troops like a bull through wet paper.

Carissa was there to greet them; she had already been around the port town and found that almost everyone had been evacuated. The tracks made it very clear; everyone had gone west in a big hurry. She was a little disappointed that the war would be delayed, she had expected that they would have to fight their way ashore. Instead, the humans had ceded the land and allowed the invaders to get a foothold in their country without so much as a cross word.

"I know that we're a formidable force, but I wasn't expecting them to run before we set a single hoof on land. What do you suggest now?" the Commissar asked the witch.

"It's pretty obvious which way they went I think we follow them, catch up to them, and wipe them out. They'll know where the rest are hiding."

"A solid plan," the Commissar replied. He took his shiny helmet off, careful not to scratch his prized curled horns. He scratched at the fur on his head, his coat being mostly blue with grey accents. "It will take the rest of the day to bring the whole force ashore. I suggest we start at dawn; I can send out scouts now, with your approval."

"I'm here to help you, Commissar. This is your army, and you are in complete control. I put the planning and the logistics fully in your capable hands," Carissa said, with a grand bow.

"So kind of you, Miss." He waved a few men over, "These men will assemble your tent and bring you anything that you need."

"That won't be necessary, as the whole town is deserted, I think that I'll stay at that inn," she pointed towards a three-story building far down the main road leading away from the shore. "I will take the highest floor. If you wish, you and some of your officers can stay in the lower floors."

"Well, I've never stayed under a real roof during a campaign; but your logic is undeniable," he said chuckling to himself. "This war will be like no other for the Mavit Tomar."

The Mavit Tomar scout soared above the plains and forests of Lourens. For hours he followed the trail till he reached the Iron Road. Then he followed the road till he found the refugees. The owl squawked that it too had seen the pack of fleeing people. He decided to move in closer to see the makeup of the group, even from this distance, it was obvious that there were many children in the crowd. He drifted lower and lower, till his shadow crossed them; that's when then they looked up and cried out in panic. They began running as well as they could; but the children slowed them to a pace that was the same as their walking pace. He easily passed them, circled around, getting lower so that he could try and decipher how many males and how many females were in the group. They all looked so much alike.

He saw one of them with a bow and thought that he was probably out of range; but just in case, he started to climb again. He'd only climbed a dozen feet when the thick arrow sank into the chest of his mount, causing them both to plummet to the ground. As he lay on the ground broken and dying, he saw them walking over to look at him. They spoke the common tongue as did almost all creatures in Xoran. They discussed him and his fate while standing over his dying body. Eventually they came to some conclusion, and one of them stepped up close to him. The man had a giant bow on his back, but he drew his sword.

"Back to hell with you, demon," he said as he drove his sword though the scout's chest.

"What the hell is it?" a woman asked.

"Not sure, but it means trouble," Tennyson answered. He stepped on the bird's chest and pulled out his 'giant killer' arrow. "Sorry, these are really hard to come by." He waved a small wagon over. He instructed the driver to load the dead Mavit Tomar scout and his owl mount on the wagon. "Make haste for Herron Castle, let the king know that this is what we face."

"Commissar, one of our scouts is overdue, he should have been back an hour ago," a drone reported.

"We have to assume that he was killed," the Commissar mused. "Prepare the men, we take wing at dawn!"

Ten thousand Mavit Tomar took to the sky at dawn. They were clad in their shiny round helmets, armor made of fish scale like plates, and each carried a ten-foot-long spear. They had long swords and daggers; their owls were fierce and ready for red meat. They soared for hours, following the trail that the evacuees had left, and then when the obvious trail ended with the start of the Iron Road, they followed that. Far below, their hunting creatures ran as fast as they could to try and keep pace with their masters. The mantis-like creatures, all about the size of a large dog, or a small pony, jumped along on their spindly legs.

The Commissar and his commanders flew far above the formation, observing both the land and their troops. Below were the cream of the crop, their mounted knights. Beneath them was this strange land of Kronos. The Commissar looked over the land, with its rich soil and unclaimed valleys. He would move here and set up a plantation. The locals would work the land, so that he would be provided with a rich lifestyle. He might even take on a second mistress with the increased wealth that he would acquire.

They had traveled for many hours, flying along the Iron Road, across plains mostly, but also crossing rivers, forests, and grassland. Every few hours a scout would land on the road and look for evidence that they were still on the trail of the fleeing citizens. Finally, they saw a group of ten or so people hobbling down the road. They were in a pass that was cut through a small stand of forest that was the border between Lourens and Margera. The Mavit Tomar sent a couple dozen cavalry down to investigate. The Commissar came down within a hundred foot, so that he could observe the interrogation.

He was surprised that they all spoke the common language spoken in Pyrros. They were very old humans, and by the looks of them, in failing health. It was clear that they couldn't keep pace with the others who were by now, hours ahead.

"So, your warriors abandon the weak to save themselves?" the lead Drone said loud enough for all to hear. He pulled an old man to his feet by his dirty, worn out shirt. "Are you really just a race of cowards?" he asked.

"No, we men of Kronos are proud and fearless," said the old man, as he plunged a long spike-like dagger into the Drone's uncovered side. "We don't fear animals, or whatever the hell you are!"

The crowd of old men and women stood defiantly on the road, each one bearing a sharp implement, and an attitude. The Mavit Tomar dismounted and a hundred of them, with swords drawn, stalked the defiant seniors. When they were fifty feet away, soldiers stormed out from the trees. The arrogant invaders were caught flat footed and unawares. As the troops came from both sides of the road, a tidal wave of arrows came from the upper reaches in the trees. The soldiers, bearing the Margera crest, were high enough to shoot down on the invaders who were hovering, and watching the proceedings. A hundred or more of the Mavit Tomar fell in the first volley, and another fifty before they could climb out of range of the archers.

From deep in the woods came a thunderous sound, steel shod hooves beating a path through the underbrush, tearing through branches, and knocking down saplings. Two hundred fully armored knights broke into the clearing; the foot soldiers parting to allow them through. At their head was King Vivek Fionn, respected warrior and longtime monarch of Margera. His armor had been shined and re-tooled for this occasion. He proudly wore his family's crest, the 'black knight on a field of red'. He wore a special helmet that was attached to his crown. The sparkling yellow gems set into the jagged gold band let everyone know who the king and protector of this land was. His eyes were sharp, despite his five plus decades of life, half of that sitting on the throne. His salt and pepper beard had been cut short so that it could not be grasped by the enemy. High above his head, he waved the sword of his fathers, an extra-large long sword, very wide at the handle, and coming to a sharp, though blunt point. Like his armor, the edges of the sword were shined to reflect every scrap of the diffused forest light. He was everything that you could want in a wartime king.

With a rallying cry echoing through the forest, they charged through the unmounted invaders. King Fionn shouted as his blade came down and bit deeply into the first of the invaders, killing him instantly. Like a madman, he chopped his way through the remainder of the standing Mavit Tomar. His men followed his example, plowing through the enemy soldiers with only a few deaths, and a handful of injuries. The king dismounted and walked toward one of the dead enemies.

"Gods, what are these things? I'll bet that this is what you get when a man fucks a goat!" he said to the roaring laughter of his men. He looked up at the thousands of mounted invaders as they circled in confusion. After some time, they broke off and headed North towards the Indigo desert.

"There are too many of them, and they've come too far to turn back. You know that, right?" Tennyson said to King Fionn.

"I do, but I'm not sure if waiting here is the not right thing to do. The trees give us a lot more protection than I thought they would. We are safe here, but the women and children are only a day ahead of us. If we can delay them long enough, they can reach the tunnels that lead to Castle Herron."

"If I were them, I would set fire to this forest first, as in, right now as we're speaking. They flew North towards the desert. If they come across something that they can drop on us, then they can stay out of our range, and we're sitting ducks."

"If they don't change direction, they'll fly right over the Oritz Quarry," said one of the Margera knights.

"Damn! We need to move as fast as we can. I think that it's going to rain!"

"Everyone, as fast as you can, head down the Iron Road going West! Our goal is to reach the entrances to the tunnels!" he called out to his men. The foot soldiers immediately gathered their packs and were quick marching down the road. The elderly were helped onto the backs of the horses, and they too were sent down the road. The man who had killed the first invader slid into the saddle behind the king.

"Nice work back there, Uncle," he said to his passenger.

"Nothing that any man of Magera wouldn't do to protect our home."

"That's why we will win," Tennyson said hopefully.

Chapter 51: King Fionn

King Vivek Fionn rode as quickly as his horse was able, chewing up the countryside with reckless abandon. He knew that the Mavit Tomar were not far behind, and he knew that the entrance to the furthest escape tunnel to Castle Herron was still miles ahead. With each passing second, he began to have hope that he and his men would reach the safety of the tunnels; but that hope was short-lived.

Man-sized boulders started raining from the heavens, many missed; but the men were riding in such tight clusters that when one was on target, it might take out several riders. Out of the corner of his eye, Vivek saw a huge chunk of granite crash into a knight, instantly crushing him and his horse, sending blood and gore in all directions.

"Men, don't cluster, spread out and keep riding!" he directed. Then men did as they were told, fanning out to make targeting individual riders all the more difficult. For many long minutes, he could hear the screams of both man and beast, and then it was over. A quick scan told him that he probably lost a fifth to a quarter of his men. He could hear the hooting of the owls, and knew they were not too far above them. When their shadows passed over, he knew their plan to flee was a lost cause.

Hundreds of giant owls, with their man-like riders dropped to ground level in front of the charging humans. Behind, several hundred more landed. The noose was drawing closed, but no one would ever accuse King Fionn and his Knights of Margera, of dying without a fight. He pulled up on the reins, while at the same time drawing his sword. His knights followed suit and prepared to face the goat-headed Mavit Tomar. Those with bows had them out with arrows nocked, waiting for a sign.

It seemed like less than a year ago that he had ridden to King Syphon's call. He trusted the man and vowed that he would 'lead' his men into battle, not 'send' them off to fight for him. Before, it was the Quell, a group of religious zealots that put no value in human life and only lived to rob, rape, and kill. They were human, and yet they treated their fellow humans worse than you would treat a rabid wolf. He had fought bands of them invading his territory for a few years before the war started, and they didn't take prisoners. These invaders were not human, and therefore, it was logical that they would value human life even less. He would not surrender his men; he would die with them on the field of battle as befit a war-time King.

Without warning or a call to battle, he spurred his horse forward, launching himself at the wall of invaders. They lowered their lances, making it sure suicide to attack them from the front. He, and the dozens of other knights who took up the charge had about a hundred yards to close before reaching the brightly shined spearheads of their enemy. They had gone about two thirds of the way when the first volley of arrows passed overhead and found soft targets to penetrate. Some of the Mavit Tomar fell immediately, with arrows to the chest, throat, and face. Dozens of them were injured to varying degrees, and many of their owl mounts suffered injuries, fatal and otherwise. The Mavit Tomar lost their composure at being struck by hundreds of arrows and allowed their lances to dip. The King urged his mount to jump at the last second. They leapt the spears and were now in the thick of the enemy's lines.

In close combat, the knights were in their element. With their large shields and long swords, they were inside the reach of the enemy's lances, and they had expertise in man to man combat. The King didn't need to watch his back, he knew his men were there to protect his unguarded rear. He swung his sword up and down, again and again, each blow finding a target in an enemy's shoulder, side, chest. He even attacked the owls if they got into the way.

The Mavit Tomar had ten times their number when their attack began. There was never any doubt as to how the fight would end. King Fionn accepted his fate; but was determined to make his death as costly as possible. The knights continued to create a wall with themselves protecting the archers. The archers continued firing till they ran out of arrows, then they drew their swords. The invader's commanders were becoming frustrated with not being able to easily roll over the humans.

One of the giant owls grabbed King Fionn's shield in its powerful beak, ripping and twisting it off his arm. He knew immediately that the arm was broken. With his good arm, he doubled his activity, both defending and striking with his longsword. He didn't need to survey the battle to know that he only had a fraction of his knights left. Far to his right, he could see the bowman, Tennyson Coe. The man was a true asset and a skilled warrior. It would be a shame that they wouldn't have more time together. He felt a spear tip enter under his ribcage, cutting into his lungs. He struck at the goat faced warrior that was holding the spear, and that allowed another enemy in the front to drive its short sword through the gap in his chest plate and the shoulder piece. He let out a last breath and looked at the sky as the creatures inflicted several more fatal wounds. His last thoughts were a prayer to Magnus that his son would be able to serve the people of Margera as their king, and that he would be a good and just leader.

Tennyson saw the king die, and though he didn't know him very well, he had quickly grown to respect the man. He was bleeding from a slash on his left thigh and had claw marks from where one of the owls had raked his back. He knew that his time was limited, and that he was just a few minutes from being overwhelmed from both sides. Looking up, he saw a single owl, a hundred feet above the battle, just circling. It was obviously the General, watching his battle plan being carried out. Tennyson decided that he would inflict the most damage that he could while he had the chance.

He ducked between a row of his fellow archers, who were now all fighting with their swords. He found a small open area, not even five feet square where he could carry out his plan. Dropping his sword, he pulled the Giant Killer bow from his back, thanked the Gods that the string was still intact, and quickly, though with precision, nocked a special arrow. He had always been a natural with the bow, and unless he was completely drunk, he could hit anything that he aimed at. He pulled the string back as far as the length of his arms would allow, anticipated the flight pattern of the hovering owl far above them, and fired. The Commissar never saw the missile, even as it passed through his owl, and then through his body, entering the groin, and exiting the right shoulder. Both bodies fell as a unit, hitting the bloodied battlefield with a sickening thud.

The Margera Thousand all died that day, but the damage that they inflicted on the Mavit Tomar would be a tale of legend for generations. If the raiders had waited for their insect-like companions to catch up with the flying cavalry, it would have been a rout. As it was, it took them almost three thousand of their elite troops, and their Commissar to take out one thousand of the humans. The Mavit Tomar would also look at this day and the lessons it offered.

Chapter 52: Chorea

Wever Bran stood on a balcony that overlooked the courtyard, which separated his personal quarters from the main chapel. Another war, and again he was sending off the army that he had assembled. He had thousands of men from all over Kronos, men who were devout and dedicated to preserving the interests of the church. Now, he was sending them off to be under the leadership of non-believers and blasphemers. He knew that the heathens and demons were coming to kill all the good men and women of the church, and those who had yet to find their way. When would he be given the time to grow this empire in the name of Magnus and the other gods?

There was a light, yet familiar hand on his shoulder. He turned to see what his assistant Lehna Miraslav wished to speak to him about. They had been together for so many years, that they had gotten to know each other pretty well. He looked at her and saw something strange in her expression, an unfamiliarity in her eyes. He thought that he knew the cause but wasn't sure. He just stared into her eyes and waited.

"It is I," she said. It was her voice, but the tone drilled through him, shaking him to the core. "What are you doing? You are giving away 'my' holy warriors?" she scolded the High Father.

"I'm doing the Church's part to protect the homeland. Demons and monsters are flooding into your creation to pillage and kill," he said.

"I know... everything. Do you doubt that my presence is everywhere, at all times?" she demanded angrily.

Wever fell to his knees and trembled before his god's wrath. "No Lord Magnus! Of course, you know everything! I thought that it would be in the church's best interest for us to support the kings in their stand against this coming evil."

"Those decisions are mine to make. I will handle these pretenders that claim that I chose them to rule. I will do it in my own time, and I don't fear 'demons' and 'monsters'," she mocked, "Such creatures are but insects before one such as I."

He looked up at her, confused and humbled, "What will you have me do, my Lord?"

"The mercenaries that Lectr Vaugh purchased will be passing not too far from here. I helped you to curse him, just as you prayed for."

"But..." he stammered.

"The merchant is now a creature of the night and will suffer your curse for a dozen lifetimes. We need to further weaken him. When his troops come through your land on the way to serve King Syphon, you must ambush and eliminate them."

"Lord?" he looked at the face of his trusted assistant, twisted with anger.

"Do as I command! Kill the mercenaries. They are bad men who've been trained to kill and destroy. Their mere existence is an affront to me!" She reached up and grabbed the High Father by the lapels of his suit. She lifted him easily off of the ground and swung him around till his feet dangled over a three-story drop. "Do as I say, and I may bless you again with my presence. Do not, and I will forsake you to your miserable fate!" She easily tossed him across the patio where he rolled into a crying heap.

Again, he felt the familiar hand on his shoulder. He dreaded lifting his face from the folds of his jacket. When he finally did, she was there still.

"Master? Are you all right?" Lehna asked.

He looked up to see the same face, though it was now the hard-working, innocent face of his trusted companion. He dried his tears on his sleeves and slowly got to his feet. She helped as much as she could and eased him into a chair.

"What's wrong Wever?" She very rarely used his first name, even when they were alone.

"I think that I'm having a crisis of faith." It hurt him to say such a thing out loud.

"You're the High Father! You've had an audience with Magnus! How can you possibly have any doubts? You need to be the rock for the rest of us to build a foundation on!" she pleaded.

"I just now spoke with our lord, Magnus," he stated.

"Really? I just missed seeing him. Such a blessing, High Father!"

"He has comanded me not to send our troops to back up the armies forming at Castle Herron," she went pale at hearing these words. "He has also instructed that when the Ursina troops pass through our land on their way to the rendezvous, we should ambush them, and if we can, wipe them out."

"I now understand your trepidation, Master. Only one as strong as you could carry out such a cruel command," she said, her hand gripping his wrist. "Whatever you order, I will work to carry them out. I don't have to agree to follow your orders, just as you don't have to understand why Magnus would order you to take on such an... unlikely mission."

He looked at her and admired her strength. He was a conniver from the start, and his ambition knew no limits. She was the perfect partner, she too was sneaky and had a twisted intelligence; but when it came to him, she was completely honest and supportive.

"Give the order for the men to stand down. Have the generals make up a plan to intercept the Ursina troops. They'll be passing through any day now. Time is of the essence."

"What will you be doing, master?" she asked.

"I need to calm down. I think I'll retire to my quarters for a while."

"Should I send one of the boys to stay with you?" she inquired.

"No, not today. I really need to be alone with my thoughts for now," he said walking towards his personal suite.

Chapter 53: Spring Storm

Anjaya walked through her sister's port into the new world. Alexina had been in Kronos for almost three weeks now. After deserting the Doreh to their own fate, she had moved inland on the wings of an Eagle and the body of a Lioness. She had soared above this strange land and admired how much of it was still open and untamed. There were miles and miles of untouched grasslands, the wind causing them to look like a vast green ocean, complete with waves. There were herds of grazing animals, their sheer numbers were their defense against predators.

Alexina told her sister about some of the cities that she had passed over. She had followed the coast that bordered the great Northern Sea and passed over the port towns of Goldport and Killburn. Both were still alive with activity, though it was obvious that they were collecting supplies and heading for the Iron Road. It seemed that the whole continent was aware that an attack was coming, and they were all fleeing.

"Where are they going, sister?" Anjaya asked of her sister.

"The humans built a new castle, especially to defend their kind against invaders like us," she laughed. "The Castle is not too far from here."

"How did you find out so much? Shouldn't they try to hide their secrets a little better?"

"When men think that they'll get a chance to touch this," she indicated her own body, "they'll divulge just about anything."

"Really? I don't see it," she said, shrugging her shoulders. "How is Carissa doing?" Anjaya asked.

"Her goat men landed and almost immediately got disgraced in battle by these hairless monkeys," Alexina informed her. "I think they are closing in on the army that opposed them, and they are planning to use their numerical superiority to finally get the job done."

"About damn time. Are we ready to bring in my secret weapon?" she asked.

"The Giants? You're crazy for those dolts."

"Each one is stronger than a hundred men and their lack of intelligence makes them very focused fighters." She looked around at trees far off, and the grassy hills all around. "Do they have those 'Bison' things near here? Once they come through, they are probably going to want to eat."

"I anticipated that sister, and there is a sizable herd just a few miles from here."

The women began clearing the ground and preparing runes to form a portal big enough to allow the Hill Giants to pass through. They were nearly done when they heard a sweet voice from their recent past.

"Spring and Summer together, how delightful!" said Chorea from behind them. They turned to see the woman, still in her ten-foot-tall form, a gown of translucent material blowing around her.

"Thank you for muting your usual radiance, Chorea," Alexina said snidely.

"Time is growing short, and I don't have much of it to spare listening to your problems," the Goddess replied. "How are your parts of the plan going?"

"The goat men are days away from the castle where King Syphon is held up," Alexina offered. "The Doreh are still a week away."

"We were getting ready to bring the Hill Giants here, right now," Anjaya explained, pointing at the runes on the freshly tilled earth.

"Let me help you," she said, making a gesture with her long delicate fingers. A portal opened up, easily thirty feet in diameter. On the other side of the huge window was a group of restless Hill Giants. When they saw the Spring Witch, over two hundred of them grunted and ambled through into a new world. Long before they were through, Chorea disappeared. Before she left, she warned the sisters that she was expecting them to coordinate their attack on Castle Herron in the next two weeks.

Chapter 54: The Week Before

Landis was walking the perimeter of the castle, giving the defenses a last review when a messenger summoned him to the planning room. He jogged along with the messenger who felt the urgency of the summons warranted a little extra speed. A thousand chores ran through his mind as they raced to the boardroom.

"Landis, the time is almost here!" King Syphon said as he approached the table. The whole map of Kronos had been carved into the table, including the mountains, lakes, rivers and such. The Ammun monk Melina had given the King a set of markers to show the locations of the various armies. Each one was carved by hand from wood, and stained dark for the opposing forces and lighter for the friendly forces. One look at the map told a story that no one wanted to hear.

"The last of the ravens have just come in, and this map is accurate to within a couple of hours." King Syphon said to Landis. These abominations riding giant owls are practically at our doorstep. It looks like they'll overtake King Fionn's army before they can reach the tunnels." He then moved his hand to a group of figures in the West. "Here are the Doreh, they are still a week away, but making good time." Then he pointed just north of the castle. "A scout has reported that two hundred giants have appeared here." He indicated the spot. "They can be here by tonight, easily."

"It looks like the sisters are trying to coordinate an attack here, at this castle."

"That's what we wanted, isn't it?" Gabriel asked.

"Yes, and no. If all of these Doreh from the West, these goat men from the East, and Giants from the North all attack at the same time, I don't think we'll be able to withstand it."

"What do you suggest, Landis?" King Syphon asked.

"Unfortunately, King Fionn is on his own, it's too late to send help," he said regretfully. "I fought these giants before, and to call them stupid is a kindness. If we lure them in ahead of the sister's schedule, we can try and eliminate them. If they all attack at the same time, we don't stand a chance."

"So... we pick a fight with 'Giants', and hope they are willing to fight us immediately. That's the plan?" Gabriel asked.

"If you have a better plan, Sire, I'd be glad to hear it." He looked at the young king, who could only shrug his shoulders. He looked to the King of Kings, who nodded in agreement.

"I'll take a few men and go out there to try and get their attention, then I'll lead them back here. Be ready to make the most of the war machines."

Kel looked thoughtful, then nodded his head, "Come back alive Landis."

Landis and his men literally ran from the room. They went to the lockers where their armor was stored, and they found that Anisha was already there. Landis was hurriedly strapping on armor and padding when she spoke.

"Don't you try to make me stay here, love. I'm as good as any man you command!" she shouted to him as she stood in the doorway, all fire and beauty.

"I know you are, get dressed!" he commanded. She smiled and started donning her own mail armor as quickly as she could. In two minutes, Landis, Anisha, and a dozen of their best knights were jogging off to the stables. The stable master had their mounts ready, and they all practically leaped into their saddles. Having mounted up, they took off to the North, ready to put themselves in harm's way.

As they rode, Landis took the opportunity to steal a few looks at his lady love. Anisha was as bold as he was, and loved fighting probably even more than he did. She rode into battle single-mindedly, her smiling face expressing calm, concentration, and capability. The only thing that she loved above war, was war at her man's side. The way that she rode her stallion, her body suspended above the saddle, her thick muscular thighs, supporting her as she rode full out. He briefly allowed his thoughts to stray to the way she rode him, and how her technique was not too dissimilar from what she was doing now.

For the better part of an hour, they rode at high speed, till the horses cried for relief. Ahead were the giants. They were impossible to hide and made no effort to be stealthy. They were feeding on Bison, and as quickly as they could grasp one of the huge beasts, they would bring it to their mouths and eat them, alive and kicking. The scene was both horrible and shocking, but Landis and Anisha had already fought the creatures back in Koregar and were not as stunned by the sight.

Landis yelled to the giants, but they couldn't hear him over the sound of the bison screaming and their own chewing. With no other ideas, he charged them and hacked at the calf of the nearest giant. He howled in pain and looked down to see the papercut-like wound to his leg. He dropped the half-eaten creature in his fist and started stomping after the little man on the horse.

"Little man cut me!" he yelled, getting the attention of the others. "Little man must die! I will eat you, little man!" The giant said, reaching down to try and grab Landis and his horse in his huge rough hands. Landis circled the giant and inflicted a few more wounds that were superficial; but served to make the giant even angrier. Anisha and the knights with them did the same. Soon, six or seven of the giants had small, but painful wounds. The other giants were closing in, trying to help their friends get their revenge, and that's when Landis cut and ran his horse as fast as he could, back towards the castle. When they saw the herd of giants heading their way, the others also turned and rode towards Castle Herron as fast as their mounts were able. Several times, Landis could almost feel the rough dry fingers grabbing at his shoulder, each one the size of a tree trunk. It only made him urge his horse on faster, to the point that he knew the horse might at any time have a heart attack and throw him to his death.

The sight on the horizon was one to behold. A dozen men, and a single woman were riding their horses at breakneck speed back to the castle, and behind them, an avalanche of Hill Giants as far as the eye could see. King Syphon looked through his telescope, a gift from Genia King, and was astonished at the sheer size of the giants. His most trusted warrior, along with the Uzor visitors from Koregar told him about their battle with the giants and they warned that there was a good chance that they would be summoned.

Kel ran to the lower levels where he was met by some of his senior knights. He let them know that it was time to prepare their defenses. He sent another man down to find the mage Danika, and to have her ready to play her part. In that short time, Landis and his group could now be seen with the naked eye, and the giants were now plainly visible. They looked like angry children, chasing after an elusive toy on the ground.

"Open the gate!" he yelled to the soldiers manning the front door.

"Sire, the enemy is coming!" a guard yelled.

"Sir Stone can fit through the gate, the giants can't!"

Landis and Anisha were first through the gate, the other knights with them were a couple of lengths behind. The giants were now only a hundred feet from the outer wall of Castle Herron. King Syphon stared at the giants; they were so big; it almost threw off his depth perception. He stared at the foot of the closest one, and when it passed the distance marker, he yelled out the order. All along the North facing wall were ballista, each with a team manning them. At his command, they all launched six-foot steel bolts with long razor-sharp tips. The giant who was chasing Landis was in the front and took the brunt of the first volley. He was struck several times in the groin, stomach, and a single bolt to the neck. Half a dozen more giants were struck by the bolts, a few of them fatally, a couple of them receiving only minor wounds.

One of the giants behind still had a bison in his hand, and in anger, hurled the nearly one-ton carcass over the wall. It struck one of the ballistae with a meaty thud, taking out not only the weapon; but the team that was firing it. The fields around the castle were cleared for a mile in every direction, to give invaders no cover. The giants were scrambling to find something to hurl at the pesky humans. A second volley of ballista bolts was sent flying as the giants were in the process of ripping apart the bodies of their dead.

Again, six or seven of the giants fell, the steel bolt finding their eyes, necks, chest, and so on. They were as strong as they were stupid, and they were able to pull the arms, legs, and heads off of their dead, and use them as ammunition. Before the third wave, heads the size of beer kegs were crashing into the interior of the castle. Arms were tossed and were able to take out several of the ballista teams. The whole front of the formerly pristine castle was now coated with the blood of giants. Hunks of meat, larger than a horse were hanging from the outer walls or were lying in the courtyard between the inner and outer walls.

The crews didn't need to have the signal given for phase two of their giant defense, the plan was already in place. A quarter mile past the walls of the castle, large trap doors opened in the grassy fields. A thousand Telnor warriors flooded out from the tunnels and massed up in position behind the giants. The Telnor were about seven feet tall, with sickly yellow skin, pointy teeth and ears, and four arms to carry shields and weapons. Danika and Jorn's servant Riken was terrifying enough when he wore his long coat and hood. A thousand Telnor in full battle armor was a sight that could give one nightmares for life. They each had twelve-foot-long spears, made of the hardwoods found only in the forests of Tel, each topped with a steel point, and blessed by their shamans. Some of the warriors carried a shield on one side and two swords on the other. Some of the fighters did without a shield, instead opting to wield four swords. A few of the larger warriors carried eight-foot-long battle axes. With the combined strength of four arms working in concert, they could use an axe much larger and deadlier than anything a human could ever swing.

It took a few minutes to get coordinated; but when all of them were out and on the move, they assumed a natural rhythm to their running. There were a thousand of the armored warriors, and yet they were quiet enough to sneak up on the pack of giants. When they were a dozen feet away, they let out a horrifying battle cry and waded into the distracted giants.

The mighty Telnor warriors launched themselves fearlessly at the giants. They were seven feet tall, but that still made them about a third the height of the Hill Giants. In their favor, the Telnor outnumbered the giants by five to one. Andor, one of the Telnor representatives who attended the King's Table was now leading the attack. He jammed his spear, using all four arms, into a giant's side. He was able to pierce the creature's thick hide, and it cried out in pain. Three more Telnor drove their spears into the giant's meaty calves and thighs. They then climbed up, using the spears as steps till they could reach the more vital areas. The ballista stopped because they didn't want to hit their allies. Now it was time for hand-to-hand combat. Hundreds of mounted knights rushed out the main gate, led by Landis.

When they were close, he pulled his sword Soulbane, and with all of his will, he summoned the spirit within. The sword disappeared and, in the sky, above him was the giant flying serpent that appeared first when he was fighting Wanaka in the Doreh arena. The serpent wrapped itself around the closest giant and started to squeeze the life out of him. At the same time, Soulbane reached down and dug his long venomous fangs into the neck of another giant. Landis had to stay out of the fray so that he could control the actions of his sword's avatar. The rest of the humans did their best to charge in and inflict what damage they could, but they did little more than annoy the giants.

King Syphon looked through his glass at the battle, trying to find any hope of their winning. The Telnor were strong enough to bring down the giants; but the process was a long one, like chopping down a Redwood. On the other hand, the humans did almost nothing to slow the brutes. He saw good knights being pummeled and ripped apart by angry Hill Giants. It was too much for him to bear, he gave the signal to sound the retreat. A boy on a large horn blew the sequence of notes that let the knights know it was time to break from combat and return to the hoped-for safety of their walls.

"Send me the mages!" he called to his men.

It took several long and heart-wrenching minutes for the magic users to appear at the king's side. All the while, he watched the serpent fight one or two giants at a time, and he watched as the Telnor fought valiantly, though many died horrible, violent deaths. He looked up when he felt them come near, he saw the girl Danika, her brother Jorn, and Lohar, the Telnor spellcaster.

"I pulled back the knights, they were getting murdered and not even slowing the giants. Now the Telnor are fighting alone, and I don't know how it's going to go," the king admitted to the trio.

"I could fire some fireballs at them, but I'd have to get pretty close," Danika said.

"Same for me, I have a few pretty good spells that I've been wanting to try; but I would have to be 'much' closer to cast them," Jorn added. They turned to the Telnor spellcaster.

"My specialty is transmuting. I don't summon things or create things. I mostly change one thing into something else," he said regretfully. They could all see the Telnor struggling with their naked eyes now. His people were the ones that were fighting and dying in front of the castle walls.

"Sire, do you have any large kegs of wine?" Jorn asked.

"Yes, I believe Herron fully stocked the castle."

"Can you turn wine into a higher proof alcohol?" Jorn asked of Lohar.

"Easily. I see where you're going!" he said with what passed for excitement for a Telnor.

"Have the kegs loaded into the trebuchet as quickly as possible," Jorn instructed the king. The situation was too dire for anyone to take notice of the break of protocol.

King Syphon gave the word, and in ten painfully long minutes, the trebuchet were all loaded with kegs of strong wine.

As they were loaded, Lohar went to each one, and using his power to its limit, changing the strong wine into nearly pure alcohol. When they were done, the king ordered the sound for the Telnor to retreat. The tones were long, and some were out of the range of human hearing, but the well-disciplined Telnor troops responded and ran for the tunnel entrances. The giants were hot on their tails, a few of them were caught trying to retreat and were crushed under the giant's dirty feet.

As soon as the Telnor were clear, the order was given to launch the kegs. As there were still well over a hundred of the giants, it was almost impossible to miss them. The kegs were each as tall as a man and five times as wide, and they had a couple of hundred gallons of liquid each. They rained down on the giants, hitting most of the ones in the middle. The giants were now in a state of total confusion, they were being pelted by tons of eye-stinging liquid, and the creatures that they were fighting were suddenly gone.

"Fire!" ordered the king. Several ballistae were set up, with their bolts wrapped in oiled rags and set on fire. They launched them into the mass of alcohol-soaked giants, and several hit the mark, causing a huge conflagration in the middle of their ranks. Their old dirty rags, along with their long oily hair went up in flames. Their howls could be heard for dozens of miles in every direction. A lot of them were fully engulfed in flame and fell smoldering to the ground. With fire so close to them, the rest of the giants panicked and ran away in all directions. The giants that got near the castle were peppered with steel bolts, but many of them ran North and East and got away.

"We got a rough count, my Lord," Gabriel said, coming up the steps to join King Syphon. "It looks like about forty-five of the giants scattered to the wind. We are sending out men to finish off the wounded right now."

"Good. We can deal with these other giants another day. I don't think that whoever brought them here will be able to corral them and get them to fight for them again." The king said.

"I agree. Now we only have two other armies to worry about."

Chapter 55: By the Gods

In the Grand Chapple, Wever Bran prayed on his knees before the altar to Magnus. Tears flooded his eyes because he knew that what he'd been commanded to do was wrong. How would killing the men of Ursina on their way to battle for the lives of everyone in Kronos serve his god's designs? Why would Magnus ask him to do things harmful to others? He had now become a man who placed curses on his enemies, a man who attacked a rival's men, seemingly out of spite. He prayed out loud for hours till his voice was raw, and only the sound of his sobbing filled the emptied chamber. Though it was strictly against god's law, he looked at the mostly ceremonial dagger that he wore at his side and contemplated plunging into his broken heart.

He was surprised when he heard a rustling sound behind him. He had given strict instructions that no one was to enter while he pleaded to Magnus for answers. Turning around, he saw a young soldier. The man was maybe twenty, and he wore the symbol of Magnus on his chest, as did all of Wever's troops. He was tall and skinny, with wiry black hair, and a chin that looked like he couldn't grow a beard for a million coins. Though everything about the man screamed innocent conscript, the look behind his eyes let Wever know immediately who it actually was. Inwardly, he prayed that Magnus had come to give him a reprieve.

"No, High Father, I'm not here to change the orders that I've given you. Instead, I've come to make sure that you carry them out. My faith in you is flagging, and I thought some last-minute encouragement might help you to do as you've been commanded."

Wearily, the High Father got to his feet. He had aged a decade in the last week, and he looked like even a mild breeze would be enough to knock him from his feet. Wever was pale, dehydrated from sobbing and drooling on himself. *How can lord Magnus ask this of me? These orders that he's given seem to run against his teachings*, he thought to himself. *I've been a servant of the church since I was a boy, and though I do not understand, I must carry out His wishes to the letter.*

"Do not doubt my faith, Lord! Please forgive me! I just needed time to collect myself. Yes, I'll see to it that your commands are carried out."

Both of them turned when they heard a third person enter the hall. Lehna Miraslav, Wever's personal assistant walked the long hall till she was close enough to join the conversation. The soldier looked at her with unbridled hatred.

"Woman! Begone!" he demanded.

"What are you trying to do here?" she asked. "You've led the High Father astray."

"Are you deaf woman?" the soldier screamed. "You'll do as I command!" the voice taking on Chorea's godly timbre.

"No, daughter. I do not take commands from you," the young woman said. "Show your true self now!" she ordered.

The soldier shuddered violently, and the glowing figure of a ten-foot-tall woman leaked out of him. Wever Bran shaded his eyes, then looked away. The light that radiated from her mostly naked body drowned out even the sunlight that shined in from the windows high above. Lehna didn't turn away, or even blink as the woman floated a few feet above them.

"I made a mistake, not keeping an eye on you at all times, Chorea."

"Chorea?" Wever squeaked.

317

"Yes, High Father. My daughter Chorea has you thinking that it was I, Magnus who has been putting evil ideas in your head."

"I never said that I was you, Father!" she exclaimed.

"She knows that to use my name falsely would be punishable by death, even for one of my daughters. She also knows my rules about direct intervention. That is why she poured honey in your ears and made 'you' commit the crimes. She thinks that her hands are clean..."

"Father!" she pleaded.

"They are not!" The words shut down the girl's argument cold, the godly voice booming throughout the chamber. "Chorea, I banish you from all the planes of man, now and forever." Wever's assistant stood there, just watching as the brilliant light of the Goddess faded into nothingness.

"I beg your forgiveness, oh great Lord Magnus!" Wever said, falling to his knees.

"There is nothing to forgive, my child. You were unfairly singled out for torment at the hands of the goddess of secrets and deceit. She will face more punishment in Wauroch; but now, we must fix at least part of what she has inflicted on my creation. In the last century, I have only spoken to three men of Kronos. I spoke with King Syphon, and yes, I restored his hand. I spoke with Landis Stone, though part of him still thinks it was in a dream... and now you. Send your soldiers, but not to fight against the men of Ursina. Order your troops to stand side by side with them to defeat the evil, that is the witches known as the Seasons."

"Of course, my Lord," Wever thought for a while. "You do not wish Kronos to be ruled by the church, and for me to report to you directly?"

"Like I have time for every cry for help? I watch what man does, but I rarely participate, and when I do, it's only to whisper truth in the ear of someone who can keep the flow of destiny on track," Lehna smiled benevolently at the High Father. "Keep this land and make the Church strong, but my religion must be one of peace and inclusion. Do not tax the people, they will give to their heart's content. It is your responsibility to make sure that they are very content."

"Thank you, my Lord. Will we meet again?" the High Father asked.

"No, we will never speak again; but know that I watch over you and your works," she said, then he could almost see the change in Lehna as the spirit of Magnus left her.

"Lehna!" he yelled to the confused woman.

"But... how did I get here?" she asked, almost falling down.

"No time for that! Make sure that my soldiers do 'not' fight the men of Ursina. In fact, they are ordered by 'The High Father', with the blessings of Magnus himself, to join the men of Ursina and fight alongside them like brothers!"

Lehna's face lit up, and she didn't say a word. She turned and ran from the chapel with all possible speed. A rider was sent with orders for the general, and peace amongst the allies, was at least for today, preserved.

Chapter 56: The Final Push

"I can't rely on you bitches to do anything right!" Lilith screamed at her sisters. "We need a coordinated attack on the humans, and by not supervising your assets, we've lost the first two encounters!"

"The Mavit Tomar didn't lose!" Carissa replied angrily.

"They lost three for every 'one' human that they killed, and their leader was killed. You lost!" She then turned on the Spring Witch, "You left those mindless Hill Giants alone with no supervision. If they were available to attack at the same time as the Doreh, and the Mavit Tomar, we would win easily. Now most of them are rotting in the sun, and the rest are roaming the countryside looking for food."

Anjaya couldn't look the others in their eyes, "I'm sorry sisters, I take full responsibility."

"That's all well and good, but we need to personally direct our remaining resources. Personally!" She turned to the Summer Witch, "That means you taking charge of the Doreh and leading them!" Lilith said firmly to her beautiful blonde sister. "I will take Anjaya to help me summon the Nephraim Swarm. We meet at the castle at dawn, the day after tomorrow."

Alexina raised her hand, causing the fifty-thousand-person army behind her to come to a halt. They were not pleased when she returned to them; but no one who had seen her fight wanted to defy her. The army was tired and irritable, they had traveled for weeks and had not found anyone to fight, and they had found very little to pillage. Their spirits picked up when they saw the castle in the distance.

The Summer Witch spoke with the chiefs and split them up so that they would be positioned to attack the castle from all four sides simultaneously. For the rest of the day, the Doreh men and women worked their way into position and then set up their tents and cooking fires. She could sense her sisters and knew that they were close by.

Carissa rode the owl, like she'd been born to it. A new Commissar had been promoted and now she rode with him above the rest of the cavalry. They still had over seven thousand of the mounted Mavit Tomar, and several thousand of the Zytlyx, their insectoid hunting dogs. She hadn't lived in the human world for hundreds of years and was just now realizing that she had underestimated them. They may not have the same resources as the other races; but they had an indomitable spirit that let them fight on, even when facing certain defeat. This time, with her guidance, the Mavit Tomar would not carelessly throw their lives away. Just then, a thought occurred to her. If they were weakened by this war, they would be susceptible to attack back in Pyrros. Just something to consider for a later date.

They didn't have to travel far before the castle came into sight. A sparkling jewel set into the Iron Road. Around the castle were tens of thousands of humans, what she presumed were the Doreh, led by her younger sister. The sheer magnitude of their encampments was enough to renew hope that their plan would still succeed. The idea was to let these humans kill each other off, and when they were weak, they could be easily exterminated. The Age of Man was just taking off, but she and her sisters wanted to crush these pesky humans and again, usher in the Age of Magic.

She signaled to the new Commissar that that they should find a spot to set down and make their own camp. Because of their mobility, they were able to set up their tents and cook fires miles from where the Doreh were. The Barbarians were completely averse to magic, and if they saw the Mavit Tomar with their curled horns, fur and cloven hooves, they would give up their attacks on the men of Kronos and would probably attack them.

Lilith had been trying to summon Chorea for the last hour. At first, her sister Anjaya had joined her; but after twenty minutes, she decided that the goddess wasn't going to be making an appearance. She looked around at the forest that her oldest sister had called home for so long and only felt pity for her. Lilith was the oldest and the strongest of the Seasons, and yet her thinking was set so far in the past that Anjaya hardly felt like she knew her anymore. All this 'Age of Magic', 'Age of Man' hogwash! She hated humans as much as her sisters did, but they were expending too much of their strength and time trying to eliminate them. She knew of a dozen uninhabited islands off the coast of Koregar where they could live in peace and luxury. She conjured a full-length mirror set in an expensive wooden frame. While her sister went on and on, she stood admiring herself. She had to admit, though she couldn't explain why, that she looked like a human. Indeed, with her silky black skin, short black hair, and voluptuous figure, she looked very much like the women of the Uzor. Her sister Alexina looked like the Doreh, with her blatant sexuality and wild blonde hair. Both Carissa and Lilith were brunettes, above average in beauty; but they looked as if they could blend into Kronos society with ease. They hated the humans, hated their weakness, and their pitiful short lives, and yet when on this plane, for some unknown reason, they would choose to emulate them.

Exhausted, Lilith finally gave up her attempts to summon Chorea. As was already discussed, they would proceed without her assistance. If she came with additional aid in the heat of battle, the sisters would consider it icing on the cake. Lilith wanted to take a break, consume something to boost her energy and lift the fog from her brain. She sat as Anjaya presented her with hot tea, laced with medicinals.

"I'll need your help to open the portal" Lilith said to her sister.

"I know. That damned goddess is unreliable, conceited, condescending..."

"The Nephraim Swarm exists on a lower plane of hell than I'm not used to accessing on my own. I know that with energy from Chorea, it would have been relatively easy. With just the two of us, we can only open it for a very limited time. As many of Hell's minions that can pass through before our doorway collapses, is all that we'll have to work with."

"Things are shaping up nicely sister. I think you worry too much," Anjaya said casually. "We will lot the humans and the goat people kill each other, then our demons will finish the rest. We can turn them loose after the battle. Let them scour this land of all life. Then we can then sit in power over a world where our kind will reign supreme!"

Lilith smiled at her sister's theatrics but couldn't deny the pleasant sounds of her vision. The two got to work, laying out the runes, setting the fire, and collecting the necessary elements. When they were done, they began casting their spell, using the power of their staffs. They sang in a forgotten language, the language of summoning.

Chapter 57: Battle of the Iron Road

"Landis, we're surrounded. There are camps on all four sides," King Herron said. Landis was standing in one of the towers looking down on the castle. In the open areas around the castle, and not a mile away, lay the huge war camps of the Doreh.

"Good! We've got them right where we want them!" he grinned, "Your Highness."

"At this point, let's go with Gabriel."

"Gabriel, what do you see out there?" he pointed at the fires off in the distance.

"Looks like they are setting up camp. They'll probably attack at dawn."

"They think that they're going to get a good night's sleep, maybe have a big breakfast, then attack us when they 're all rested and fresh," Landis said, looking at the young leader.

"They 'do' want to kill us... so, I'm thinking that we 'don't' let them rest or sleep. Not even for a minute," Gabriel said, smiling.

Hundreds of asses, horses, and even cattle ran through the Doreh camps as fast as they could. Each one of them had bales of burning hay strapped to their backs. The poor creatures ran with the thought that if they ran faster, they would be able to escape the fire. They became insane with the pain and fear as they tore through the camps, ignoring or trampling anything in their way. They set thousands of tents on fire, they crushed hundreds, perhaps thousands of men under their hooves. In general, they turned the Doreh camps into fiery mayhem.

King Syphon handed his looking glass back to Landis, trying not to laugh too hard.

"Good work. Do we have anything else planned for our uninvited guests?"

For the Doreh, the night was a long one. Every hour or so, flaming arrows would appear seemingly out of nowhere, setting more of their tents on fire. By morning light, they looked worn out instead of rested, and their attitudes had gone from positive in anticipation of the coming battle, to resolving that it would be a grinder. Just as the sun was coming up, the remainder of the tents that were not burned overnight were packed, and the whole of the armies pulled into closer range. All morning and through the afternoon, they worked on their siege engines. They piled tree trunks and bound them into battering rams. Hundreds of ladders were made, each tall enough to get a man over the outer wall of the castle.

They had gathered the materials and had done a lot of the work as they had traveled across the country. Now that they were beneath the walls of the enemy, they only had to assemble the machines. The trebuchet and siege towers were mostly built, but they still took all day to assemble. When they were done, they sent out Alexina and a few of the tribal chiefs. She called out to have the commander of the castle present himself for terms. King Syphon went to the wall and looked down on the gathered barbarians.

"You're King Syphon, are you not?" she called out.

"I am," he replied.

"I am Alianna Ragnar, leader of the united Doreh clans of Hadon. Come to ask for your surrender!" she yelled up to him.

"Strange. I thought that your name was Alexina, the Summer Witch!" he yelled back. The Doreh around her looked at her in surprise. Their people had always been violently against magic, to the point of killing anyone who showed any aptitude for it. They all regarded Alexina with skeptical stares.

"He says that you're a witch!" said the barbarian to her left, his hand on his axe handle. She pulled her double-sided axe, swung it and took the man's head off before he could react. She looked at the half dozen other men who were accompanying her, they all held their tongues.

"That's right, friends! She's a witch, she's not even human. She's good with an axe, but deadlier still with her magic! She can summon demons and change a man into a worm! Beware!" the king bellowed. Alexina's face, though beautiful was contorted with rage.

"Attack!" she screamed. She rode her horse back to the Doreh lines, the other chiefs in tow. "Attack! Attack now!" She rode up to the wall of tall, blonde warriors. Her horse reared up, and she held her bloody, double-sided axe high above her head.

The horde had not heard the accusations, they just knew that the time that they'd been preparing for had finally arrived. Thousands of men charged forward, war paint on and weapons drawn. Others carried ladders, and teams of mounted men were pulling the trebuchet and siege towers. The word went around the castle like a wave, all the Doreh, still over forty-five thousand of them, surged forward. Their pale faces were marked with black ash, and red berry juice, to show their war faces and to instill fear in their enemies. They rushed forward till they reached about one hundred feet from the walls, and then the ground gave way beneath them. All around the castle, a thirty-foot-wide by twenty-foot-deep moat had been dug. The bottom was full of sewer water, and the top of the trench had been covered by a layer of thin branches and less than a foot of dirt. It looked like firm ground from a distance, and even at close range; but it didn't have the strength to support a man, much less a horse or siege weapon.

Thousands of men and horses fell into the ditches, with the rest of the horde surging behind them. As soon as they fell in, the arrows started flying. Every inch of the outer wall of Castle Herron had an archer, and they had orders to keep firing till they ran out of arrows. The Doreh held up their shields and they fought through the shit filled trench; but many hundreds of them fell from arrow wounds.

Alexina was incensed. She had only lost once in her life, and it was an experience she vowed never to repeat. She pulled one of the flying squirrels from a cage on her personal wagon and whispered into its ear. She launched the creature, and it rose up into the sky as quickly as it could, then took off eastward. The creature took no note of the blood and destruction that it flew over. It flew over the tens of thousands of Doreh barbarians, then over the lush countryside for more than a mile till it reached the camp of the goat headed Mavit Tomar. The creature circled around, and when it found its mistress, it landed lightly on her shoulder. Squeaking in its quiet language, the messenger let her know that the Doreh were on the move.

"Damn that girl!" Carissa cursed. "Commissar!" she called to the leader of her forces. "We ride now!" She rushed off to collect her mount.

"Brothers! It's time to take our revenge on these 'humans' and claim them as slaves. Take their land, their wealth, and make it ours! Each one of you will have new servants, and if you wish, a land gift here in this new world!" The men roared in approval at the mention of their coming rewards. "Free the Zytlyx and don your armor! We attack immediately!"

In short order, thousands of Mavit Tomar took to the air, their owls flying low so that the insect creatures they controlled wouldn't stray from the mission. They reached the outer edge of the Doreh occupation when the Mavit Tomar took to the skies. They lifted their hellish hunting hounds and dropped them over the walls of the castle. A few of the owls were shot and fell to the ground, but most evaded the volley of arrows and started circling above the battlefield. The chaos caused by the Zytlyx within the castle walls gave the Doreh invaders a much-needed reprieve. They still struggled to cross the trench, but they had fewer arrows flying in their direction.

One of the Zytlyx almost landed squarely on Landis. The creature was huge, well over a hundred pounds, despite its thin body and spindly limbs. As soon as it hit the stone of the wall where Landis was leading the defense, it reared up and grabbed on to his armor with four of its six legs. The head was a bit smaller than a human head, but the multi-faceted eyes were each as large as an apple. Their crescent-shaped pincers took up most of their face and were dark green like their bodies. The pincers snapped at Landis, trying to rip a hunk of flesh from his face or neck. Landis pushed the creature away, and before it hit the ground, Soulbane was in his hand. He swung the sword, and the creature lost its head in a flash of sharpened steel. The head on the ground continued to snap aimlessly, and the six, stick-like limbs continued to claw for whatever they could snag. Landis jammed his sword into the thorax and lifted the whole corpse over the edge of the castle wall so that it dropped it on the heads of the Doreh below. Going up and down the walkway, he found several more of his men fighting off the Zytlyx with varying degrees of success. He chopped and hacked off the thin green limbs, severed the shiny round heads, and helped toss a dozen more of the beasts over the edge.

Jorn ran up the steps that brought him to the highest tower of Castle Herron. From that vantage point, he could see the whole of the battlefield. The castle was being besieged on all sides, though the largest force, including the hovering Mavit Tomar were attacking the main entrance that faced the Iron Road. No one knew that he'd gone up on the tower, the young mage went unnoticed by friend and foe alike. He looked up at the sky and saw the heavy dark clouds that extended as far as he could see in every direction. This made him smile. Jorn could sense the water in the clouds above, millions of gallons, just waiting to fall on the fertile land of Khatuna. Closing his eyes, he began chanting his spell. He moved his hands as part of the spell, summoning the powers that were now a part of him and had been refined with years of training. The clouds above started to bend to his will. They grew darker and darker, till they reached the point that they could no longer hold their watery burden. The rain began; but again, and again, Jorn willed the water to fly back up into the clouds. It would freeze, then fall, then fly up for another coating of water, then fall and freeze again. He did this till the air was full of hail the size of a man's fist.

When Jorn finally allowed the hail to fall, he directed it so that it struck the mass of humans, and the Mavit Tomar who were riding their giant owls. The castle seemed to have an invisible umbrella, the hail falling on all sides, but not on Castle Herron proper. The rock-hard chunks of ice picked up speed, and when they struck, the effects were devastating. The Mavit Tomar were pelted mercilessly, they and their mounts falling from the sky like so many wounded ducks. The barbarians tried hiding behind their shields; but with huge chunks of ice pelting them at high velocity, many were getting stoned to death. The Doreh were surprised as giant owls, and men who looked like they were part animal fell amongst them. Most died on impact, but those that only suffered superficial wounds were swarmed by the Doreh and killed for being the spawn of evil. For an hour, ice fell from the sky, killing thousands apon thousands of the barbarians, and effectively halting their advance. When every last drop of moisture had been wrung from the heavens, and hurled at the enemy, the skies parted, and it was again a beautiful sunny day. The scene was surreal. An army huddled under their siege weapons, and shields, the ground covered in spheres of clear ice. There were bloody and broken bodies lying everywhere, including the corpses of the Mavit Tomar and their feathered mounts.

When the spell was complete, an exhausted Jorn almost fell to the stone roof of the tower. He had expended all his energy and could only smile at his sister before falling into a deep slumber. She had a couple of men, including Gabriel Herron, carry the young mage to his chambers. King Syphon looked to Landis, and they both smiled, knowing that Jorn had tilted the scale in their favor. The odds were still against them, but now they started to have real hope.

The tunnels opened not too far from the barbarian's rear lines. Half a dozen doors on each side of the castle were thrown open, and from each, thousands of the Uzor rushed forth. Anisha Bkar was the first one out of her tunnel, and behind her, over a thousand strong Uzor warriors who would fight with her to the end. To the side, she saw another tunnel door open, and Wanaka ran out, his trusty sword Panther Claw already in-hand. He wore little armor compared to his men, he always complained that a helm interfered with his vision. Anisha thought it was so that the enemy could see the 'crazy' in his eyes.

The barbarians were still shell shocked from the long and bloody hail storm. They were completely shocked to see their old enemies, the Uzor, attacking them from behind. For centuries, they had scrimmaged with the black peoples to their South; and they had found that in war, they were evenly matched. That's why, for generations, there had been no open war between them. The Doreh had hoped that they would be invading a 'soft' population, men that would put up a minimal fight, then roll over and play dead. Instead, they were not only being prevented from advancing; but were being attacked from behind.

Anisha charged forward, wearing full plate armor instead of the leather armor that she normally wore. Across her chest was the white panther, to symbolize the spirit of her people. Her helmet and plate were all shined to a mirror-like finish and her long saber was sharpened so fine that it could cut a human hair lengthwise. The closest barbarian heard her war cry and turned just in time to watch as she slashed him with her sword, spilling his innards on the foreign soil. She ignored his look of shock, and moved on to the next, and the next. A few more fell before the barbarians turned to face this new, yet familiar threat.

The Doreh were tired, hungry, and frustrated by losing men and not having the chance to fight back. They saw the thousands of enemy troops rushing at them and gave a collective sigh of relief. The two armies smashed together like dueling tsunamis. Alexina had vanished when the hail started, the Doreh were now leaderless again; but their nature was to fight to the death, and to always press forward. Their mighty axes chopped into the Uzor knights, and they used their shields both for defense and as battering rams against their foes.

The Uzor were well-trained warriors, and well led by the King's Champion. The hero went without a shield and carried a second sword in his offhand. Wanaka was like a human whirlwind, taking off hands, chopping into shoulders, and slicing through torsos. He would no sooner kill a man, than two would take his place. The Uzor sent by King Lollondo were roughly twenty-thousand men, all delivered through portals by Linea Bkar and the Anant twins. They had waited over a week for this moment. This was their chance to fight a neighbor that had been raiding small towns in Koregar since before they were born. They followed Wanaka and fed off his nearly inhuman energy. There were rumors that he had fought a white champion to a standstill when he was a captive of the Doreh; but none of them believed that. To them, Wanaka was immortal, unbeatable, a force of nature.

Another thousand Uzor fighters dutifully followed Anisha. She was second only to Wanaka in reputation as a fighter. She was not known as a berserker, but instead for her artistry with a sword. The way that she moved during battle was closer to dancing than combat. She weaved her way past a man's guard, slit his throat, and was on to the next before he realized that he was dead. She used her enemy, both alive and dead, to control space in the battle. Because of her size, compared to the giant blonde Doreh, she would use them as shields and strike at them from angles that they couldn't anticipate.

The battle had started with a frenetic pace, but soon it developed its own rhythm, and the more experienced warriors changed to a pace that they could sustain for a longer period. Night was closing in and the Doreh were no closer to leaving than they were at the beginning of the day. Anisha was able to let her mind wander a bit while the fighting went on. She stole a glance downfield and saw that Wanaka was still out front, tearing into the enemy like a dog on a fresh bone. He never seemed to tire, and she was amazed at how his pace was still higher than anyone else's on either side of the conflict. She wondered how her lover Landis was doing on the other side of the castle. She didn't fear for his life, he was such a complete champion, that perhaps even the gods themselves could not kill him.

Landis was the first one out the front gate. Far up in the castle, a young man was blowing a horn, which was the signal to begin the attack. The Uzor would be popping out of the tunnels and attacking the enemy from behind. He had over fifteen thousand knights and men at his side, and with the Uzor, they just might make it. There were thousands of men unaccounted for, they just didn't have time to cross the countryside before the Doreh and the Mavit Tomar arrived.

Landis charged out of the gate with his shield up, sword in hand, and a grim expression on his face. In the many years that he had paid his bills with his sword, he had never been, or at least never seen himself as a leader. Now again, he found himself responsible not only for his own life but for the lives of the men who followed him. He yelled for the charge and then led the men into battle; knowing many, if not all of them might fall today. He guided his men in an effort to drive a wedge in the enemy ranks, to use their speed and the element of surprise to break the enemy's spirit. He led by example, using his enchanted sword that felt as light as a feather but was sharper than broken glass He ripped through the barbarian ranks, cutting men down, then stepping over them to kill more men. His sword glided gracefully through the steamy, foul air, inflicting fatal wounds by twisting ever so slightly at the last moment. It felt strange to him that he was not completely in control, but the inhuman accuracy of the weapon made his fights shorter and allowed him to face even greater odds. His mind might occasionally wander a bit, his arms and legs had a mind of their own.

Two of the barbarians had sought him out. Landis was obviously the leader of the defenders and was by far the toughest opponent to on the field. When he had killed off the last of three men that he had been fighting simultaneously, Landis looked up to see Gunner Sigifrid and Agnar Yoren. Gunner was known to run blindly into battle, relying on his size and berserker rage to carry him through. If the last month had taught him one thing, it was that sometimes it made sense to exercise caution. Agnar spun his extra-large war axes in his hands. He looked at the smaller, heavily armored man, and he couldn't believe that Landis posed as much of a threat as his reputation would warrant. The two were accustomed to battling side by side and fighting in close quarters, despite their large size.

Landis had never experienced fear in battle. He understood caution, and though he at times took chances, he never took foolish chances. He felt that one on one, he could defeat either of the men in front of him. Two on one with quality opponents, he had to devote his full attention and effort to the fight. Agnar was fast and strong, and Landis needed both his shield and sword to fend off his attacks. Gunner was just strong, and even when blocking his attacks, Landis could feel vibrations throughout his whole body. The two Doreh warriors were closing the distance with Landis, their constant attacks forcing him to take a step back, then another step. His foot caught on one of the thousands of dead that littered the fields surrounding the castle, and he fell backward. Agnar tried to pounce on him, only to be kicked in the testicles by Landis' steel-covered foot. Gunner slammed his huge broadsword down on Landis and impacted against his shield, cracking it in half.

Gunner was about to deliver what he intended to be a death blow when another longsword intercepted his swing. The Doreh looked up to see a black warrior, dressed in armor that was unlike the armor worn by the Uzor. King Syphon smiled at the giant blonde man's frustration. He hacked at the larger man, each time getting closer to connecting with flesh. Landis rolled to his feet so that two of Kronos' deadliest swordsmen were now fighting shoulder to shoulder.

King Syphon had a small buckler attached to his left arm so that his hand was free to grasp the long handle of his sword.

Like Gunner, he used both hands and was able to generate more speed and power than a one-armed attack. The Doreh was having trouble with Kel's fighting style, it was too much like his own. He was not used to a foe that was strong enough to make him go on the defensive. Single-mindedly, Kell Syphon chopped at the tall blonde warrior. He was so fast and relentless, that Gunner had no chance to go on offense, where he felt most comfortable. Kel chopped downward at the Doreh so many times, that when he finally changed attack angles, it caught his opponent by complete surprise. Dozens of downward chops, then without warning, a spin and a horizontal slash across the man's midsection. The look in Gunner's eyes showed that he knew he'd been beaten. Like a tree falling before the woodsman's axe, he keeled over, landing face-first on the blood-soaked ground.

King Syphon looked up from his victory, to see that Landis had finished his opponent perhaps a few seconds prior. He was proud of his ability, but he was not ashamed to acknowledge the mastery of Landis Stone in combat. He heard a frightening cackle and noticed a new threat that was brewing off in the distance. A tall figure stood above the fray, and chaos swirled around her. She was easily ten feet tall, her long blonde hair pulled back by a golden tiara Each of her six arms carried a long sword with a spur at the end. The mercenary and the king fought their way closer till they could see the extent of what they were now up against. The creature was female, her full bosom and thin waist gave way to a snake's body that was twenty feet long. They could tell that she had once been the Season known as Alexina, the Summer Witch. Now, she appeared as a Marilith, a demon from one of the lower planes of hell.

Apparently, her strength was commensurate with her size. Every swing of one of her great swords sent men flying. She had started by attacking the men of Kronos; but when the Doreh saw who she really was, they too turned their attacks on her.

Now she indiscriminately struck out at any human that got within range. Landis had heard tales of such beasts when he was a child, and if he remembered correctly, she couldn't use magic in this form; but while she was in this demon form, she was resistant to most spells and magic. He wasn't sure if that included his enchanted blade, but as a leader, it was his task to charge in and find out.

Running in close, he ducked under her arms and thrust his sword into her gut. Though he pushed with all his might, he struck the reptilian scales and was only able to score a superficial wound. The demoness howled in rage and slashed at him with two of her six arms. Landis had to roll on the ground to avoid losing his head. Getting up, he chopped again at the snake portion of her body, and again found the hide to be tough and highly resistant to damage. She attacked again, and Landis was barely able to get his shield and sword up in time to block her swing. Before she could retract her arms, he swung at one of the lower arms and found that the sword was able to bite deeply into the parts of her that were still human.

Alexina howled in pain, the blood flowing freely from a deep gash on her forearm. Landis didn't even see the tail that caught him from the side and threw his considerable weight a dozen feet or more. Luckily, there was a crowd of Doreh fighters to break his fall. Quickly as possible, he untangled himself from the others and ran in to confront the demoness. Landis slashed at her, catching the demoness in one of her armpits, opening a vicious cut that started bleeding profusely. When she tried to attack, he blocked her strikes, though the force rocked him, and he felt like he was suffering from a hundred small fractures in his arms and back.

The demoness was ready to strike again when an arrow found her right eye. Her screams of pain could be heard for miles, the whole battlefield halted for a moment and all eyes looked in her direction. Landis turned to see King Herron nocking another arrow and preparing to fire. Landis took advantage of the distraction and swung his blade as hard as he could. The sword cut through one of her lower wrists, completely severing the hand. He quickly chopped at a second hand, not quite severing it; but he did enough that it hung from the arm like a loose hunk of meat. Several more arrows struck her, none were able to penetrate that deeply, but they served to enrage her even more.

Alexina whipped her tail around at near the speed of sound, and though Landis saw it coming and was able to duck, a soldier behind him was not so lucky. The soldier's head came off cleanly and was propelled a hundred feet or more off into the crowd. Those who were not close enough to the demon continued their individual fights. The ground was red with blood, and every time Landis cut the demoness, she got weaker. Soon all her arms were dripping from a hundred different cuts, and she was having trouble keeping her good eye open. Her tail still whipped around and took out a soldier here or there. Landis climbed her till he was eye to eye with her. He dropped his shield and gripped his sword with both hands and with all his strength he chopped at her neck. The blade bit deeply, causing black gore to spew from the wound and her tongue to hang from the side of her twisted mouth. He chopped again and again till the head came free from her body. As her body fell, he jumped forward and landed in a standing position, with a sword in one hand and a severed head in the other.

Holding up the bloody head, he turned to his men, "Men of Kronos! Attack! Fight till these invaders, these hellspawn are defeated! Not even demons from the depths of Hell will keep us from victory!" The crowd of soldiers erupted in cheers, then returned to fighting with renewed purpose.

Chapter 58: Magic

Lilith and Anjaya strained to keep the portal open. In doing so, they expended nearly all their energies. The gateway was a direct connection between Kronos and the seventh circle of hell. Demons anxiously surged through the gateway into the world of men. There were several different types of demons, but what they had in common was their cruelty and the pleasure that they took from torturing their victims. They were the most violent of demons, and they lived only to kill. They feared neither pain nor death.

The sisters finally ran out of energy and had to let the portal close. They smiled at what they had accomplished though. Thousands of the lower demons had been ushered through into this pristine land dominated by man. Mounting their horses, the witches addressed the horde of twisted, evil creatures.

"We've summoned you here to pillage and destroy this land! I command you to follow us and kill any human that you meet. Consume their flesh, devour their souls, and leave no one alive!" Lilith yelled. The demons all growled in agreement and started following the sisters. There were hundreds of Balor, demons that resembled Minotaur with large bat wings. They carried long swords and whips and were the generals. They commanded hundreds of Imps, Bone Devils, Lemure, and Pit Fiends. Many of the creatures could fly, and the Balor made sure that they didn't get too far ahead of the others.

They had traveled for hours when the sisters felt a wave of loss. The four of them were deeply connected, and when their younger sister lost her head, they felt her pain. The void that she left filled the remaining seasons with unimaginable hate. They didn't cry, it wasn't in their nature. Feelings of sadness for the loss of a loved one were alien to them. What they did feel was a burning need for revenge. As much as they hated the humans before, they now hated them a thousand times more. They spurred their horses on, running them ragged for the remaining distance to Castle Herron.

A pitched battle was still raging. The Doreh were more than cut in half. Most of them didn't know that they had been tricked into this war by a demon, so they continued to fight. The Uzor forces were devastated, and the Kronos soldiers were a quarter of what they started with. The demons threw themselves into the middle, killing friend and foe alike. When a wave of Hellspawn descended on them, the humans ceased their own fights and turned to take on the new menace. Now Uzor and Doreh were fighting shoulder to shoulder against a common enemy. Demons and devils came as a wave from the North, attacking with tooth and claw, spiked tails, and sharpened horns. Landis saw the shift in the tide of battle and saw his chance to unite the men of this new world.

"Men of Kronos, men of Tychon, now is the time for us to put aside our differences. We must band together to kill these witches and their demons!" He ran over to where the large head of Alexina lay on the muddy, bloody soil. It was the face of a beautiful woman, twisted into the demon that she really was. He held the bloody head by the long blonde hair and yelled to the others. "This is what we fight! Demons! Witches! Follow me, if we want our people to go on, if we want a world for our children, we must unite! Put aside whatever your reasons are to fight each other and pledge your swords, your axes, your bows, to sending these fiends back to hell!" he yelled, standing on top of the now lifeless body of the Summer Witch.

Every man and woman, regardless of the banner that they had sworn to that morning, were now in a single army set on defeating the evil of the remaining Seasons. Lilith saw a human standing on her sister's corpse, and this sent her into a mindless rage. She charged forward on her horse, trying to get through her own demons to personally attack Landis. When she reached him, her horse reared, and she held up her staff to summon any of its power that had returned since closing the portal. She was beautiful, with pale white skin and black robes that showed what looked like a woman's tender skin. He knew that inside she was exactly like the foul creature that he stood upon.

Summoning a ball of fire, she launched it at the defiant knight. He held up his shield and was blasted back by the force of the fireball. He shook his head, and with effort, rose again to his feet. She launched another fireball, this one he was more prepared for, but still, his shield was starting to turn red with the extended time that he had to use it to block the flames. The fireballs were coming faster than he could recover, Lilith soon had him on his knees, sweating, tired, and singed. She was about to finish him off when an unfamiliar voice sounded. A sweet female voice that cut through the hell was being unleashed all about them.

"So, you like to play with fire?" Lilith looked up to see a tall, beautiful brunette in a bright red dress. She sneered at the woman as nothing more than a distraction. She was about to launch against Landis again when the woman spoke again. "I like fire too!" Danika fired a fireball at the witch which struck her full in the face.

Lilith got up and laughed condescendingly at the young mage. "Child, I'm a creature of fire. It'll take a lot more than that to harm me."

"You want more?" Danika asked. "I can give you more. More than you thought was possible!" This time, she took an extra half a second to summon a fire so hot that it burned a deep blue. When it struck Lilith, she was knocked backward, and she had a worried look on her face. Danika walked forward and touched the gem on her amulet. Its power was to repeat the last spell that she had cast. From her hand, and without casting or conjuring, she launched another bright blue fireball. She repeated the process, again, and again, and again. As Danika was walking forward, she kept up her assault. Lilith was being hit with fireballs more potent than any she could conjure, at a rate of several per second. Her beautiful face, with the youth that she had stolen from her disciples, began to melt and char. She screamed in horror and pain but the attack from Danika was relentless. The staff the old woman carried at first smoldered, then burst into flame, till the jewel it carried fell to the ground.

Now Lilith was the one on the ground, cowering and holding up her arms to try and fend off the fire. Her hair burned, her dress burned, and finally, her skin melted and released the evil spirit that had been inside. When Danika finally stopped the barrage, there was nothing but an oily, black puddle on the ground, with a shiny blue diamond nearby.

Danika had been focused on her opponent to such a degree, that when she looked up, she was almost surprised by the legion of devils and demons that were ready to avenge their mistress. She summoned a wave of fire and let it fan out before her. The demons weren't affected by her flames till she increased the heat and soon, they were being blasted with fires much hotter than the hells that they had come from. The Bone Devils cracked and broke apart, the Lemure melted and the Shadow Demons were blasted by the sheer energy, despite their ethereal nature. The Imps and Pit Fiends laughed and pressed forward, intent on taking out the young sorceress.

The demons were almost upon Danika when a bolt of lightning hit the first one and bounced to the next and the next and a hundred more. Danika looked to the left, and there was Linea Bkar, lightning flying from her fingertips. The Uzor sorceress looked supremely confident as she lashed out, killing demons by the dozen with her magic. Danika looked around and found that everyone was with her. Though nearly drained, her brother had her back. Wanaka, the Uzor champion was there, Father Sebastienne was healing those who could be saved with all his gods given power. Kings Syphon and Herron were there, each was dispatching demons, and leading men into battle. That woman, Anisha Bkar was there, fighting as well or better than most men; she was both heroic and beautiful at the same time.

Landis was there, as he always was. He had said that he loved her; but in the end, he was more in love with his honor. When she met him, he was a sellsword, a man who would fight for money, throwing in with whatever cause paid the most. He had changed a lot since then. His brother died at the hands of the Quell, and he also lost his wife and child to the savages of the Quell. Both tragedies were enough to make most men either crumble into uselessness, or as in Landis' case, rise to the occasion. He was now a knight, a man that served the kings of Kronos, and served the will of the gods. She had loved him; she loved him still. She knew that these things happened, that sometimes you meet that certain person, who your heart tells you is the one that you've been waiting for. She knew that she was still young, and that having her heart broken was to be expected, that it would happen to everyone at some time in their life. She looked at Landis and knew that she would never feel this way again. And that was okay.

Danika gave her attention back to the task at hand. Demons were almost on her. She reached down in the well of sadness and frustration that had been filling her soul recently and released the demi-god. A massive fist appeared in the air above the massed demons. It was the size of a house, and though it was semi-transparent, it caused everyone on the field to stop and stare. A wicked light burned in Danika's eyes as the fist rose up, then came crashing down on the heads of at least a dozen demons. The ground shook with the impact, causing many to lose their footing. The fist rose up to fifty feet or so, and again came crashing down. It was as if Danika had grown to a hundred feet tall and was busily squashing her enemies. The fist rose and crashed down, and each time, an earthquake shook the ground for hundreds of yards in every direction. The look on her face was that of a child, experiencing power for the first time, crushing ants under its boot. The demons tried running or flying away; but she flattened her hand, and the giant hand came down like a fly swatter, knocking imps and Balor out of the air. The crushed bodies of the demons littered the battlefield, and the humans all stopped to watch the incredible sight. Danika was using her hands to direct the spell, and the giant disembodied hand was following her every movement. She had a manic look in her eyes, her smile was wide and bordering on evil. Cracks formed in the walls of the castle, the ground shook so much that everyone on both sides had difficulty standing. The giant hand began growing as Danika poured in her power, and soon, the entire little valley was under the shadow of Danika's palm.

Landis was trying desperately to get his men to flee, to move away from the impending danger. Jorn ran towards his sister, to see if he could get her to dial down the power of her attack. That's when it happened. The Hand of God disappeared in an instant, and Danika fell to her knees. Jorn could see that the Spring Witch was at her side, with her knife buried in Danika's chest. She pulled the blade out, and the young mage's blood poured out onto the already bloody ground. Anjaya grabbed a fistful of Danika's wavy black hair and was about to slit her throat when she felt Jorn's knife enter her heart. Then a most interesting thing happened. As she stood there, knife in one hand, her victim's hair in the other, and a ten-inch blade buried to the hilt in her black heart; she felt her life force being sucked out of her perfect body. The knife that the old Telnor mage had given him was enchanted to always hit its target, and to drink the life of whomever it struck. Anjaya dropped everything and tried her best to remove the blade; but it was thirsty and was determined to keep drinking from her till its thirst was quenched. In the course of a minute, her face went from victory and satisfaction, to pain, then horror, and finally resignation. She toppled over dead, face first into the bloody muck, next to the young woman that she had so gleefully murdered.

Jorn ran to his sister. Falling to his knees, he rolled her over to look for any signs of life. He stared into her vacant eyes and knew without needing to check that she was gone. They had been together in the womb, and almost constantly since then. Now, for the first time in his life, he was truly alone. He wept over the loss of his sister as the battle raged on.

The demons had been greatly decreased by Danika's spell, and the combined numbers of the humans on the field made it a very close battle. Landis knew that his good friend was dead, but now was not the time to deal with it. He'd have to mourn her later. He looked at the enemy and looked at the remaining men. The battle was now only to the North of the castle, the rest of the armies had worked their way to where the action was taking place. He wondered if they had enough men to finish off the demons, and gods forbid, if the Doreh still wanted to fight when their shared enemy was gone. Just then, he heard the trumpets.

Chapter 59: Help from the North

Everyone looked up to see not one but two armies, riding hard towards them. With banners flying in the dying sun and trumpets announcing their entrance to the conflict, the forces of O'Bell came from the Northeast, and an army of trained mercenaries, mixed with the Church's army rode in from the Northwest. Altogether, they numbered four to five thousand men, and four thousand women.

The cavalry rode with spears lowered, visors down, and thunder in their hooves. They tore through the ranks of the demons like a hot knife through butter, and made several passes, each time, reducing the number of demons. Behind them came the thousands of archers, pike men, knights, and infantry. The men who had been fighting for a full day, let their swords dip, and they watched as the reinforcements mopped up the remains of the demon horde.

When the fighting was done, Landis walked over to the remaining Doreh fighters. There were only a few thousand of the fifty thousand that had landed on the shores of Tebron more than a month ago. They were leaderless, tired, and in no state-of-mind to continue the hostilities. They were disarmed and were ordered to march through a portal provided by Linea Bkar. Once they were all back in Hadon, she closed the rip in space and turned to King Syphon.

"I could use a drink, your highness," she said wearily.

"As could we all, I would presume," he replied.

"An army of all women?" Linea asked of Lydia O'Bell, who still sat a horse.

"We use men for procreation and manual labor; but a woman's place is in battle," she said merrily.

"You almost missed all of the fighting, Lydia," Kell chimed in. "The Southern armies are nearly wiped out, and our allies, the Uzor and the Telnor suffered massive casualties among the soldiers that they sent."

"I'm sorry Kel, but we were accosted by dozens of giants on the way here. They were tougher than you can imagine," she replied.

"We can imagine," Gabriel Herron corrected her.

"All the same, I'm glad you arrived," Landis said to the group. "I lost a dear friend today, and you prevented my losing more. Pardon me, I need to pay my respects," he said. They caught the forming of tears in the corners of his eyes. Lydia knew that for a man like that to well up, the loss must have been particularly close to home.

Landis walked over to a tent that had been set up to tend to the dead. Among the bodies clad in shining armor, and white tunics was a girl in a bright red dress. In death, Danika looked younger. She reminded him of the child that he and his brother had met so many years ago. Landis wondered how much his breaking up with her had to do with her lying dead now. Did she fight carelessly? Did she enter the battle, never intending to live beyond today? He would never wonder these things aloud. Not to his woman Anisha, and certainly not to his friend Jorn.

Jorn stood over the body, his tears were cried out for now and his sadness had turned to numbness. At times, she was a substitute mother to him, bossing him around and in general, being more mature than he was. They had lost their parents, then they lost the Archmage who taught them so much, and now he had lost his sister. He knew that he would go on; but at least for now, he didn't want to. He begged the gods to make a trade. To take him and bring her back. The gods were not listening today.

Chapter 60: Conclusion

Reinhold Lothar watched as his partners fell beneath the swords of the 'soft' men of Kronos. There were still thousands of his countrymen left on the field; but the momentum was now firmly with the other side. His leader had shown herself to be the demon that she had always been. In his mind, it was time to cut his losses.

The king was dead, the battle commanders were all dead, and Alianna had shown herself to be witch and a demon. No one noticed as he reached the edge of the fighting, and just drifted away towards the hills to the West. If he cut his hair, and adopted the clothes of Kronos, he could with some small effort, fit in. Long before the battle was officially over, Reinhold was miles away, and on his way to a new life.

Carissa felt empty. Stepping through the small portal, she was once again alone in her stark white castle in the northern hills of Pyrros. Before she was just separated from her sisters, and part of her always thought that they would eventually be reunited. Now, three of them were dead, and she felt more alone than she had at any time in her very long life.

She would have to keep an eye out for the Mavit Tomar. Ten thousand of their crack troops, along with mounts and hunting animals had joined her in a mission to invade and raid the new world. Now, all of them were dead, their corpses rotting in the sun of a country very far from their homeland. The Tsar would not be pleased. Not pleased at all. Despite her weariness and the fact that her magic was nearly drained from overuse, she would have to start preparing for the eventual visit of the Tsar, or more likely, his elite guard. She had gone from having the Mavit Tomar as unfriendly but mostly neutral neighbors, to having them as enemies. Instead of ridding the world of men and all the man-like races, she was again forced to retreat and hide behind her milky-white stone walls.

Wanaka looked at Anisha the way a big brother would look at a younger sister. Though their ages were not too far apart, she had always called him 'master'. He had trained her and turned her from an angry, hard to control young woman, into a seasoned and skillful warrior. She stood there in a grassy field, littered with the dead and dying. She was covered head to toe in the blood of her enemies, and looked both tired, and relieved to be alive. He walked over to her.

"You did good, Ani," he said to her. "What are you and Linea going to do now?"

"I imagine she's going back to her position as the king's councilor and sorceress," she replied.

"But what about you? You've never left your sister's side since childhood."

"I'm an adult now, and I'm going wherever my man goes," she looked at her former master, her face showing peace with her decision.

"Where's he going?" Wanaka asked.

"I don't know." She waved at Landis who was a hundred feet away, motioning him to come over to her and Wanaka. "Dear, what's next?" She touched his cheek and saw the sadness in his eyes.

"One of the Seasons escaped. Tens of thousands of my people, your people, even the damned Doreh, died for their amusement. I want to hunt her down and deliver the justice that's due her."

"She is supposed to live on another continent that is ever further to the East of here," Wanaka added. "A place with no people, just creatures that walk like men."

"If it can be reached by boat, then I'll go there and do what needs to be done."

"We'll go there," Anisha corrected him. She smiled warmly and fell into his arms.

"Yes dear. We'll do it together."

Linea Bkar walked up to the only people that she really knew on this continent. Her sister, the white devil, and the king's champion. They looked like they were in a discussion; but she didn't mind intruding. This war that she had never wanted to participate in was essentially over and she wanted to go home. She looked at her sister, the one that had protected her till her magic reached the point where she was the more feared of the two. Anisha the strong melted into the arms of the white foreigner. So many Uzor had petitioned to be her mate, and yet this man was the one that she chose.

"It's time to go. I can summon a portal and have what remains of our army return to Koregar," Linea said to them.

"I need to say my goodbyes, then I'll be ready to go," Wanaka told the sorceress. "I need to report to the king as soon as possible. I will tell him that the men of Uzor fought alongside the men of Kronos, and handily defeated the Doreh!"

"Sister?" Linea asked of Anisha.

"You're being provocative, Lin!" Anisha snapped. "You know my heart. He will understand that I've served for many years, and now I seek my own happiness."

"You're staying with this..." Linea was not sure how to end her sentence.

"This man, this good man," Anisha answered. "He may be of Kronos; but he has the heart of an Uzor! I will follow him, and if necessary, die at his side defending this new world."

"If you're asking for my blessing, you don't have it!" she growled at her sister. "Your duty is to the king, first and foremost, then to the Uzor! I only fight next to these white devils because they kill the Doreh, and that in the end, makes our people safer," Linea said with hate in her eyes. "You would sleep with the enemy? It puts bile in my mouth to just call you 'sister'," she said, not caring who was present.

"I'm truly sorry that you feel that way," Anisha said with sorrow in her voice. "When, and it the ice in your heart melts, seek me out. I will always be your sister," and with that, she walked away.

Linea turned to Wanaka as the Uzor troops were starting to gather around them. Linea looked at the familiar faces, and for a minute, felt at home. She looked at the only one that was closer to the royal family than she was.

"Am I wrong?" she challenged Wanaka.

"Your feelings are what they are," he replied. "I'm a simple man, I try not to judge anyone. Your sister seems happy, and Landis is a good man. He's the only one who has every defeated me since becoming the king's champion."

"You're better than I am, Wanaka. I look at that man, and all I see is a well-groomed Doreh. I don't think that I could ever call him 'family'."

"I hope your feelings are worth losing a sister. Are we ready to go?" he asked of Linea. "I've said my good-byes and King Syphon has thanked us profusely for helping to defeat the Doreh."

"I've created a portal, and they were marched through it," she replied. "I hope they don't mind that they were sent to a rival clan's territory. Should be interesting to see a couple thousand from the Friodor clan, dropped deep in the heart of the Engal clan's lands," she laughed at the thought of more of the white devils killing each other. "We will go to the square outside of the king's courtyard."

She produced a large portal and held it open while the Uzor warriors ran through. There were thousands remaining, and it took a long time, even at a run, to get them all through. There was enough time for Wanaka to say goodbye to his student, and to the man who had won her heart. Wanaka was the second to last through, Linea walked through tiredly, after expending so much energy to hold open the portal. Her last action was to look back through to see her sister, standing there in the arms of 'that man'. Perhaps she was better off without a sister.

"Did I mention that you did a good job on this fortress?" King Syphon said to Gabriel, as they stood on the walkway of the outer wall.

"You did, but I never tire of hearing it," he joked. "It'll take a ton of repairs, and it no longer has that 'like new' smell." He looked out over the devastation, and a look of sadness crossed his usually cheerful face. "We can't release the men till the bodies are burnt. The carrion are having their fill, and yet there are still tens of thousands of them to be dealt with."

"We have no choice; we can't bury that many. Strange," the king remarked. "They fought to the death in battle; but now they'll be burned together, friend and foe together on the same pyre."

"There are few that need to be buried. I believe that Danika Anant was the difference between winning or losing this day."

"I know that you 'liked' her," the king said.

"I didn't know her that well; but she was a beauty, and her strength was very appealing. We must also have a service for King Fionn, and Tennyson Coe. We lost good people."

"We must sure that they'll never be forgotten."

Many days travel from the Iron Road, Roku sat meditating in the master's balcony. His sister Melina approached and sat very close to him. He opened his eyes; his expression was a little perturbed.

"Even if I were roaming the infinite, I would sense that you're invading my personal space. Can you move back a little?"

"Were you?" she asked as she slid backward a foot.

"Were I what?" he asked.

"Were you exploring the many planes of existence, roaming the infinite?"

"No, though I was touching the minds of some of our acquaintances. For all intents and purposes, the war is over."

"That's a great thing!" she said happily. "It's good that things are getting back to normal."

"I didn't say that," he quipped.

"What do you mean?"

"Things are not returning to the way they were. Many worlds that had once been one, then were separated, are now and forever one again."

"Really?" She looked at her big brother thoughtfully, "What do you think tore them apart in the first place... and what could put them back together?"

"I don't know, and we may never know," he replied. "The Old Gods have spoken to some of the people of Kronos, and they claim to have made this world; but the Uzor claim the same thing, and I imagine that every people believe that their gods are the only true gods. I'm not sure that these heavenly creatures have the power to weave the fabric of time and space like we've experienced."

"You think that maybe whoever created the universe, may have also spawned the Old Gods?"

"In this, I'm like an ant wondering how the Smith forges a sword. Do the gods, have gods of their own?" he asked, giving his sister a rare smile.

Author's Note:

I've written four books so far in this series, then re-wrote and edited them to the point that I forget that Landis and the twins are not real people. I hope you were able to read the first book and that you enjoyed reading this sequel. I am imagining more volumes for the series, along with solo adventures for some of my favorite characters.

Self-publishing is a very daunting pursuit, and I won't pretend that I'm doing everything correctly yet. I appreciate your delving into my imagination, and I would value any feedback that you might have, positive or negative. Please drop by my website and sign up for the newsletter. I will try to include interesting content along with announcing new material that is coming out. If you would be so kind as to leave a review, that would be also be appreciated as it would let others know what to expect from one of my books, (and yes, its helps the search algorithim).

Check out my website: MarkRGoodrum.com

Email: markgoodrum@MarkRGoodrum.com

Instagram: **mrgintl**

Facebook:
https://www.facebook.com/profile.php?id=100094028413995

Twitter: @MarkRGoodrum

Made in United States
Troutdale, OR
10/18/2024

23904670R00197